NICE WORK

A Novel

David Lodge

David Lodge (signature)

SECKER &
WARBURG
LONDON

First published in England 1988 by
Martin Secker & Warburg Limited
Michelin House, 81 Fulham Road, London SW3 6RB

British Library Cataloguing in Publication data

Lodge, David.
  Nice work.
  I. Title
  823'.914 [F]
ISBN 0–436–25667–3

Lyrics are quoted by permission from

"The Power Of Love" (De Rouge/Mende/Applegate) © 1985 SBK Songs Ltd, 3–5 Rathbone Place, London W1P 1DA

"Come Give Me Your Hand" (De Rouge/Mende/Rush) © 1983 SBK Songs Ltd, 3–5 Rathbone Place, London W1P 1DA

"Surrender" (Rush/Klapperton) © 1985 SBK Songs Ltd, 3–5 Rathbone Place, London W1P 1DA

Set in Monophoto Plantin 10½ pt
and printed in Great Britain by
Richard Clay Ltd, Bungay, Suffolk

To Andy and Marie,
in friendship and gratitude

Author's Note

Perhaps I should explain, for the benefit of readers who have not been here before, that Rummidge is an imaginary city, with imaginary universities and imaginary factories, inhabited by imaginary people, which occupies, for the purposes of fiction, the space where Birmingham is to be found on maps of the so-called real world.

I am deeply grateful to several executives in industry, and to one in particular, who showed me around their factories and offices, and patiently answered my often naive questions, while this novel was in preparation.

D.L.

Upon the midlands now the industrious muse doth fall,
The shires which we the heart of England well may call.
DRAYTON: *Poly-Olbion* (Epigraph to
Felix Holt the Radical, by George Eliot)

"Two nations; between whom there is no intercourse and no sympathy;
who are as ignorant of each other's habits, thoughts and feelings, as if
they were dwellers in different zones, or inhabitants of different
planets; who are formed by a different breeding, and fed by different
food, and ordered by different manners . . ."

"You speak of —" said Egremont hesitatingly.
BENJAMIN DISRAELI: *Sybil; or, the Two Nations*

ONE

If you think . . . that anything like a romance is preparing for you, reader, you were never more mistaken. Do you anticipate sentiment, and poetry, and reverie? Do you expect passion, and stimulus, and melodrama? Calm your expectations, reduce them to a lowly standard. Something real, cool and solid lies before you; something unromantic as Monday morning, when all who have work wake with the consciousness that they must rise and betake themselves thereto.

CHARLOTTE BRONTË: Prelude to *Shirley*

1

Monday January 13th, 1986. Victor Wilcox lies awake, in the dark bedroom, waiting for his quartz alarm clock to bleep. It is set to do this at 6.45. How long he has to wait he doesn't know. He could easily find out by groping for the clock, lifting it to his line of vision, and pressing the button that illuminates the digital display. But he would rather not know. Supposing it is only six o'clock? Or even five? It could be five. Whatever it is, he won't be able to get to sleep again. This has become a regular occurrence lately: lying awake in the dark, waiting for the alarm to bleep, worrying.

Worries streak towards him like enemy spaceships in one of Gary's video games. He flinches, dodges, zaps them with instant solutions, but the assault is endless: the Avco account, the Rawlinson account, the price of pig-iron, the value of the pound, the competition from Foundrax, the incompetence of his Marketing Director, the persistent breakdowns of the core blowers, the vandalising of the toilets in the fettling shop, the pressure from his divisional boss, last month's accounts, the quarterly forecast, the annual review . . .

In an effort to escape this bombardment, perhaps even to doze awhile, he twists onto his side, burrows into the warm plump body of his wife, and throws an arm round her waist. Startled, but still asleep, drugged with Valium, Marjorie swivels to face him. Their noses and foreheads bump against each other; there is a sudden flurry of limbs, an absurd pantomime struggle. Marjorie puts up her fists like a pugilist, groans and pushes him away. An object slides off the bed on her side and falls to the floor with a thump. Vic knows what it is: a book entitled *Enjoy Your Menopause*, which one of Marjorie's friends at the Weight Watchers' club has lent her, and which she has been reading in bed, without much show of conviction, and falling asleep over, for the past week or two. On retiring to bed Vic's last action is normally to detach a book from Marjorie's nerveless fingers, tuck her arms under the covers and turn out her bedside lamp, but he must have neglected the first of these chores last night, or perhaps *Enjoy Your Menopause* was concealed under the coverlet.

He rolls away from Marjorie, who, now lying on her back, begins to snore faintly. He envies her that deep unconsciousness, but cannot afford to join her in it. Once, desperate for a full night's sleep, he had accepted her offer of a Valium, sluicing it down with his usual nightcap, and moved about the next morning like a diver walking on the seabed. He made a mistake of two percentage points in a price for steering-boxes for British Leyland before his head cleared. *You shouldn't have mixed it with whisky*, Marjorie said. *You don't need both.* Then I'll stick to whisky, he said. *The Valium lasts longer*, she said. Too bloody long, if you ask me, he said. I lost the firm five thousand pounds this morning, thanks to you. *Oh, it's my fault, is it?* she said, and her lower lip began to tremble. Then to stop her crying, anything to stop that, he had to buy her the set of antique-look brass fire-irons she had set her heart on for the lounge, to give an extra touch of authenticity to the rustic stone fireplace and the imitation-log gas fire.

Marjorie's snores become louder. Vic gives her a rude, exasperated shove. The snoring stops but, surprisingly, she does not wake. In other rooms his three children are also asleep. Outside, a winter gale blusters against the sides of the house and swishes the branches of trees to and fro. He feels like the captain of a sleeping ship, alone at the helm, steering his oblivious crew through dangerous seas. He feels as if he is the only man awake in the entire world.

The alarm clock cheeps.

Instantly, by some perverse chemistry of his body or nervous system, he feels tired and drowsy, reluctant to leave the warm bed. He presses the snooze button on the clock with a practised finger and falls effortlessly asleep. Five minutes later, the alarm wakes him again, cheeping insistently like a mechanical bird. Vic sighs, hits the Off button on the clock, switches on his bedside lamp (its dimmer control turned low for Marjorie's sake) gets out of bed and paddles through the deep pile of the bedroom carpet to the *en suite* bathroom, making sure the connecting door is closed before he turns on the light inside.

Vic pees, a task requiring considerable care and accuracy since the toilet bowl is lowslung and tapered in shape. He does not greatly care for the dark purplish bathroom suite ("Damson", the estate agent's brochure had called the shade) but it had been one of the things that attracted Marjorie when they bought the house two years ago – the bathroom, with its kidney-shaped handbasin and goldplated taps and sunken bath and streamlined loo and bidet. And, above all, the fact that it was *"en suite"*. *I've always wanted an en suite bathroom*, she would say to visitors, to her friends on the phone, to, he wouldn't be surprised, tradesmen on the doorstep or strangers she accosted in the street. You would think *"en suite"* was the most beautiful phrase in any language, the lengths Marjorie went to introduce it into her conversation. If they made a perfume called *En Suite*, she would wear it.

Vic shakes the last drops from his penis, taking care not to sprinkle the shaggy pink nylon fitted carpet, and flushes the toilet. The house has four toilets, a cause of concern to Vic's father. *FOUR toilets?* he

4

said, when first shown over the house. *Did I count right?* What's the matter, Dad? Vic teased. Afraid the water table will go down if we flush them all at once? *No, but what if they start metering water, eh? Then you'll be in trouble.* Vic tried to argue that it didn't make any difference how many toilets you had, it was the number of times you flushed them that mattered, but his father was convinced that having so many toilets was an incitement to unnecessary peeing, therefore to excessive flushing.

He could be right, at that. At Gran's house, a back-to-back in Easton with an outside toilet, you didn't go unless you really had to, especially in the winter. Their own house in those days, a step up the social ladder from Gran's, had its own indoor toilet, a dark narrow room off the half-landing that always niffed a bit, however much Sanilav and Dettol his mother poured into the bowl. He remembered vividly that yellowish ceramic bowl with the trademark "Challenger", the big varnished wooden seat that was always pleasantly warm to the bum, and a long chain dangling from the high cistern with a sponge-rubber ball, slightly perished, on the end of it. He used to practise heading, flicking the ball from wall to wall, as he sat there, a constipated schoolboy. His mother complained of the marks on the distemper. Now he is the proud owner of four toilets – damson, avocado, sunflower and white, all centrally heated. Probably as good an index of success as any.

He steps onto the bathroom scales. Ten stone two ounces. Quite enough for a man only five feet five and a half inches tall. Some say – Vic has overheard them saying it – that he tries to compensate for his short stature by his aggressive manner. Well, let them. If it wasn't for a bit of aggression, he wouldn't be where he is now. Though how long he will stay there is far from certain. Vic frowns in the mirror above the handbasin, thinking again of last month's accounts, the quarterly forecast, the annual review . . . He runs hot water into the dark purple bowl, lathers his face with shaving foam from an aerosol can, and begins to scrape his jaw with a safety razor, using a Wilkinson's Sword blade. Vic believes fervently in buying British, and has frequent rows with his eldest son, Raymond, who favours a disposable plastic razor manufactured in France. Not that this is the only bone of contention between them, no, not by a long chalk. The principal constraint on the number of their disagreements is, indeed, the comparative rarity of their encounters, Raymond invariably being asleep when Vic leaves for work and out when he returns home.

Vic wipes the tidemark of foam from his cheeks and fingers the shaven flesh appraisingly. Dark brown eyes stare back at him. Who am I?

He grips the washbasin, leans forward on locked arms, and scans the square face, pale under a forelock of lank brown hair, flecked with grey, the two vertical furrows in the brow like a clip holding the blunt nose in place, the straight-ruled line of the mouth, the squared-off jaw. You know who you are: it's all on file at Division.

Wilcox: Victor Eugene. *Date of Birth*: 19 Oct. 1940. *Place of Birth*: Easton, Rummidge, England. *Education*: Endwell Road Primary School, Easton; Easton Grammar School for Boys; Rummidge College of Advanced Technology. MI Mech. Eng. 1964. *Marital Status*: married (to Marjorie Florence Coleman, 1964). *Children*: Raymond (*b.* 1966), Sandra (*b.* 1969), Gary (*b.* 1972). *Career*: 1962–64, apprentice, Vanguard Engineering; 1964–66, Junior Production Engineer, Vanguard Engineering; 1966–70, Senior Engineer, Vanguard Engineering; 1970–74 Production Manager, Vanguard Engineering; 1974–78, Manufacturing Manager, Lewis & Arbuckle Ltd; 1978–80, Manufacturing Director, Rumcol Castings; 1980–85, Managing Director, Rumcol Castings. *Present Position*: Managing Director, J. Pringle & Sons Casting & General Engineering.

That's who I am.

Vic grimaces at his own reflection, as if to say: come off it, no identity crises, please. Somebody has to earn a living in this family.

He shrugs on his dressing-gown, which hangs from a hook on the bathroom door, switches off the light, and softly re-enters the dimly lit bedroom. Marjorie has, however, been woken by the sound of plumbing.

"Is that you?" she says drowsily; then, without waiting for an answer, "I'll be down in a minute."

"Don't hurry," says Vic. *Don't bother* would be more honest, for he prefers to have the kitchen to himself in the early morning, to prepare his own simple breakfast and enjoy the first cigarette of the day undisturbed. Marjorie, however, feels that she must put in an appearance downstairs, however token, before he leaves for work, and there is a sense in which Vic understands and approves of this gesture. His own mother was always first up in the mornings, to see husband and son off to work or college, and continued the habit almost till the day she died.

As Vic descends the stairs, a high-pitched electronic squeal rises from below. The pressure of his foot on a wired pad under the stair-carpet has triggered the burglar alarm, which Raymond, amazingly, must have remembered to set after coming in at God knows what hour last night. Vic goes to the console beside the front door and punches in the numerical code that disarms the apparatus. He has fifteen seconds to do this, before the squeal turns into a screech and the alarm bell on the outside wall starts yammering. All the houses in the neighbourhood have these alarms, and Vic admits that they are necessary, with burglaries increasing in frequency and boldness all the time, but the system they inherited from the previous owners of the house, with its magnetic contacts, infra-red scanners, pressure pads and panic buttons, is in his opinion over-elaborate. It takes about five minutes to set it up before you retire to bed, and if you come back downstairs for something you have to cancel it and start all over again. *The sufferings of the rich*, Raymond sneered when Vic was complaining of this one day – Raymond, who despises his parents' affluence while continuing to enjoy its comforts and conveniences, such as rent-free centrally heated accommodation, constant hot water, free laundry service, use of mother's car, use of TV, video recorder, stereo system, etcetera etcetera. Vic feels his blood pressure rising at the thought of his eldest son, who dropped out of university four months ago and has not been usefully occupied since, now swaddled in a duvet upstairs, naked except for a single gold earring, sleeping off last night's booze. Vic shakes his head irritably to rid his mind of the image.

He opens the inner front door that leads to the enclosed porch and glances at the doormat. Empty. The newspaper boy is late, or perhaps there is no paper today because of a strike. An infra-red scanner winks its inflamed eye at him as he goes into the lounge in search of reading matter. The floor and furniture are littered with the dismembered carcasses of the *Mail on Sunday* and the *Sunday Times*. He picks up the Business Section of the *Times* and takes it into the kitchen. While the kettle is boiling he scans the front page. A headline catches his eye: "LAWSON COUNTS THE COST AS TAX HOPES FADE."

Nigel Lawson, the Chancellor, is this weekend closeted with his Treasury team assessing the danger to his economic strategy from last week's rise in interest rates, and the sharp rise in unemployment.

So what else is new?

The kettle boils. Vic makes a pot of strong tea, puts two slices of white bread in the toaster, and opens the louvres of the venetian blinds on the kitchen window to peer into the garden. A grey, blustery morning, with no frost. Squirrels bound across the lawn like balls of fluff blown by the wind. Magpies strut from flowerbed to flowerbed, greedily devouring the grubs that he turned up in yesterday's gardening. Blackbirds, sparrows, robins, and other birds whose names Vic doesn't know, skip and hop about at a discreet distance from the magpies. All these creatures seem very much at home in Vic's garden, although it is only two miles from the city centre. One morning not

7

long ago he saw a fox walking past this same window. Vic tapped on the pane. The fox stopped and turned his head to look at Vic for a moment, as if to say, *Yes?* and then proceeded calmly on his way, his brush swaying in the air behind him. It is Vic's impression that English wildlife is getting streetwise, moving from the country into the city where the living is easier – where there are no traps, pesticides, hunters and sportsmen, but plenty of well-stocked garbage bins, and house-wives like Marjorie, softhearted or softheaded enough to throw their scraps into the garden, creating animal soup-kitchens. Nature is joining the human race and going on the dole.

Vic has eaten his two slices of toast and is on his third cup of tea and his first cigarette of the day when Marjorie shuffles into the kitchen in her dressing-gown and slippers, a scarf over her curlers, her pale round face puffy with sleep. She carries the *Daily Mail*, which has just been delivered.

"Smoking," she says, in a tone at once resigned and reproachful, condensing into a single word an argument well-known to both of them. Vic grunts, the distillation of an equally familiar rejoinder. He glances at the kitchen clock.

"Shouldn't Sandra and Gary be getting up? I won't waste my breath on Raymond."

"Gary doesn't have school today. The teachers are on strike."

"*What?*" he says accusingly, his anger at the teachers somehow getting displaced onto Marjorie.

"Industrial action, or whatever they call it. He brought a note home on Friday."

"Industrial *in*action, you mean. You don't see teachers out on the picket line, in the cold and the rain, have you noticed? They're just sitting around in their warm staff rooms, chewing the fat, while the kids are sent home to get into mischief. That's not action. It's not an industry, either, come to that. It's a profession and it's about time they started to act like professionals."

"Well . . ." says Marjorie placatingly.

"What about Sandra? Is the Sixth Form College taking 'industrial action' too?"

"No, I'm taking her to the doctor's."

"What's the matter with her?"

Marjorie yawns evasively. "Oh, nothing serious."

"Why can't she go on her own? A girl of seventeen should be able to go to the doctor's without someone to hold her hand."

"I don't go in with her, not unless she wants me to. I just wait with her."

Vic regards his wife suspiciously. "You're not going shopping with her afterwards?"

Marjorie blushes. "Well, she needs a new pair of shoes . . ."

"You're a fool, Marje!" Vic exclaims. "You spoil that girl something rotten. All she thinks about is clothes, shoes, hairstyles. What kind of A-Levels do you think she's going to get?"

"I don't know. But if she doesn't want to go to University . . ."

"What does she want to do, then? What's the latest?"

"She's thinking of hairdressing."

"Hairdressing!" Vic puts as much contempt into his voice as he can muster.

"Anyway, she's a pretty girl, why shouldn't she enjoy clothes and so on, while she's young?"

"Why shouldn't *you* enjoy dressing her up, you mean. You know you treat her like a doll, Marje, don't you?"

Rather than answer this question, Marjorie reverts to an earlier one. "She's been having trouble with her periods, if you must know," she says, imputing a prurient inquisitiveness to Vic, although she is well aware that such gynaecological disclosures are the last thing he wants, especially at this hour of the morning. The pathology of women's bodies is a source of great mystery and unease to Vic. Their bleedings and leakages, their lumps and growths, their peculiarly painful-sounding surgical operations – scraping of wombs, stripping of veins, amputation of breasts – the mere mention of such things makes him wince and cringe, and lately the menopause has added new items to the repertory: the hot flush, flooding, and something sinister called a bloat. "I expect he'll put her on the pill," says Marjorie, making herself a fresh pot of tea.

"What?"

"To regulate her periods. I expect Dr Roberts will put Sandra on the pill."

Vic grunts again, but this time his intonation is ambiguous and uncertain. He has a feeling that his womenfolk are up to something. Could the real purpose of Sandra's visit to the doctor's be to fix her up with contraception? With Marjorie's approval? He knows he doesn't approve himself. Sandra having sex? At seventeen? With whom? Not that spotty youth in the army surplus overcoat, what's his name, Cliff, not him for God's sake. Not with anyone. An image of his daughter in the act of love, her white knees parted, a dark shape above her, flashes unbidden into his head and fills him with rage and disgust.

He is conscious of Marjorie's watery blue eyes scanning him speculatively over the rim of her teacup, inviting further discussion of Sandra, but he can't face it, not this morning, not with a day's work ahead of him. Not at any time, to be honest. Discussion of Sandra's sex-life could easily stray into the area of his and Marjorie's sex-life, or rather

9

the lack of it, and he would rather not go into that. Let sleeping dogs lie. Vic compares the kitchen clock with his watch and rises from the table.

"Shall I do you a bit of bacon?" says Marjorie.

"No, I've finished."

"You ought to have a cooked breakfast, these cold mornings."

"I haven't time."

"Why don't we get a microwave? I could cook you a bit of bacon in seconds with a microwave."

"Did you know," says Vic, "that ninety-six per cent of the world's microwave ovens are made in Japan, Taiwan or Korea?"

"Everybody we know has got one," says Marjorie.

"Exactly," says Vic.

Marjorie looks unhappily at Vic, uncertain of his drift. "I thought I might price some this morning," she says. "After Sandra's shoes."

"Where would you put it?" Vic enquires, looking round at the kitchen surfaces already cluttered with numerous electrical appliances – toaster, kettle, coffee-maker, food-processor, electric wok, chip-fryer, waffle-maker . . .

"I thought we could put the electric wok away. We never use it. A microwave would be more useful."

"Well, all right, price them but don't buy. I can get one cheaper through the trade."

Marjorie brightens. She smiles, and two dimples appear in her pasty cheeks, still shiny from last night's application of face cream. It was her dimples that first attracted Vic to Marjorie twenty-five years ago, when she worked in the typing pool at Vanguard. These days they appear infrequently, but the prospect of a shopping expedition is one of the few things that are guaranteed to bring them out.

"Just don't expect *me* to eat anything cooked in it," he says.

Marjorie's dimples fade abruptly, like the sun going behind a cloud. "Why not?"

"It's not proper cooking, is it? My mother would turn in her grave."

Vic takes the *Daily Mail* with him to the lavatory, the one at the back of the house, next to the tradesmen's entrance, with a plain white suite, intended for the use of charladies, gardeners and workmen. By tacit agreement, Vic customarily moves his bowels in here, while Marjorie uses the guest cloakroom off the front hall, so that the atmosphere of the *en suite* bathroom remains unpolluted.

Vic smokes a second cigarette as he sits at stool, and scans the *Daily Mail*. Westland and Heseltine are still making the headlines. STOP THE NO. 10 WHISPERS. MAGGIE'S BID TO COOL OFF BATTLE. He flicks through the inside pages. MURDOCH FACING UNION CLASH. THE IMAM'S CALL TO PRAYER MAKES THE VICAR TALK OF BEDLAM. HEARTACHE AHEAD FOR THE BRIDE WHO MARRIED TWICE. WE'RE IN THE SUPER-LEAGUE OF NATIONS. Hang about.

Britain is back in the Super-League of top industrial nations, it is claimed today. Only Germany, Holland, Japan and Switzerland can now match us for economic growth, price stability and strong balance of payments, says Dr David Lomax, the Natwest's economic adviser.

"Match" presumably means "beat". And since when was *Holland* an industrial superpower? Even so, it must be all balls, a mirage massaged from statistics. You only have to drive through the West Midlands to see that if we are in the Super-League of top industrial nations, somebody must be moving the goalposts. Vic is all in favour of backing Britain, but there are times when the *Mail*'s windy chauvinism gets on his tits. He takes a drag on his cigarette and taps the ash between his legs, hearing a faint hiss as it hits the water. 100 M.P.G. FAMILY CAR LOOKING GOOD IN TESTS.

Trials have been started by British Leyland of their revolutionary light-weight aluminium engine for a world-beating family car capable of 100 miles per gallon.

When was the last time we were supposed to have a world-beating aluminium engine? The Hillman Imp, right? Where are they now, the Hillman Imps of yesteryear? In the scrapyards, every one, or nearly. And the Linwood plant a graveyard, grass growing between the assembly lines, corrugated-iron roofs flapping in the wind. A car that nobody wanted to buy, built on a site chosen for political not commercial reasons, hundreds of miles from its component suppliers. He turns to the City Pages. HOW TO GET UP A HEAD OF ESTEEM.

What has been designated Industry Year has got off to a predictably silly start. Various bodies in Manufacturing Industry are working themselves into one of their regular lathers about the supposed low social esteem bestowed upon engineers and engineering.

Vic reads this article with mixed feelings. Industry Year is certainly a lot of balls. On the other hand, the idea that society undervalues its engineers is not.

It is 7.40 when Vic emerges from the lavatory. The tempo of his actions begins to accelerate. He strides through the kitchen, where

Marjorie is listlessly loading his soiled breakfast things into the dishwasher, and runs up the stairs. Back in the *en suite* bathroom, he briskly cleans his teeth and brushes his hair. He goes into the bedroom and puts on a clean white shirt and a suit. He has six business suits, which he wears in daily rotation. He used to think five was enough, but acquired an additional one after Raymond wisecracked, "If that's the charcoal grey worsted, it must be Tuesday." Today it is the turn of the navy blue pinstripe. He selects a tie diagonally striped in dark tones of red, blue and grey. He levers his feet into a pair of highly polished black calf Oxfords. A frayed lace snaps under too vigorous a tug, and he curses. He rummages in the back of his wardrobe for an old black shoe with a suitable lace and uncovers a cardboard box containing a brand-new clock radio, made in Hong Kong, sealed in a transparent plastic envelope and nestling in a polystyrene mould. Vic sighs and grimaces. Such discoveries are not uncommon at this time of year. Marjorie has a habit of buying Christmas presents early, hiding them away like a squirrel, and then forgetting all about them.

When he comes downstairs again, she is hovering in the hall.

"Who was the clock radio for, then?"

"What?"

"I found a brand-new clock radio at the back of the wardrobe."

Marjorie covers her mouth with her hand. "Sst! I *knew* I'd got something for your Dad."

"Didn't we give him a Christmas present, then?"

"Of course we did. You remember, you rushed out on Christmas Eve and got him that electric blanket . . . Never mind, it will do for next year."

"Hasn't he already got a clock radio? Didn't we give him one a few years ago?"

"Did we?" says Marjorie vaguely. "Perhaps one of the boys would like it, then."

"What they need is a clock with a bomb attached to it, not a radio," says Vic, patting his pockets, checking for wallet, diary, keyring, calculator, cigarettes and lighter.

Marjorie helps him on with his camelhair overcoat, a garment she persuaded him to buy against his better judgment, for it hangs well below his knees and, he thinks, accentuates his short stature, as well as making him look like a prosperous bookie. "When will you be home?" she enquires.

"I don't know. You'd better keep my dinner warm."

"Don't be too late."

She closes her eyes and tilts her face towards him. He brushes her lips with his, then jerks his head in the direction of the first floor. "Get that idle shower out of bed."

"They need sleep when they're growing, Vic."

"Raymond's not *growing*, for Christ's sake. He stopped growing years ago, unless he's growing a beer belly, which wouldn't surprise me."

"Well, Gary's still growing."

"Make sure he does some homework today."

"Yes, dear."

Vic is quite sure she has no intention of carrying out his instructions. If she hadn't arranged to take Sandra to the doctor's Marjorie would probably go back to bed herself, now, with a cup of tea and the *Daily Mail*. A few weeks before, he'd returned home soon after getting to work because he'd left some important papers behind, and found the house totally silent, all three children and their mother sound asleep at 9.30 in the morning. No wonder the country is going to the dogs.

Vic passes through the glazed porch and out into the open air. The cold wind ruffles his hair and makes him flinch for a moment, but it is refreshing after the stale warmth of the house, and he takes a deep breath or two on his way to the garage. As he approaches the garage door it swings open as if by magic – in fact by electricity, activated by a remote-control device in Vic's pocket – a feat that never fails to give him a deep, childlike pleasure. Inside, the gleaming dark blue Jaguar V12, Registration Number VIC 100, waits beside Marjorie's silver Metro. He backs the car out, shutting the garage door with another touch on the remote control. Marjorie has now appeared at the lounge window, clutching her dressing-gown across her bosom with one hand and waving timidly with the other. Vic smiles conciliatingly, puts the automatic gear lever into Drive, and glides away.

Now begins the best half-hour of the day, the drive to work. In fact it is not quite half-an-hour – the journey usually takes twenty-four minutes, but Vic wishes it were longer. It is an interval of peace between the irritations of home and the anxieties of work, a time of pure sensation, total control, effortless superiority. For the Jaguar is superior to every other car on the road, Vic is convinced of that. When Midland Amalgamated headhunted him for the MD's job at Pringle's they offered him a Rover 3500 Vanden Plas, but Vic stuck out for the Jaguar, a car normally reserved for divisional chairmen, and to his great satisfaction he had got one, even though it wasn't quite new. It had to be a British car, of course, since Pringle's did so much business with the local automotive industry – not that Vic has ever driven a foreign car: foreign cars are anathema to him, their sudden invasion of British roads in the 1970s marked the beginning of the region's economic ruin in his view – but he has to admit that you don't have a lot of choice in British cars when it comes to matching the top-of-the-range

Mercedes and BMWs. In fact the Jag is just about the only one that can really wipe the smiles off their drivers' faces, unless you're talking Rolls-Royce or Bentley.

He pauses at the T-junction where Avondale Road meets Barton Road, on which the rush-hour traffic is already beginning to thicken. The driver of a Ford Transit van, though he has priority, hangs back respectfully to let Vic filter left. Vic nods his thanks, turns left, then right again, picking his way through the broad, tree-lined residential streets with practised ease. He is skirting the University, whose tall redbrick clock-tower is occasionally visible above trees and rooftops. Though he lives on its doorstep, so to speak, Vic has never been inside the place. He knows it chiefly as a source of seasonal traffic jams about which Marjorie sometimes complains (the University day begins too late and finishes too early to inconvenience Vic himself) and of distractingly pretty girls about whose safety he worries, seeing them walking to and fro between their halls of residence and the Students' Union in the evenings. With its massive architecture and landscaped grounds, guarded at every entrance by watchful security staff, the University seems to Vic rather like a small city-state, an academic Vatican, from which he keeps his distance, both intimidated by and disapproving of its air of privileged detachment from the vulgar, bustling industrial city in which it is embedded. His own *alma mater*, situated a few miles away, was a very different kind of institution, a dingy tower block, crammed with machinery and lab benches, overlooking a railway marshalling yard and a roundabout on the inner ring road. In his day a College of Advanced Technology, it has since grown in size and been raised to the status of a university, but without putting on any airs and graces. And quite right too. If you make college too comfortable nobody will ever want to leave it to do proper work.

Vic leaves the residential area around the University and filters into the traffic moving sluggishly along the London Road in the direction of the City Centre. This is the slowest part of his morning journey, but the Jaguar, whispering along in automatic, takes the strain. Vic selects a cassette and slots it into the four-speaker stereo system. The voice of Carly Simon fills the interior of the car. Vic's taste in music is narrow but keen. He favours female vocalists, slow tempos, lush arrangements of tuneful melodies in the jazz–soul idiom. Carly Simon, Dusty Springfield, Roberta Flack, Dionne Warwick, Diana Ross, Randy Crawford and, more recently, Sade and Jennifer Rush. The subtle inflexions of these voices, honeyed or slightly hoarse, moaning and whispering of women's love, its joys and disappointments, soothe his nerves and relax his limbs. He would of course never dream of playing these tapes on the music centre at home, risking the derision

of his children. It is a very private pleasure, a kind of musical mas-
turbation, all part of the ritual of the drive to work. He would enjoy it
more, though, if he were not obliged to read at the same time, in the
rear windows of other cars, crude reminders of a more basic sexuality.
YOUNG FARMERS DO IT IN THEIR WELLIES. WATER SKIERS DO IT STANDING
UP. HOOT IF YOU HAD IT LAST NIGHT. It, it, it. Vic's knuckles are white
as he grips the steering wheel. Why should decent people have to put
up with this crap? There ought to be a law.

Now Vic has reached the last traffic lights before the system of
tunnels and flyovers that will conduct him without further interruption
through the centre of the city. A red Toyota Celica draws up beside
him, then inches forward as its driver rides his clutch, evidently
intending a quick getaway. The lights turn to amber and the Toyota
darts forward, revealing, wouldn't you know it, a legend in its rear
window, HANG GLIDERS DO IT IN MID AIR. Vic waits law-abidingly for
the green light, then presses the accelerator hard. The Jaguar surges
forward, catches the Toyota in two seconds, and sweeps effortlessly
past – Carly Simon, by happy coincidence, hitting a thrilling crescendo
at the very same moment. Vic glances in his rear-view mirror and
smiles thinly. Teach him to buy a Jap car.

It won't, of course. Vic is well aware of the hollowness of his small
victory, a huge thirsty 5.3-litre engine pitted against the Toyota's
economical 1.8. But never mind common sense for the moment, this is
the time of indulgence, suspended between home and work, the time
of effortless motion, cushioned in real leather, insulated from the noise
and fumes of the city by the padded coachwork, the tinted glass, the
sensuous music. The car's long prow dips into the first tunnel. In and
out, down and up. Vic threads the tunnels, switches lanes, swings out
onto a long covered ramp that leads to a six-lane expressway thrust
like a gigantic concrete fist through the backstreets of his boyhood.
Every morning Vic drives over the flattened site of his Gran's house
and passes at chimney-pot level the one in which he himself grew up,
where his widower father still stubbornly lives on in spite of all Vic's
efforts to persuade him to move, like a sailor clinging to the rigging of
a sinking ship – buffeted, deafened and choked by the thundering
torrent of traffic thirty yards from his bedroom window.

Vic swings on to the motorway, going north-west, and for a few
miles gives the Jaguar its head, moving smoothly up the outside lane
at 90, keeping a watchful eye on the rear-view mirror, though the
police rarely bother you in the rush hour, they are as eager as anyone
to keep the traffic flowing. To his right and left spreads a familiar
landscape, so familiar that he does not really see it, an expanse of
houses and factories, warehouses and sheds, railway lines and canals,

piles of scrap metal and heaps of damaged cars, container ports and lorry parks, cooling towers and gasometers. A monochrome landscape, grey under a low grey sky, its horizons blurred by a grey haze.

Vic Wilcox has now, strictly speaking, left the city of Rummidge and passed into an area known as the Dark Country – so called because of the pall of smoke that hung over it, and the film of coaldust and soot that covered it, in the heyday of the Industrial Revolution. He knows a little of the history of this region, having done a prize-winning project on it at school. Rich mineral deposits were discovered here in the early nineteenth century: coal, iron, limestone. Mines were sunk, quarries excavated, and ironworks sprang up everywhere to exploit the new technique of smelting iron ore with coke, using limestone as a flux. The fields were gradually covered with pitheads, foundries, factories and workshops, and rows of wretched hovels for the men, women and children who worked in them: a sprawling, unplanned, industrial conurbation that was gloomy by day, fearsome by night. A writer called Thomas Carlyle described it in 1824 as *"A frightful scene . . . a dense cloud of pestilential smoke hangs over it forever . . . and at night the whole region becomes like a volcano spitting fire from a thousand tubes of brick."* A little later, Charles Dickens recorded travelling *"through miles of cinder-paths and blazing furnaces and roaring steam engines, and such a mass of dirt, gloom and misery as I never before witnessed."* Queen Victoria had the curtains of her train window drawn when she passed through the region so that her eyes should not be offended by its ugliness and squalor.

The economy and outward appearance of the area have changed considerably since those days. As the seams of coal and iron were exhausted, or became unprofitable to work, mining and smelting diminished. But industries based on iron – casting, forging, engineering, all those kinds of manufacturing known generically as "metal-bashing" – spread and multiplied, until their plant met and merged with the expanding industrial suburbs of Rummidge. The shrinkage of heavy industry, and the development of new forms of energy, have reduced the visible pollution of the air, though the deadlier fumes of leaded petrol exhaust, drifting from the motorways with which the whole area is looped and knotted, thicken the characteristic grey haziness of the Midlands light. Nowadays the Dark Country is not noticeably darker than its neighbouring city, and of country there is precious little to be seen. Foreign visitors sometimes suppose that the region gets its name not from its environmental character but from the complexions of so many of its inhabitants, immigrant families from India, Pakistan and the Caribbean, drawn here in the boom years of the fifties and sixties, when jobs were plentiful, and now bearing the brunt of high un-employment.

All too soon it is time to slow down and leave the motorway, de-scending into smaller-scale streets, into the congestion of traffic lights, roundabouts, T-junctions. This is West Wallsbury, a district domin-ated by factories, large and small, old and new. Many are silent, some derelict, their windows starred with smashed glass. Receiverships and closures have ravaged the area in recent years, giving a desolate look to its streets. Since the election of the Tory Government of 1979, which allowed the pound to rise on the back of North Sea oil in the early eighties and left British industry defenceless in the face of foreign competition, or (according to your point of view) exposed its inef-ficiency (Vic inclines to the first view, but in certain moods will admit the force of the second), one-third of all the engineering companies in the West Midlands have closed down. There is nothing quite so forlorn as a closed factory – Vic Wilcox knows, having supervised a shutdown himself in his time. A factory is sustained by the energy of its own functioning, the throb and whine of machinery, the clash of metal, the unceasing motion of the assembly lines, the ebb and flow of workers changing shifts, the hiss of airbrakes and the growl of diesel engines from wagons delivering raw materials at one gate, taking away finished goods at the other. When you put a stop to all that, when the place is silent and empty, all that is left is a large, ramshackle shed – cold, filthy and depressing. Well, that won't happen at Pringle's, hopefully, as they say. Hopefully.

Vic is very near his factory now. A scarlet neon sign, *Susan's Sauna*, subject of many nudge-nudge jokes at work, but to Vic merely a useful landmark, glows above a dingy shop-front. A hundred yards further on, he turns down Coney Lane, passes Shopfix, Atkinson Insulation, Bitomark, then runs alongside the railings that fence the Pringle site until he reaches the main entrance. It is a long fence, and a large site. In its heyday, in the post-war boom, Pringle's employed four thousand men. Now the workforce has shrunk to less than a thousand, and much of the plant is in disuse. There are buildings and annexes that Vic has never been inside. It is cheaper to let them rot than to clear them away.

Vic hoots impatiently at the barrier; the security man's face appears at the window and flashes an ingratiating smile. Vic nods grimly back. Bugger was probably reading a newspaper. His predecessor had been fired at Vic's insistence just before Christmas when, returning un-expectedly to the factory at night, he found the man watching a port-able TV instead of the video monitors he was paid to watch. It looks as though this one is not much of an improvement. Perhaps they should employ another security firm. Vic makes a mental note to raise the matter with George Prendergast, his Personnel Director.

The barrier is raised and he drives to his personal parking space next to the front entrance of the office block. He checks the statistics of his journey on the digital dashboard display. Distance covered: 9.8 miles. Journey time: 25 mins. 14 secs. Average for the morning rush-hour. Petrol consumption: 17.26 m.p.g. Not bad – would have been better if he hadn't put the Toyota in its place.

Vic pushes through the swing doors to the reception lobby, a reasonably impressive space, its walls lined with light oak panelling installed in a more prosperous era. The furniture is looking a bit shabby, though. The clock on the wall, an irritating type with no numbers on its face, suggests that the time is just before half-past eight. Doreen and Lesley, the two telephonist–receptionists, are taking off their coats behind the counter. They smile and simper, patting their hair and smoothing their skirts.

"Morning Mr Wilcox."

"Morning. Think we could do with some new chairs in here?"

"Oh yes, Mr Wilcox, these are ever so hard."

"I didn't mean *your* chairs, I mean for visitors."

"Oh . . ." They don't know quite how to react. He is still Mr New Broom, slightly feared. As he pushes through the swing doors and walks down the corridor towards his office, he can hear them spluttering with stifled laughter.

"Good morning, Vic." His secretary, Shirley, smirks from behind her desk, self-righteous at being at her post before the boss, even though she is at this moment inspecting her face in a compact mirror. She is a mature woman with piled hair of an improbable yellow hue, and a voluptuous bosom on which her reading glasses, retained round her neck by a chain, rest as upon a shelf. Vic inherited her from his predecessor, who had evidently cultivated an informal working relationship. It was not with any encouragement from himself that she began to address him as Vic, but he was obliged to concede the point. She had worked for Pringle's for years, and Vic was heavily dependent on her know-how while he eased himself into the job.

"Morning, Shirley. Make us a cup of coffee, will you?" Vic's working day is lubricated by endless cups of instant coffee. He hangs up his camelhair coat in the anteroom that connects his office with Shirley's, and passes into the former. He shrugs off the jacket of his suit and drapes it over the back of a chair. He sits down at his desk and opens his diary. Shirley comes in with coffee and a large photograph album.

18

"I thought you'd like to see Tracey's new portfolio," she says.

Shirley has a seventeen-year-old daughter whose ambition is to be a photographic model, and she is forever thrusting glossy pictures of this well-developed young hussy, crammed into skimpy swimsuits or revealing underwear, under Vic's nose. At first, he suspected her of trying to curry favour by pandering to his lust, but later came to the conclusion that it was genuine parental pride. The silly bitch really couldn't see that there was anything dubious about turning your daughter into a pin-up.

"Oh yes?" he says, with scarcely concealed impatience. Then, as he opens the portfolio: "Good Christ!"

The pouting, weak-chinned face under the blonde curls is familiar enough, but the two huge naked breasts, thrust towards the camera like pink blancmanges tipped with cherries, are a new departure. He turns the stiff, polythene-covered pages rapidly.

"Nice, aren't they?" says Shirley fondly.

"You let someone take pictures of your daughter like this?"

"I was there sort of thing. In the studio."

"I'll be frank with you," says Vic, closing the album and handing it back. "I wouldn't let *my* daughter."

"I don't see the harm," says Shirley. "People think nothing of it nowadays, topless sort of thing. You should have seen the beach at Rhodes last summer. And even television. If you've got a beautiful body, why not make the most of it? Look at Sam Fox!"

"Who's he?"

"She. Samantha Fox. You *know*!" Incredulity raises Shirley's voice an octave. "The top Page Three girl. D'you know how much she earned last year?"

"More than me, I don't doubt. And more than Pringle's will make this year, if you waste any more of my time."

"Oh, you," says Shirley roguishly, adept at receiving reprimands as if they are jokes.

"Tell Brian I want to see him, will you?"

"I don't think he's in yet."

Vic grunts, unsurprised that his Marketing Director has not yet arrived. "As soon as he is, then. Let's do some letters in the mean-time."

The telephone rings. Vic picks up the receiver. "Wilcox."

"Vic?"

The voice of Stuart Baxter, chairman of Midland Amalgamated's Engineering and Foundry Division, sounds faintly disappointed. He was hoping, no doubt, to be told that Mr Wilcox wasn't in yet, so that he could leave a message for Vic to ring back, thus putting him on the

19

defensive, knowing that his divisional chief knew that he, Vic, hadn't been at his desk as early as him, Stuart Baxter. Vic becomes even more convinced that this was the motive for the call as it proceeds, because Stuart Baxter has nothing new to communicate. They had the same conversation the previous Friday afternoon, about the disappointing figures for Pringle's production in December.

"There's always a downturn in December, Stuart, you know that. With the long Christmas holiday."

"Even allowing for that, it's well down, Vic. Compared to last year."

"And it's going to be well down again this month, you might as well know that now."

"I'm sorry to hear you say that, Vic. It makes life very difficult for me."

"We haven't got the foundry on song, yet. The core blowers are always breaking down. I'd like to buy a new machine, fully automated, to replace the lot."

"Too expensive. You'd do better to buy in from outside. It's not worth investing in that foundry."

"The foundry has a lot of potential. It's a good workforce. They do nice work. Any road, it's not just the foundry. We're working on a new production model for the whole factory – new stock control, new purchasing policy. Everything on computer. But it takes time."

"Time is what we haven't got, Vic."

"Right. So why don't we both get back to work now, instead of nattering on like a couple of housewives over the garden fence?"

There is a momentary silence on the line, then a forced chuckle, as Stuart Baxter decides not to take offence. Nevertheless he *has* taken offence. It was probably a foolish thing to say, but Vic shrugs off any regret as he puts the receiver down. He is not in the business of ingratiating himself with Stuart Baxter. He is in the business of making J. Pringle & Sons profitable.

Vic flicks a switch on his telephone console and summons Shirley, whom he had gestured out of the office while Baxter was talking, to take some letters. He leafs through the file of correspondence in his In-tray, the two vertical lines in his brow above the nose drawing closer together as he concentrates on names, figures, dates. He lights a cigarette, inhales deeply, and blows two plumes of smoke through his nostrils. Outside the sky is still overcast, and the murky yellow light that filters through the vertical louvres of the window blinds is hardly enough to read by. He switches on his desk lamp, casting a pool of light on the documents. Through walls and windows comes a muffled compound noise of machinery and traffic, the soothing, satisfying sound of men at work.

2

And there, for the time being, let us leave Vic Wilcox, while we travel back an hour or two in time, a few miles in space, to meet a very different character. A character who, rather awkwardly for me, doesn't herself believe in the concept of character. That is to say (a favourite phrase of her own), Robyn Penrose, Temporary Lecturer in English Literature at the University of Rummidge, holds that "character" is a bourgeois myth, an illusion created to reinforce the ideology of capitalism. As evidence for this assertion she will point to the fact that the rise of the novel (the literary genre of "character" *par excellence*) in the eighteenth century coincided with the rise of capitalism; that the triumph of the novel over all other literary genres in the nineteenth century coincided with the triumph of capitalism; and that the modernist and postmodernist deconstruction of the classic novel in the twentieth century has coincided with the terminal crisis of capitalism.

Why the classic novel should have collaborated with the spirit of capitalism is perfectly obvious to Robyn. Both are expressions of a secularised Protestant ethic, both dependent on the idea of an autonomous individual self who is responsible for and in control of his/her own destiny, seeking happiness and fortune in competition with other autonomous selves. This is true of the novel considered both as commodity and as mode of representation. (Thus Robyn in full seminar spate.) That is to say, it applies to novelists themselves as well as to their heroes and heroines. The novelist is a capitalist of the imagination. He or she invents a product which consumers didn't know they wanted until it was made available, manufactures it with the assistance of purveyors of risk capital known as publishers, and sells it in competition with makers of marginally differentiated products of the same kind. The first major English novelist, Daniel Defoe, was a merchant. The second, Samuel Richardson, was a printer. The novel was the first mass-produced cultural artefact. (At this point Robyn, with elbows tucked into her sides, would spread her hands outwards from the wrist, as if to imply that there is no need to say more. But of course she always has much more to say.)

According to Robyn (or, more precisely, according to the writers who have influenced her thinking on these matters) there is no such thing as the "self" on which capitalism and the classic novel are founded – that is to say, a finite, unique soul or essence that constitutes a person's identity; there is only a subject position in an infinite web of discourses – the discourses of power, sex, family, science, religion, poetry, etc. And by the same token, there is no such thing as an author, that is to say, one who originates a work of fiction *ab nihilo*. Every text is a product of intertextuality, a tissue of allusions to and citations of other texts; and, in the famous words of Jacques Derrida (famous to people like Robyn, anyway), *"il n'y a pas de hors-texte"*, there is nothing outside the text. There are no origins, there is only production, and we produce our "selves" in language. Not *"you are what you eat"* but *"you are what you speak"* or, rather *"you are what speaks you"*, is the axiomatic basis of Robyn's philosophy, which she would call, if required to give it a name, "semiotic materialism". It might seem a bit bleak, a bit inhuman ("antihumanist, yes; inhuman, no," she would interject), somewhat deterministic ("not at all; the truly determined subject is he who is not aware of the discursive formations that determine him. Or her," she would add scrupulously, being among other things a feminist), but in practice this doesn't seem to affect her behaviour very noticeably – she seems to have ordinary human feelings, ambitions, desires, to suffer anxieties, frustrations, fears, like anyone else in this imperfect world, and to have a natural inclination to try and make it a better place. I shall therefore take the liberty of treating her as a character, not utterly different in kind, though of course belonging to a very different social species, from Vic Wilcox.

Robyn rises somewhat later than Vic this dark January Monday. Her alarm clock, a replica of an old-fashioned instrument purchased from Habitat, with an analogue dial and a little brass bell on the top, rouses her from a deep sleep at 7.30. Unlike Vic, Robyn invariably sleeps until woken. Then worries rush into her consciousness, as into his, like clamorous patients who have been waiting all night for the doctor's surgery to open; but she deals with them in a rational, orderly manner. This morning she gives priority to the fact that it is the first day of the winter term, and that she has a lecture to deliver and two tutorials to conduct. Although she has been teaching now for some eight years, on and off, although she enjoys it, feels she is good at it, and would like to go on doing it for the rest of her life if possible, she always feels a twinge of anxiety at the beginning of a new term. This does not disturb her self-confidence: a good teacher, like a good actress, should not be immune from stage fright. She sits up in bed for a moment, doing some complicated breathing and flexing of the abdominal muscles, learned in yoga classes, to calm herself. This exercise is rendered easier to perform by the fact that Charles is not lying beside her to observe and ask ironic questions about it. He left the previous evening to drive to Ipswich, where his own term is due to begin today at the University of Suffolk.

And who is Charles? While Robyn is getting up, and getting ready for the day, thinking mostly about the nineteenth-century industrial novels on which she has to lecture this morning, I will tell you about Charles, and other salient facts of her biography.

She was born, and christened Roberta Anne Penrose, in Melbourne, Australia, nearly thirty-three years ago, but left that country at the age of five to accompany her parents to England. Her father, then a young academic historian, had a scholarship to pursue post-doctoral research into nineteenth-century European diplomacy at Oxford. Instead of returning to Australia, he took a post at a university on the South Coast of England, where he has been ever since, now occupying a personal Chair. Robyn has only the dimmest memories of the country of her birth, and has never had the opportunity to refresh or renew them, Professor Penrose's characteristic response to any suggestion that the family should revisit Australia being a shudder.

Robyn had a comfortable childhood, growing up in a pleasant, unostentatious house with a view of the sea. She attended an excellent direct-grant grammar school (which has since gone independent, much to Robyn's disgust) where she was Head Girl and Captain of Games and which she left with four A grades at A-Level. Though urged by the school to apply for a place at Oxbridge, she chose instead to go to Sussex University, as bright young people often did in the 1970s, because the new universities were considered exciting and innovatory places to study at. Under the umbrella of a degree course in English Literature, Robyn read Freud and Marx, Kafka and Kierkegaard, which she certainly couldn't have done at Oxbridge. She also set about losing her virginity, and accomplished this feat without difficulty, but without much pleasure, in her first term. In her second, she was recklessly promiscuous, and in her third she met Charles.

(Robyn kicks off the duvet and gets out of bed. She stands upright in her long white cotton nightgown from Laura Ashley, scratches her bottom through the cambric, and yawns. She goes to the window, treating the rugs spread on the sanded and waxed pine floorboards as stepping-stones, pulls back the curtain, and peers out. She looks up at the grey clouds scudding across the sky, down at a vista of narrow back gardens, some neat and trim with goldfish ponds and brightly painted play equipment, others tatty and neglected, cluttered with broken appliances and discarded furniture. It is an upwardly mobile street of nineteenth-century terraced cottages, where houseproud middle-class owners rub shoulders with less tidy and less affluent working-class occupiers. A gust of wind rattles the sash window and the draught makes Robyn shiver. She has not double-glazed the house

23

in order to preserve its architectural integrity. Clutching herself, she skips to the door from rug to rug, like a Scottish country dancer, across the landing and into the bathroom, which has smaller windows and is warmer.)

The Sussex campus, with its tastefully harmonised buildings in the modernist-Palladian style, arranged in elegant perspective at the foot of the South Downs a few miles outside Brighton, was much admired by architects, but had a somewhat disorienting effect on the young people who came to study there. Toiling up the slope from Falmer railway station, you had the Kafkaesque sensation of walking into an endlessly deep stage set where apparently three-dimensional objects turned out to be painted flats, and reality receded as fast as you pursued it. Cut off from normal social intercourse with the adult world, relieved of inhibition by the ethos of the Permissive Society, the students were apt to run wild, indulging in promiscuous sex and experimenting with drugs, or else turned melancholy mad. Robyn's generation, coming up to university in the early 1970s, immediately after the heroic period of student politics, were oppressed by a sense of belatedness. There were no significant rights left to demand, no taboos left to break. Student demonstrations developed an ugly edge of gratuitous violence. So did student parties. In this climate, shrewd and sensitive individuals with an instinct for self-preservation looked around for a partner and pair-bonded. By living in what their parents called sin, they nailed their colours to the mast of youthful revolt, while enjoying the security and mutual support of old-fashioned matrimony. Sussex, some long-haired, denim-clad veteran of the sixties complained, was looking more and more like a housing estate for first-time buyers. It was full of couples holding hands and plastic carrier bags that were as likely to contain laundry and groceries as books and revolutionary pamphlets. One of these couples consisted of Robyn and Charles. She had looked around, and chosen him. He was clever, personable, and, she thought, probably loyal (she had not been proved wrong). It was true that he had been educated at a public school, but he managed to disguise this handicap very well.

(Robyn, her white nightdress billowing round her hips, sits on the loo and pees, mentally rehearsing the plot of Mrs Gaskell's *Mary Barton* (1848). Rising from the toilet, she pulls the nightdress over her head and steps into the bath, not first pulling the chain of the toilet because that would affect the temperature of the water coming through the showerhead on the end of its flexible tube, with which she now hoses herself down. She palpates her breasts as she washes, checking for lumps. She steps from the bath, stretching for a towel in one of those ungainly, intimate postures so beloved of Impressionist painters and deplored by the feminist art historians Robyn admires. She is tall and womanly in shape, slender of waist, with smallish round breasts, heavier about the hips and buttocks.)

In their second year, Robyn and Charles moved off campus and set up house in a small flat in Brighton, commuting to the University by local train. Robyn took an active part in student politics. She ran successfully for the Vice-Presidentship of the Student Union. She organised an all-night telephone counselling service for students in despair about their grades or love-lives. She spoke frequently in the Debating Society in favour of progressive causes such as abortion, animal rights, state education and nuclear disarmament. Charles led a more subdued and private life. He kept the flat tidy while Robyn was out doing good works, and always had a cup of cocoa or a bowl of soup ready for her when she returned home, tired but invariably triumphant. At the end of the first term of her third year, Robyn resigned from all her commitments in order to prepare for Finals. She and Charles worked hard and, despite the fact that they were pursuing the same course, without rivalry. In their Final Examinations, Robyn obtained a First – her marks, she was unofficially informed, were the highest ever achieved by a student in the School of European Studies in its short history – and Charles an extremely high Upper Second. Charles was not jealous. He was used to living in the shade of Robyn's achievements. And in any case his degree was good enough to earn him, as Robyn's did for her, a Major State Studentship to do postgraduate research. The idea of doing research and pursuing an academic career was common ground to both of them; indeed they had never considered any alternative.

They had got used to living in Brighton, and saw no reason to uproot themselves, but one of their tutors took them aside and said, "Look, this place hasn't got a proper research library, and it's not going to get one. Go to Oxbridge." He had seen the writing on the wall: after the oil crisis of 1973 there wasn't going to be enough money to keep all the universities enthusiastically created or expanded in the booming sixties in the style to which they had become accustomed. Not many people perceived this quite so soon.

(Robyn, a dressing-gown over her underclothes and slippers on her feet, descends the short dark staircase to the ground floor and goes into her narrow and extremely untidy kitchen. She lights the gas stove, and makes herself a breakfast of muesli, wholemeal toast and decaffeinated coffee. She thinks about the structure of Disraeli's *Sybil; or, the Two Nations* (1845), until the sound of the *Guardian* dropping onto the doormat sends her scurrying to the front door.)

So Robyn and Charles went to Cambridge to do their PhDs.

Intellectually it was an exciting time to be a research student in the English Faculty. New ideas imported from Paris by the more adventurous young teachers glittered like dustmotes in the Fenland air: structuralism and poststructuralism, semiotics and deconstruction, new mutations and graftings of psychoanalysis and Marxism, linguistics and literary criticism. The more conservative dons viewed these ideas and their proponents with alarm, seeing in them a threat to the traditional values and methods of literary scholarship. Battle was joined, in seminars, lectures, committee meetings and the review pages of scholarly journals. It was revolution. It was civil war. Robyn threw herself enthusiastically into the struggle, on the radical side naturally. It was like the sixties all over again, in a new, more austerely intellectual key. She subscribed to the journals *Poètique* and *Tel Quel* so that she could be the first person on the Trumpington Road to know the latest thoughts of Roland Barthes and Julia Kristeva. She forced her mind through the labyrinthine sentences of Jacques Lacan and Jacques Derrida until her eyes were bloodshot and her head ached. She sat in lecture theatres and nodded eager agreement as the Young Turks of the Faculty demolished the idea of the author, the idea of the self, the idea of establishing a single, univocal meaning for a literary text. All this of course took up a great deal of time and delayed the completion of Robyn's thesis on the nineteenth-century industrial novel, which had to be constantly revised to take the new theories into account.

Charles was not quite so committed to the new wave. He supported it, naturally – otherwise he and Robyn could hardly have continued to co-habit – but in a more detached spirit. He chose a subject for his PhD – the idea of the Sublime in Romantic poetics – which sounded reassuringly serious to the traditionalists and off-puttingly dry to the Young Turks, but which neither party knew much about, so Charles was not drawn into the front-line controversy in his own research. He delivered his dissertation on time, was awarded his doctorate, and was lucky enough to obtain a lectureship in the Comparative Literature Department at the University of Suffolk, "the last new job in Romanticism this century", as he was wont to describe it, with justifiable hyperbole.

(Robyn scans the front-page headline of the *Guardian*, "LAWSON DRAWN INTO FRAY OVER WESTLAND", but does not linger over the text beneath. It is enough for her to know that things are going badly for Mrs Thatcher and the Tory party; the details of the Westland affair do not engage her interest. She turns at once to the Women's page, where there is a Posy Simmonds strip cartoon adroitly satirising middle-aged, middle-class liberals, an article on the iniquities of the

Unborn Children (Protection) Bill, and a report on the struggle for women's liberation in Portugal. These she reads with the kind of pure, trance-like attention that she used to give, as a child, to the stories of Enid Blyton. A column entitled "Bulletin" informs her that Marilyn French will be discussing her new book, *Beyond Power: Women, Men and Morals*, at a public meeting to be held later in the week in London, and it crosses Robyn's mind, not for the first time, that it is a pity she lives so far from the metropolis where such exciting events are always happening. This thought reminds her of why she is living in Rummidge, namely her job, and makes her guiltily aware that time is passing. She puts her soiled breakfast things in the sink, already crammed with the relics of last night's supper, and hurries upstairs.)

Charles' success in landing a job provoked in Robyn the first twinge of jealousy, the first spasm of pique, to mar their relationship. She had grown used to being the dominant partner, the teachers' favourite, the Victrix Ludorum. Her grant had expired, and she was still some way off completing her PhD dissertation. However, she had her sights fixed on higher things than the University of Suffolk, a new "plateglass" university with a reputation for student vandalism. Her supervisor and other friends in the Faculty encouraged her to think that she would get an appointment at Cambridge eventually if she could hang on. She hung on for two years, existing on fees for supervising undergraduates and an allowance from her father. She finished, at last, her thesis, and was awarded her PhD. She competed successfully for a post-doctoral research fellowship at one of the less fashionable women's colleges. It was for three years only, but it was a promising stepping-stone to a proper appointment. She got a contract to turn her thesis on the Industrial Novel into a book, and settled enthusiastically to the task. Her personal life did not change much. Charles continued to live with her in Cambridge, commuting by car to Ipswich to teach his classes, and staying there for a night or two each week.

Then, in 1981, all hell broke loose in the Cambridge English Faculty. An extremely public row about the denial of tenure to a young lecturer associated with the progressive party opened old wounds and inflicted new ones on this always thin-skinned community. Long-standing friendships were broken, new enmities established. Insults and libel suits were exchanged. Robyn was almost ill with excitement and outrage. For a few weeks the controversy featured in the national and even international press, up-market newspapers carrying spicy stories about the leading protagonists and confused attempts to explain the difference between structuralism and poststructuralism to the man on the Clapham omnibus. To Robyn it seemed that critical theory had at last moved to its rightful place, centre-stage, in the theatre of history, and she was ready to play her part in the drama. She put her name down to speak in the great debate about the state of the English Faculty that was held in the University Senate; and in the *Cambridge University Reporter* for 18th February, 1981, occupying a column and half of small print, sandwiched between contributions from two of the University's most distinguished professors, you may find Robyn's impassioned plea for a radical theorisation of the syllabus.

(Robyn straightens the sheet on the bed, shakes and spreads the duvet. She sits at her dressing-table and vigorously brushes her hair, a mop of copper-coloured curls, natural curls, as tight and springy as coiled steel. Some would say her hair is her finest feature, though Robyn herself secretly hankers after something more muted and malleable, hair that could be groomed and styled according to mood – drawn back in a severe bun like Simone de Beauvoir's, or allowed to fall to the shoulders in a Pre-Raphaelite cloud. As it is, there is not much she can do with her curls except, every now and again, crop them brutally short just to demonstrate how inadequately they represent her character. Her face is comely enough to take short hair, though perfectionists might say that the grey-green eyes are a little close-set, and the nose and chin are a centimetre longer than Robyn herself would have wished. Now she rubs moisturiser into her facial skin as protection against the raw wintry air outside, coats her lips with lip-salve, and brushes some green eyeshadow on her eyelids, pondering shifts of point of view in Charles Dickens' *Hard Times* (1854). Her simple cosmetic operations completed, she dresses herself in opaque green tights, a wide brown tweed skirt and a thick sweater loosely knitted in muted shades of orange, green and brown. Robyn generally favours loose dark clothes, made of natural fibres, that do not make her body into an object of sexual attention. The way they are cut also disguises her smallish breasts and widish hips while making the most of her height: thus are ideology and vanity equally satisfied. She contemplates her image in the long looking-glass by the window, and decides that the effect is a little too sombre. She rummages in her jewellery box where brooches, necklaces and earrings are jumbled together with enamel lapel badges expressing support for various radical causes – *Support the Miners, Crusade for Jobs, Legalise Pot, A Woman's Right To Choose* – and selects a silver brooch in which the CND symbol and the Yin sign are artfully entwined. She pins it to her bosom. She takes from the bottom of her wardrobe a pair of calf-length fashion boots in dark brown leather and sits on the edge of the bed to pull them on.)

When the dust settled in Cambridge, however, it seemed that the party of reaction had triumphed. A University committee charged to investigate the case of the young lecturer determined that there had been no administrative malpractice. The man himself departed to take up a more remunerative and prestigious post elsewhere, and his friends and supporters fell silent, or retired, or resigned and took jobs in America. One of the latter group, somewhat the worse for drink at his farewell party, advised Robyn to get out of Cambridge too. "This place is finished," he said, meaning that Cambridge would be a less interesting place for his own absence from it. "Anyway, you'll never get a job here, Robyn. You're a marked woman."

Robyn decided she would not put this gloomy prediction to further test. Her research fellowship was coming to an end, and she could not bear the prospect of "hanging on" for another year as a freelance supervisor of undergraduates, sponging on her parents. She began to look for a university job outside Cambridge.

But there were no jobs. While Robyn had been preoccupied with the issues of contemporary literary theory and its repercussions on the Cambridge English Faculty, the Conservative Government of Mrs Thatcher, elected in 1979 with a mandate to cut public spending, had set about decimating the national system of higher education. Universities everywhere were in disarray, faced with swingeing cuts in their funding. Required to reduce their academic staff by anything up to 20%, they responded by persuading as many people as possible to take early retirement and freezing all vacancies. Robyn considered herself lucky to get a job for one term at one of the London colleges, deputising for a woman lecturer on maternity leave. There followed an awful period of nearly a year when she was unemployed, searching the back pages of the *Times Higher Educational Supplement* in vain every week for lectureships in nineteenth-century English Literature.

The previously unthinkable prospect of a non-academic career now began to be thought – with fear, dismay and bewilderment on Robyn's part. Of course she was aware, cognitively, that there was a life outside universities, but she knew nothing about it, nor did Charles, or her parents. Her younger brother, Basil, in his final year of Modern Greats at Oxford, spoke of going into the City when he graduated, but Robyn considered this was just talk, designed to ward off *hubris* about his forthcoming examinations, or an Oedipal teasing of his academic father. When she tried to imagine herself working in an office or a bank, her mind soon went blank, like a cinema screen when the projector breaks down or the film snaps. There was always schoolteaching, of course, but that would entail the tiresome business of acquiring a Postgraduate Certificate of Education, or else working in the independent sector, to which she had ideological objections. In any case, teaching English literature to schoolchildren would only remind her daily of the superior satisfactions of teaching it to young adults.

Then, in 1984, just when Robyn was beginning to despair, the job at Rummidge came up. Professor Philip Swallow, Head of the English Department at Rummidge University, had been elected Dean of the Arts Faculty for a three-year term; and since the duties of this office, added to his Departmental responsibilities, drastically reduced his contribution to undergraduate teaching, he was by tradition allowed to appoint a temporary lecturer, at the lower end of the salary scale, as what was quaintly termed "Dean's Relief". Thus a three-year lectureship in English Literature was advertised, Robyn applied, was interviewed along with four other equally desperate and highly qualified candidates, and was appointed.

Glory! Jubilation! Huge sighs of relief. Charles met Robyn off the train from Rummidge with a bottle of champagne in his hand. The three years stretching ahead seemed like a long time, then, worth buying a little house in Rummidge for (Robyn's father lent her the money for the deposit) rather than paying rent. Besides, Robyn had faith that, somehow or other, she would be kept on when her temporary appointment came to an end. She was confident that she could make her mark on the Rummidge Department in three years. She knew she was good, and it wasn't long before she privately concluded that she was better than most of her colleagues – more enthusiastic, more energetic, more productive. When she arrived she had already published several articles and reviews in academic journals, and shortly afterwards her much-revised thesis appeared under the imprint of Lecky, Windrush and Bernstein. Entitled *The Industrious Muse: Narrativity and Contradiction in the Industrial Novel* (the title was foisted on her by the publishers, the subtitle was her own) it received enthusiastic if sparse reviews, and the publishers commissioned another book provisionally entitled, *Domestic Angels and Unfortunate Females: Woman as Sign and Commodity in Victorian Fiction*. She was a popular and conscientious teacher, whose optional courses on women's writing were oversubscribed. She performed her share of administrative duties efficiently. Surely they couldn't just let her go at the end of the three years?

(Robyn goes into her long narrow living-room, formed by knocking down the dividing wall between the front and back parlours of the little house, which also serves as her study. There are books and periodicals everywhere – on shelves, on tables, on the floor – posters and reproductions of modern paintings on the walls, parched-looking potted plants in the fireplace, a BBC micro and monitor on the desk, and beside it sheaves of dot-matrix typescript of early chapters of *Domestic Angels and Unfortunate Females* in various drafts. Robyn picks her way across the floor, putting her shapely boots down carefully in the spaces between books, back numbers of *Critical Inquiry* and *Women's*

30

Review, LP albums by Bach, Philip Glass and Phil Collins (her musical tastes are eclectic) and the occasional wineglass or coffee cup, to the desk. She lifts from the floor a leather Gladstone bag, and begins to load it with the things she will need for the day: well-thumbed, much underlined and annotated copies of *Shirley*, *Mary Barton*, *North and South*, *Sybil*, *Alton Locke*, *Felix Holt*, *Hard Times*; her lecture notes – a palimpsest of holograph revisions in different-coloured inks, beneath which the original typescript is scarcely legible; and a thick sheaf of student essays marked over the Christmas vacation.

Returning to the kitchen, Robyn turns down the thermostat of the central heating and checks that the back door of the house is locked and bolted. In the hall she wraps a long scarf round her neck and puts on a cream-coloured quilted cotton jacket, with wide shoulders and inset sleeves, and lets herself out by the front door. Outside, in the street, her car is parked, a red six-year-old Renault Five with a yellow sticker in its rear window, *"Britain Needs Its Universities."* It was formerly her parents' second car, sold to Robyn at a bargain price when her mother replaced it. It runs well, though the battery is getting feeble. Robyn turns the ignition key, holding her breath as she listens to the starter's bronchial wheeze, then exhales with relief as the engine fires.)

Three years didn't seem such a long time when one of them had elapsed, and although Robyn was satisfied that she was highly valued by her colleagues, the talk at the University these days was all of further cuts, of tightening belts, deteriorating staff–student ratios. Still, she was optimistic. Robyn was naturally optimistic. She had faith in her star. Nevertheless, the future of her career was a constant background worry as the days and weeks of her appointment at Rummidge ticked away like a taxi meter. Another was her relationship with Charles.

What was it, exactly, this relationship? Hard to describe. Not a marriage, and yet more like marriage than many marriages: domesticated, familiar, faithful. There was a time, early in their days at Cambridge, when a brilliant and handsome research student from Yale made a determined pitch for Robyn, and she had been rather dazzled and excited by the experience (he wooed her with a heady mixture of the latest postfreudian theoretical jargon and devastatingly frank sexual propositions, so she was never quite sure whether it was Lacan's symbolic phallus he was referring to or his own real one). But in the end she pulled back from the brink, conscious of Charles' silent but reproachful figure hovering on the edge of her vision. She was too honest to deceive him and too prudent to exchange him for a lover whose interest would probably not last very long.

When Charles obtained his post at Suffolk, there had been a certain amount of pressure from both sets of parents for them to get married. Charles was willing. Robyn indignantly rejected the suggestion. "What are you implying?" she demanded from her mother. "That I should go and keep house for Charles in Ipswich? Give up my PhD and live off Charles and have babies?" "Of course not, dear," said her mother. "There's no reason why you shouldn't still have your own career. If that's what you want." She managed to imbue this last phrase with a certain pitying incomprehension. She herself had never aspired to a career, finding complete satisfaction in acting as her husband's typist and research assistant in the time she had left over from gardening and housekeeping. "Certainly it's what I want," said Robyn, so fiercely that her mother let the subject drop. Robyn had a reputation in the family for being strong-willed, or, as her brother Basil less flatteringly put it, "bossy". There was a much-told tale of her Australian infancy that was held to be prophetic in this respect – about how at the age of three she had, by the sheer force of her will, compelled her uncle Walter (who was taking her for a walk to the local shops at the time) to put all the money he had on his person into a charity collecting-box in the shape of a plaster-of-Paris boy cripple; as a result of which the uncle, too embarrassed to admit to this folly and borrow from his relatives, had run out of petrol on the way back to his sheep station. Robyn herself, needless to say, interpreted this anecdote in a light more favourable to herself, as anticipating her later commitment to progressive causes.

Charles found a *pied-à-terre* in Ipswich and continued to keep his books and most of his other possessions in the flat at Cambridge. Naturally they saw less of each other, and Robyn was aware that this did not cause her to repine as much as perhaps it should have done. She began to wonder if the relationship was not, very very slowly, dying a natural death, and whether it would not be sensible to terminate it quickly. She put this calmly and rationally to Charles one day, and calmly and rationally he accepted it. He said that although he was personally quite happy with things as they were, he understood her doubts and perhaps a trial separation would resolve them one way or the other.

(Robyn drives her red Renault zigzag across the south-west suburbs of Rummidge, sometimes with the flow of rush-hour traffic, sometimes against – though the rush hour is almost over. It is 9.20 a.m. as Robyn reaches the broad tree-lined streets that border the Univey. She takes a short cut down Avondale Road, and passes the five-bedroom detached house of Vic Wilcox without a glance, for she does not know him from Adam, and the house is outwardly no different from any of the other modern executive dwellings in this exclusive residential district: red brick and white paint, "Georgian" windows, a tarmac drive and double garage, a burglar alarm prominently displayed on the front elevation.)

So Charles moved his books and other possessions to Ipswich, which Robyn found rather inconvenient, since she was in the habit of borrowing his books, and occasionally his sweaters. They remained good friends, of course, and called each other up frequently on the telephone. Sometimes they met for lunch or a theatre in London, on neutral ground, and both looked forward to these meetings as if they were occasions of almost illicit pleasure. Neither was short of opportunities to form new relationships, but somehow neither of them could be bothered to do so. They were both busy people, preoccupied with their work – Robyn with her supervisions and the completion of her PhD, Charles with the demands of his new job – and the thought of having to adjust to another partner, to study their interests and minister to their needs, wearied them in anticipation. There were so many books and periodicals to be read, so many abstruse thoughts to be thought.

There was sex of course, but although both of them were extremely interested in sex, and enjoyed nothing better than discussing it, neither of them, if the truth be told, was quite so interested in actually having it, or at any rate in having it very frequently. They seemed to have burned up all their lust rather rapidly in their undergraduate years. What was left was sex in the head, as D. H. Lawrence called it. He had meant the phrase pejoratively, of course, but to Robyn and Charles D. H. Lawrence was a quaint, rather absurd figure, and his fierce polemics did not disturb them. Where else would the human subject have sex but in the head? Sexual desire was a play of signifiers, an infinite deferment and displacement of anticipated pleasure which the brute coupling of the signifieds temporarily interrupted. Charles himself was not an imperious lover. Calm and svelte, stealthy as a cat in his movements, he seemed to approach sex as a form of research, favouring techniques of foreplay so subtle and prolonged that Robyn occasionally dozed off in the middle of them, and would wake with a guilty start to find him still crouched studiously over her body, fingering it like a box of index cards.

During their trial separation, Robyn became deeply involved in a Women's Group at Cambridge who met regularly but informally to discuss women's writing and feminist literary theory. It was an article of faith with this circle that women must free themselves from the erotic patronage of men. That is to say, it was not true, as every novel, film, and TV commercial implied, that a woman was incomplete without a man. Women could love other women, and themselves. Several

33

members of the group were lesbians, or tried hard to be. Robyn was quite sure she was not; but she enjoyed the warmth and companionship of the group, the hugging and kissing that accompanied their meetings and partings. And if her body occasionally craved a keener sensation, she was able to provide it herself, without shame or guilt, theoretically justified by the writings of radical French feminists like Hélène Cixous and Luce Irigaray, who were very eloquent on the joys of female auto-eroticism.

Robyn had two casual heterosexual encounters at this time, both one-night stands after rather drunken parties, both unsatisfactory. She took no new live-in lover, and as far as she was aware, neither did Charles. So then it became a question, what was the point of separation? It was just costing them a lot of money in phone calls and train tickets to London. Charles moved his books and sweaters back to Cambridge and life went on much as before. Robyn continued to give much of her time and emotional energy to the Women's Group, but Charles did not object; after all, he considered himself a feminist too.

But when, two years later, Robyn was appointed to Rummidge, they had to split up again. It was impossible to commute from Rummidge to Ipswich or *vice versa*. The journey, by road or rail, was one of the most tedious and inconvenient it was possible to contrive in the British Isles. To Robyn, it seemed a providential opportunity to make another – this time decisive – break with Charles. Much as she liked him, much as she would miss his companionship, it seemed to her that the relationship had reached a dead end. There was nothing new in it to be discovered, and it was preventing them from making new discoveries elsewhere. It had been a mistake to get together again – a symptom of their immaturity, their enslavement to Cambridge. Yes (she swelled with the certainty of this insight) it had been Cambridge, not desire, that had reunited them. They were both so obsessed with the place, its gossip and rumours and intrigues, that they wanted to spend every possible moment together there, comparing notes, exchanging opinions: who was in, who out, what X said about Y's review of P's book about Q. Well, she was sick and tired of the place, tired of its beautiful architecture housing vanity and paranoia, glad to exchange its hothouse atmosphere for the real if smoky air of Rummidge. And to make the break with Cambridge somehow entailed breaking finally with Charles. She informed him of this conclusion, and with his usual calm he accepted it. Later she wondered if he was counting on her not sticking to her resolution.

Rummidge was a new leaf, a blank page, in Robyn's life. She had at the back of her mind the thought that some new male companion might figure in it. But no such person manifested himself. All the men in the University seemed to be married or gay or scientists, and Robyn had no time or energy to look further afield. She was fully stretched preparing her classes, on a whole new range of subjects, marking her essays, researching *Domestic Angels and Unfortunate Females*, and making herself generally indispensable to the Department. She was fulfilled and happy, but, occasionally, a little lonely. Then sometimes she would pick up the telephone and natter to Charles. One day she rashly invited him to stay for a weekend. She had in mind a purely platonic visit – there was a guestroom in the little house; but in the event, perhaps inevitably, they ended up in bed together. And it was nice to have someone else caress your body, and release the springs of pleasure hidden within it, instead of having to do the job yourself. She had forgotten how nice it was, after so long an interval. It seemed, after all, that they were indispensable to each other; or, if that was putting it too strongly, they fulfilled a mutual need.

They did not go back to "living together" even in the purely conceptual sense of many academic couples they knew, separated by their jobs. When Charles came to visit, he did so as a guest, and when he departed he left no possessions behind him. However, on these occasions they invariably slept together. An odd relationship, undoubtedly. Not a marriage, not a living-together, not an affair. More like a divorce in which the two parties occasionally meet for companionship and sexual pleasure without strings. Robyn is not sure whether this is wonderfully modern and liberated of them, or rather depraved.

So these are the things that are worrying Robyn Penrose as she drives through the gates of the University, with a nod and a smile to the security man in his little glass sentry box: her lecture on the Industrial Novel, her job future, and her relationship with Charles – in that order of conspicuousness rather than importance. Indeed, her uneasiness about Charles scarcely counts as a conscious worry at all; while the worry about the lecture is, she is well aware, a trivial and mechanical one. It is not that she does not know what to say, it is that there is not enough time to say all she knows. After all, she worked on the nineteenth-century industrial novel for something like ten years, and even after publishing her book she went on accumulating ideas and insights about the subject. She has boxes full of notes and file cards on it. She probably knows more about the nineteenth-century industrial novel than anyone else in the entire world. How can all that knowledge be condensed into a fifty-minute lecture to students who know almost nothing about it? The interests of scholarship and pedagogy are at odds here. What Robyn likes to do is to deconstruct the texts, to probe the gaps and absences in them, to uncover what they are *not* saying, to expose their ideological bad faith, to cut a cross-section through the twisted strands of their semiotic codes and literary conventions. What the students want her to do is to give them some basic facts that will enable them to read the novels as simple straightforward reflections of "reality", and to write simple, straightforward, exam-passing essays about them.

Robyn parks her car in one of the University's landscaped car parks, lugs her Gladstone bag from the front passenger seat, and makes her way to the English Department. Her gait is deliberate and stately. She holds her head erect, her red-gold curls like a torch burning in the grey, misty atmosphere. You would not think her unduly burdened with worries, if you watched her crossing the campus, smiling at people she knows, her eyes bright, her brow unfurrowed. And indeed, she carries them lightly, her worries. She has youth, she has confidence, she regrets nothing.

She passes into the foyer of the Arts Block. Its stairs and passages are crowded with students; the air is loud with their shouts and laughter as they greet each other on the first day of the new term. Outside the Department Office she meets Bob Busby, the Department's representative on the local committee of the Association of University Teachers, pinning a sheet of paper to the AUT noticeboard. The notice is headed "ONE DAY STRIKE – WED. JANUARY 15TH". Unbuttoning her coat, and unwinding her scarf, she reads over his shoulder: *"Day of Action . . . protest against cuts . . . erosion of salaries . . . pickets will be mounted at every entrance to the University . . . volunteers should give their names to Departmental representatives . . . other members are asked to stay away from the campus on the Day of Action."*

"Put me down for picketing, Bob," says Robyn.

Bob Busby, who is having trouble digging a drawing-pin out of the noticeboard, swivels his black beard towards her. "Really? That's jolly decent of you."

"Why?"

"Well, you know, a young temporary lecturer . . ." Bob Busby looks slightly embarrassed. "No one would blame you if you wanted to keep a low profile."

Robyn snorts indignantly. "It's a matter of principle!"

"Right then. I'll put you down." He resumes work on the drawing-pin.

"Good morning, Bob. Good morning, Robyn."

They turn to face Philip Swallow, who has evidently just arrived, since he is wearing his rather grubby anorak and carrying a battered briefcase. He is a tall, thin, stooped man, with silvery grey hair, deeply receding at the temples, curling over his collar at the back. Robyn has been told that he once had a beard, and he is forever fingering his chin as if he missed it.

"Oh, hallo, Philip," says Bob Busby. Robyn merely says, "Hallo." She is always uncertain how to address her Head of Department. "Philip" seems too familiar, "Professor Swallow" too formal, "Sir" impossibly servile.

"Had a good vac, both of you? All set to return to the fray? Jolly good." Philip Swallow utters these platitudes without waiting for, or appearing to expect, a reply. "What are you up to, Bob?" His face falls as he reads the heading of the notice. "Do you really think a strike is going to do any good?"

"It will if everyone rallies round," says Bob Busby. "Including those who voted 'Against' in the ballot."

"I was one of them, I don't mind admitting," says Philip Swallow.

"Why?" Robyn boldly interjects. "We must *do* something about the cuts. Not just accept them as if they're inevitable. We must protest."

"Agreed," says Philip Swallow. "I just doubt the effectiveness of a strike. Who will notice? It's not as if we're like bus drivers or air traffic controllers. I fear the general public will find they can get along quite well without universities for a day."

"They'll notice the pickets," says Bob Busby.

"A very sticky wicket," says Philip Swallow.

"Pickets. I said, they'll notice the pickets," says Bob Busby, raising his voice against the surrounding hubbub.

"Hmm, mounting pickets, are we? Going the whole hog." Philip Swallow shakes his head, looking rather miserable. Then, with a slightly furtive glance at Robyn, "Have you got a moment?"

"Yes, of course." She follows him into his office.

"Have a good vac?" he says again, divesting himself of his coat.

"Yes, thanks."

"Do sit down. Go anywhere interesting? North Africa? Winter sports?" He grins encouragingly, as if to intimate that a positive reply would cheer him up.

"Good Lord, no."

"I hear they have very cheap packages to the Gambia in January."

"I couldn't afford the time, even if I had the money," says Robyn. "I had a lot of marking to catch up on. Then I was interviewing all last week."

"Yes, of course."

"What about you?"

"Oh, well, I, er, don't do admissions any more. Used to, of course – "

"No," says Robyn, smiling. "I mean, did *you* go anywhere interesting?"

"Ah. I had an invitation to a conference in Florida," says Philip Swallow wistfully. "But I couldn't get a travel grant."

"Oh dear, what a shame," says Robyn, without being able to work up much genuine compassion for this misfortune.

According to Rupert Sutcliffe, the most senior member of the Department, and its most pertinacious gossip, there was a time not so long ago when Philip Swallow was forever swanning around the globe on some conference jaunt or other. Now it seems that the cuts have clipped his wings. "And quite right, too," Rupert Sutcliffe declared. "A waste of time and money, in my opinion, those conferences. *I've* never attended an international conference in my life." Robyn nodded polite approval of this abstention, while privately guessing that Rupert Sutcliffe had not been embarrassed by a large number of invitations. "Mind you," Sutcliffe added, "I don't think it's just lack of funds that has kept him at home lately. I have a hunch that Hilary read him the riot act."

"Mrs Swallow?"

"Yes. He used to get up to all kinds of high jinks on those trips, by all accounts. I suppose I ought to tell you: Swallow has a bit of a weakness where women are concerned. Forewarned is forearmed." Sutcliffe tapped the side of his long nose with his index finger as he uttered these words, dislodging his spectacles and causing them to crash into his tea-cup – for this conversation took place in the Senior Common Room, not long after Robyn's arrival at Rummidge. Looking at Philip Swallow now, as he seats himself in a low, upholstered chair facing her, Robyn has difficulty in recognising the jet-set philanderer of Rupert Sutcliffe's description. Swallow looks tired and careworn and slightly seedy. She wonders why he has invited her into his office. He smiles nervously at her and combs a phantom beard with his fingers. Suddenly a portentous atmosphere has been established.

"I just wanted to say, Robyn . . . As you know, your present appointment is a temporary one."

Robyn's heart leaps with hope. "Yes," she says, interlocking her hands to stop them from trembling.

"For three years only. You're a third of the way into your second year, with another full year still to run from next September." He states these facts slowly and carefully, as if they might somehow have slipped her mind.

"Yes."

"I just wanted to say that, we would of course be very sorry to lose you, you've been a tremendous asset to the Department, even in the short time you've been here. I really mean that."

"Thank you," says Robyn dully, untwining her fingers. "But?"

"But?"

"I think you were going to say something beginning with *But*."

"Oh. Ah. Yes. But I just wanted to say that I, we, shouldn't at all blame you if you were to start applying for jobs elsewhere now."

"There aren't any other jobs."

"Well, not at this moment in time, perhaps. But you never know, something may turn up later in the year. If so, perhaps you should go in for it. I mean, you shouldn't feel under any obligation to complete the three years of your contract here. Much as we should regret losing you," he says again.

"What you mean is: there's no chance of my being kept on after the three years are up."

Philip Swallow spreads his hands and shrugs. "No chance at all, as far as I can see. The University is desperate to save on salaries. They're talking about another round of early retirements. Even if someone were to leave the Department, or drop dead – even if you were to, what's the expression, take out a contract on one of us" – he laughs to show that this is a joke, displaying a number of chipped and discoloured teeth, set in his gums at odd angles, like tombstones in a neglected churchyard – "even then, I very much doubt whether we should get a replacement. Being Dean, you see, I'm very aware of the financial constraints on the University. Every day I have the Heads of other Departments in here bellyaching about lack of resources, asking for replacements or new appointments. I have to tell them that the only way we can meet our targets is an absolute freeze. It's very hard for young people in your position. Believe me, I do sympathise."

He reaches out and puts a hand comfortingly on Robyn's pair. She looks at the three hands with detachment, as if they are a still life. Is this the long-delayed, much-heralded pass? Is there a promotions-and-appointments couch somewhere in the room? It seems not, for Philip Swallow immediately removes his hand, stands up and moves to the window. "It's no fun being Dean, these days, I can tell you. All you do is give people bad news. And, as Shakespeare observed, the nature of bad news infects the teller."

"When it concerns the fool or coward." Robyn recklessly recites the next line from *Anthony and Cleopatra*, but fortunately Philip Swallow appears not to have heard. He is staring down gloomily into the central quadrangle of the campus.

"I feel as if, by the time I retire, I shall have lived through the entire life-cycle of post-war higher education. When I was a student myself, provincial universities like Rummidge were a very small show. Then in the sixties, it was all expansion, growth, new building. Would you believe our biggest grouse in the sixties was about the noise of construction work? Now it's all gone quiet. Won't be long before they're sending in the demolition crews, no doubt."

"I'm surprised you don't support the strike, then," says Robyn tartly. But Philip Swallow evidently thinks she said something entirely different.

"Exactly. It's like the Big Bang theory of the universe. They say that at a certain point it will stop expanding and start contracting again, back into the original primal seed. The Robbins Report was our Big Bang. Now we've gone into reverse."

Robyn glances surreptitiously at her watch.

"Or perhaps we've strayed into a black hole," Philip Swallow continues, evidently enchanted with his flight of astronomical fancy.

"If you'll excuse me," says Robyn, getting to her feet. "I have to get ready for a lecture."

"Yes, yes, of course. I'm sorry."

"It's all right, only I –"

"Yes, yes, my fault entirely. Don't forget your bag." With smiles, with nods, with evident relief that an awkward interview is over, Philip Swallow ushers her out of his office.

Bob Busby is still busy at his bulletin board, rearranging old notices around the new one, like a fussy gardener tidying a flower bed. He cocks an inquisitive eyebrow at Robyn as she passes.

"Is it your impression that Philip Swallow is a bit hard of hearing?" she asks him.

"Oh yes, it's been getting worse lately," says Bob Busby. "It's high-frequency deafness, you know. He can hear vowels but not consonants. He tries to guess what you say to him from the vowels. Usually he guesses what he happens to be thinking about himself, at the time."

"It makes conversation rather a hit-or-miss affair," says Robyn.

"Anything important, was it?"

"Oh no," says Robyn, disinclined to share her disappointment with Bob Busby. She smiles serenely and moves on.

There are several students slouching against the wall, or sitting on the floor, outside her room. Robyn gives them a wry look as she approaches, having a pretty good idea of what they want.

"Hallo," she says, by way of a general greeting as she fishes for her door key in her coat pocket. "Who's first?"

"Me," says a pretty, dark-haired girl wearing an outsize man's shirt like an artist's smock over her jeans and sweater. She follows Robyn into her room. This has the same view as Philip Swallow's, but is smaller – indeed, rather too small for all the furniture it contains: a desk, bookcases, filing cabinets, a table and a dozen or so unstacked stacking chairs. The walls are covered with posters illustrative of various radical causes – nuclear disarmament, women's liberation, the protection of whales – and a large reproduction of Dante Gabriel Rossetti's painting, "The Lady of Shalott", which might seem incongruous unless you have heard Robyn expound its iconic significance as a matrix of male stereotypes of the feminine.

The girl, whose name is Marion Russell, comes straight to the point. "I need an extension for my assessed essay."

Robyn sighs. "I thought you might." Marion is a persistent defaulter in this respect, though not without reason.

"I did two jobs in the vac, you see. The Post Office, as well as the pub in the evenings."

Marion does not qualify for a maintenance grant because her parents are well off, but they are also estranged, from each other and from her, so she is obliged to support herself at university with a variety of part-time jobs.

"You know we're only supposed to give extensions on medical grounds."

"Well, I did get a terrible cold after Christmas."

"I don't suppose you got a medical certificate?"

"No."

Robyn sighs again. "How long do you want?"

"Ten days."

"I'll give you a week." Robyn opens a drawer in her desk and takes out the appropriate chit.

"Thanks. Things will be better this term. I've got a better job."

"Oh?"

"Fewer hours, but better pay."

"What is it?"

"Well, it's sort of . . . modelling."

Robyn stops writing and looks sharply at Marion. "I hope you know what you're doing."

Marian Russell giggles. "Oh it's nothing like that."

"Like what?"

"You know. Porn. Vice."

"Well, that's a relief. What is it you model, then?"

Marion Russell drops her eyes and blushes slightly. "Well, it's sort of underwear."

Robyn has a vivid mental image of the girl before her, now so pleasantly and comfortably dressed, sheathed in latex and nylon, the full fetishistic ensemble of brassière, knickers, suspender belt and stockings with which the lingerie industry seeks to truss the female body, and having to parade at some fashion show in front of leering men and hardfaced women from department stores. Waves of compassion and

41

outrage fuse with delayed feelings of self-pity for her own plight, and society seems for a moment a huge conspiracy to exploit and oppress young women. She feels a choking sensation in her chest, and a dangerous pressure in her tear-ducts. She rises and clasps the astonished Marion Russell in her arms.

"You can have two weeks," she says, at length, sitting down and blowing her nose.

"Oh, thanks, Robyn. That's super."

Robyn is rather less generous with the next supplicant, a young man who broke his ankle falling off his motorbike on New Year's Eve, but even the least deserving candidate gets a few days' respite, for Robyn tends to identify with the students against the system that assesses them, even though she is herself part of the system. Eventually they are all dealt with, and Robyn is free to prepare for her lecture at eleven. She opens her Gladstone bag, pulls out the folder containing her notes, and settles to work.

3

The University clock strikes eleven, its chimes overlapping with the chimes of other clocks, near and far. All over Rummidge and its environs, people are at work – or not, as the case may be.

Robyn Penrose is making her way to Lecture Room A, along corridors and down staircases thronged with students changing classes. They part before her, like waves before the prow of a stately ship. She smiles at those she recognises. Some fall in behind her, and follow her to the lecture theatre, so that she appears to be leading a little procession, a female Pied Piper. She carries under one arm her folder of lecture notes, and under the other a bundle of books from which to read illustrative quotations. No young man offers to carry this burden for her. Such gallantry is out of fashion. Robyn herself would disapprove of it on ideological grounds, and it might be interpreted by other students as creeping.

Vic Wilcox is in a meeting with his Marketing Director, Brian Everthorpe, who answered Vic's summons at 9.30, complaining of contraflow holdups on the motorway, and whom Vic, himself dictating letters at 9.30, told to come back at eleven. He is a big man, which in itself doesn't endear him to Vic, with bushy sideboards and RAF-style moustache. He wears a three-piece suit with an old-fashioned watch-chain looped across his waistcoated paunch. He is the most senior, and the most complacent, member of the management team Vic inherited.

"You should live in the city, like me, Brian," says Vic. "Not thirty miles away."

"Oh, you know what Beryl is like," says Brian Everthorpe, with a smile designed to seem rueful.

Vic doesn't know. He has never met Beryl, said to be Everthorpe's second wife, and formerly his secretary. As far as he knows, Beryl may not even exist, except as an excuse for Brian Everthorpe's delinquencies. *Beryl says the kids need country air. Beryl was poorly this morning and I had to run her to the doctor's. Beryl sends her apologies – she forgot to give me your message.* One day, quite soon in fact, Brian Everthorpe is going to have to concentrate his mind on the difference between a wife and an employer.

In a café in a covered shopping precinct at the centre of Rummidge,

Marjorie and Sandra Wilcox are sipping coffee, debating what colour shoes Sandra should buy. The walls of the café are covered with tinted mirrors, and soft syncopated music oozes from speakers hidden in the ceiling.

"I think a beige," says Marjorie.

"Or that sort of pale olive," says Sandra.

The shopping precinct is full of teenagers gathered in small clusters, smoking, gossiping, laughing, scuffling. They look at the goods in the shiny, illuminated shopwindows, and wander in and out of the boutiques, but do not buy anything. Some stare into the café where Marjorie and Sandra are sitting.

"All these kids," says Marjorie disapprovingly. "Wagging it, I suppose."

"On the dole, more likely," says Sandra, suppressing a yawn, and checking her appearance in the mirrored wall behind her mother's back.

Robyn arranges her notes on the lectern, waiting for latecomers to settle in their seats. The lecture theatre resonates like a drum with the chatter of a hundred-odd students, all talking at once, as if they have just been released from solitary confinement. She taps on the desk with an inverted pencil and clears her throat. A sudden hush falls, and a hundred faces tilt towards her – curious, expectant, sullen, apathetic – like empty dishes waiting to be filled. The face of Marion Russell is absent, and Robyn cannot suppress a tiny, ignoble twinge of resentment at this ungrateful desertion.

"I've been looking at your expense account, Brian," says Vic, turning over a small pile of bills and receipts.

"Yes?" Brian Everthorpe stiffens slightly.

"It's very modest."

Everthorpe relaxes. "Thank you."

"I didn't mean it as a compliment."

Everthorpe looks puzzled. "Sorry?"

"I'd expect the Marketing Director of a firm this size to claim twice as much for overnight stays."

"Ah, well, you see, Beryl doesn't like being on her own in the house at night."

"But she has your kids with her."

"Not during term, old man. We send them away to school – have to, living in the depths of the country. So I prefer to drive back home after a meeting, no matter how far it is."

"Your mileage is pretty modest, too, isn't it?"

"Is it?" Brian Everthorpe, beginning to get the message, stiffens again.

"In the 1840s and 1850s," says Robyn, "a number of novels were published in England which have a certain family resemblance. Raymond Williams has called them 'Industrial Novels' because they dealt with social and economic problems arising out of the Industrial Revolution, and in some cases described the nature of factory work. In their own time they were often called 'Condition of England Novels', because they addressed themselves directly to the state of the nation. They are novels in which the main characters debate topical social and economic issues as well as fall in and out of love, marry and have children, pursue careers, make or lose their fortunes, and do all the other things that characters do in more conventional novels. The Industrial Novel contributed a distinctive strain to English fiction which persists into the modern period – it can be traced in the work of Lawrence and Forster, for instance. But it is not surprising that it first arose in what history has called 'the Hungry 'Forties'.

"By the fifth decade of the nineteenth century the Industrial Revolution had completely dislocated the traditional structure of English society, bringing riches to a few and misery to the many. The agricultural working class, deprived of a subsistence on the land by the enclosures of the late eighteenth and early nineteenth centuries, thronged to the cities of the Midlands and the North where the economics of *laissez-faire* forced them to work long hours in wretched conditions for miserable wages, and threw them out of employment altogether as soon as there was a downturn in the market.

"The workers' attempt to defend their interests by forming trades unions was bitterly resisted by the employers. The working class met even stiffer resistance when they tried to secure political representation through the Chartist Movement."

Robyn glances up from her notes and sweeps the audience with her eyes. Some are busily scribbling down every word she utters, others are watching her quizzically, chewing the ends of their ballpoints, and those who looked bored at the outset are now staring vacantly out of the window or diligently chiselling their initials into the lecture-room furniture.

"The People's Charter called for universal male suffrage. Not even those far-out radicals could apparently contemplate the possibility of universal *female* suffrage."

All the students, even those who have been staring out of the window, react to this. They smile and nod or, in a friendly sort of way, groan and hiss. It is what they expect from Robyn Penrose, and even

45

the rugby-playing boys in the back row would be mildly disappointed if she didn't produce this kind of observation from time to time.

Vic Wilcox asks Brian Everthorpe to stay for a meeting he has arranged with his technical and production managers. They file into the office and sit round the long oak table, slightly in awe of Vic, serious men in chain-store suits, with pens and pencils sticking out of their breast pockets. Brian Everthorpe takes a chair at the far end of the table, slightly withdrawn as if to mark his difference from the engineers. Vic sits at the head of the table, in his shirtsleeves, half a cup of cold coffee at his right hand. He unfolds a sheet of computer printout.

"Does anybody know," he says, "how many different products this firm made last year?" Silence. "Nine hundred and thirty-seven. That's about nine hundred too many, in my opinion."

"You mean different specs, don't you? Not products," says the technical manager, rather boldly.

"All right, different specs. But every new specification means that we have to stop production, retool or reset the machines, stop a flow line, or whatever. That costs time, and time is money. Then the operatives are more likely to make mistakes when setups are constantly changing, and that leads to increased wastage. Am I right?"

"There were two climactic moments in the history of the Chartist Movement. One was the submission of a petition, with millions of signatures, to Parliament in 1839. Its rejection led to a series of industrial strikes, demonstrations, and repressive measures by the Government. This is the background to Mrs Gaskell's novel *Mary Barton* and Disraeli's *Sybil*. The second was the submission of another monster petition in 1848, which forms the background to Charles Kingsley's *Alton Locke*. 1848 was a year of revolution throughout Europe, and many people in England feared that Chartism would bring revolution, and perhaps a Terror, to England. Any kind of working-class militancy tends to be presented in the fiction of the period as a threat to social order. This is also true of Charlotte Brontë's *Shirley* (1849). Though set at the time of the Napoleonic wars, its treatment of the Luddite riots is clearly an oblique comment on more topical events."

Three black youths with huge, multicoloured knitted caps pulled over their dreadlocks like tea-cosies lean against the plateglass window of the shopping-precinct café, drumming a reggae beat on it with their finger-tips until shooed away by the manageress.

"I hear there was more trouble in Angleside at the weekend," says

Marjorie, wiping the milky foam of the cappuccino from her lips with a dainty tissue.

Angleside is the black ghetto of Rummidge, where youth unemployment is 80%, and rioting endemic. There are long queues in the Angleside Social Security office this morning, as every morning. The only job vacancies in Angleside are for interviewers in the Social Security office, where the furniture is screwed to the floor in case the clients should try to assault the interviewers with it.

"Or maybe oyster," says Sandra dreamily. "To go with my pink trousers."

"My point is simply this," says Vic. "We're producing too many different things in short runs, meeting small orders. We must rationalise. Offer a small range of standard products at competitive prices. Encourage our customers to design their systems around *our* products."

"Why should they?" says Brian Everthorpe, tipping his chair back on its rear legs and hooking his thumbs in his waistcoat pockets.

"Because the product will be cheap, reliable and available at short notice," says Vic. "If they want something manufactured to their own spec, OK, but we insist on a thumping great order or a high price."

"And if they won't play?" says Brian Everthorpe.

"Then let them go elsewhere."

"I don't like it," says Brian Everthorpe. "The small orders bring in the big ones."

The heads of the other men present have been swivelling from side to side, like spectators at a tennis match, during this argument. They look fascinated but slightly frightened.

"I don't believe that, Brian," says Vic. "Why should anybody order long when they can order short and keep their inventory down?"

"I'm talking about goodwill," says Brian Everthorpe. "Pringle's has a slogan –"

"Yes, I know, Brian," says Vic Wilcox. "*If it can be made, Pringle's will make it.* Well, I'm proposing a new slogan. *If it's profitable, Pringle's will make it.*"

"Mr Gradgrind in *Hard Times* embodies the spirit of industrial capitalism as Dickens saw it. His philosophy is utilitarian. He despises emotion and the imagination, and believes only in Facts. The novel shows, among other things, the disastrous effects of this philosophy on Mr Gradgrind's own children, Tom, who becomes a thief, and Louisa, who nearly becomes an adulteress, and on the lives of working people in the city of Coketown which is made in his image, a dreary place containing:

*several streets all very like one another, and many more streets still
more like one another, inhabited by people equally like one another, who
all went in and out at the same hours, with the same sound upon the
same pavements, to do the same work, and to whom every day was the
same as yesterday and tomorrow, and every year the counterpart of the
last and the next.*

"Opposed to this alienated, repetitive way of life, is the circus – a
community of spontaneity, generosity and creative imagination. '*You
mutht have us, Thquire,*' says the lisping circus master, Mr Sleary,
to Gradgrind. '*People mutht be amuthed.*' It is Cissie, the despised
horserider's daughter adopted by Gradgrind, who proves the redemp-
tive force in his life. The message of the novel is clear: the alienation
of work under industrial capitalism can be overcome by an infusion
of loving kindness and imaginative play, represented by Cissie and
the circus."

Robyn pauses, to allow the racing pens to catch up with her discourse, and to give emphasis to her next sentence: "Of course, such a
reading is totally inadequate. Dickens' own ideological position is
riddled with contradiction."

The students who have been writing everything down now look up
and smile wryly at Robyn Penrose, like victims of a successful hoax.
They lay down their pens and flex their fingers, as she pauses and
shuffles her notes preparatory to the next stage of her exposition.

In Avondale Road, the Wilcox boys have risen from their beds at last
and are making the most of their unsupervised occupancy of the house.
Gary is eating a heaped bowl of cornflakes in the kitchen, while reading
Home Computer propped up against the milk bottle and listening via
the hall and two open doors to a record by UB40 playing at maximum
volume on the music centre in the lounge. In his bedroom Raymond is
torturing his electric guitar, which is plugged into an amplifier as big
as an upended coffin, grinning fiendishly as he produces howls and
wails of feedback. The whole house vibrates like a sounding-box.
Ornaments tremble on shelves and glassware tinkles in sideboards. A
tradesman who has been ringing at the front door for several minutes
gives up and goes away.

"It is interesting how many of the industrial novels were written by
women. In their work, the ideological contradictions of the middle-
class liberal humanist attitude to the Industrial Revolution take on a
specifically sexual character."

48

At the mention of the word "sexual", a little ripple of interest stirs the rows of silent listeners. Those who have been daydreaming or carving their initials into the desktops sit up. Those who have been taking notes continue to do so with even greater assiduousness. People cease to cough or sniff or shuffle their feet. As Robyn continues, the only interference with the sound of her voice is the occasional ripping noise of a filled-up page of A4 being hurriedly detached from its parent pad.

"It hardly needs to be pointed out that industrial capitalism is phallocentric. The inventors, the engineers, the factory owners and bankers who fuelled it and maintained it, were all men. The most commonplace metonymic index of industry – the factory chimney – is also metaphorically a phallic symbol. The characteristic imagery of the industrial landscape or townscape in nineteenth-century literature – tall chimneys thrusting into the sky, spewing ribbons of black smoke, buildings shaking with the rhythmic pounding of mighty engines, the railway train rushing irresistibly through the passive countryside – all this is saturated with male sexuality of a dominating and destructive kind.

"For women novelists, therefore, industry had a complex fascination. On the conscious level it was the Other, the alien, the male world of work, in which they had no place. I am, of course, talking about middle-class women, for all women novelists at this period were by definition middle-class. On the subconscious level it was what they desired to heal their own castration, their own sense of lack."

Some of the students look up at the word "castration", admiring the cool poise with which Robyn pronounces it, as one might admire a barber's expert manipulation of a cut-throat razor.

"We see this illustrated very clearly in Mrs Gaskell's *North and South*. In this novel, the genteel young heroine from the south of England, Margaret, is compelled by her father's reduced circumstances to take up residence in a city called Milton, closely based on Manchester, and comes into social contact with a local mill-owner called Thornton. He is a very pure kind of capitalist who believes fanatically in the laws of supply and demand. He has no compassion for the workers when times are bad and wages low, and does not ask for pity when he himself faces ruin. Margaret is at first repelled by Thornton's harsh business ethic, but when a strike of workers turns violent, she acts impulsively to save his life, thus revealing her unconscious attraction to him, as well as her instinctive class allegiance. Margaret befriends some of the workers and shows compassion for their sufferings, but when the crunch comes she is on the side of the master. The interest Margaret takes in factory life and the processes of manufacturing – which her

49

mother finds sordid and repellent – is a displaced manifestation of her unacknowledged erotic feelings for Thornton. This comes out very clearly in a conversation between Margaret and her mother, who complains that Margaret is beginning to use factory slang in her speech. She retorts:

> '*And if I live in a factory town, I must speak factory language when I want it. Why, Mamma, I could astonish you with a great many words you never heard in your life. I don't believe you know what a knobstick is.*'
>
> '*Not I, child. I only know it has a very vulgar sound; and I don't want to hear you using it.*''

Robyn looks up from the copy of *North and South* from which she has been reading this passage, and surveys her audience with her cool, grey-green eyes. "I think we all know what a knobstick is, metaphorically."

The audience chuckles gleefully, and the ballpoints speed across the pages of A4 faster than ever.

"Any more questions?" says Vic Wilcox, looking at his watch.

"Just one point, Vic," says Bert Braddock, the Works Manager. "If we rationalise production like you say, will that mean redundancies?"

"No," says Vic, looking Bert Braddock straight in the eye. "Rationalisation will mean growth in sales. Eventually we'll need more men, not fewer." Eventually perhaps, if everything goes according to plan, but Braddock knows as well as Vic that some redundancies are inevitable in the short term. The exchange is purely ritual in function, authorising Bert Braddock to reassure anxious shop stewards if they start asking awkward questions.

Vic dismisses the meeting and, as the men file out, stands up and stretches. He goes to the window, and fiddles with the angle of the louvred blinds. Staring out across the car park, where silent, empty cars wait for their owners like patient pets, he ponders the success of the meeting. The telephone console on his desk buzzes.

"It's Roy Mackintosh, Wragcast," says Shirley.

"Put him on."

Roy Mackintosh is MD of a local foundry that has been supplying Pringle's with castings for many years. He has just heard that Pringle's is not reordering, and has phoned to enquire the reason.

"I suppose someone is undercutting us," he says.

"No, Roy," says Vic. "We're supplying ourselves now."

"From that old foundry of yours?"

"We've made improvements."

"You must have . . ." Roy Mackintosh sounds suspicious. After a certain amount of small talk, he says casually. "Perhaps I might drop by some time. I'd like to have a look at this foundry of yours."

"Sure." Vic does not welcome this proposal, but protocol demands a positive response. "Tell your secretary to fix it with mine."

Vic goes into Shirley's office, shrugging on the jacket of his suit. Brian Everthorpe, who is hanging over Shirley's desk, straightens up guiltily. Griping about the boss, no doubt.

"Hallo, Brian. Still here?"

"Just off." Smiling blandly, he tugs the points of his waistcoat down over his paunch and sidles out of the office.

"Roy Mackintosh wants to look round the foundry. When his secretary rings, put him off as long as you decently can. Don't want the whole world knowing about the KW."

"OK," says Shirley, making a note.

"I'm just going over there now, to see Tom Rigby. I'll drop into the machine shop on my way."

"Right," says Shirley, with a knowing smile. Vic's frequent but unpredictable visits to the shop floor are notorious.

Robyn's student, Marion Russell, wearing a long, shapeless black overcoat and carrying a plastic holdall, hurriedly enters a large building in the commercial centre of Rummidge and asks the security man at the desk for directions. The man asks to see inside her bag and grins at the contents. He motions her towards the lift. She takes the lift to the seventh floor and walks along a carpeted corridor until she comes to a room whose door is slightly ajar. The noises of men talking and laughing and the sound of champagne corks popping filter out into the corridor. Marion Russell stands at the threshold and peeps cautiously round the edge of the door, surveying the arrangement of people and furniture as a thief might case a property for ease of entry and swiftness of escape. Satisfied, she retraces her steps until she comes to a Ladies' cloakroom. In the mirror over the washbasins she applies pancake makeup, lipstick and eyeliner, and combs her hair. Then she locks herself in one of the cubicles, puts her bag on the toilet seat, and takes out the tools of her trade: a red satin basque with suspenders attached, a pair of black lace panties, black fishnet stockings and shiny high-heeled shoes.

"The writers of the industrial novels were never able to resolve in fictional terms the ideological contradictions inherent in their own situation in society. At the very moment when they were writing about these problems, Marx and Engels were writing the seminal texts in which the political solutions were expounded. But the novelists had never heard of Marx and Engels – and if they had heard of them and their ideas, they would probably have recoiled in horror, perceiving the threat to their own privileged position. For all their dismay at the squalor and exploitation generated by industrial capitalism, the novelists were in a sense capitalists themselves, profiting from a highly commercialised form of literary production."

The campus clock begins to strike twelve, and its muffled notes are audible in the lecture theatre. The students stir restlessly in their seats, shuffling their papers and capping their pens. The spring-loaded clips of looseleaf folders snap shut with a noise like revolver shots. Robyn hastens to her conclusion.

"Unable to contemplate a political solution to the social problems they described in their fiction, the industrial novelists could only offer narrative solutions to the personal dilemmas of their characters. And these narrative solutions are invariably negative or evasive. In *Hard Times* the victimised worker Stephen Blackpool dies in the odour of sanctity. In *Mary Barton* the working-class heroine and her husband go off to the colonies to start a new life. Kingsley's Alton Locke emigrates after his disillusionment with Chartism, and dies shortly after. In *Sybil*, the humble heroine turns out to be an heiress and is able to marry her well-meaning aristocratic lover without compromising the class system, and a similar stroke of good fortune resolves the love stories in *Shirley* and *North and South*. Although the heroine of George Eliot's *Felix Holt* renounces her inheritance, it is only so that she can marry the man she loves. In short, all the Victorian novelist could offer as a solution to the problems of industrial capitalism were: a legacy, a marriage, emigration or death."

As Robyn Penrose is winding up her lecture, and Vic Wilcox is commencing his tour of the machine shop, Philip Swallow returns from a rather tiresome meeting of the Arts Faculty Postgraduate Studies Committee (which wrangled for two hours about the proposed revision of a clause in the PhD regulations and then voted to leave it unchanged, an expenditure of time that seemed all the more vain since there are scarcely any new candidates for the PhD in arts subjects anyway these days) to find a rather disturbing message from the Vice-Chancellor's office.

His secretary Pamela reads it off her memo pad: "The VC's PA rang to say could they have your nomination for the Industry Year Shadow Scheme."

"What in God's name is that?"

Pamela shrugs. "I don't know. I've never heard of it. Shall I ring Phyllis Cameron and ask her?"

"No, no, don't do that," says Philip Swallow, nervously fingering his beardless chin. "Last resort. Don't want to make the Arts Faculty look incompetent. We're in enough trouble already."

"I'm sure *I* never saw a letter about it," says Pamela defensively.

"No, no, my fault, I'm sure."

It is. Philip Swallow finds the VC's memorandum, its envelope still unopened, at the bottom of his In-tray, trapped between the pages of a brochure for Bargain Winter Breaks in Belgium which he had picked up from a local travel agency some weeks ago. His casual treatment of this missive is not entirely surprising, since its external appearance hardly conveys an idea of its august addresser. The brown manila envelope, originally despatched to the University by an educational publishing firm, whose name and address, printed on the top left-hand corner, has been partially defaced, is creased and tattered. It has already been used twice for the circulation of internal mail and resealed by means of staples and Sellotape.

"Sometimes I think the VC takes his economy drive a little too far," says Philip, gingerly extracting the stencilled memorandum from its patched and disintegrating container. The document is dated 1st December, 1985. "Oh dear," says Philip, sinking into his swivel seat to read it. Pamela reads it with him, peering over his shoulder.

From: The Vice-Chancellor   *To*: Deans of all Faculties
Subject: INDUSTRY YEAR SHADOW SCHEME
    As you are no doubt aware, 1986 has been designated Industry
    Year by the Government. The DES, through the UGC, have
    urged the CVCP to ensure that universities throughout the UK –

"He does love acronyms, doesn't he," Philip murmurs.

"What?" says Pamela.

"All these initials," says Philip.

"It's supposed to save paper and typing time," says Pamela. "We had a memo round about it. Acrowhatsits to be used whenever possible in University correspondence."

    – make a special effort in the coming year to show themselves
    responsive to the needs of industry, both in terms of collaboration
    in research and development, and the provision of well-trained
    and well-motivated graduates for recruitment to industry.
    A working party was set up last July to advise on this Univer-
    sity's contribution to IY, and one of its recommendations,

approved by Senate at its meeting of November 18th, is that each Faculty should nominate a member of staff to "shadow" some person employed at senior management level in local manufacturing industry, nominated through CRUM, in the course of the winter term.

"I don't remember it coming up at that meeting of Senate," says Philip. "Must have been passed without discussion. What's CRUM?"
"Confederation of Rummidge Manufacturers?" Pamela hazarded.
"Could be. Good try, Pam."

There is a widespread feeling in the country that universities are "ivory tower" institutions, whose staff are ignorant of the realities of the modern commercial world. Whatever the justice of this prejudice, it is important in the present economic climate that we should do our utmost to dispel it. The SS will advertise our willingness to inform ourselves about the needs of industry.

"The SS? Got his own stormtroopers, now, has he, the VC?"
"I think it stands for Shadow Scheme," says Pamela.
"Yes, I'm afraid you're probably right."

A Shadow, as the name implies, is someone who follows another person about all day as he goes about his normal work. In this way a genuine, inward understanding of that work is obtained by the Shadow, which could not be obtained by a simple briefing or organised visit. Ideally, the Shadow should spend an uninterrupted week or fortnight with his opposite number, but if that is impracticable, a regular visit of one day a week throughout the term would be satisfactory. Shadows will be asked to write a short report of what they have learned at the end of the exercise.
Action: Nominations to reach the VC's Office by Wednesday 8th January, 1986.

"Oh dear," says Philip Swallow, once more, when he has finished reading the memorandum.
Anxiety makes him want to pee. He hurries to the Male Staff toilet and finds Rupert Sutcliffe and Bob Busby already ensconced at the three-stall urinal.
"Ah, well met," says Philip, taking his place between them. In front of his nose dangles a hexagonal rubber handle suspended from a chain, installed a year or two earlier when the University removed all automatic flushing systems from its men's cloakrooms as an economy

measure. Someone in the Works and Buildings Department, haunted by the thought of these urinals gushing pointlessly at regular intervals all through the hours of darkness, Sundays and public holidays, had hit on this means of reducing the University's water rate. "I need a volunteer," says Philip, and briefly explains the Shadow Scheme.

"Not my cup of tea, I'm afraid," says Rupert Sutcliffe. "What are you laughing at, Swallow?"

"Cup of pee. Very good, Rupert, I must admit."

"Tea. I said cup of *tea*," says Rupert Sutcliffe frostily. "Traipsing round a factory all day is not mine. I can't think of anything more wearisome." Buttoning up his fly (Sutcliffe's trousers date back to that era, and look it) he retreats to the washbasins on the other side of the room.

"Bob, what about you?" says Philip, swivelling his head in the opposite direction. Bob Busby has also concluded his business at the urinal, but is adjusting his dress with a great deal of fumbling and knee-flexing, as if his member is of such majestic size that it can be coaxed back into his Y-fronts only with the greatest difficulty.

"Quite impossible this term, Philip. With all the extra AUT work on top of everything else." Bob Busby stretches out a hand in front of Philip's face and pulls the chain. The cistern flushes, sending a fine spray over Philip's shoes and trouser bottoms, and the swinging handle released by Busby hits him on the nose. The protocol of chain-pulling in multiple-occupancy urinals has not been thought through by the Works and Buildings Department.

"Who shall I nominate, then?" says Philip Swallow plaintively. "I've got to have a name by 4.30 this afternoon. There isn't time to consult other Departments."

"Why not do it yourself?" Rupert Sutcliffe suggests.

"Don't be absurd. With all the work I have as Dean?"

"Well, the whole idea is pretty absurd," says Sutcliffe. "What has the Faculty of Arts to do with Industry Year, or Industry Year to do with the Faculty of Arts?"

"I wish you'd put that question to the Vice-Chancellor, Rupert," says Philip. "*What has the FA to do with IY, or IY with the FA?*"

"I'm sure I don't know what you're talking about."

"Just my little joke," says Philip to Sutcliffe's departing back. "Not much to joke about when you're Dean of sweet FA," he continues to Bob Busby, who is carefully combing his hair in the mirror. "It's responsibility without power. You know, I ought to be able to *order* one of you to do this shadow nonsense."

"You can't," says Bob Busby smugly. "Not without asking for nominations and holding a Department meeting to discuss it first."

"I know, and there isn't time."

"Why don't you ask Robyn Penrose?"

"The most junior member of the Department? Surely it wouldn't –"

"It's right up her street."

"Is it?"

"Of course – her book on the Victorian industrial novel."

"Oh, *that*. It's hardly the same . . . Still, it's a thought, Bob."

Later that day, much later, when Shirley and the other office staff have gone home, and Vic sits alone in the administration block, working in his darkened office by the light of a single desk lamp, he gets a call from Stuart Baxter.

"You've heard about Industry Year, Vic?"

"Enough to know it's a waste of time and money."

"I'm inclined to agree with you. But the Board feels that we've got to go along with it. Good PR for the Group, you know. Our chairman is dead keen. I've been asked to co-ordinate initiatives –"

"What do you want me to do?" Vic cuts in impatiently.

"I was coming to that, Vic. You know what a shadow is, don't you?"

When Stuart Baxter has finished telling him, Vic says: "No way."

"Why not, Vic?"

"I don't want some academic berk following me about all day."

"It's only one day a week, Vic, for a few weeks."

"Why me?"

"Because you're the most dynamic MD in the division. We want to show them the best."

Vic knows this compliment is totally insincere, but he has no wish to disown it. It could be useful to remind Stuart Baxter of it some time in the future.

"I'll think about it," he says.

"Sorry, Vic. I've got to tie it up now. Seeing the Chairman tonight at a function."

"Left it a bit late, haven't you?"

"To tell you the truth, my secretary fucked up. Lost the letter."

"Oh yes?" says Vic sceptically.

"I'd be very grateful if you'd co-operate."

"You mean, it's an order?"

"Don't be silly, Vic. We're not in the Army."

Vic keeps Baxter in suspense for a few moments, while he reviews the advantages of having him under an obligation. "About that automatic core blower . . ."

"Send me a Capex and I'll run it up the flagpole."

"Thanks," says Vic. "Will do."

"And the other?"

"All right."

"Great! The name of your shadow is Dr Robin Penrose."

"A medic?"

"No."

"Not a shrink, for Christ's sake?"

"No, I understand he's a lecturer in English Literature."

"English *what*?"

"Don't know much else about him – only got the message this afternoon."

"Jesus wept."

Stuart Baxter chuckles. "Read any good books lately, Vic?"

TWO

Mrs Thornton went on after a moment's pause: "Do you know anything of Milton, Miss Hale? Have you seen any of our factories? our magnificent warehouses?"

"No," said Margaret. "I have not seen anything of that description as yet."

Then she felt that, by concealing her utter indifference to all such places, she was hardly speaking the truth; so she went on: "I dare say, papa would have taken me before now if I had cared. But I really do not find much pleasure in going over manufactories."

ELIZABETH GASKELL: *North and South*

1

Ten days later, at eight-thirty in the morning of Wednesday, 22nd January, Robyn Penrose set off in a snowstorm and an ill humour to begin her stint as the University of Rummidge Faculty of Arts Industry Year Shadow, or URFAIYS as she was designated in memoranda emanating from the Vice-Chancellor's Office. One of these documents had informed her that she was to be attached to a Mr Victor Wilcox, Managing Director of J. Pringle & Sons, for one day a week during the remainder of the winter term, and she had chosen Wednesdays for this undertaking since it was the day she normally kept free from teaching. By the same token it was a day she normally spent at home, catching up on her marking, preparation and research, and she bitterly resented having to sacrifice it. For this reason above all others she had come very close to declining Philip Swallow's proposal to nominate her for the Shadow Scheme. After all, if the University wasn't going to keep her on (Swallow's request had come, rather tactlessly, later in the very same day on which he had communicated this gloomy prognosis) why should she put herself out to oblige the University?

"Exactly!" said Penny Black the following evening, as she peeled off her jeans in the women's changing-room at the University Sports Centre. "I don't understand why you agreed to do it." Penny was a feminist friend of Robyn's from the Sociology Department, with whom she played squash once a week.

"I wish I hadn't, now," said Robyn. "I wish I'd told him to, to . . ."

"To stick his shadow scheme up his ass. Why didn't you?"

"I don't know. Well, I do, really. A little voice, a nasty, calculating little voice whispered in my ear that one day I'm going to need a reference from Swallow."

"You're right, honey. That's how they screw us, these men in authority. It's a power trip. Damn these hooks and eyes."

Penny Black fumbled with the fastenings of her bra, reversed around her waist like a belt. Succeeding, she rotated the garment, levered her formidable breasts into the cups and thrust her arms through the shoulderstraps. Latex smacked lustily against solid flesh. Playing squash was the only time Penny wore a bra – without it, as she said, her boozums would bounce from wall to wall faster than the ball.

"Oh, I wouldn't say that about Swallow," Robyn demurred. "To be fair, he doesn't seem to *have* much power. He was practically begging me to agree."

"So why didn't you bargain with him? Why didn't you say you'd be his fucking shadow if he'd give you tenure?"

"Don't be ridiculous, Penny."

"What's ridiculous?"

"Well, A, he's not in a position to give it to me, and B, I wouldn't stoop to that sort of thing."

"You British!" said Penny Black, shaking her head in despair. She herself was British, in fact, but having spent several years as a graduate student in California, where she had been converted to radical feminism, she now thought of herself as spiritually an American, and tried as far as possible to speak like one. "Well," she continued, pulling on a red Amazon sports shirt, "you'll just have to sweat out your hostility on the squash court." Her dark, tousled head popped out of the collar, a grinning Jill-in-the-box: "Pretend the ball is one of Swallow's."

A middle-aged grey-haired woman swathed in a bath-towel nodded a greeting to Robyn as she passed between the sauna and the showers. Robyn smiled radiantly back, hissing between her teeth, "For God's sake keep your voice down, Penny, that's his wife."

Charles was amused by this story when Robyn rang him up later that evening. But, like Penny, he was surprised Robyn had agreed to be nominated as Arts Faculty Shadow.

"It's not your sort of thing, is it?"

"Well, I *am* supposed to be an expert on the industrial novel. Swallow made a great point of that."

"But not in a *realist* sort of way. I mean, you're not suggesting that there's any possible *relevance –*"

"No, no, of course not," said Robyn, anxious to disown the taint of realism. "I'm just trying to explain the pressure that was put on me." She was beginning to feel that she had made a mistake, and allowed herself to be exploited. It was a rare sensation for Robyn, and all the more unpleasant for that.

This suspicion hardened into certainty in the days that followed. She woke on the morning appointed for her initiation into the Shadow Scheme with a heavy heart, which the weather did nothing to lighten. "Oh no," she groaned, pulling the bedroom curtain aside on a sky swirling with snowflakes, like a shaken paperweight. A thin layer already covered the frost-hardened ground, and clung delicately to tree-branches, clothes-lines and back-garden bric-à-brac. She was tempted to use the weather as an excuse to postpone her visit to J. Pringle & Sons, but the work ethic that had carried her successfully through so many years of study and so many examinations now exerted its leverage on her conscience once more. She had already postponed the exercise by one week, because of the AUT strike. Another cancellation would look bad.

Over breakfast (no *Guardian* was delivered, doubtless because of the snow) she pondered the question of what clothes to wear for the occasion. She possessed a boiler suit bought recently from Next, which seemed in theory appropriate, but it was bright orange, with a yellow flower appliquéd on the bib, and it might, she thought, lack dignity. On the other hand, she wasn't going to show excessive respect by wearing her olive-green tailored interview suit. What did a liberated woman wear to visit a factory? It was a nice semiotic problem. Robyn was well aware that clothes do not merely serve the practical purpose of covering our bodies, but also convey messages about who we are, what we are doing, and how we feel. However, she did in the end let the weather partly determine her choice: a pair of elephant-cord trousers tucked Cossack-style into her high boots, and a chunky-knit cardigan with a shawl collar worn over a Liberty print blouse. On top of this outfit she wore her cream-coloured quilted cotton jacket and a Russian-style hat made of artificial fur. Thus attired, she ventured out into the blizzard.

The little Renault already looked sculpted out of snow, and the key would not turn in the frozen door-lock. She freed it with a patent squirt imported from Finland, and hastily discontinued, called Superpiss. Charles had given it to her for a joke, suggesting she use it as a visual aid to introduce Saussurean linguistics to first-year undergraduates, holding the tube aloft to demonstrate that what is onomatopoeia in one language community may be obscenity in another. The snow adhering to the car windows created a sepulchral gloom inside, and Robyn spent several minutes brushing it off before she attempted to start the engine. Amazingly, perversely, and rather to her regret (a flat battery would have been a cast-iron excuse to abort the visit) the engine fired. With the Rummidge *A to Z* open on the passenger seat beside her, she set off to find J. Pringle & Sons, somewhere on the other side of the city: the dark side of Rummidge, as foreign to her as the dark side of the moon.

Because of the weather Robyn decides not to use the motorway, and, finding the residential backstreets treacherous and strewn with abandoned vehicles, she joins a long, slow-moving convoy of traffic on the Outer Ring – not a purpose-built road, this, but a motley string of suburban shopping streets and main roads, where the snow has already been churned into filthy curds and whey. She feels as if she is negotiating the entrails of the city in the slow, peristaltic procession. Stopping and starting, grinding forward in low gear, she passes shops,

63

offices, tower blocks, garages, car marts, churches, fast-food outlets, a school, a bingo hall, a hospital, a prison. Shocking, somehow, to come across this last, a gloomy Victorian gaol in the middle of an ordinary suburb where double-decker buses pass and housewives with shopping bags and pushchairs go about their mundane business. Prison is just a word to Robyn, a word in a book or a newspaper, a symbol of something – the law, hegemony, repression (*"The prison motif in* Little Dorrit *is a metaphorical articulation of Dickens' critique of Victorian culture and society" – Discuss*). Seeing it there, foursquare in soot-streaked stone, with its barred windows, great studded iron door, and high walls trimmed with barbed wire, makes her think with a shudder of the men cooped up inside in cramped cells smelling of sweat and urine, rapists and pimps and wife-beaters and child-molesters among them, and her heart sinks under the thought that crime and punishment are equally horrible, equally inevitable – unless men should change, all become like Charles, which seems unlikely.

The convoy crawls on. More shops, offices, garages, takeaways. Robyn passes a cinema converted into a bingo hall, a church converted into a community centre, a Co-op converted into a Freezer Centre. This part of the city lacks the individual character of Robyn's own suburb, where healthfood stores and sportswear boutiques and alternative bookshops have sprung up to cater for the students and liberal-minded yuppies who live there; and still more does it lack the green amenities of the residential streets around the University. There are few trees and no parks to be seen. There are occasional strips of terraced houses, whose occupants seem to have given up the unequal struggle against the noise and pollution of the Ring Road, and retreated to their back rooms, for the frontages are peeling and dilapidated and the curtains sag in the windows with a permanently drawn look. Here and there an effort has been made at renovation, but always in deplorable taste, "Georgian" bay windows or Scandinavian-style pine porches clapped on to the Victorian and Edwardian façades. The shops are either flashy or dingy. The windows of the former are piled with cheap mass-produced goods, banks of conjunctival TVs twitching and blinking in unison, blinding white fridges and washing-machines, ugly shoes, ugly clothes, and unbelievably ugly furniture, all plastic veneers and synthetic fabrics. The windows of the dingy shops are like cemeteries for unloved and unwanted goods – limp floral print dresses, yellowing underwear, flyblown chocolate boxes and dusty plastic toys. The people slipping and sliding on the pavements, spattered with slush by the passing traffic, look stoically wretched, as if they expect no better from life. A line from D. H. Lawrence – was it *Women in Love* or *Lady Chatterley*? – comes into Robyn's head, *"She felt in a wave of terror the grey, gritty hopelessness of it all.*" How she wishes she were back in her snug little house, tapping away on her word-processor, dissecting the lexemes of some classic Victorian novel, delicately detaching the hermeneutic code from the proairetic code, the cultural from the symbolic, surrounded by books and files, the gas fire hissing and a cup of coffee steaming at her elbow. She passes launderettes, hairdressers, betting shops, Sketchleys, Motaparts, Currys, a Post Office, a DIY Centre, a Denture Centre, an Exhaust Centre. An exhaustion centre is what she will soon be in need of. The city seems to stretch on and on – or is she going round and round the Ring Road in an endless loop? No, she is not. She is off the Ring Road. She is lost.

Robyn thinks she must be in Angleside, because the faces of the people slithering on the pavements or huddled miserably at bus-stops are mostly swarthy and dark-eyed, and the bright silks of saris, splashed with mud, gleam beneath the hems of the women's drab topcoats. The names on the shopfronts are all Asian. Nanda General Stores. Sabar Sweet Centre. Rajit Brothers Import Export. Punjabi Printers Ltd. Usha Saree Centre. Halted at a red light, Robyn consults her *A to Z*, but before she has found the place on the map, the lights have changed and cars are hooting impatiently behind her. She takes a left turn at random, and finds herself in an area of derelict buildings, burned out and boarded up, the site, she realises, of the previous year's rioting. Caribbean faces now preponderate on the pavements. Youths in outsize hats, lounging in the doorways of shops and cafés, with hands thrust deep into their pockets, gossip and smoke, jog on the spot to keep warm, or lob snowballs at each other across the road, over the roofs of passing cars. How strange it is, strange and sad, to see all these tropical faces amid the slush and dirty snow, the grey gritty hopelessness of an English industrial city in the middle of winter.

Halted on the inside lane, Robyn catches the eye of a young West Indian with Rastafarian dreadlocks, hunched in the entrance of a boarded-up shop, and smiles: a friendly, sympathetic, anti-racist smile. To her alarm the young man immediately straightens up, takes his hands out of the pockets of his black leather jacket, and comes over to her car, stooping to bring his head level with the window. He mouths something through the glass which she cannot hear. The car in front moves forward a few yards, but when Robyn inches forward in turn the young man lays a restraining hand on the Renault's wing. Robyn leans across the passenger seat and winds the window down a little way. "Yes?" she says, her voice squeaky with suppressed panic.

"Yow want soom?" he says in a broad Rummidge accent.

"What?" she says blankly.

"Yow want soom?"

"Some what?"

"The weed, man, wudjerthink?"

"Oh," says Robyn, as the penny drops. "No thank you."

"Somethin' else? Smack? Speed? Yow nime it."

"No, really, it's very kind of you, but –" The car ahead moves forward again and the car behind hoots impatiently. "Sorry – I can't stop!" she cries and lets out the clutch. Mercifully the traffic progresses for fifty yards before it stalls again, and the Rasta does not pursue her further, but Robyn keeps a nervous eye on her rear-view mirror.

Robyn sees a roadsign to West Wallsbury, the area in which J. Pringle & Sons is situated, and gratefully follows it. But the snow, which has been slight in the past half-hour, suddenly begins to fall fast and furiously again, limiting her vision. She finds herself on a dual carriageway, almost a motorway, raised above the level of the neighbouring houses, and with no apparent exits. She is forced to go faster than she would choose by the intimidating bulk of lorries nudging up behind her, their radiator grilles looming like cliffs in her rear-view mirror, the drivers high above, out of sight. Every now and again one of these vehicles swings out and surges past, spattering her side windows with filth and making the little Renault stagger under the impact of displaced air. How can these men (of course they are all men) drive their juggernauts at such insane speeds in such dreadful conditions? Frightened, Robyn clings to the steering wheel like a helmsman in a storm, her head craned forward to peer past the flailing windscreen wipers at the road ahead, ribbed with furrows of yellow-brown slush. At the last possible moment, she glimpses a slip-road to her left and swerves down it. At the bottom there is a roundabout, which she circles twice, trying to make sense of the direction signs. She takes an exit at random and pulls up at the side of the road to consult her *A to Z*, but there are no street names visible which would enable her to orient herself. Seeing the glow of a red and yellow Shell sign ahead, she drives on and pulls into the forecourt of a self-service petrol station.

Inside the little shop, a doleful Asian youth wearing finger mittens, walled in behind racks of cheap digital watches, ballpoint pens, sweets, and music cassettes, shakes his head and shrugs when she asks him the name of the street. "Do you mean to say that you don't know the name of the street your own garage is in?" she says sharply, exasperation overcoming sensitivity to racial minorities.

"An't my garridge," says the youth in a broad Rummidge accent. "Oi juss work 'ere."

"Well, do you know if this is West Wallsbury?"

The youth admits that it is. Does he know the way to J. Pringle & Sons? He shakes his head again.

"Pringle's? I'll take you there."

Robyn turns to face a man who has just entered the shop: tall, heavily built, with bushy sideboards and moustache, a sheepskin coat open over his three-piece suit.

"With pleasure," he adds, smiling and looking Robyn up and down.

"If you would just show me the route on this map," says Robyn, without returning the smile, "I'd be most grateful."

"I'll take you. Just let me settle with Ali Baba here."

"I have a car of my own, thank you."

"I mean you can follow me."

"I couldn't put you to that trouble. If you would just –"

"No trouble, my love. I'm going there myself." Seeing the doubtful expression on Robyn's face, he laughs. "I work there."

"Oh well, in that case . . . Thank you."

"And what brings *you* to Pringle's?" says the man, as he signs his credit card slip with a flourish. "Going to work for us, too? Secretary?"

"No."

"Pity. But you're not a customer, I think?"

"No."

"So . . . what? Are you going to make me play twenty questions?"

"I'm from Rummidge University. I'm, er, taking part in, that is to say . . . I'm on a kind of educational visit."

The man freezes in the act of stowing away his wallet. "You're never Vic Wilcox's shadow?"

"Yes."

He gapes at her for a moment, then chortles and slaps his thigh. "My word, Vic's in for a surprise."

"Why?"

"Well, he was expecting . . . someone rather different. Older." He snorts with suppressed laughter. "Less attractive."

"Perhaps we should get on," says Robyn frostily. "I'm going to be very late."

"No wonder, in this weather. I'm a bit late myself. Motorway was a shambles. I'm Brian Everthorpe, by the way. Marketing Director at Pringle's." He produces a small card from his waistcoat pocket and presents it.

Robyn reads aloud: "Riviera Sunbeds. Daily and weekly rental."

"Oops, somebody else's card, got mixed up with mine," says Brian Everthorpe, exchanging the card with another. "Nice little business that, as a matter of fact, Riviera Sunbeds. I know the people. I can arrange a discount if you're interested."

"No thank you," says Robyn.

"You get a marvellous tan. Good as a trip to Tenerife, and a fraction of the cost."

"I never sunbathe," says Robyn. "It gives you skin cancer."

"If you believe the newspapers," says Brian Everthorpe, "everything nice is bad for you." He opens the door of the shop and a flurry of snow blows in. "That's my Granada over there by pump number two. Just get on my tail and stick to it, as the bee said to the pollen."

Brian Everthorpe led Robyn a tortuous route through streets lined with factories and warehouses, many of them closed down, some displaying "For Sale" or "For Lease" signs on them, some derelict beyond the hope of restoration, with snow blowing through their smashed windows. There was not a soul to be seen on the pavements. She was glad of Everthorpe's guidance, though she disliked his manners and resented his evident desire to stage-manage her arrival at Pringle's. At the entrance to the factory, he engaged the man controlling the barrier in some kind of argument, then got out of his car to speak to Robyn. She lowered her window.

"Sorry, but the security johnny insists that you sign the visitors' book. He's afraid Vic'll bawl him out otherwise. Bit of a martinet, Vic, I should warn you." His eye lit upon the little tube on the dashboard. "Superpiss! What's that for?" he chortled.

"It's for unfreezing car locks," said Robyn, hastily stowing it away in the glove compartment. "It's made in Finland."

"I'd rather use my own," said Brian Everthorpe, enjoying the joke hugely. "It costs nothing, and it's always on tap."

Robyn got out of the car and looked through railings across the car park to a brick office block and a tall windowless building behind it, a prospect almost as depressing as the prison she had seen that morning. Only the carpet of snow relieved its drabness, and that was being rolled up by a man driving a small tractor with a scoop on the front.

"Where are the chimneys?" she asked.

"What chimneys?"

"Well, you know. Great tall things, with smoke coming out of them."

Brian Everthorpe laughed. "We don't need 'em. Everything runs on gas or electricity." He looked at her quizzically. "Ever been inside a factory before?"

"No," said Robyn.

"I see. A virgin, eh? Factorywise, I mean." He grinned and stroked his whiskers.

"Where's the Visitors' Book?" Robyn enquired coldly.

After she had signed in, Brian Everthorpe directed her to the section of the car park reserved for visitors, and waited for her at the entrance to the Administration Block. He ushered her into an overheated wood-panelled lobby.

"This is Dr Penrose," he said to the two women behind the reception desk. They gaped at her as if she was an alien from outer space, as she shook the snow from her fur cap and quilted jacket. "I'll tell Mr Wilcox she's here," said Brian Everthorpe, and Robyn thought she saw him wink for some inscrutable reason. "Take a seat," he said, indicating a rather threadbare sofa of the kind Robyn associated with very old-fashioned cinema foyers. "I won't be a tick. Can I take your coat?" The way he looked her up and down made Robyn wish she had kept it on.

"Thanks, I'll keep it with me."

Everthorpe left, and Robyn sat down. The two women behind the reception desk avoided her eye. One was typing and the other was operating the switchboard. Every minute or so the telephone operator intoned in a bored sing-song, "J. Pringle & Sons good morning kin I 'elp yew?", and then, "Puttin' yew threw," or "Sorree, there's no reply." Between calls she murmured inaudibly to her companion and stroked her platinum-blonde hair-do as if it were an ailing pet. Robyn looked around the room. There were framed photographs and testimonials on the panelled walls, and some bits of polished machinery in a glass case. On a low table in front of her were some engineering trade magazines and a copy of the *Financial Times*. It seemed to her that the world could not possibly contain a more boring room. Nothing her eye fell upon aroused in her the slightest flicker of interest, except a bulletin board with removable plastic letters which declared, under the day's date: "*J. Pringle & Sons welcomes Dr Robin Penrose, Rummidge University.*" Noticing that the two women were now looking at her, Robyn smiled and said, "It's Robyn with a 'y' actually." To her bewilderment they both dissolved into giggles.

2

Vic Wilcox was dictating letters to Shirley when Brian Everthorpe knocked and put his head round the door, grinning, for some reason, from sideburn to sideburn.

"Visitor for you, Vic."

"Oh?"

"Your shadow."

"He's late."

"Well, not surprising, is it, in this weather?" Brian Everthorpe came uninvited into the room. "The motorway was a shambles."

"You should move further in, Brian."

"Yes, well, you know what Beryl is like about the country . . . This shadow caper: what happens exactly?"

"You know what happens. He follows me about all day."

"What, everywhere?"

"That's the idea."

"What, even to the Gents?" Brian Everthorpe exploded with laughter as he uttered this question.

Vic looked wonderingly at him and then at Shirley, who arched her eyebrows and shrugged incomprehension. "You feeling all right, Brian?" he enquired.

"Quite all right, thanks, Vic, quite all right." Everthorpe coughed and wheezed and wiped his eyes with a silk handkerchief which he wore, affectedly, in his breast pocket. "You're a lucky man, Vic."

"What are you talking about?"

"Your shadow. But what will your wife say?"

"What's it got to do with Marjorie?"

"Wait till you see her."

"Marjorie?"

"No, your shadow. Your shadow's a bird, Vic!"

Shirley gave a little squeak of surprise and excitement. Vic stared speechlessly as Brian Everthorpe elaborated.

"A very dishy redhead. I prefer bigger boobs, myself, but you can't have everything." He winked at Shirley.

"Robin!" said Shirley. "It can be a girl's name, can't it? Though they spell it different. With a 'y' sort of thing."

"In the letter it was 'Robin' with an 'i'," said Vic.

"An easy mistake," said Brian Everthorpe.

"Stuart Baxter said nothing about a woman," said Vic.

"I'll bring her in. Seeing's believing."

"Let me find that letter first," said Vic, riffling blindly through the papers in his Pending-tray, playing for time. He felt anger surging through his veins and arteries. A lecturer in English Literature was bad enough, but a *woman* lecturer in English Literature! It was a ludicrous mistake, or else a calculated insult, he wasn't sure which, to send such a person to shadow him. He wanted to rage and swear, to shout down the telephone and fire off angry memoranda. But something in Brian Everthorpe's demeanour restrained him.

"How old is she sort of thing?" Shirley asked Brian Everthorpe.

"I dunno. Young. In her thirties, I'd say. Shall I bring her in?"

"Go and find that letter, first," Vic said to Shirley. She went into her office, followed, to his relief, by Brian Everthorpe. Everthorpe was getting a lot of mileage out of the mix-up, trying to make him look foolish. Vic could imagine him spreading the story all round the works. "*You should have seen his face when I told him! I couldn't help laughing. Then he went spare. Shirley had to cover her ears . . .*" No, better to limit the damage, control his anger, make nothing of it, pretend he didn't mind.

He rose from his desk and went through the anteroom into Shirley's office. High up on one wall were some glazed panels. They were painted over, but someone had scraped away a small area of paint, exposing the clear glass. Shirley was peering through this spyhole, balanced precariously on top of a filing cabinet, steadied by the hand of Brian Everthorpe on her haunch. "Hmm, not a bad-looking wench," she was saying. "If you like that type."

"You're just jealous, Shirley," said Brian Everthorpe.

"Me, jealous? Don't be daft. I like her boots, mind."

"What in God's name are you doing up there?" Vic said.

Brian Everthorpe and Shirley turned and looked at him.

"A little dodge of your predecessor," said Brian Everthorpe. "He liked to look over his visitors before a meeting. Reckoned it gave him a psychological advantage." He removed his hand from Shirley's rump, and assisted her to the ground.

"I couldn't find that letter," she said.

"You mean you can see into reception from there?" said Vic.

"Have a dekko," said Brian Everthorpe.

Vic hesitated, then sprang onto the filing cabinet. He applied his eye to the hole in the paint and gazed, as if through a telescope already fixed and focused, at the young woman seated on the far side of the lobby. She had copper-coloured hair, cut short as a boy's at the back, with a mop of curls tilted jauntily forward at the front. She sat at her ease on the sofa, with her long, booted and pantalooned legs crossed at

71

the ankles, but the expression on her face was bored and haughty. "I've seen her before," he said.

"Oh, where?" said Shirley.

"I don't know." She was like a figure in a dream that he could not quite recall. He stared at the topknot of red-gold curls, straining to remember. Then she yawned suddenly, like a cat, revealing two rows of white, even teeth, before she covered her mouth. She lifted her head as she did this, and seemed to look straight at him. Embarrassed, feeling too like a Peeping Tom for comfort, he scrambled to the floor.

"Let's stop playing silly buggers," he said, striding back into his office. "Show the woman in."

Brian Everthorpe threw open the door of Vic Wilcox's office and motioned Robyn across the threshold with a flourish. "Doctor Penrose," he announced, with a smirk.

The man who rose from behind a large polished desk on the far side of the room, and came forward to shake Robyn's hand, was smaller and more ordinary-looking than she had expected. The term "Managing Director" had suggested to her imagination some figure more grand and gross, with plump, flushed cheeks and wings of silver hair, a rotund torso sheathed in expensively tailored suiting, a gold tiepin and cufflinks, and a cigar wedged between manicured fingers. This man was stocky and wiry, like a short-legged terrier, his face was pale and drawn, with two vertical worry-lines scored into the brow above the nose, and the hank of dark, flat hair that fell forward across his brow had clearly never had the attention of an expert barber. He was in shirtsleeves, and the shirt did not fit him very well, the buttoned cuffs hanging down over his wrists, like a schoolboy's whose clothes had been purchased with a view to his "growing into" them. Robyn almost smiled with relief as she appraised his advancing figure – she already heard herself describing him to Charles or Penny as "a funny little man" – but the strength of his handshake, and the glint in his dark brown eyes, warned her not to underestimate him.

"Thanks, Brian," he said to the hovering Everthorpe. "I expect you've got work to do."

Everthorpe departed with obvious reluctance. "See you later, I hope," he said unctuously to Robyn, as he closed the door.

"Like some coffee?" said Wilcox, taking her coat and hanging it on the back of the door.

Robyn said she would love some.

"Have a seat." He indicated an upright armchair drawn up at an angle to his desk, to which he now returned. He flicked a switch on a console and said, "Two coffees, please, Shirley." He thrust a cigarette pack in her direction. "Smoke?"

Robyn shook her head. He lit one himself, sat down and swivelled his chair to face her. "Haven't we met before?" he said.

"Not that I'm aware of."

"I've a feeling I've seen you recently."

"I can't imagine where that would be."

Wilcox continued to stare at her through a cloud of smoke. If it had been Everthorpe, she would have dismissed this performance as a clumsy pass, but Wilcox seemed teased by some genuine memory.

"I'm sorry I'm a bit late," she said. "The roads were terrible, and I got lost."

"You're a week late," he said. "I was expecting you last Wednesday."

"Didn't you get my message?"

"About halfway through the morning."

"I hope I didn't inconvenience you."

"You did, as a matter of fact. I'd cancelled a meeting."

He did not lighten this rebuke with a smile. Robyn felt herself growing warm with resentment of his rudeness, mingled with the consciousness that her own conduct had not been entirely blameless. Her original plan for the previous Wednesday had been to put in an hour or two of picket duty very early in the morning, and then go on to her appointment at Pringle's. But on the picket line Bob Busby had pointed out to her that the Shadow Scheme was official University business and that she would be strike-breaking if she kept her appointment. Of course it was and of course she would! *Stupida!* She punched her head with her fist in self-reproach. She was inexperienced in the protocol of industrial action, but only too pleased to have an excuse to put off her visit to Pringle's for a week.

"I'm sorry," she said to Wilcox. "It was a bit chaotic at the University last Wednesday. We had a one-day strike on, you see. The switchboard wasn't operating normally. It took me ages to phone."

"That's where I saw you!" he exclaimed, sitting up in his chair, and pointing a finger at her like a gun. "You were standing outside the University gates at about eight o'clock in the morning, last Wednesday."

"Yes," said Robyn. "I was."

"I drive past there every day on my way to work," he said. "I was held up there last Wednesday. Put two minutes on my journey time, it did. You were holding a banner." He pronounced this last word as if it denoted something unpleasant.

"Yes, I was picketing."

What fun it had been! Stopping cars and thrusting leaflets through the drivers' windows, turning back lorries, waving banners for the

73

benefit of local TV news cameras, cheering when a truck driver decided not to cross the picket line, thawing one's fingers round a mug of thermos-flask coffee, sharing the warm glow of camaraderie with colleagues one had never met before. Robyn had not felt so exalted since the great women's rally at Greenham Common.

"What were you striking about? Pay?"

"Partly. That and the cuts."

"You want no cuts and more pay?"

"That's right."

"Think the country can afford it?"

"Certainly," said Robyn. "If we spent less on defence –"

"This company has several defence contracts," said Wilcox. "We make gearbox casings for Challenger tanks, and con-rods for Armoured Personel Carriers. If those contracts were cancelled, I'd have to lay off men. Your cuts would become ours."

"You could make something else," said Robyn. "Something peaceful."

"What?"

"I can't say what you should make," said Robyn irritably. "It's not my business."

"No, it's mine," said Wilcox.

At that moment his secretary came into the room with two cups of coffee, which she distributed in a pregnant silence, shooting curious, covert glances at each of them. When she had gone, Wilcox said, "Who were you trying to hurt?"

"Hurt?"

"A strike has to hurt someone. The employers, the public. Otherwise it has no effect."

Robyn was about to say, "The Government," when she saw the trap: Wilcox would find it easy enough to argue that the Government had not been troubled by the strike. Nor, as Philip Swallow had predicted, had the general public been greatly inconvenienced. The students' Union had supported the strike, and its members had not complained about a day's holiday from lectures. The University, then? But the University wasn't responsible for the cuts or the erosion of lecturers' salaries. Faster than a computer, Robyn's mind reviewed these candidates for the target of the strike and rejected them all. "It was only a one-day strike," she said at length. "More of a demonstration, really. We got a lot of support from other trade unions. Several lorry-drivers refused to cross the picket lines."

"What were they doing – delivering stuff?"

"Yes."

"I expect they came back the next day, or the next week?"

74

"I suppose so."

"And who paid for the extra deliveries? I'll tell you who," he went on when she did not answer. "Your University – which you say is short of cash. It's even shorter, now."

"They docked our salaries," said Robyn. "They can pay for the lorries out of that."

Wilcox grunted as if acknowledging a debating point, from which she deduced that he was a bully and needed to be stood up to. She did not think it necessary to tell him that the University administration had been obliged to circulate all members of staff with a memorandum asking them, if they had been on strike, to volunteer the information (since there was no other way of finding out) so that their pay could be docked. It was rumoured that the number of staff who had responded was considerably smaller than the number of participants in the strike claimed by the AUT. "Do you have many strikes here?" she asked, in an effort to shift the focus of conversation.

"Not any more," said Wilcox. "The employees know which side their bread is buttered. They look around this area, they see the factories that have closed in the past few years, they know how many people are out of work."

"You mean, they're afraid to strike?"

"Why should they strike?"

"I don't know – but if they wanted to. For higher wages, say?"

"This is a very competitive industry. A strike would plunge us deep into the red. The division could close us down. The men know that."

"The division?"

"The Engineering and Foundry Division of Midland Amalgamated. They own us."

"I thought J. Pringle & Sons were the owners."

Wilcox laughed, a gruff bark. "Oh, the Pringle family got out years ago. Took their money and ran, when the going was good. The company's been bought and sold twice since then." He took a brown manila folder from a drawer and passed it to her. "Here are some tree diagrams showing how we fit into the conglomerate, and the management structure of the company. D'you know much about business?"

"Nothing at all. But isn't that supposed to be the point?"

"The point?"

"Of the Shadow Scheme."

"I'm buggered if I know what the point is," said Wilcox sourly. "It's just a PR stunt, if you ask me. You teach English literature, don't you?"

"Yes."

"What's that? Shakespeare? Poetry?"

75

"Well, I do teach a first-year course that includes some –"

"We did *Julius Caesar* for O-Level," Wilcox interjected. "Had to learn great chunks of it by heart. Hated it, I did. The master was a toffee-nosed southerner, used to take the pi – used to make fun of our accents."

"My field is the nineteenth-century novel," said Robyn. "And women's studies."

"Women's studies?" Wilcox echoed with a frown. "What are they?"

"Oh, women's writing. The representation of women in literature. Feminist critical theory."

Wilcox sniffed. "You give degrees for that?"

"It's one part of the course," said Robyn stiffly. "It's an option."

"A soft one, if you ask me," said Wilcox. "Still, I suppose it's all right for girls."

"Boys take it too," said Robyn. "And the reading load is very heavy, as a matter of fact."

"Boys?" Wilcox curled a lip. "Nancy boys?"

"Perfectly normal, decent, intelligent young men," said Robyn, struggling to control her temper.

"Why aren't they studying something useful, then?"

"Like mechanical engineering?"

"You said it."

Robyn sighed. "Do I really have to tell you?"

"Not if you don't want to."

"Because they're more interested in ideas, in feelings, than in the way machines work."

"Won't pay the rent, though, will they – ideas, feelings?"

"Is money the only criterion?"

"I don't know a better one."

"What about happiness?"

"Happiness?" Wilcox looked startled, caught off balance for the first time.

"Yes, I don't earn much money, but I'm happy in my job. Or I would be, if I were sure of keeping it."

"Why aren't you?"

When Robyn explained her situation, Wilcox seemed more struck by her colleagues' security than by her own vulnerability. "You mean, they've got jobs for life?" he said.

"Well, yes. But the Government wants to abolish tenure in the future."

"I should think so."

"But it's essential!" Robyn exclaimed. "It's the only guarantee of academic freedom. It's one of the things we were demonstrating for last week."

"Hang about," said Wilcox. "*You* were demonstrating in support of the other lecturers' right to a job for life?"

"Partly," said Robyn.

"But if they can't be shifted, there'll never be room for you, no matter how much better than them you may be at the job."

This thought had crossed Robyn's mind before, but she had suppressed it as ignoble. "It's the principle of the thing," she said. "Besides, if it wasn't for the cuts, I'd have had a permanent job by now. We should be taking more students, not fewer."

"You think the universities should expand indefinitely?"

"Not indefinitely, but –"

"Enough to accommodate all those who want to do women's studies?"

"If you like to put it that way, yes," said Robyn defiantly.

"Who pays?"

"You keep bringing everything back to money."

"That's what you learn from business. There's no such thing as a free lunch. Who said that?"

Robyn shrugged. "I don't know. Some right-wing economist, I suppose."

"Had his head screwed on, whoever he was. I read it in the paper somewhere. There's no such thing as a free lunch." He gave his gruff bark of a laugh. "Someone always has to pick up the bill." He glanced at his watch. "Well, I suppose I'd better show you round the estate. Just give me a few minutes, will you?" He stood up, seized his jacket and thrust his arms into the sleeves.

"Aren't I supposed to follow you everywhere?" said Robyn, rising to her feet.

"I don't think you can follow me where I'm going," said Wilcox.

"Oh," said Robyn, colouring. Then, recovering her poise, she said, "Perhaps you would direct me to the Ladies."

"I'll get Shirley to show you," said Wilcox. "Meet me back here in five minutes."

Jesus wept! Not just a lecturer in English literature, not just a *woman* lecturer in English literature, but a trendy lefty feminist lecturer in English literature! A *tall* trendy leftist feminist lecturer in English literature! Vic Wilcox scuttled into the Directors' Lavatory as if into a place of sanctuary. It was a large, dank, chilly room, empty at this moment, which had been lavishly appointed, in more prosperous times, with marble washbasins and brass taps, but was now badly in need of

77

redecoration. He stood at the urinal and peed fiercely at the white ceramic wall, streaked with rusty tear-stains from the corroding pipes. What the hell was he going to do with this woman every Wednesday for the next two months? Stuart Baxter must be off his trolley, sending someone like that. Or was it a plot?

It was strange, strange and ominous, that he had seen her before, outside the University last week. Her hair, glowing like a brazier through the early-morning mist, her high boots and her cream-coloured quilted jacket with its exaggerated shoulders, had drawn his gaze as he sat impatiently in a line of cars while the pickets argued with the driver of an articulated wagon that was trying to enter the University. She had been standing on the pavement, holding some silly banner – *"Education Cuts Are Not Comic"*, or something like that – talking and laughing excitedly with a big-bosomed woman stuffed into a scarlet ski-suit and pink moon boots, and he remembered thinking to himself: so it's finally happened – designer industrial action. The two women, the copperhead in particular, had seemed to epitomise everything he most detested about such demonstrations – the appropriation of working-class politics by middle-class style. And now he was stuck with her for two months.

There was a marble-topped table in the centre of the flagged floor, bearing, like an altar, a symmetrical arrangement of clothes brushes and men's toiletries that Vic had never seen anyone disturb since he came to Pringle's. In his anger and frustration, he picked up a long, curved clothes brush and banged it down hard on the surface of the table. It broke in half.

"Shit!" said Vic, aloud.

As if on cue, a cistern flushed and the door of one of the WC cubicles opened to reveal the emerging figure of George Prendergast, the Personnel Director. This was not a total surprise, since Prendergast suffered from Irritable Bowel Syndrome and was frequently to be encountered in the Directors' Lavatory, but Vic had thought he was alone, and felt rather foolish standing there with the stump of the clothes brush, like an incriminating weapon, in his fist. For the sake of appearances, he picked up another brush and began swatting at the sleeves and lapels of his suit.

"Smartening yourself up for your Shadow, Vic?" said Prendergast jocularly. "I hear she's quite a, er, that is . . ." Catching sight of Vic's expression, he faltered into silence. His pale blue eyes peered anxiously at Vic through thick rimless spectacles. He was the youngest of the senior management team and rather overawed by Vic.

"Have you seen her?" Vic demanded.

"Well, no, not actually seen, but Brian Everthorpe says –"

"Never mind what Brian Everthorpe says, he's only interested in the size of her tits. She's a women's libber, if you don't mind, a bloody communist too, I shouldn't be surprised. She had one of those CND badges on. What in the name of Christ am I –" He stopped, struck by a sudden thought. "George – can I borrow your phone?"

"Of course. Something wrong with yours?"

"No, I just want to make a private call. Give me a couple of minutes, will you? Brush yourself down while you're waiting. Here." He thrust the clothes brush into the bewildered Prendergast's hand, patted him on the shoulder, and made tracks for the Personnel Director's Office by a circuitous route that did not take him past his own.

"Mr Prendergast's just popped out," said his secretary.

"I know," said Vic, striding past her and shutting the door of Prendergast's room behind him. He sat down at the desk and dialled Stuart Baxter's private number. Luckily he was in.

"Stuart – Vic Wilcox here. My shadow's just arrived."

"Oh yes? What's he like?"

"She, Stuart, she. You mean you didn't know?"

"Honest to God," said Stuart Baxter, when he had finished laughing, "I had no idea. Robyn with a 'y', well, well. Is she good-looking?"

"That's the only thing anybody seems to be interested in. My managers are poncing about like gigolos and the secretaries are beside themselves with jealousy." This was admittedly an exaggeration, but he wanted to emphasise the potentially disruptive effect of Robyn Penrose's presence. "Christ knows what will happen when I take her onto the shop floor," he said.

"So she *is* good-looking."

"Some might say so, I suppose. More to the point, she's a Communist."

"What? How d'you know?"

"Well, a left-winger, anyway. You know what those university types are like, on the arts side. She's a member of CND."

"That's not a crime, Vic."

"No, but we do have MoD contracts. She's a security risk."

"Hmm," said Stuart Baxter. "Not exactly secret weapons you're making, are they, Vic? Gearbox casings for tanks, engine components for trucks . . . Any of your people had to be vetted? Have you signed the Official Secrets Act?"

"No," Vic admitted. "But it's better to be safe than sorry. I think you ought to get her taken off the scheme."

After a brief pause for thought, Stuart Baxter said, "No can do, Vic. There'd be the most almighty row if we appeared to be sabotaging an

Industry Year project simply because this bird is a member of CND. I can just see the headlines – RUMMIDGE FIRM SLAMS DOOR ON RED ROBYN. If you catch her stealing blueprints, let me know, and I'll do something about it."

"Thanks a lot," said Vic flatly. "You're a great help."

"Why be so negative, about it, Vic? Relax! Enjoy the girl's company. I should be so lucky." Stuart Baxter chuckled, and put down the phone.

3

"Well – what did you make of it?" Vic Wilcox demanded, an hour or so later, when they were back in his office after what he had referred to as "a quick whistle round the works".

Robyn sank down on to a chair. "I thought it was appalling," she said.

"Appalling?" He frowned. "What d'you mean, appalling?"

"The noise. The dirt. The mindless, repetitive work. The . . . everything. That men should have to put up with such brutalising conditions –"

"Now just a minute –"

"Women, too. I did see women, didn't I?" She had a blurred memory of brown-skinned creatures vaguely female in shape but unsexed by their drab, greasy overalls and trousers, working alongside men in some parts of the factory.

"We have a few. I thought you were all for equality?"

"Not equality of oppression."

"*Oppression?*" He gave a harsh, derisive laugh. "We don't force people to work here, you know. For every unskilled job we advertise, we get a hundred applicants – more than a hundred. Those women are glad to work here – go and ask 'em if you don't believe me."

Robyn was silent. She felt confused, battered, exhausted by the sense-impressions of the last hour. For once in her life, she was lost for words, and uncertain of her argumentative ground. She had always taken for granted that unemployment was an evil, a Thatcherite weapon against the working class; but if this was employment then perhaps people were better off without it. "But the noise," she said again. "The dirt!"

"Foundries are dirty places. Metal is noisy stuff to work with. What did you expect?"

What *had* she expected? Nothing, certainly, so like the satanic mills of the early Industrial Revolution. Robyn's mental image of a modern factory had derived mainly from TV commercials and documentaries: deftly edited footage of brightly coloured machines and smoothly moving assembly lines, manned by brisk operators in clean overalls, turning out motor cars or transistor radios to the accompaniment of Mozart on the sound track. At Pringle's there was scarcely any colour, not a clean overall in sight, and instead of Mozart there was a deafening demonic cacophony that never relented. Nor had she been able to comprehend what was going on. There seemed to be no logic or direction to the factory's activities. Individuals or small groups of men worked on separate tasks with no perceptible relation to each other. Components were stacked in piles all over the factory floor like the contents of an attic. The whole place seemed designed to produce, not goods for the outside world, but misery for the inmates. What Wilcox called the machine shop had seemed like a prison, and the foundry had seemed like hell.

"There are two sides to our operation," he had explained, when he led her out of the office block and across a bleak enclosed courtyard, where footsteps had scored a diagonal path through the snow, towards a high windowless wall of corrugated iron. "The foundry, and the machine shop. We also do a bit of assembly work – small engines and steering assemblies, I'm trying to build it up – but basically we're a general engineering firm, supplying components to the motor industry mostly. Parts are cast in the foundry or bought in and then we machine 'em. The foundry was allowed to go to pot in the seventies and Pringle's started purchasing from outside suppliers. I'm trying to make our foundry more efficient. So the foundry is a cost-centred operation, and the engineering side is profit-centred. But if all goes well, in time we should be able to sell our castings outside and make a profit on them too. In fact we've got to, because a really efficient foundry will produce more castings than we can use ourselves."

"What exactly is a foundry?" said Robyn, as they reached a small, scarred wooden door in the corrugated-iron wall. Wilcox halted, his hand on the door. He stared at her incredulously.

"I told you I didn't know anything about . . ." She was going to say "industry", but it occurred to her that this admission would come oddly from an expert on the Industrial Novel. "This sort of thing," she concluded. "I don't suppose *you* know a lot about literary criticism, do you?"

Wilcox grunted and pushed open the door to let her through. "A foundry is where you melt iron or other metal and pour it into moulds to make castings. Then in the machine shop we mill and grind them and bore holes in them so that they can be assembled into more complex products, like engines. Are you with me?"

"I think so," she said coldly. They were walking along a broad corridor between glass-partitioned offices, lit by bleak fluorescent strip lighting, where sallow-faced men in shirtsleeves stared at computer terminals or pored over sheets of printout.

"This is production control," said Wilcox. "I don't think there'd be much point trying to explain it to you now."

Some of the men in the offices looked up as they passed, nodded to Wilcox and eyed Robyn curiously. Few smiled.

"We should really have started at the foundry," said Wilcox, "since that's the first stage of our operation. But the quickest way to the foundry is through the machine shop, especially in this weather. So you're seeing the production process in reverse." He pushed through another battered-looking swing door and held it open for her. She plunged into the noise as into a tank of water.

The machine shop was an enormous shed with machines and work benches laid out in a grid pattern. Wilcox led her down the broad central aisle, with occasional detours to left and right to point out some particular operation. Robyn soon gave up trying to follow his explanations. She could hardly hear them because of the din, and the few words and phrases that she did catch – "tolerances to five thou", "cross-boring", "CNC machine", "indexes round" – meant nothing to her. The machines were ugly, filthy and surprisingly old-fashioned in appearance. The typical operation seemed to be that the man took a lump of metal from a bin, thrust it into the machine, closed some kind of safety cage, and pulled a lever. Then he opened the cage, took out the part (which now looked slightly different) and dropped it into another bin. He did all this as noisily as possible.

"Does he do the same thing all day?" she shouted to Wilcox, after they had watched one such man at work for some minutes. He nodded. "It seems terribly monotonous. Couldn't it be done automatically?"

Wilcox led her to a slightly quieter part of the shop floor. "If we had the capital to invest in new machines, yes. And if we cut down the number of our operations – for the part he's making it wouldn't be worth automating. The quantities are too small."

"Couldn't you move him to another job occasionally?" she said, with a sudden burst of inspiration. "Move them all about, every few hours, just to give them a change?"

"Like musical chairs?" Wilcox produced a crooked smile.

"It seems so awful to be standing there, hour after hour, doing the same thing, day after day."

"That's factory work. The operatives like it that way."

"I find that hard to believe."

"They don't like being shunted about. You start moving men about from one job to another, and they start complaining, or demanding to be put on a higher grade. Not to mention the time lost changing over."

"So it comes back to money again."

"Everything does, in my experience."

"Never mind what the men want?"

"They prefer it this way, I'm telling you. They switch off, they daydream. If they were smart enough to get bored, they wouldn't be doing a job like this in the first place. If you want to see an automated process, come over here."

He strode off down one of the aisles. The blue-overalled workers reacted to his passage like a shoal of minnows in the presence of a big fish. They did not look up or catch his eye, but there was a perceptible tremor along the work benches, a subtle increase in the carefulness and precision of their movements as the boss passed. The foremen behaved differently. They came hurrying forward with obsequious smiles as Wilcox stopped to ask about a bin of components with "WASTE" chalked on the side, or squatted beside a broken-down machine to discuss the cause with an oily-pawed mechanic. Wilcox made no attempt to introduce Robyn to anyone, though she was aware that she was an object of curiosity in these surroundings. On all sides she saw glazed abstracted eyes click suddenly into sharp focus as they registered her presence, and she observed sly smiles and muttered remarks being exchanged between neighbouring benches. The content of these remarks she could guess all too easily from the pin-ups that were displayed on walls and pillars everywhere, pages torn from soft-porn magazines depicting glossy-lipped naked women with bulging breasts and buttocks, pouting and posturing indecently.

"Can't you do something about these pictures?" she asked Wilcox.

"What pictures?" He looked around, apparently genuinely puzzled by the question.

"All these pornographic pin-ups."

"Oh, those. You get used to them. They don't register, after a while."

That, she realised, was what was peculiarly degrading and depressing about the pictures. Not just the nudity of the girls, or their poses, but the fact that nobody was looking at them, except herself. Once these images must have excited lust – enough to make someone take the trouble to cut them out and stick them up on the wall; but after a day or two, or a week or two, the pictures had ceased to arouse, they had become familiar – faded and tattered and oil-stained, almost indistinguishable from the dirt and debris of the rest of the factory. It made the models' sacrifice of their modesty seem poignantly vain.

"There you are," said Wilcox. "Our one and only CNC machine."

"What?"

"Computer-numerically controlled machine. See how quickly it changes tools?"

Robyn peered through a Perspex window and watched things moving round and going in and out in sudden spasms, lubricated by spurts of a liquid that looked like milky coffee.

"What's it doing?"

"Machining cylinder heads. Beautiful, isn't it?"

"Not the word I'd choose."

There was something uncanny, almost obscene, to Robyn's eye, about the sudden, violent, yet controlled movements of the machine, darting forward and retreating, like some steely reptile devouring its prey or copulating with a passive mate.

"One day," said Wilcox, "there will be lightless factories full of machines like that."

"Why lightless?"

"Machines don't need light. Machines are blind. Once you've built a fully computerised factory, you can take out the lights, shut the door and leave it to make engines or vacuum cleaners or whatever, all on its own in the dark. Twenty-four hours a day."

"What a creepy idea."

"They already have them in the States. Scandinavia."

"And the Managing Director? Will he be a computer too, sitting in a dark office?"

Wilcox considered the question seriously. "No, computers can't think. There'll always have to be a man in charge, at least one man, deciding what should be made, and how. But these jobs" – he jerked his head round at the rows of benches – "will no longer exist. This machine here is doing the work that was done last year by twelve men."

"O brave new world," said Robyn, "where only the managing directors have jobs."

This time Wilcox did not miss her irony. "I don't like making men redundant," he said, "but we're caught in a double bind. If we don't modernise we lose competitive edge and have to make men redundant, and if we *do* modernise we have to make men redundant because we don't need 'em any more."

"What we should be doing is spending more money preparing people for creative leisure," said Robyn.

"Like women's studies?"

"Among other things."

"Men like to work. It's a funny thing, but they do. They may moan about it every Monday morning, they may agitate for shorter hours and longer holidays, but they need to work for their self-respect."

"That's just conditioning. People could get used to life without work."

"Could *you*? I thought you enjoyed your work."

"That's different."

"Why?"

"Well, it's nice work. It's meaningful. It's rewarding. I don't mean in money terms. It would be worth doing even if one wasn't paid anything at all. And the conditions are decent – not like this." She swept her arm round in a gesture that embraced the oil-laden atmosphere, the roar of machinery, the crash of metal, the whine of electric trolleys, the worn, soiled ugliness of everything.

"If you think this is rough, wait till you see the foundry," said Wilcox, with a grim smile, and set off again at his brisk terrier's trot.

Even this warning did not prepare Robyn for the shock of the foundry. They crossed another yard, where hulks of obsolete machinery crouched, bleeding rust into their blankets of snow, and entered a large building with a high vaulted roof hidden in gloom. This space rang with the most barbaric noise Robyn had ever experienced. Her first instinct was to cover her ears, but she soon realised that it was not going to get any quieter, and let her hands fall to her sides. The floor was covered with a black substance that looked like soot, but grated under the soles of her boots like sand. The air reeked with a sulphurous, resinous smell, and a fine drizzle of black dust fell on their heads from the roof. Here and there the open doors of furnaces glowed a dangerous red, and in the far corner of the building what looked like a stream of molten lava trickled down a curved channel from roof to floor. The roof itself was holed in places, and melting snow dripped to the floor and spread in muddy puddles. It was a place of extreme temperatures: one moment you were shivering in an icy draught from some gap in the outside wall, the next you felt the frightening heat of a furnace's breath on your face. Everywhere there was indescribable mess, dirt, disorder. Discarded castings, broken tools, empty canisters, old bits of iron and wood, lay scattered around. Everything had an improvised, random air about it, as if people had erected new machines just where they happened to be standing at the time, next to the debris of the old. It was impossible to believe that anything clean and new and mechanically efficient could come out of this place. To Robyn's eye it resembled nothing so much as a medieval painting of hell – though it was hard to say whether the workers looked more like devils or the damned. Most of them, she observed, were Asian or Caribbean, in contrast to the machine shop where the majority had been white.

Wilcox led her up a twisted and worn steel staircase to a prefabricated office perched on stilts in the middle of the building, and introduced her to the general manager, Tom Rigby, who looked her up and down once and then ignored her. Rigby's young assistant regarded her with more interest, but was soon drawn into a discussion about production schedules. Robyn looked around the office. She had never seen a room that had such a forlorn, unloved look. The furniture was dirty, damaged and mismatched. The lino on the floor was scuffed and torn, the windows nearly opaque with grime, and the walls looked as if they had never been repainted since the place was constructed. Fluorescent strip lighting relentlessly illuminated every sordid detail. The only splash of colour in the drab decor was the inevitable pin-up, on the wall above the desk of Rigby's young assistant: last year's calendar, turned to the page for December, depicting a grinning topless model tricked out in fur boots and ermine-trimmed bikini pants. Apart from her, the only item in the room that didn't look old and obsolete was the computer over which the three men were crouched, talking earnestly.

Bored, she stepped outside, onto a steel gallery overlooking the factory floor. She surveyed the scene, feeling more than ever like Dante in the Inferno. All was noise, smoke, fumes and flames. Overalled figures, wearing goggles, facemasks, helmets or turbans, moved slowly through the sulphurous gloom or crouched over their inscrutable tasks beside furnaces and machines.

"Here – Tom said you'd better put this on."

Wilcox had appeared at her side. He thrust into her hands a blue plastic safety helmet with a transparent visor.

"What about you?" she asked, as she put it on. He shrugged and shook his head. He hadn't even got a coat or overall to cover his business suit. Some kind of macho pride, presumably. The boss must appear invulnerable.

"Visitors have to," said Tom Rigby. "We're responsible, like."

A very loud hooter started bleating frantically, and made Robyn jump.

Rigby grinned: "That's the KW, they've got it going again."

"What was the matter with it?" said Wilcox.

"Just a valve, I think. You should show her." He jerked his head in Robyn's direction. "Something worth seeing, the KW, when she's on song."

"What's a KW?" Robyn asked.

"Kunkel Wagner Automatic Moulding Line," said Wilcox.

"The boss's pride and joy," said Rigby. "Only installed a few weeks back. You should show her," he said again to Wilcox.

"All in due course," said Wilcox. "The pattern shop first."

The pattern shop was a haven of relative peace and quiet, reminiscent of cottage industry, a place where carpenters fashioned the wooden shapes that contributed the first stage of the moulding process. After that she saw men making sand moulds, first by hand, and then with machines that looked like giant waffle-irons. It was there that she saw women working alongside the men, lifting the heavy-looking mouldings, reeking of hot resin, from the machines, and stacking them on trolleys. She listened uncomprehendingly to Wilcox's technical explanations about the drag and the cope, core boxes and coffin moulds. "Now we'll have a dekko at the cupola," he shouted. "Watch your step."

The cupola turned out to be a kind of gigantic cauldron erected high in one corner of the building where she had earlier noticed what looked like volcanic lava trickling downwards. "They fill it up continuously with layers of coke and iron – scrap-iron and pig-iron – and limestone, and fire it with oxygenated air. The iron melts, picking up the correct amount of carbon from the coke, and runs out of the tap-hole at the bottom." He led her up another tortuous steel staircase, its steps worn and buckled, across improvised bridges and ricketty gangways, up higher and higher, until they were crouching next to the very source of the molten metal. The white-hot stream flowed down a crudely-fashioned open conduit, passing only a couple of feet from Robyn's toecaps. It was like a small pinnacle in Pandemonium, dark and hot, and the two squatting Sikhs who rolled their white eyeballs and flashed their teeth in her direction, poking with steel rods at the molten metal for no discernible purpose, looked just like demons on an old fresco.

The situation was so bizarre, so totally unlike her usual environment, that there was a kind of exhilaration to be found in it, in its very discomfort and danger, such as explorers must feel, she supposed, in a remote and barbarous country. She thought of what her colleagues and students might be doing this Wednesday morning – earnestly discussing the poetry of John Donne or the novels of Jane Austen or the nature of modernism, in centrally heated, carpeted rooms. She thought of Charles at the University of Suffolk, giving a lecture, perhaps, on Romantic landscape poetry, illustrated with slides. Penny Black would be feeding more statistics on wife-beating in the West Midlands into her data-base, and Robyn's mother would be giving a coffee morning for some charitable cause in her Liberty-curtained lounge with a view of the sea. What would they all think if they could see her now?

"Something funny?" Wilcox yelled in her ear, and she realised that she was grinning broadly at her own thoughts. She straightened her features and shook her head. He shot her a suspicious glance, and continued his commentary: "The molten metal is received into that holding furnace down there. Its temperature is regulated electrically, so we only use what we need. Before I installed it, they had to use all the iron they melted, or else waste it." He stood up abruptly, and without explanation or offer of assistance, set off on the descent to the factory floor. Robyn followed as best she could, her high-heeled boots skidding on the slippery surfaces, polished by generations of men grinding black sand underfoot. Wilcox waited impatiently for her at the bottom of the final staircase. "Now we can have a look at the KW," he said, marching off again. "Better hurry, or they'll soon be knocking off for lunch."

"I thought the man in the office, Mr Rigby, said it was a new machine," was Robyn's first comment, when they stood before its massive bulk. "It doesn't look new."

"It's not *new*," said Wilcox. "I can't afford to buy machines like that brand new. I got it second-hand from a foundry in Sunderland that closed down last year. A snip, it was."

"What does it do?"

"Makes moulds for cylinder blocks."

"It seems quieter than the other machines," said Robyn.

"It's not running at the moment," Wilcox said, with a pitying look. "What's up?" he demanded, addressing the back of a blue-overalled worker who was standing beside the machine.

"Fookin' pallet's jammed," said the man, without turning his head. "Fitter's workin' on it."

"Watch your language," said Wilcox. "There's a lady present."

The man turned round and looked at Robyn with startled eyes. "No offence," he muttered.

The hooter recommenced its strident blasts.

"Right – here we go," said Wilcox.

The workman manipulated some knobs and levers, closed a cage, stood back, and pressed a button on a console. The huge complex of steel shuddered into life. Something moved forward, something turned over, something began to make a most appalling noise, like a pneumatic drill greatly amplified. Robyn covered her ears. Wilcox jerked his head to indicate that they should move on. He led her up some stairs to a steel gallery from which he said they would get a bird's-eye-view of the operation. They overlooked a platform on which several men were standing. A moving track brought to the platform, from the machine that was making the appalling noise, a series of boxes containing moulds shaped out of black sand (though Wilcox called it green). The men lowered core moulds made of orange sand into the boxes, which were turned over and joined to boxes containing the other half of the moulds (the bottom half was the drag, the top the cope – the first bit of jargon she had managed to master) and moved forward on the track to the casting area. Two men brought the molten metal from a holding furnace to the moulds. It was contained in huge ladles suspended from hoists which they guided with pushbutton controls on the end of electric cables, held in one hand. The other hand grasped a kind of huge steering wheel attached to the side of the ladle, which they turned to tip the molten metal into the small holes in the mould-boxes. The two men, working in rotation, turn and turn about, moved with the slow deliberate gait of astronauts or deep-sea divers. She couldn't see their features, because they wore facemasks and goggles – not without reason, for when they tipped the ladles to pour, white-hot metal splashed like pancake batter and sparks flew through the air.

"Do they do that job all day?" Robyn asked.

"All day, every day."

"It must be frightfully hot work."

"Not so bad in winter. But in summer . . . the temperature can go up to a hundred and twenty Fahrenheit down there."

"Surely they could refuse to work in conditions like that?"

"They could. The office staff start whingeing if it gets above eighty. But those two are men." Wilcox gave this noun a solemn emphasis. "The track makes a ninety-degree turn down there," he went on, shooting out an arm to point, "and the castings go into a cooling tunnel. And the end of it, they're still hot, but hard. The sand gets shaken off them at the knockout."

The knockout was aptly named. It certainly stunned Robyn. It seemed to her like the anus of the entire factory: a black tunnel that extruded the castings, still encased in black sand, like hot, reeking, iron turds, onto a metal grid that vibrated violently and continuously to shake off the sand. A gigantic West Indian, his black face glistening with sweat, bracing himself with legs astride in the midst of the fumes and the heat and the din, dragged the heavy castings from the grid with a steel rod, and attached them to hooks on a conveyor belt by which they were carried away, looking now like carcasses of meat, to another stage of the cooling process.

It was the most terrible place she had ever been in in her life. To say that to herself restored the original meaning of the word "terrible": it provoked terror, even a kind of awe. To think of being that man, wrestling with the heavy awkward lumps of metal in that maelstrom of heat, dust and stench, deafened by the unspeakable noise of the vibrating grid, working like that for hour after hour, day after day . . . That he was black seemed the final indignity: her heart swelled with the recognition of the spectacle's powerful symbolism. He was the noble savage, the Negro in chains, the archetype of exploited humanity, quintessential victim of the capitalist-imperialist-industrial system. It was as much as she could do to restrain herself from rushing forward to grasp his hand in a gesture of sympathy and solidarity.

★

"You have a lot of Asians and Caribbeans working in the foundry, but not so many in the other part," Robyn observed, when they were back in the peaceful calm and comparative luxury of Wilcox's office.

"Foundry work is heavy work, dirty work."

"So I noticed."

"The Asians and some of the West Indians are willing to do it. The locals aren't any more. I've no complaints. They work hard, especially the Asians. It's like poetry, Tom Rigby says, when they're working well. Mind you, they have to be handled carefully. They stick together. If one walks out, they all walk out."

"It seems to me the whole set-up is racist," said Robyn.

"Rubbish!" said Wilcox angrily. He pronounced it "Roobish" – it was a word in which his Rummidge accent was particularly noticeable. "The only race trouble we have is between the Indians and the Pakis, or the Hindus and the Sikhs."

"You just admitted blacks do all the worst jobs, the dirtiest, hardest jobs."

"Somebody's got to do them. It's supply and demand. If we were to advertise a job today – a labouring job in the foundry – I guarantee we'd have two hundred black and brown faces at the gates tomorrow morning, and maybe one white."

"And what if you advertise a skilled job?"

"We have plenty of coloureds in skilled jobs. Foremen, too."

"Any coloured managers?" Robyn asked.

Wilcox fumbled for a cigarette, lit it, and exhaled smoke through his nostrils like an angry dragon. "Don't ask me to solve society's problems," he said.

"Who is going to solve them, then," said Robyn, "if it isn't people with power, like you?"

"Who said I have power?"

"I should have thought it was obvious," said Robyn with an airy gesture that embraced the room and its furnishings.

"Oh, I have a big office, and a secretary, and a company car. I can hire and, with a bit more difficulty, fire people. I'm the biggest cog in this particular machine. But a small cog in a much bigger one – Midland Amalgamated. They can get rid of me whenever they like."

"Isn't there something called a golden handshake?" Robyn enquired drily.

"A year's salary, two if I was lucky. That doesn't last for ever, and it's not easy to psych yourself up to get another job after you've been given the push. I've seen it happen to a lot of good MDs that got fired. It wasn't their fault, usually, that the firm was doing badly, but they had to carry the can. You can have the greatest ideas in the world for improving competitive edge, but you have to rely on other people to carry them out, from senior managers down to labourers."

"Perhaps if everybody had a stake in the business, they would work better," said Robyn.

"How d'you mean?"

"Well, if they had a share in the profits."

"And in the losses, too?"

Robyn pondered this awkward point. "Well," she shrugged, "that's the trouble with capitalism, isn't it? It's a lottery. There are winners and losers."

"It's the trouble with life," said Wilcox, looking at his watch. "We'd better get some lunch."

Lunch was, in its way, as obnoxious to the senses as everything else in the factory. Rather to Robyn's surprise, there were no special eating arrangements for management. "Pringle's used to have a Directors' Dining Room, with their own cook," Wilcox explained as he led her through the drab corridors of the administration block, and out across a yard where fresh snow was already covering the footpath that had been cleared. "I used to have lunch there occasionally when I worked for Lewis & Arbuckle – marvellous grub, it was. And there was a separate restaurant for middle management, too. All that went by the board with the first wave of redundancies. Now there's just the canteen."

"Well, it's more democratic," said Robyn approvingly.

"Not really," said Wilcox. "My senior managers go to the local pub, and the men prefer to bring their own snap. So it's mostly technical and clerical who eat here." He ushered her into a dismal canteen with strip lighting, Formica-topped tables and moulded plastic stacking chairs. The windows were steamed over, and there was a smell in the air that reminded Robyn nauseatingly of school dinners. The food was predictably stodgy – steak pie or fish fried in batter, chips, boiled cabbage and tinned peas, sponge pudding and custard – but it was astonishingly cheap: 50p for the whole menu. Robyn wondered why more workmen didn't take advantage.

"Because they'd have to take off their overalls," said Wilcox, "and they can't be bothered. They'd rather sit on the factory floor and eat their snap, without even washing their hands. You don't want to get too sentimental about the operatives, you know," he went on. "They're a pretty crude lot. They seem to like dirt. We put new toilets in the fettling shop last November. In two weeks they were all vandalised. Disgusting it was, what they did to those toilets."

"Perhaps it was a form of revenge," said Robyn.

"Revenge?" Wilcox stared. "Revenge against who? Me, for giving them new toilets?"

"Revenge against the system."

"What system?"

"The factory system. It must generate enormous resentment."

"Nobody forces them to work here," said Wilcox, stabbing the crust of his steak pie with a fork.

"That's what I mean, it's the return of the repressed. It's unconscious."

"Oh? Who says?" Wilcox enquired, cocking his eyebrow.

"Freud, for one," said Robyn. "Sigmund Freud, the inventor of psychoanalysis."

"I know who you mean," said Wilcox sharply. "I'm not completely solid between the ears, you know, even if I do work in a factory."

"I wasn't implying that you were," said Robyn, flushing. "Have you read Freud, then?"

"I don't get much time for reading," said Wilcox, "but I've a rough idea what he was about. Said everything came down to sex, didn't he?"

"That's a rather over-simplified way of putting it," said Robyn, disinterring some overcooked fish from its carapace of orange batter.

"But basically right?"

"Well, not entirely wrong," said Robyn. "The early Freud certainly thought libido was the prime mover of human behaviour. Later he came to think the death instinct was more important."

"The death instinct – what's that?" Wilcox arrested the transfer of a morsel of meat to his mouth to put this question.

"It's hard to explain. Essentially it's the idea that unconsciously we all long for death, for non-being, because being is so painful."

"I often feel like that at five o'clock in the morning," said Wilcox. "But I snap out of it when I get up."

Not long after they got back to Wilcox's office, Brian Everthorpe appeared at the door. His face was flushed and his waistcoat seemed perceptibly tighter than ever across his paunch.

"Hallo, Vic. We were expecting you down at the Man in the Moon. But no doubt you had a nice *tête-à-tête* lunch somewhere a bit more upmarket, eh? The King's Head, was it?" He leered at Robyn, and masked a belch with the back of his hand.

"We ate in the canteen," said Wilcox coldly.

Everthorpe fell back a pace, in exaggerated astonishment. "You never took her to that hole, Vic?"

"Nothing wrong with it," said Wilcox. "It's clean and it's cheap."

"How did you enjoy the food?" Everthorpe enquired of Robyn. "Not exactly cordon blue, is it?"

Robyn sat down in an armchair. "It's part of the factory, I suppose."

"Very diplomatic. Next time – there will be a next time, I hope? Next time, get Vic to take you to the King's Head Carvery. If he won't, I will."

"Did you want to see me about something?" said Wilcox impatiently.

"Yes, a little idea I've had. I think we ought to have a calendar. You know, something to give customers at the end of the year. Great advertisement for the firm. It's up there on the wall three hundred and sixty-five days a year."

"What kind of calendar?" said Wilcox.

"Well, you know, the usual sort of thing. Birds with boobs." He glanced at Robyn and winked. "Tasteful, you know, nothing crude. Like the Pirelli calendar. Collectors' items they are, you know."

"Are you off your trolley?" said Wilcox.

"I know what you're going to say," said Everthorpe, holding up his pink, fleshy palms placatingly. "'We can't afford it.' But I wasn't thinking of hiring the Earl of Lichfield and a lot of London models. There's a way we can get it done cheap. You know Shirley has a daughter who does modelling?"

"Wants to do it, you mean."

"Tracey's got what it takes, Vic. You should see her portfolio."

"I have. She looks like a double helping of pink blancmange, and about as exciting. Did Shirley put you up to this?"

"No, Vic, it was my own idea," said Everthorpe, looking hurt. "Of course, I've discussed it with Shirley. She's all in favour."

"Yes, I bet she is."

"My idea is, we use the same girl – Tracey, that is – for each month, but with different backgrounds according to the season."

"Very original. Won't the photographer have his own ideas?"

"Ah, but that's where the other part of my plan comes in. You see, I belong to a photographic club –"

"Excuse me," said Robyn, standing up. The two men, who had temporarily forgotten her presence in the heat of argument, turned their heads and looked at her. She addressed herself to Everthorpe. "Do I understand that you're proposing to advertise your products with a calendar that degrades women?"

"It won't degrade them, my dear, it will . . . ." Everthorpe groped for a word.

"Celebrate them?" Robyn helped him out.

"Exactly."

"Yes, I've heard that one before. But you *are* proposing to use

94

pictures of naked women, or one naked woman – like the pin-ups that are plastered all over the factory?"

"Well, yes, but classier. Good taste, you know. None of your *Penthouse*-style crotch shots. Just tit and bum."

"What about a bit of prick and bum, too?" said Robyn.

Everthorpe looked satisfyingly taken aback. "Eh?" he said.

"Well, statistically, at least ten percent of your customers must be gay. Aren't they entitled to a little porn too?"

"Ha, ha," Everthorpe laughed uneasily. "Not many queers in our line of business, are there, Vic?"

Wilcox, who was following this conversation with amused interest, said nothing.

"Or what about the women who work in the offices where these calendars are stuck up?" Robyn continued. "Why should they have to look at naked women all the time? Couldn't you dedicate a few months of the year to naked men? Perhaps you'd like to pose yourself, along with Tracey?"

Vic Wilcox guffawed.

"I'm afraid you've got it wrong, darling," said Everthorpe, struggling to retain his poise. "Women aren't like that. They're not interested in pictures of naked men."

"*I* am," said Robyn. "I like them with hairy chests and ten-inch pricks." Everthorpe gaped at her. "You're shocked, aren't you? But you think it's perfectly all right to talk about women's tits and bums and stick pictures of them up all over the place. Well, it isn't all right. It degrades the women who pose for them, it degrades the men who look at them, it degrades sex."

"This is all very fascinating," said Wilcox, looking at his watch, "but I've got a meeting in here in about five minutes time, with my technical manager and his staff."

"I'll talk to you later," said Brian Everthorpe huffily. "When there's less interference."

"I'm afraid it's a non-starter, Brian," said Wilcox.

"Stuart Baxter didn't think so," said Everthorpe, fluffing out his sideboards with the back of his hand.

"I don't give a monkey's what Stuart Baxter thinks," said Wilcox.

"I'll talk to you again, when your shadow, or your guardian angel, or whatever she is, will let me get a word in edgewise." Everthorpe strode out of the office.

Robyn, whose legs felt suddenly weak as the adrenalin drained out of her, sat down. Wilcox, who had been frowning after the departing figure of Everthorpe, turned and almost smiled. "I quite enjoyed that," he said.

"You agree with me, then?"

"I think we'd make ourselves a laughing-stock."

"I mean about the principle. The exploitation of women's bodies."

"I don't have much time for that sort of thing myself," said Wilcox. "But some men never grow up."

"You could do something about it," said Robyn. "You're the boss. You could ban all pin-ups from the factory."

"I could, if I was completely barmy. All I need is a wildcat strike over pin-ups."

"You could set an example, at least. There's one of those girlie calendars in your secretary's office."

"Is there?" Wilcox looked genuinely surprised. He jumped up from his swivel chair and went into the adjoining office. A few moments later he returned, scratching his chin thoughtfully. "Funny, I never noticed it. Gresham's Pumps gave it to us."

"Are you going to take it down, then?"

"Shirley says the Gresham's buyer likes to see it on the wall when he visits. No point offending a customer."

Robyn tossed her head scornfully. She was disappointed, having glimpsed the possibility of returning from this expedition into the cultural heart of darkness with some creditable achievement to report to Charles and Penny Black.

Wilcox turned on some lights above the board table on the other side of the room. He went to the window, where the daylight was already fading, and looked out between the vertical louvres of the blind. "It's snowing again. Maybe you should be on your way. The roads will be difficult."

"It's only half past two," said Robyn. "I thought I was supposed to stay with you all day."

"Suit yourself," he said, with a shrug. "But I warn you, I work late."

While Robyn was hesitating, the office began to fill up with men wearing drab suits and dull ties and with the pasty complexions that seemed to be common to everybody who worked in the factory. They came in diffidently, nodded respectfully to Wilcox, and looked askance at Robyn. They sat down at the table, and took out of their pockets packets of cigarettes, lighters and calculators, placing these objects carefully in front of them as if they were necessary equipment for some game they were about to play.

"Where shall I sit?" said Robyn.

"Anywhere you like," said Wilcox.

Robyn took a seat at the opposite end of the table from Wilcox. "This is Dr Robyn Penrose, of Rummidge University," he said. As though given permission to stare at her, the men all turned their heads

96

simultaneously in her direction. "You've all heard of Industry Year, I suppose. And you all know what a shadow is. Well, Dr Penrose is my Industry Year Shadow." He looked round the table as if daring anyone to smile. No one did. He explained the Shadow Scheme briefly, and concluded, "Just carry on as if she wasn't there."

This they seemed to find no difficulty in doing, once the meeting started. The subject was Wastage. Wilcox began by stating that the percentage of products rejected by their own inspectors was five per cent, which he considered far too high, and another one per cent was returned by customers. He listed various possible causes – defective machines, careless workmanship, poor supervision, faulty lab tests – and asked the head of each department to identify the main cause of waste in their own area. Robyn found the discussion hard to follow. The managers spoke in cryptic, allusive utterances, using technical jargon that was opaque to her. The adenoidal whine of their accents dulled her hearing, and the smoke of their cigarettes made her eyes smart. She grew bored, and gazed out of the window, at the fading winter light and the fluttering descent of the snow. The snow was general all over Rummidge, she mused, playing variations on a famous passage by James Joyce to divert herself. It was falling on every part of the dark, sprawling conurbation, on the concrete motorways, and the treeless industrial estates, falling softly upon the lawns of the University campus and, further westward, upon the dark mutinous waters of the Rummidge–Wallsbury Canal. Then suddenly she was listening with attention again.

They were discussing a machine that was continually breaking down. "It's the operative's fault," one of the managers was saying. "He's just not up to the job. He doesn't set the indexes properly, so it keeps jamming."

"What's his name?" Wilcox demanded.

"Ram. He's a Paki," said one.

"No, he's not, he's Indian," said another.

"Well, whatever. Who can tell the difference? They call him Danny. Danny Ram. He was moved on to the job when we were short-handed last winter, and up-graded from labourer."

"Let's get rid of him, then," said Wilcox. "He's causing a bottleneck. Terry – see to it, will you?"

Terry, a heavily built man smoking a pipe, took it out of his mouth and said, "We haven't got a basis to fire him."

"Rubbish. He's been trained, hasn't he?"

"I'm not sure."

"Check it out. If he hasn't, train him, even if he can't grasp it. Are you with me?"

Terry nodded.

"Then each time he fails to set the machine properly, you give him a proper warning. On the third warning, he's fired. Shouldn't take more than a fortnight. All right?"

"Right," said Terry, putting his pipe back between his teeth.

"The next question," said Wilcox, "is quality control in the machine shop. Now I've got some figures here –"

"Excuse me," said Robyn.

"Yes, what is it?" said Wilcox, looking up impatiently from his spreadsheet.

"Do I understand that you are proposing to pressure a man into making mistakes so that you can sack him?"

Wilcox stared at Robyn. There was a long silence, such as falls over a saloon bar in a Western at moments of confrontation. Not only did the other men not speak; they did not move. They did not appear even to breathe. Robyn herself was breathing rather fast, in short, shallow pants.

"I don't think it's any of your business, Dr Penrose," said Wilcox at last.

"Oh, but it is," said Robyn hotly. "It's the business of anyone who cares for truth and justice. Don't you see how wrong it is, to trick this man out of his job?" she said, looking round the table. "How can you sit there, and say nothing?" The men fiddled uneasily with their cigarettes and calculators, and avoided meeting her eye.

"It's a management matter in which you have no competence," said Wilcox.

"It's not a management matter, it's a moral issue," said Robyn.

Wilcox was now pale with anger. "Dr Penrose," he said, "I think you've got the wrong idea about your position here. You're a shadow, not an inspector. You're here to learn, not to interfere. I must ask you to keep quiet, or leave the meeting."

"Very well, I'll leave," said Robyn. She gathered up her belongings in a strained silence, and left the room.

"Meeting over?" said Shirley, with a bright, meaningless smile.

"No, it's still going on," said Robyn.

"You're leaving early, then? I don't blame you, in this weather. Coming back tomorrow, are you?"

"Next week," said Robyn. "Every Wednesday – that's the arrangement." She was very doubtful whether this arrangement would continue, but it suited her purpose to conceal the row that had just occurred. "Do you know a worker in the factory called Danny Ram?" she asked, in a casual tone of voice.

"Can't say I do. What's his job?"

98

"I'm not sure. He operates some kind of machine."

"Well, most of them do, don't they?" said Shirley, with a laugh. "Quite a change for you, isn't it, this kind of place? After the University, I mean."

"Yes, quite a change."

"This Ram a friend of yours, is he?" Shirley's curiosity, and perhaps suspicion, had been aroused.

"No, but I think he's the father of one of my students," Robyn improvised.

"You could ask Betty Maitland in Accounts," said Shirley. "Two doors along the corridor."

"Thanks," said Robyn.

Betty Maitland very obligingly looked up Danny Ram on the payroll (his name was actually Danyatai Ram) and told Robyn that he worked in the foundry. Since the only way she knew to the foundry was the route of her guided tour earlier that day, she was obliged to retrace it.

In the machine shop, without Victor Wilcox to escort her, Robyn was as conspicuous in her high-fashion boots, her cord breeches and her cream-coloured quilted jacket, as some rare animal, a white doe or a unicorn, would have been in the same place. Wolf-whistles and catcalls, audible in spite of the mechanical din, followed her as she hurried through the factory. The more the men whistled, the more ribald their remarks, the faster she walked; but the faster she walked, the more of a sexual object, or sexual quarry, she became, twisting and turning between the rows of benches (for she soon lost her bearings), stumbling over piles of metal parts, skidding on the oily floor, her cheeks as red as her hair, the wings of her nostrils white, her eyes fixed steadfastly ahead, refusing to meet the gaze of her tormentors. *"'Allo, darlin', lookin' for me? Fancy a bit of that, Enoch? Show us yer legs! Coom over 'ere and 'old me tool, will yow?"*

At last she found the exit at the far end of the enormous shed, and burst out into a dark courtyard, littered with the hulks of abandoned machinery, which she remembered from the morning. She paused for a moment under a feeble electric light to recover her self-possession, drawing the clean cold air into her lungs, before plunging once more into the third circle of this industrial inferno. With no daylight at all penetrating to the interior of the foundry, it looked more hellish than ever, its furnaces glowing fiercely in the smoky gloom. Here the workers were fewer than in the machine shop, and shyer – perhaps because they were mostly Asian. They avoided her glance, and turned away at her approach, as though her presence vaguely alarmed them. "Danny Ram?" she called after them. "Do you know where Danny Ram works?" They shook their heads, rolled their eyes, grinned nervously, and went about their inscrutable business. At last she came across a white man, nonchalantly lighting his cigarette from a twelve-inch flame shooting out of a gas jet, who was prepared to answer her question. "Danny Ram?" he said, holding his head aslant to avoid being scorched, "Yeah, I know 'im. Woi?"

"I have a message for him."

"'E's over theer," said the man, straightening up, and pointing to a thin, rather depressed-looking Asian standing beside a complicated piece of machinery. It was making so much noise, and absorbing his attention so completely, that he didn't register Robyn's approach.

"Mr Ram?" she said, touching his sleeve.

He started and swivelled round. "Yes?" he mouthed, staring.

"I have some important information for you," she shouted.

"Information?" he repeated wonderingly. "Who are you, please?"

Fortunately the machine came to the end of its cycle at this point and she was able to continue in a more normal tone of voice. "It doesn't matter who I am. The information is confidential, but I think you ought to know. They're going to try and sack you." The man began to tremble slightly inside his overalls, which were stiff with grease and dirt. "They're going to keep finding fault with your work, and giving you warnings, so they can sack you. Understand? Fore-warned is forearmed. Don't tell anyone I told you." She smiled encouragingly, and extended her hand. "Goodbye."

The man wiped his hands ineffectually on his hips and gave her a limp handshake. "Who are you?" he said. "How do you know this?"

"I'm a shadow," said Robyn. The man looked mystified, and slightly awestruck, as if he thought the word denoted some kind of supernatural messenger. "Thank you," he said.

To avoid running the gauntlet of the machine shop again, Robyn made her way back to the car park by going round the outside of the building, but the paths were covered with drifting snow and the going was difficult. She got lost in the labyrinth of yards and passageways that separated the numerous buildings, many of them apparently disused or derelict, that covered the factory site, and there was nobody around to direct her. At last, after about twenty minutes' wandering, her feet soaking wet inside her leaking boots, and her leg muscles aching from wading through the snow, she arrived at the car park outside the administration block, and found her car. She brushed a thick layer of snow from its windows, and, with a sigh of relief, got behind the wheel. She turned the ignition key. Nothing happened.

"Fuck," said Robyn, aloud to herself, alone in the middle of the frozen car park. "Bum. Tit."

If it was the battery it must have finally given up the ghost, because there wasn't even the faintest wheeze or whisper from the starter motor. Whatever it was, she could do nothing about it herself, since she hadn't the remotest idea what went on under the bonnet of the Renault. She got wearily out of the car and tramped across the car park to the reception lobby, where she asked the receptionist with peroxided hair if she could phone the AA. While she was dialling, Wilcox passed in the corridor beyond, saw her, checked, and came in.

"Still here?" he said, lifting an eyebrow.

Robyn nodded, holding the receiver to her ear.

"She's phoning the AA," said the peroxide blonde. "Car won't start."

"What's the problem?" said Wilcox.

"Nothing happens when I turn the key. It's completely dead."

"Let's have a look at it," said Wilcox.

"No, no," said Robyn. "Please don't bother. I'll manage."

"Come on." He jerked his head in the direction of the car park. "You won't get the AA to come for hours on a day like this."

The engaged tone bleeping in Robyn's ear confirmed the good sense of this judgment, but she put down the receiver reluctantly. The last thing she wanted at this juncture was to be under an obligation to Wilcox.

"Don't you want to get your overcoat?" she asked, as they passed through the swing doors into the freezing outside air.

Wilcox shook his head impatiently. "Where's your car?"

"The red Renault over there."

Wilcox set off in a straight line, indifferent to the snow that covered his thin black shoes and clung to his trouser bottoms.

"Why did you buy a foreign car?" he said.

"I didn't buy it, my parents gave it to me, when they changed it."

"Why did they buy it, then?"

"I don't know. Mummy liked it, I suppose. It's a good little car."

"So's the Metro. Why not buy a Metro if you want a small car? Or a Mini? If everybody who bought a foreign car in the last ten years had bought a British one instead, there wouldn't be seventeen per cent unemployment in this area." He made a sweeping gesture with his arm that took in the wilderness of derelict factories beyond the perimeter fence.

As a subscriber to *Marxism Today*, Robyn had suffered occasional qualms of guilt because she didn't cycle to work instead of driving, but she had never been attacked for owning a foreign car before. "If British cars were as good as foreign ones, people would buy them," she said. "But everyone knows they're hopelessly unreliable."

"Rubbish," said Wilcox. *Roobish*. "They used to be, I grant you, some models, but now our quality control is as good as anybody's. Trouble is, people love to sneer at British products. Then they have the gall to moan about the unemployment figures." His breath steamed, as though his anger were condensing in the frigid air. "What does your father drive?" he said.

"An Audi," said Robyn.

Wilcox grunted contemptuously, as if he had expected no better.

They came up to the Renault. Wilcox told her to get in and release the bonnet catch. He opened the bonnet and disappeared behind it. After a moment or two she heard him call, "Turn the ignition key," and when she did so, the engine fired.

Wilcox lowered the bonnet and pushed it shut with the palm of his hand. He came to the driver's window, brushing snow from his suit.

"Thank you very much," said Robyn. "What was it?"

"Loose electrical connection," he said. "Looked as if someone had pulled out the HT lead, actually."

"Pulled it out?"

"I'm afraid we get a bit of vandalism here, and practical joking. Was the car locked?"

"Maybe not every door. Anyway, thanks very much. I hope you won't catch cold," she said, encouraging him to leave. But he lingered by the window, inhibiting her from winding it up.

"I'm sorry if I was a bit sharp at the meeting this afternoon," he said gruffly.

"That's all right," said Robyn; though it wasn't all right, she told herself, it wasn't all right at all. She fiddled with the choke button to avoid having to look at him.

"Only sometimes you have to use methods that look a bit dodgy, for the good of the firm."

"I don't think we should ever agree about that," said Robyn. "But this is hardly the time or the place . . ." Out of the corner of her eye she saw a man in a white coat floundering through the snow towards them, and in some intuitive way this increased her anxiety to be off.

"Yes, you'd better be on your way. I'll see you next Wednesday, then?"

Before Robyn could reply, the man in the white coat had called out, "Mr Wilcox! Mr Wilcox!" and Wilcox turned to face him.

"Mr Wilcox, you're wanted in the foundry," said the man breathlessly, as he came up. "There's been a walkout."

"Goodbye," said Robyn, and let out the clutch. The Renault shot forward and slewed from side to side in the snow as she drove fast towards the gates. In her rear-view mirror she saw the two men hurrying back towards the administration block.

THREE

"People mutht be amuthed. They can't be alwayth a learning, nor yet they can't be alwayth a working. They an't made for it."

CHARLES DICKENS: *Hard Times*

"The drive back was quite horrendous," said Robyn. "Swirling snow. Roads like skating-rinks. Abandoned cars strewn all over the place. It took me two and a half hours to get home."

"God," said Charles sympathetically.

"I felt absolutely exhausted and filthy – my feet were soaking wet, my clothes reeked of that ghastly factory, and my hair was full of soot. All I wanted was to wash my hair and take a long, hot bath. I'd just eased myself into it – oh, what bliss! – when the doorbell rang. Well, I thought, too bad, I'm not going to answer it. I couldn't imagine who it could be, anyway. But the bell went on ringing and ringing. I began to think perhaps it was a real emergency. Anyway, after a while I couldn't stand it any longer, lying there and listening to the bloody bell, so I got out of the bath, dried myself after a fashion, put on a bathrobe, and went downstairs to open the door. Who d'you think it was?"

"Wilcox?"

"How clever of you to guess. He was in a towering rage, pushed his way into the house most rudely, and didn't even bother to wipe his feet. They were covered in snow, and left great wet footprints on the hall carpet. When I took him into the living-room he even had the cheek to look round and say to himself, loud enough for me to hear, 'What a tip!'"

Charles laughed. "Well, you must admit, dear, you aren't the world's tidiest housekeeper."

"I never claimed to be," said Robyn. "I have more important things to do than housework."

"Oh, absolutely," said Charles. "What did Wilcox want, then?"

"Well, it was about Danny Ram, of course. It seems that as soon as I left he told his workmates what the management were up to, and they all walked out in protest. It was pretty silly of him, actually. I mean, it didn't take Wilcox long to work out who had tipped him off."

"So Wilcox had come straight round to complain?"

"More than complain. He demanded that I go back to the factory next morning and tell Danny Ram and his mates that I'd made a mistake, and that there was no plot to sack him."

"Good Lord, what a nerve! Would you move over a bit?"

Robyn, who was lying naked, face down on the bed, wriggled over towards the centre of the mattress. Charles, who was also naked, knelt astride her legs and poured aromatic oil from Body Shop onto her shoulders and down her spine. Then, capping the bottle carefully, he put it aside and began working the oil into Robyn's neck and shoulders with his long, supple, sensitive fingers. Charles had come to stay for the weekend following Robyn's visit to Pringle's, and this was their customary way of rounding off Saturday evening, after an early film at the Arts Laboratory followed by an excellent cheap supper at one of the local Asian restaurants. It began as a real massage, and turned almost imperceptibly into an erotic one. Robyn and Charles were into non-penetrative sex these days, not because of AIDS (which to heterosexuals was only a cloud on the horizon, no bigger than a man's hand, in the winter of 1986) but for reasons both ideological and practical. Feminist theory approved, and it solved the problem of contraception, Robyn having renounced the pill on health grounds and Charles regarding condoms as unaesthetic (though Robyn, like the thoroughly liberated young woman she was, always had a packet handy should the need arise). At the moment they were still at the non-erotic stage of the massage. The bedroom was dimly lit and cosily warm, the radiators being supplemented by an electric fire. Robyn supported her head, turned sideways, on a pillow, and conversed with Charles over her shoulder, as he rubbed and stroked.

"You refused, I presume?" said Charles.

"Well, yes, at first."

"Only at first?"

"Well, after a while he stopped trying to bully me, when he saw that it wouldn't do any good, and began to use real arguments. He said that if the walkout settled into a strike, the whole factory would be brought to a standstill. The Asian workers are very clannish, he said, and very stubborn. Once they get an idea into their heads, it's hard to shift it."

"Racist talk," said Charles.

"Well, I know," said Robyn. "But they're so Neanderthal in that respect, the whole management, that after a while you only notice the grosser examples of prejudice. Anyway, Wilcox said a strike could drag on for weeks. The foundry would stop supplying the machine shop. The whole factory would grind to a halt. Midland Amalgamated might decide to cut their losses by closing it down altogether. Then hundreds of men would be thrown out of work, with no hope of getting another job. All because of me, was the implication. Of course, I told him it was his fault in the first place. If he hadn't plotted to trick Danny Ram out of his job, none of it would have happened."

"Quite," said Charles, running the edges of his hands up and down Robyn's vertebrae.

"He had got me a bit worried, though, I must admit. I mean, I'd only intended to put Danny Ram on his guard, not to provoke a major industrial dispute."

"Did Wilcox admit he was in the wrong?"

"Well, exactly, that was crucial. I said to him, look, you're asking me to lie, to say something I said was untrue, when it wasn't. What are *you* going to do?"

"And what did he say?"

"'Anything, within reason.' So I said, all right, I want an admission that it's immoral to get rid of a worker the way you proposed to get rid of Danny Ram, and I want an undertaking that you won't do it again. Well, he looked pretty sick at that, but he swallowed hard, and agreed. So I reckon I achieved something at the end of the day. But what a day!"

"Do you trust him to keep his word?"

Robyn considered this for a moment. "Yes, I do, as a matter of fact."

"In spite of the way he was going to treat the Indian?"

"He honestly didn't see it was immoral, you know, until I protested. It's not uncommon, apparently, to get rid of people like that. There's no procedure for remedial training. If someone's promoted to a higher-level job, and they're not up to it, there's no way of dealing with the problem. Don't you think that's incredible?"

"Not really, it applies to several full professors I can think of at Suffolk," said Charles. "Except you can't fire them."

Robyn sniggered. "I know what you mean . . . Anyway, I got him to agree to fix up Danny Ram with some special training."

"Did you, by golly!" Charles paused in his ministrations, with a hand on each of Robyn's firm round buttocks. "You really are a remarkable girl, Robyn."

"Woman," Robyn corrected him, but without rancour. She was pleased with the success of her story and the heroic role she had fashioned for herself in it. She had concealed from Charles some qualms of conscience about collaborating in the cover-up about Danny Ram. As a piece of action in a Victorian novel she might have judged it harshly as a case of one bourgeois supporting another when the chips were down, but she had persuaded herself that it was for the greater good of the factory workers – not to save Wilcox's skin – that she had lied; and the conditions she had imposed on Wilcox were a guarantee of her good faith.

"So that was the story we agreed on: I would tell Danny Ram that I'd got the wrong end of the stick at the meeting, and misunderstood the discussion, which was *really* about the need to give him special training, not to sack him."

"And did you?" Charles now dismounted from his position astride Robyn's legs in order to massage them. He kneaded the backs of her thighs and stroked the muscles of her calves, he flexed her ankles, scratched the soles of her feet and, gently parting the interstices of her toes, moistened the hollow spaces between them with with his oiled fingers.

"Absolutely. The next morning at seven-thirty sharp, Wilcox was at my door again, with his enormous Jaguar, to drive me to the factory. He didn't say a word to me for the whole journey. Rushed me into his office, with the secretaries and so on all skipping out of his way like frightened rabbits, and goggling at me as if I was some kind of terrorist he'd put under citizen's arrest. Then he and two of his cronies took me to a special meeting with the Asian foundry workers, in the canteen. There must have been about seventy of them, including Danny Ram, in their ordinary clothes, not overalls. Danny Ram gave me a scared kind of smile when I came in. There were some whites there too. Wilcox said they were shop stewards come to observe, deciding whether to make the strike official. So I said my piece to Danny, but really to all of them. I must say it stuck in my throat when I had to apologise, but I went through with it. Then we withdrew into another room, the canteen manageress's office I think it was, while the Asians deliberated. After about twenty minutes they sent a delegation to say that they were prepared to go back to work providing Danny was guaranteed his job back after retraining and on condition they were given five minutes paid washing-up time at the end of their shift. Then they went out and Wilcox and his cronies went into a huddle. Wilcox was furious, he said the washing-up time business had nothing to do with the original dispute, and that the shop stewards had put them up to it, but the other two said that the workers had to get something out of the walkout or they'd lose face, so they should settle. After a while Wilcox agreed to offer two minutes, and finally settled for three, but with ill-grace I must say. After all, I *had* lied to get him off the hook, and I didn't like doing it, but I didn't get a word of thanks, or any other kind of word. He stalked out of the room after the meeting without so much as a goodbye. The Personnel Manager drove me back to the University, an incredibly boring man who talked to me all the time about his Irritable Bowel Syndrome. I got back to the University just in time for a ten o'clock tutorial on *Middlemarch*. It was a rather weird feeling, actually. I thought it must be like coming off a night shift. The day was just starting for the Department, the students were still yawning and rubbing the sleep out of their eyes, but I felt as if I had been up for hours and hours. I suppose I was emotionally drained by the drama of the meeting and the negotiations. I had a ridiculous urge to tell the students all about it, but of course I didn't. I don't think it was one of my better tutorials, though. My mind was on other things."

Robyn fell silent. The massage had reached its erotic stage. Without being prompted, she rolled over on to her back. Charles' practised index finger gently probed and stroked her most sensitive parts. Quite soon she reached a very satisfying climax. Then it was Charles' turn.

Robyn's massage technique was more energetic than Charles'. She splashed oil all down his back and began to pummel him vigorously with the edges of her palms. "Ow! Ooh!" he exclaimed pleasurably, as the rather plump cheeks of his buttocks vibrated under this assault.

"You've got a horrible pimple on your bottom, Charles," she said. "I'm going to squeeze it."

"Oh, no, don't," he groaned. "You hurt so when you do that." But the note of protest was partly feigned.

Robyn pinched the pimple between her two forefingers and pressed hard. Charles yelled and his eyes filled with water. "There, all gone," said Robyn, swabbing away the residue of the pimple with a piece of cotton wool. She stopped pummelling, and began to stroke and smooth the backs of his thighs. Charles stopped whimpering into his pillow. He closed his eyes and his breathing became regular. "Will you go back next week?" he murmured. "To the factory, I mean?"

"I shouldn't think so," said Robyn. "Turn over, Charles."

2

At about the same time that evening, Vic Wilcox was restively watching television with his younger son, Gary, in the lounge of the five-bedroomed, four-lavatoried neo-Georgian house on Avondale Road. Marjorie was upstairs in bed, reading *Enjoy Your Menopause*, or, more likely, had already fallen asleep over it. Raymond was out boozing somewhere with his cronies, and Sandra was at a disco with the spotty Cliff. Gary was too young to go out on a Saturday night and Vic was . . . not too old, of course, but disinclined. He did not care for the noisy, false bonhomie of pubs and clubs; he had always regarded the cinema as primarily a convenience for courting couples in the winter months, and had ceased to patronise it shortly after getting married; and he had never been a theatre- or concert-goer. When he worked for Vanguard, he and Marjorie had belonged to a rather gay crowd of other young managers and their wives, who used to meet regularly in each other's houses on Saturday nights; but it turned out that there was a lot of hanky-panky going on at those parties, or after them, or in between them, and the circle eventually broke up in an atmosphere of scandal and recrimination. Since those days, Vic had moved on and up the career ladder to a point where he seemed to have no friends any more, only business acquaintances, and all social life was an extension of work. His idea of pleasure on a Saturday night was to sit in front of the telly, with a bottle of scotch conveniently to hand, watching "Match of the Day", and discussing the finer points of the game with his younger son.

But this winter there was no "Match of the Day", owing to a dispute between the Football League and the TV companies. The Football League had got greedy and demanded a hugely increased fee for broadcasting rights, and the TV companies had called their bluff. Vic's satisfaction at the administration of this business lesson was tempered by a sense of personal deprivation. Football on television was about the only form of escape he had left, and it was also one of the few topics on which he could hold a reasonably amicable conversation with his sons. When Raymond was a kid, he used to take him to watch Rummidge City, but gave that up when, at some time in the nineteen-seventies, football grounds were entirely taken over by tribes of foul-mouthed juvenile delinquents. Now even televised soccer was denied him, and he was obliged to sit with Gary on a Saturday night watching old films and TV dramas that were either boring or embarrassing.

The one they were watching now looked as if it was just about to change from being boring to being embarrassing. The hero and heroine were dancing cheek to cheek to a stereo in the girl's apartment. You could tell by the kind of music, and the look of dreamy lust on their faces, that before long they would be in bed together, with nothing on, writhing about under the bedcovers, or even on top of the bedcovers, uttering the usual obligatory moans and sighs. The decline of soccer and the increase of explicit sex in the media seemed to be reciprocally related symptoms of national decline, though Vic sometimes thought he was the only one who had noticed the coincidence. You saw things on television nowadays that would have been under-the-counter pornography when he was a lad. It made family viewing an anxious and uncomfortable business. "You don't want to watch any more of this, do you?" he said to Gary, with affected casualness.

"It's all right," said Gary, slumped in an armchair, without taking his eyes from the screen. His hand moved rhythmically from a bag of potato crisps to his mouth and back again.

"Let's see what's on the other channels."

"No, Dad, don't!"

Overriding Gary's protest, Vic played a short scale on the buttons of the remote control. The other channels were showing: a documentary about sheepdogs, a repeat of an American detective series about (Vic remembered it) a murdered prostitute, and another feature film the hero and heroine of which were already in bed together and wrestling energetically under the bedcovers. Vic quickly switched back to the first channel, where the girl was now slowly unbuttoning her blouse in front of a mirror while the man looked lasciviously over her shoulder. It was only a matter of time, Vic thought, before he scored a pornographic jackpot, simulated copulation on all four channels simultaneously.

"You don't want to watch any more of this crap," he said, pressing the Off button.

"Oh, *Dad!*"

"Anyway, it's time you were in bed," said Vic. "It's gone half past eleven."

"It's Saturday, Dad," Gary whined.

"No matter. You need a lot of sleep at your age."

"You just want to watch it on your own, don't you?" said Gary slyly.

Vic gave a derisive laugh. "Watch that rubbish? No, I'm off to bed, and so are you."

Vic was now obliged to follow his son upstairs to bed, though he wasn't sleepy and would, indeed, left to himself, have gone on watching the film, just to keep himself up to date on the decline of public decency. To add to his irritation, Marjorie was still awake when he got to the bedroom, and seemed disposed to talk. She chattered away through the open door of the bathroom as he brushed his teeth, about redecorating the lounge and buying loose covers for the three-piece suite; and when he came back into the bedroom to put on his pyjamas she asked him if he liked her new nightdress. It was a semi-transparent effort in peach-coloured nylon, with narrow shoulder straps and a deeply plunging neckline that revealed a considerable expanse of Marjorie's pale, freckled bosom. The dark circles round her flat nipples showed through the thin material like two stains. There was something else unfamiliar about her appearance, though he couldn't put his finger on it.

"A bit flimsy for this weather, isn't it?" he said.

"But do you like it?"

"It's all right."

"It's supposed to be the *Dynasty* look."

Vic grunted. "Don't talk to me about television."

"Why, what've you been watching?"

"The usual crap." Vic climbed into bed and switched off his bedside lamp. "You're very talkative tonight," he remarked. "Is the Valium losing its effect?"

"I haven't taken it yet," said Marjorie, turning off the lamp on her side. Her reason became all too clear when she laid a hand on his thigh under the bedclothes. At the same moment he became aware that she had drenched herself in a powerful scent, and realised that she had looked different sitting up in bed because she wasn't wearing curlers. "Vic," she said. "It's a long time since we . . . you know."

He pretended not to understand. "What?"

"You *know*." Marjorie rubbed his thigh with the back of her hand. It was something she used to do in their courting days, giving him a hard-on like a bar of pig-iron. Now his member didn't even stir.

"I thought you'd gone off it," he muttered.

"It was only a phase. Part of the change of life. It says so in the book." She switched on her bedside lamp and reached for *Enjoy Your Menopause*.

"For God's sake, Marjorie!" he grumbled. "What are you doing?"

"Where are my glasses . . .? Ah, yes, here it is. Listen. '*You may feel a revulsion against marital relations for a while. This is quite normal, and nothing to worry about. With time, and patience, and an understanding partner, your lib, libby –*'"

"Libido," said Vic. "Freud invented it before he discovered the death instinct."

"'*Your libido will return, stronger than ever.*'" Marjorie replaced the book on the bedside table, took off her glasses, turned out the light, and sank down in the bed beside him.

"You mean, you've got it back?" Vic asked flatly.

"Well, I don't know," she said. "I mean, I won't, will I, not till we try? I think we ought to give it a try, Vic."

"Why?"

"Well, it's natural for married couples. You used to want to . . ." There was a dangerous quaver in Marjorie's voice.

"Everything comes to an end," he said desperately. "We're getting on."

"But we're not old, Vic, not that old. The book says –"

"Fuck the book," said Vic.

Marjorie began to cry.

Vic sighed, and turned on his bedside lamp. "Sorry, love," he said. "Only you can't expect me to suddenly . . . get all interested, out of the blue. I thought we were past all that. So we're not – good – but give me time to readjust. OK?"

Marjorie nodded, and blew her nose daintily on a paper tissue.

"I have my own problems, you know," he said.

"I know, Vic," said Marjorie. "I know you have a lot of worries at work."

"That silly bitch from the University has caused me no end of trouble . . . then there's Brian Everthorpe with his daft idea of a calendar, which he claims Stuart Baxter approves of. Why is Brian Everthorpe in Stuart Baxter's confidence, I'd like to know?"

"As long as it's not me," Marjorie sniffed.

He leaned over and planted a dry kiss on her cheek, before turning out the light again. "'Course it's not you," he said.

But of course it was. It was years since he had felt any unforced desire for Marjorie, and now he couldn't even force it. When she seemed to be going off sex because of her time of life he'd been secretly relieved. The buxom, dimpled girl he'd married had become a middle-aged podge with tinted hair and too much make-up. Her roly-poly body embarrassed him when he happened to see it naked, and as for her mind, well that was almost as embarrassing when she exposed it. It would be futile to complain of this, for there was no way she could change herself, become clever and witty and sophisticated, any more than she could become tall and slim and athletic. He had married Marjorie for what she was, a simple, devoted, docile young woman, with the kind of plump good looks that quickly run to fat, and he was in honour bound to put up with her. Vic had old-fashioned ideas about marriage. A wife was not like a car: you couldn't part-exchange her when the novelty wore off, or the bodywork started to go. If you discovered you'd made a mistake, too bad, you just had to live with it. The one thing you couldn't do, he thought grimly, was make love to it.

Even that arrogant, interfering women's libber from the University was more of a turn-on than poor old Marjorie. If her ideas were barmy, at least they were ideas, whereas Marjorie's idea of an idea was something she had about wallpaper or loose covers. Of course she was young, which always helped, and good-looking in a way, if you liked that type of hairstyle, with the neck shaved like a boy's, which he didn't, and ignored the ridiculous Cossack's get-up. She'd looked a bit more normal in her bathrobe, when he drove round to her house that evening in a cold fury, taking hair-raising risks with the Jaguar in the ice and snow, and practically battered her door down.

He'd gone with no other intention than to scare the shit out of her and relieve his own feelings. He meant to tell her that the Shadow Scheme was cancelled, and that he would be telling the University the reason why. It was only when he came face to face with her that he'd thought of persuading her to undo the damage she'd caused instead. It was probably a stroke of luck that she was having a bath at the time. It put her at a disadvantage, not being properly dressed.

Vic's memory presented to him with surprising vividness the image of Robyn Penrose, her copper curls damp, her feet bare, swathed in a white towelling bathrobe that gaped as she stooped to light the gas-fire in her cluttered living-room, giving him a glimpse of a gently sloping breast and the profile of a pink nipple, for she appeared to have nothing on under the robe. To his surprise, and almost dismay, his penis stiffened at the recollection. At the same moment, Marjorie, reaching probably for his hand, to give it a friendly squeeze, found his penis instead, giggled and murmured, "Ooh, you are interested after all, then?"

Then he had no option but to go through with it, though as Marjorie gasped and grunted beneath him he was only able to come by imagining he was doing it to Robyn Penrose, sprawled on the rug in front of her gas fire, her bathrobe cast aside to reveal that indeed she was wearing nothing underneath it, yes, that was sweet revenge on the silly stuck-up cow for making him Brian Everthorpe's butt and interrupting his meetings with damnfool questions and telling tales on the shopfloor and nearly destroying six months' patient coaxing of the foundry back to efficiency – yes, that was good, to have her there on the floor amid the incredible litter of books and dirty coffee cups and wineglasses and album sleeves and copies of *Spare Rib* and *Marxism Today*, stark naked, her bush as fiery red as her topknot, thrashing and writhing underneath him like the actresses in the TV films, moaning with pleasure in spite of herself as he thrust and thrust and thrust.

When he rolled off Marjorie she gave a sigh – whether of satisfaction or relief, he couldn't tell – pulled down her nightdress, and waddled off to the bathroom. He himself felt only guilt and depression, like he used to feel as a lad when he wanked off. That he'd been able to make love to his wife only by whipping up crude fantasies about a woman he had every reason to detest was bad enough; but the bitterest thought was that, had she known what he'd done, Robyn Penrose would have nodded smugly at so complete a confirmation of her feminist prejudices. So far from having had his revenge, Vic felt that he had suffered a moral defeat. It had not been a good week, he reflected gloomily, listening to Marjorie sloshing water about in the bidet, and then filling a glass at the sink to help swallow her Valium. He nearly called out to her to bring one for him, too.

As Marjorie came back into the bedroom, the noise of the front door closing made him spring upright in the bed. "Is that Sandra?" he said.

"I expect so, what's the matter?"

"I forgot all about her."

It was his usual practice to wait up until Sandra came in on a Saturday night, partly to reassure himself that she had got home safely, and partly to see Cliff, the acne ace, off the premises. But because Gary had manoeuvred him into going to bed early, he had forgotten all about his daughter.

"She's all right. Cliff always sees her home."

"That's what I'm worried about. He's probably downstairs now." He threw back the covers and fumbled under the bed for his slippers.

"Where are you going?" Marjorie said.

"Downstairs."

"Leave them alone for heaven's sake, Vic," said Marjorie, with a surprising show of spirit. "You'll make yourself look ridiculous. They're only having a cup of coffee or something. Don't you trust your own daughter?"

"I don't trust that Cliff," Vic said. But after a few moments' hesitation, sitting on the edge of the bed, he got slowly back under the blankets and turned out the light for, it felt like, the ninety-seventh time that night. "Youths like him are only interested in one thing," he said.

"Cliff's all right. Anyway, you're a fine one to talk." Marjorie sniggered, and nudged him with her elbow. "You didn't half go it just now."

Vic said nothing, thankful that the darkness concealed the expression on his face.

"It was nice, though, wasn't it?" Marjorie murmured drowsily.

Vic grunted a vague assent which appeared to satisfy her. The Valium, coming on top of the unwonted sexual exercise, soon worked its effect. Marjorie's breathing became deep and regular. She was asleep.

Vic must have dozed off himself. He was woken by a sound like the beating of his own heart, and when he checked his alarm clock the digital display showed the time to be one-fifteen. The heart-beat, he quickly realised, was actually the throb of the bass notes on a record someone was playing on the music centre in the lounge. A clip from the film he'd watched earlier that evening replayed itself in his head, with Sandra and Cliff standing in for the infatuated couple dancing cheek to cheek. He levered himself out of bed, groped for his slippers and, as his eyes accommodated to the darkness, took his dressing-gown from behind the bathroom door and quietly left the bedroom. The landing and front hall were dark, but a dim light over the burglar-alarm control box guided him down the stairs. He could hear the sound of music, though no light was visible under the lounge door. He opened it and went in.

Vic felt like a white explorer who had stumbled on a cave where some nomadic tribe had bivouacked for the night. The only light in the room came from the gas flames licking round the imitation logs in the hearth, casting a fitful illumination over half-a-dozen figures sprawled in a semi-circle on the floor. He switched on the main ceiling light. Six young men, one of them Raymond, with cans of lager and smouldering cigarettes in their fists, blinked and gaped up at him.

"'Ullo, Dad," said Raymond, with the vague geniality that was the usual sign that he had been drinking.

"What's going on?" Vic demanded, tugging the cord of his dressing-gown tight.

"Jus' brought a few of the lads back," said Raymond.

Vic had seen them all before at one time or another, though he didn't know their names, since Raymond never bothered to introduce them, nor did they seem capable of introducing themselves. They did not get to their feet now, or show any other sign of respect or discomfiture. They reclined on the floor in the shabby overcoats and Doc Marten boots that they never seemed to take off, and gaped apathetically at him from under their sticky punk haircuts. Like Raymond, they were all college dropouts, or youths who hadn't been able to summon up the energy even to start college. They lived on the dole and on their parents, and spent their time drinking in pubs or pricing amplifiers in the Rummidge music stores; for they all played electric guitars of various shapes and sizes, and nourished the fantasy of

116

forming a "band" one day, in spite of the fact that none of them could read music and the collective noise they made was so dire that they could seldom find anywhere to rehearse. Just to look at them made Vic want to start campaigning for the restoration of National Service, or the workhouse, or transportation – anything to encourage these idle young sods to get off their backsides and into some honest work.

"Where's Sandra?" he asked Raymond. "Did she come in?"

"Gone t' bed. Came in a while ago."

"And whatsisname?"

"Cliff went home." As usual, Raymond did not look Vic in the eye as he spoke, but down at his own feet, rocking his head slightly to the rhythm of the music. Vic looked round the room, feeling self-conscious now, standing there in his pyjamas and dressing-gown – garments he was fairly confident none of these youths had worn since attaining the age of puberty. "That my lager?" he enquired, feeling mean even as he uttered the question.

"Yeah, d'you mind?" said Raymond. "I'll replace it when I get me next giro."

"I don't mind you drinking the lager," said Vic, "as long as you don't puke all over the carpet."

"That was Wiggy," said Raymond, recognising the allusion to an incident some months earlier. "He doesn't go around with us any more."

"Learned some sense, has he?"

"Nah. He got married." Raymond grinned and glanced slyly at his friends, who seemed to find this idea as amusing as he did. They belched and guffawed, or shook their shoulders in silent laughter.

"God help his wife, is all I can say," said Vic. He stepped over several pairs of outstretched legs to reach the stereo, and turned down the volume and bass controls. "Keep this low," he said, "or you'll wake your mother."

"A'right," said Raymond mildly, though he knew as well as Vic that only a bomb would wake Marjorie now. He added, as Vic made his way to the door, "Turn the light out, will you, Dad?"

As he climbed the stairs, Vic thought he heard the sound of stifled laughter coming from the lounge. It was a sound he was getting increasingly tired of.

The following morning Vic, while engaged in cleaning the road salt off the underside of his car with a pressure hose in the front drive, saw several of last night's nomads leave, and by dint of staring hard even compelled two of them to mutter a greeting. Under an agreement negotiated some time ago, Raymond was allowed to have friends to stay in the house overnight only on condition that they slept in his room. This clause, intended to limit the number of his guests, had quite failed of its intended effect since, however many there were, they all somehow managed to squeeze themselves into the available space, curled up on the floor in sleeping bags or wrapped in their overcoats in (as Vic imagined the scene) a snoring, farting, belching heap. From this foetid nest they would emerge, singly and at intervals, in the course of Sunday morning, to pee, not always accurately, in one of the lavatories of the house, and help themselves lavishly to cornflakes in the kitchen, before sloping off to their next pub rendezvous. As usual, Raymond was the last to rise this morning; indeed, he was still having his breakfast when Vic drove off to fetch his father for lunch.

Since Vic's elder sister, Joan, had married a Canadian and gone to live in Winnipeg twenty-five years ago, the responsibility of looking after their parents had fallen to him. Mr Wilcox Senior had retired in 1975 after working all his life, first as a toolmaker, later as a stores supervisor, for one of the largest engineering companies in Rummidge. Vic's mother had died six years later, of cancer, but Mr Wilcox insisted on staying on in the terraced house in Ebury Street he had married into, old-fashioned and inconvenient as it was. Bringing him round to Avondale Road for Sunday lunch was a regular ritual.

Every time Vic drove down Ebury Street, it seemed a little more dejected, but on this overcast January Sunday, with a slow thaw in progress, it seemed especially depressing. Decay had set in at each end of the street, as if the molars had been the first to go in a row of teeth, and was creeping slowly towards the middle, where a few of the long-term residents, like his father, still remained stubbornly rooted. Some of the houses were squats, some were boarded up, and others were occupied by poor immigrants. To this latter group Mr Wilcox had a curiously divided attitude. Those he knew personally he spoke of in terms of the warmest regard; the rest he anathematised as "bloody blacks and coloureds" who had brought the neighbourhood down. Vic had tried on several occasions to explain to his father that their presence in Ebury Street was an effect, not a cause – that the cause was the expressway striding over the rooftops only thirty yards away on its great bulging concrete legs – but without success. Come to think of it, he had never succeeded in changing his father's mind about anything.

Vic drew into the gutter, still clogged with dirty packed snow, and parked outside number 59. Some Caribbean children throwing slushy snowballs at each other desisted for a moment to stare at the big shiny car, as well they might. The Jaguar seemed almost obscenely opulent alongside the bangers parked in this street, old rust-eaten Escorts and Marinas sagging on their clapped-out shock-absorbers. Vic would have felt more comfortable driving Marjorie's Metro, but he knew that his father got a kick out of being collected in the Jag. It was a message to the neighbours: *Look, my son is rich and successful. I'm not like you, I don't have to live on this shit-heap. I can move out any time I like. I just happen to like living in my own house, the house I've always lived in.*

Vic knocked on the front door. His father opened it almost immediately, neatly dressed in his Sunday best: a checked sports jacket with grey flannels, a woolly cardigan under the jacket, collar and tie, and brown shoes gleaming like freshly gathered conkers. His thin grey hair was slicked down with haircream, which, Vic reflected, thinking of Raymond's friends, seemed to be coming back into fashion – not that fashion had anything to do with Mr Wilcox's use of it.

"I'll just get my coat," he said, "I was airing it. D'you want to come in?"

"I might as well," said Vic.

The air seemed almost as damp and chill in the hall as outside on the pavement. "You ought to let me put central heating in this house," Vic said, as he followed the dark shape of his father – short and broad-shouldered like his own, but with less flesh on the bones – down the hall. Correctly predicting the reply, he silently mouthed it in unison.

"I don't 'old with central 'eating."

"You wouldn't have to air your clothes in front of the kitchen stove."

"It's bad for the furniture."

Somewhere Mr Wilcox had picked up the idea that central heating dried up the glue in furniture, causing it eventually to collapse and disintegrate. The fact that Vic's furniture was still intact after many years in a centrally heated environment had not shaken this conviction, and of course it could not be pointed out to Mr Wilcox that his own furniture, mostly bought from the Co-op in the nineteen-thirties, was in any case hardly worth careful preservation.

The back kitchen was at least cosy and warm, which was just as well, since Mr Wilcox virtually wintered in it, sitting in his high-backed armchair facing the stove, with the TV perched precariously on top of the sideboard and a pile of the old books and magazines he bought from jumble sales within easy reach. The door of the solid-fuel boiler was open, and in front of it a navy-blue overcoat was slumped like a drunk over the back of an upright chair. Mr Wilcox closed the door of the boiler with a bang, and Vic helped him on with the coat.

"You could do with a new one," he said, noticing the threadbare cuffs.

"You can't get material like this any more," said Mr Wilcox. "That thing you've got on doesn't look as if it's got any warmth in it."

Vic was wearing a quilted gilet over a thick sweater. "It's warmer than it looks," he said. "Nice for driving – leaves your arms free."

"How much was it?"

"Fifteen pounds," said Vic, halving the actual price.

"Good God!" Mr Wilcox exclaimed.

Whenever his father asked him the price of anything, Vic always halved it. This formula, he found, ensured that the old man was agreeably scandalised without being really upset.

"Picked up an interesting book yesterday," said Mr Wilcox, brandishing a volume with limp red covers, somewhat soiled and creased. "Only cost me fivepence. 'Ave a look."

The book was the *AA Guide to Hotels and Restaurants 1958*. "Bring it with you, Dad," said Vic. "We'd better be on our way, or the dinner'll spoil."

"Did you know, in 1958 you could get bed and breakfast in a one-star hotel in Morecambe for seven-and-six a night?"

"No, Dad, I didn't."

"How much d'you reckon it would cost now. Seven quid?"

"Easily," said Vic. "More like twice that."

"I don't know how folk manage these days," said Mr Wilcox, with gloomy satisfaction.

Sunday lunch, or dinner as Vic called it in deference to his father, hardly varied through the year, also in deference to Mr Wilcox: a joint of beef or lamb, with roast potatoes and sprouts or peas, followed by apple crumble or lemon meringue pie. Once Marjorie had experimented with *coq au vin* from a recipe in a magazine, and Mr Wilcox had sighed unhappily as his plate was put before him and said afterwards that it was very nice but he had never been much of a one for foreign food and there was nothing like the good old English roast. Marjorie had taken the hint.

After lunch they sat in the lounge and Mr Wilcox diverted himself and, he fondly supposed, the rest of the family, by reading aloud extracts from the *AA Guide to Hotels and Restaurants*, and inviting them to guess the 1958 rate for a week's half board at the best hotel in the Isle of Wight or the price of bed and breakfast at a class A boarding house in Rhyl. "I don't even know what seven-and-six *means*, Grandpa," said Sandra irritably, while Gary had to be restrained from giving his grandfather a patronising lecture on inflation. Sandra and Gary squabbled over the TV, Sandra wanting to watch the *Eastenders* omnibus and Gary wanting to play a computer game. He had a black-and-white set of his own upstairs, but the game required colour. When Vic upheld Sandra's claim, Gary sulked and said it was time he had a colour set of his own. Mr Wilcox asked how much the set in the living-room cost and Vic, looking fiercely at the rest of the family, said two hundred and fifty pounds. Marjorie was reading, with great concentration and hardly moving her lips at all, a mail-order brochure that had come with her credit-card account and kept proposing to purchase various items of useless gadgetry – a keyring that bleeped when you whistled for it, an alarm clock that stopped bleeping if you shouted at it, an inflatable neck-pillow for sleeping on aeroplanes, a battery-operated telescopic tie-rack, a thermostatically controlled waxing machine for removing unwanted hair, and a jacuzzi conversion kit for the bathtub – until Mr Wilcox's relentless quiz about 1958 hotel prices reminded her of summer holidays and she began to go through the Sunday papers and the TV guides cutting out coupons for brochures. Sandra said she was sick of family holidays and why didn't they buy their own apartment in Spain or Majorca, then they could all go separately and stay with their friends, a proposal enthusiastically backed up by Raymond, who came in from the kitchen, where he had been eating his warmed-up lunch because as usual he had come in from the pub too late to sit down at table. He also asked Vic if he would lend him and his mates two hundred and fifty pounds to have a "demo tape" of their band made, a request Vic had the satisfaction of turning down flat. Caught in the crossfire between a parent who regarded all non-essential expenditure as a form of moral turpitude and a wife and children who would spend his annual salary five times over if given the chance, Vic gave up the attempt to read the Sunday papers and relieved his feelings by going outside and shovelling away the slush on the front drive. Nothing depressed him more than the thought of summer holidays: a fortnight of compulsory idleness, mooning about in the rain in some dreary English seaside resort, or looking for a bit of shade on a sweltering Mediterranean beach. Weekends were bad enough. By this point on a Sunday afternoon he was itching to get back to the factory.

3

For Robyn and Charles weekends were for work as well as recreation, and the two activities tended to blend into each other at certain interfaces. Was it work or recreation, for instance, to browse through the review pages of the *Observer* and the *Sunday Times*, mentally filing away information about the latest books, plays, films, and even fashion and furniture (for nothing semiotic is alien to the modern academic critic)? A brisk walk in Wellington boots to feed the ducks in the local park was, however, definitely recreation; and after a light lunch (Robyn cooked the omelettes and Charles dressed the salad), they settled down for a few hours' serious work in the congested living-room–study, before it would be time for Charles to drive back to Suffolk. Robyn had a stack of essays to mark, and Charles was reading a book on Deconstruction which he had agreed to review for a scholarly journal. The gas fire hissed and popped in the the hearth. A harpsichord concerto by Haydn tinkled quietly on the stereo. Outside, as the light faded from the winter sky, melting snow dripped from the eaves and trickled down the gutters. Robyn, looking up from Marion Russell's overdue assessed essay on *Tess of the D'Urbervilles* (which was actually not at all bad, so perhaps the modelling job was turning out to be a sensible decision), caught Charles' abstracted gaze and smiled.

"Any good?" she enquired, nodding at his book.

"Not bad. Quite good on the de-centring of the subject, actually. You remember that marvellous bit in Lacan?" Charles read out a quotation: "'*I think where I am not, therefore I am where I think not . . . I am not, wherever I am the plaything of my thought; I think of what I am wherever I don't think I am thinking.*'"

"Marvellous," Robyn agreed.

"There's quite a good discussion of it in here."

"Isn't that where Lacan says something interesting about realism?"

"Yes: '*This two-faced mystery is linked to the fact that the truth can be evoked only in that dimension of alibi in which all "realism" in creative works takes its virtue from metonymy.*'"

Robyn frowned. "What d'you think that *means*, exactly? I mean, is 'truth' being used ironically?"

"Oh, I think so, yes. It's implied by the word 'alibi', surely? There is no 'truth', in the absolute sense, no transcendental signified. Truth is just a rhetorical illusion, a tissue of metonymies and metaphors, as

Nietzsche said. It all goes back to Nietzsche, really, as this chap points out." Charles tapped the book on his lap. "Listen. Lacan goes on: '*It is likewise linked to this other fact that we accede to meaning only through the double twist of metaphor when we have the unique key: the signifier and the signified of the Saussurian formula are not at the same level, and man only deludes himself when he believes that his true place is at their axis, which is nowhere.*'"

"But isn't he making a distinction there between 'truth' and 'meaning'? Truth is to meaning as metonymy is to metaphor."

"How?" It was Charles' turn to frown.

"Well, take Pringle's, for example."

"Pringle's?"

"The factory."

"Oh, that. You seem quite obsessed with that place."

"Well, it's uppermost in my mind. You could represent the factory realistically by a set of metonymies – dirt, noise, heat and so on. But you can only grasp the *meaning* of the factory by metaphor. The place is like hell. The trouble with Wilcox is that he can't see that. He has no metaphorical vision."

"And what about Danny Ram?" said Charles.

"Oh, poor old Danny Ram, I don't suppose he has any metaphorical vision either, otherwise he couldn't stick it. The factory to him is just another set of metonymies and synecdoches: a lever he pulls, a pair of greasy overalls he wears, a weekly pay packet. That's the truth of his existence, but not the meaning of it."

"Which is . . .?"

"I just told you: hell. Alienation, if you want to put it in Marxist terms."

"But –" said Charles. But he was interrupted by a long peal on the doorbell.

"Who on earth can that be?" Robyn wondered, starting to her feet.

"Not your friend Wilcox, again, I hope," said Charles.

"Why should it be?"

"I don't know. Only you made him sound a bit . . ." Charles, uncharacteristically, couldn't find the epithet he wanted.

"Well, you needn't look so apprehensive," said Robyn, with a grin. "He won't eat you." She went to the window and peeped out at the front porch. "Good Lord!" she exclaimed. "It's Basil!"

"Your brother?"

"Yes, and a girl." Robyn did a hop, skip and jump across the cluttered floor and went to open the front door, while Charles, displeased at the interruption, marked his place in the book and stowed it away in his briefcase. The little he knew about Basil did not suggest that deconstruction was a likely topic of conversation in the next hour or two.

Basil's decision to go into the City, announced to an incredulous family in his last undergraduate year at Oxford, had not been an idle threat. He had joined a merchant bank on graduating and after only three years' employment was already earning more than his father, who had related this fact to Robyn at Christmas with a mixture of pride and resentment. Basil himself had not been at home for Christmas, but skiing in St Moritz. It was in fact some time since Robyn had seen her brother, because, for their parents' sake, they deliberately arranged their visits home to alternate rather than coincide, and they had little desire to meet elsewhere. She was struck by the change in his appearance: his face was fatter, his wavy corn-coloured hair was neatly trimmed, and he seemed to have had his teeth capped – all presumably the results of his new affluence. Everything about him and his girlfriend signified money, from their pastel-pale, luxuriously thick sheepskin coats that seemed to fill the threshold when she opened the front door, to the red C-registration BMW parked at the kerb behind Charles' four-year-old Golf. Underneath the sheepskin coats Basil was wearing an Aquascutum cashmere sports jacket, and his girlfriend, whose name was Debbie, an outfit remarkably like one designed by Katherine Hamnett illustrated in that day's *Sunday Times*. This classy attire was explained partly by the fact that they had been to a hunt ball in Shropshire the previous evening, and had decided on impulse to call in on their way back to London.

"A hunt ball?" Robyn repeated, with a raised eyebrow. "Is this the same man whose idea of a good night out used to be listening to a punk band in a room over a pub?"

"We all have to grow up, Rob," said Basil. "Anyway, it was partly business. I made some useful contacts."

"It was a real lark," said Debbie, a pretty pale-faced girl with blonde hair cut like Princess Diana's, and a figure of almost anorexic slimness. "Held in a sorter castle. Just like a horror film, wonnit?" she said to Basil. "Suits of armour and stuffed animals' heads and everyfink."

At first Robyn thought that Debbie's Cockney accent was some sort of joke, but soon realised that it was authentic. In spite of her Sloaney clothes and hair-do, Debbie was decidedly lower-class. When Basil mentioned that she worked in the same bank as himself, Robyn assumed that she was a secretary or typist, but was quickly corrected by her brother when he followed her out to the kitchen where she was making tea.

"Good Lord, no," he said. "She's a foreign-exchange dealer. Very smart, earns more than I do."

"And how much is that?" Robyn asked.

"Thirty thousand, excluding bonuses," said Basil, his arms folded smugly across his chest.

Robyn stared. "Daddy said you were getting disgustingly rich, but I didn't realise just how disgusting. What do you do to earn that sort of money?"

"I'm in capital markets. I arrange swaps."

"Swaps?" The word reminded her of Basil when he was her kid brother, a gangling boy in scuffed shoes and a stained blazer, sorting conkers or gloating over his stamp collection.

"Yes. Suppose a corporate has borrowed x thousands at a fixed rate of interest. If they think that interest rates are going to fall, they could execute a swap transaction whereby we pay them a fixed rate and they pay us LIBOR, that's the London Interbank Offered Rate, which is variable . . ."

While Basil told Robyn much more than she wanted to know, or could understand, about swaps, she busied herself with the teacups and tried to conceal her boredom. He was anxious to assure her that he was only earning less than Debbie because he had started later. "She didn't go to University, you see."

"No, I thought she probably didn't."

"Not many spot dealers are graduates, actually. They've usually left school at sixteen and gone straight into the bank. Then somebody sees that they've got what it takes and gives them a chance."

Robyn asked what it took.

"The barrow-boy mentality, they call it. Quick wits and an appetite for non-stop dealing. Bonds are different, you have to be patient, spend a long time preparing a package. There are lulls. I couldn't last for half-an-hour in Debbie's dealing room – fifty people with about six telephones in each hand shouting across the room things like '*Six hundred million yen 9th of January!*' All day. It's a madhouse, but Debbie thrives on it. She comes from a family of bookies in Whitechapel."

"Is it serious, then, between you and Debbie?"

"What's serious?" said Basil, showing his capped teeth in a bland smile. "We don't have anybody else, if that's what you mean."

"I mean, are you living together?"

"Not literally. We both have our own houses. It makes sense to have a mortgage each, the way property prices are going up in London. How much did you pay for this place, by the way?"

"Twenty thousand."

"Good God, it would fetch four times that in Stoke Newington. Debbie bought a little terraced house there two years ago, just like this, for forty thousand, it's worth ninety now . . ."

"So property governs sexuality in the City these days?"

"Hasn't it always, according to Saint Karl?"

"That was before women liberated themselves."

"Fact is, we're both too knackered after work to be interested in anything more energetic than a bottle of wine and a hot bath. It's a long day. Twelve hours – sometimes more if things get lively. Debbie is usually at her desk by seven."

"Whatever for?"

"She does a lot of business with Tokyo . . . So we tend to work hard on our own all week and live it up together at the weekend. What about you and Charles? Isn't it time you got hitched?"

"Why d'you say that?" Robyn demanded.

"I was thinking, as we saw you through your front window from the pavement, that you looked just like some comfortably married couple."

"We're not into marriage."

"I say, do people still say 'into' like that, up here in the rust belt?"

"Don't be a metropolitan snob, Basil."

"Sorry," he said, with a smirk that showed he wasn't. "You've been very faithful, anyway."

"We don't have anyone else, if that's what you mean," she said drily.

"And how's the job?"

"In jeopardy," said Robyn, leading the way back to the living-room. Debbie, perched on the arm of Charles's chair, her hair falling over her eyes, was showing him a little gadget like a pocket quartz alarm clock.

"Is Lapsang Suchong all right?" Robyn asked, setting down the tea tray, and thinking to herself that Debbie probably favoured some brand advertised on television by chimps or animated teapots, brewed so strong you could stand the teaspoon up in it.

"Love it," said Debbie. She really was a very difficult person to get right.

"Very interesting," said Charles politely, handing Debbie's gadget back to her. It apparently informed her of the state of the world's principal currencies twenty-four hours a day, but as it only worked within a fifty-mile radius of London its liquid-crystal display was blank.

"I get ever so nervy when I'm outside of the range," she said. "At home I sleep with it under my pillow, so if I wake in the middle of the night I can check on the yen–dollar rate."

"So what's this about your job?" Basil asked Robyn.

Robyn explained briefly her situation, while Charles provided a more emotive gloss. "The irony is that she's easily the brightest person in the Department," he said. "The students know it, Swallow knows it, the other staff know it. But there's nothing anybody can do about it, apparently. That's what this government is doing to the universities: death by a thousand cuts."

"What a shame," said Debbie. "Why doncher try somethink else?"

"Like the money market?" Robyn enquired sardonically, though Debbie seemed to take the suggestion seriously.

"No, love, it's too late, I'm afraid. You're burned out at thirty-five, they reckon, in our game. But there must be something else you could do. Start a little business!"

"A business?" Robyn laughed at the absurdity of the idea.

"Yeah, why not? Basil could arrange the finance, couldn't you darl?"

"No problem."

"And you can get a government grant, forty quid a week and free management training for a year, too," said Debbie. "Friend of mine did it after she was made redundant. Opened a sports shoe boutique in Brixton with a bank loan of five thousand. Sold out two years later for a hundred and fifty grand and went to live in the Algarve. Has a chain of shops out there now, in all them time-share places."

"But I don't want to run a shoe shop or live in the Algarve," said Robyn. "I want to teach women's studies and poststructuralism and the nineteenth-century novel and write books about them."

"How much do you get for doing that?" Basil asked.

"Twelve thousand a year, approximately."

"Good God, is that all?"

"I don't do it for the money."

"No, I can see that."

"Actually," said Charles, "there are a great many people who live on half that."

"I'm sure there are," said Basil, "but I don't happen to know any of them. Do you?"

Charles was silent.

"I do," said Robyn.

"Who?" said Basil. "Tell me one person you know, I mean *know*, not just know of, somebody you talked to in the last week, who earns less than six thousand a year." His expression, both amused and belligerent, reminded Robyn of arguments they used to have when they were younger.

"Danny Ram," said Robyn. She happened to know that he earned a hundred and ten pounds a week, because she had asked Prendergast, the Personnel Director at Pringle's.

"And who's Danny Ram?"

"An Indian factory worker." Robyn derived considerable satisfaction from uttering this phrase, which seemed a very effective putdown

127

of Basil's arrogant cynicism; but of course she then had to explain how she came to be acquainted with Danny Ram.

"Well, well," said Basil, when she had finished a brief account of her experiences at Pringle's, "So you've done your bit to make British industry even less competitive than it is already."

"I've done my bit to bring some social justice to it."

"Not that it will make any difference in the long run," said Basil. "Companies like Pringle's are batting on a losing wicket. Maggie's absolutely right – the future for our economy is in service industries, and perhaps some hi-tech engineering."

"Finance being one of the service industries?" Charles enquired.

"Naturally," said Basil, smiling. "And you ain't seen nothing yet. Wait till the Big Bang."

"What's that?" said Robyn.

Basil and Debbie looked at each other and burst out laughing. "I don't believe it," said Basil. "Don't you read the newspapers?"

"Not the financial pages," said Robyn.

"It's some kind of change in the rules of the Stock Exchange," said Charles, "that will allow people like Basil to make even more money than they do already."

"Or lose it," said Basil. "Don't forget there's an element of risk in our job. Unlike women's studies or critical theory," he added, with a glance at Robyn. "That's what makes it more interesting, of course."

"It's just a glorified form of gambling, isn't it?" said Charles.

"That's right. Debbie gambles with a stake of ten to twenty million pounds every day of the week, don't you my sweet?"

"'Sright," said Debbie. "Course, it's not like having a flutter on a horse. You don't *see* the money, and it's not yours anyway, it's the bank's."

"But twenty million!" said Charles, visibly shaken. "That's nearly the annual budget of my University."

"You should see Debbie at work, Charles," said Basil. "It would open your eyes. You too, Rob."

"Yeah, why not?" said Debbie. "I could probably fix it."

"It might be interesting," said Charles, rather to Robyn's surprise.

"Not to me, I'm afraid," she said.

Basil glanced at his watch, extending his wrist just long enough to show that it was a Rolex. "Time we were off."

He insisted that they went outside into the slushy street to admire his BMW. It had a sticker in the rear window saying BOND DEALERS DO IT BACK TO BACK. Robyn asked what it meant.

Debbie giggled. "Back to back is like a loan that's made in one currency and set against an equal loan in another."

128

"Oh, I see, it's a metaphor."

"What?"

"Never mind," said Robyn, hugging herself against the damp chill of the evening.

"It's also a joke," said Basil.

"Yes, I see that a joke is intended," said Robyn. "It must rather pall on people following you down the motorway."

"Nobody stays that close for long," said Basil. "This is a very fast car. Well, goodbye, sister mine."

Robyn submitted to a kiss on the cheek from Basil, then from Debbie. After a moment's hesitation and a little embarrassed laugh, Debbie brushed Charles' cheek with her own, and jumped into the passenger seat of the car. Charles and Basil waved vaguely to each other as they parted.

"You don't really want to visit that bank, do you?" Robyn said to Charles, as they returned to the house.

"I thought it might be interesting," said Charles. "I thought I might write something about it."

"Oh well, that's different," said Robyn, closing the front door and following Charles back into the living room. "Who for?"

"I don't know, *Marxism Today* perhaps. Or the *New Statesman*. I've been thinking lately I might try and supplement my income with a little freelance journalism."

"You've never done anything like that before," said Robyn.

"There's always a first time."

Robyn stepped over the soiled tea things on the floor and crouched by the gasfire to warm herself. "What did you make of Debbie?"

"Rather intriguing."

"Intriguing?"

"Well, so childlike in many ways, but handling millions of pounds every day."

"I'm afraid Mummy will consider Debbie what she calls 'common' – if Basil ever dares take her home."

"You rather gave the impression that you thought her common yourself."

"Me?" said Robyn indignantly.

"You patronised her terribly."

"Nonsense!"

"You may not think so," said Charles calmly. "But you did."

Robyn did not like to be accused of snobbery, but her conscience was not entirely easy. "Well, what can you talk about to people like that," she said defensively. "Money? Holidays? Cars? Basil's just as bad. He's become quite obnoxious, as a matter of fact."

"Mmm."

"Don't let's ever become rich, Charles," said Robyn suddenly anxious to mend the little breach that had opened up between them.

"I don't think there's any danger of that," Charles said, rather bitterly, Robyn thought.

FOUR

"I know so little about strikes, and rates of wages, and capital, and labour, that I had better not talk to a political economist like you."

"Nay, the more reason," said he eagerly. "I shall be only too glad to explain to you all that may seem anomalous or mysterious to a stranger; especially at a time like this, when our doings are sure to be canvassed by every scribbler who can hold a pen."

Elizabeth Gaskell: *North and South*

1

The following Wednesday morning, Robyn found herself back in Vic Wilcox's office, rather to her own surprise, and certainly to Wilcox's, to judge from the expression on his face as Shirley ushered her in.

"You again?" he said, looking up from his desk.

Robyn did not advance into the room, but stood just inside the door, stripping off her gloves. "It's Wednesday," she said. "You didn't send a message telling me not to come."

"I didn't think you'd have the nerve to show your face in this place again, to tell you the truth."

"I'll go away, if you like," said Robyn, with one glove off and one on. "Nothing would please me more."

Wilcox resumed flicking through the contents of a file that was open on his desk. "Why did you come then?"

"I agreed to come every Wednesday for the rest of this term. I wish I hadn't, but I did. If you want to cancel the arrangement, that's fine by me."

Wilcox looked at her in a calculating kind of way. After a long pause he said, "You might as well stay. They might send me somebody even worse."

His rudeness was provocation enough to walk out, but Robyn hesitated. She had already expended a lot of time and energy in the past couple of days wondering whether to go back to Pringle's, expecting from hour to hour a message from Wilcox or the VC's office that would settle the question. No message had come. Penny Black, whose advice she had sought after squash on Monday evening, had urged her to go back – "if you don't, he'll think he's won" – so she had gone back. And now the voice of prudence counselled her to stay. Wilcox evidently hadn't lodged a formal complaint about her conduct the previous Wednesday, but if she resigned from the Shadow Scheme it would all come out. Though she wasn't ashamed of her intervention on behalf of Danny Ram (and Penny had been deeply impressed) there had been, she privately acknowledged, something slightly Quixotic about it, and she didn't relish the prospect of having to explain and justify it to Philip Swallow or the VC. She came further into the room and peeled off her remaining glove.

"As long as one thing is understood," said Wilcox. "Everything you see or hear while you're shadowing me is confidential."

"All right," said Robyn.

"Don't take your coat off yet – we may be going out." He spoke to Shirley on his intercom: "Phone Foundrax and ask if Norman Cole can spare me a few minutes this morning, will you?"

For once, Wilcox himself put on an overcoat, an expensive-looking camelhair garment that, like most of his clothes, seemed designed for a man with longer arms and legs. In the lobby they ran into Brian Everthorpe, swaggering in from the car park, huffing and puffing and rubbing his pink hands together. Robyn hadn't seen him since the previous Wednesday – mercifully he hadn't been present at the meeting with the Asian workers, though he must have heard about it.

"Hallo, Vic, I see your beautiful shadow is back, she must be a glutton for punishment. How are you, my dear? Get home all right last week, did you?"

"I managed," Robyn said coldly. Something knowing about his grin made her suspect that he had been responsible for tampering with her car.

"Bad on the motorway was it this morning, Brian?" said Wilcox, glancing at his watch.

"Terrible."

"I thought so."

"Always the same, Wednesday mornings."

"See you," said Wilcox, slicing through the swing doors.

Robyn followed him outside. After the weekend's partial thaw, the weather had turned bitterly cold again. The remnants of last week's blizzard had frozen into corrugated patches of ice on the car park, but Wilcox's Jaguar was just outside the office block, in a bay that had been neatly scraped clean and dry. The car was long and low and luxuriously upholstered. When Wilcox turned the ignition key, a female vocalist sang out with startling clarity and resonance, as if she were concealed, complete with orchestra, in the back seat-well: "*Maybe I'm a dreamer, maybe just a fool –*" Wilcox, evidently embarrassed to have his musical tastes thus revealed, snapped off the stereo system with a quick movement of his hand. The car glided away, ice crackling under its tyres. As he drove, he explained the background to the morning's business, an appointment with the Managing Director of a firm called Foundrax, situated not far away.

Pringle's and Foundrax both supplied a manufacturer of diesel-powered pumps, Rawlinson's, with components – Pringle's with cylinder blocks, Foundrax with cylinder heads. Recently Rawlinson's had asked Pringle's to drop their prices by five per cent, claiming that they had had a quote from another firm at that level. "Of course, they may be bluffing. They're amost certainly bluffing about the size of the

134

discount. Prices ought to be going up, not down, what with the cost of pig-iron and scrap these days. But competition is so ferocious it's possible another company is trying to get some of the action by offering a silly price. The question is, how silly? And who are they? That's why I'm going to see Norman Cole. I want to find out if Rawlinson's are asking for the same sort of reduction on his cylinder heads."

The offices of the Foundrax factory had, like Pringle's, an air of being embalmed in an earlier era, the late fifties or early sixties. There was the same dull reception foyer done out in light oak veneer and worn-looking splay-legged furniture, the same trade magazines spread on the low tables, the same (it seemed to Robyn's inexpert eye) bits of polished machinery in dusty display cases, the same permanent waves on the heads of the secretaries, including the one who, casting curious glances at Robyn, escorted them to Norman Cole's office. Like Wilcox's, this was a large, colourless room, with an executive desk on one side, and on the other a long board table at which he invited them to sit.

Cole was a portly, bald-headed man who blinked a great deal behind his glasses, and smoked a pipe – or rather he poked, scraped, blew into, sucked on and frequently applied burning matches to a pipe. Not much smoke was produced by all this activity. He exuded instead a rather false air of bonhomie. "Ha, ha!" he exclaimed, when Wilcox explained Robyn's presence. "I'll believe you, Vic. Thousands wouldn't." He turned to Robyn: "And what is it you do at the University, Miss er . . ."

"Doctor," said Wilcox, "she's Dr Penrose."

"Oh, on the medical side, are you?"

"No, I teach English Literature," said Robyn.

"And women's studies," said Wilcox, with a grimace.

"I don't go in for women's studies, ha, ha," said Cole. "But I like a good book. I'm on *The Thornbirds* at the moment." He looked expectantly at Robyn.

"I'm afraid I haven't read it," said Robyn.

"So how's business, Norman?" Wilcox said.

"Mustn't grumble," said Cole.

The conversation about trade continued desultorily for some minutes. The secretary brought in a tray with coffee and biscuits. Vic raised the topic of some charity fund-raising function the two men were involved in. Cole glanced at his watch. "Anything special I can do for you, Vic?"

"No, I'm just making a few calls to give this young lady an idea of the scope of our business," said Vic. "We won't take up any more of your time. Oh, while I'm here – you haven't had a letter from Rawlinson's buyer lately, by any chance?"

135

Cole lifted an eyebrow and blinked at Robyn.

"It's all right," said Wilcox. "Dr Penrose understands that nothing we say goes beyond these four walls."

Cole took out of his pocket an implement like a miniature Swiss Army knife, and began to poke at the bowl of his pipe. "No," he said. "Not to my knowledge. What would it be about?"

"Asking for a reduction on your prices. In the order of five per cent."

"I don't recollect anything," said Cole. He interrupted his excavations to flick a switch on his telephone console and ask his secretary to bring in the Rawlinson file. "Having some trouble with Rawlinson's, then, Vic?"

"Someone's trying to undercut us," Wilcox said. "I'd like to know who it is."

"A foreign firm, perhaps," Cole suggested.

"I don't believe a foreign firm could do it cheaper," said Wilcox. "Why would they bother, anyway? The quantities are too small. What are you thinking of? Germany? Spain?"

Cole unscrewed the mouthpiece of his pipe and peered into the barrel. "I'm just guessing in the dark," he said. "Far East, perhaps, Korea."

"No," said Wilcox, "by the time you added on the cost of shipping it wouldn't make sense. It's another British company, you can bet on that."

The secretary brought in a thick manila file and laid it reverently on Norman Cole's desk. He glanced inside. "No, nothing untoward there, Vic."

"How much are you asking for your cylinder heads, as a matter of interest?"

Norman Cole exposed two rows of nicotine-stained teeth in a broad grin. "You wouldn't expect me to answer that, Vic."

Vic returned the smile with a visible effort. "I'll be off, then," he said, getting to his feet and holding out his hand.

"Taking your shadow with you?" said Cole, grinning and blinking.

"What? Oh. Yes, of course," said Wilcox, who had clearly forgotten Robyn's existence.

"You can leave her here if you like, ha, ha," said Cole, shaking Wilcox's hand. He shook Robyn's hand as well. "*The Fourth Protocol*, that's another good one," he said. "Have you read it?"

"No," said Robyn.

When they were outside in the car, Wilcox said, "Well, what did you make of Norman Cole?"

"I didn't think much of his literary taste."

"He's an accountant," said Wilcox. "Managing Directors in this

business are either engineers or accountants. I don't trust accountants."

"He did seem a bit shifty," said Robyn. "All that fiddling with his
pipe is an excuse to avoid eye contact."

"Shifty is the word," said Wilcox. "I began to get suspicious when
he started talking about Korea. As if anyone in Korea would be interested in Rawlinson's business."

"You think he's hiding something, then?"

"I think he may be the mysterious third party," said Wilcox, as he
swung the Jaguar out of the Foundrax car park and slotted into a gap
in the traffic on the main road, between a yellow van conveying Riviera
Sunbeds and a Dutch container truck.

"You mean the one offering a five per cent reduction?"

"Supposed to be offering five per cent. He might only be offering
four."

"But why would he do that? You said nobody could make a profit at
that price."

"There could be all kinds of motives," said Wilcox. "Perhaps he's
desperate for orders, even loss-making orders, just to keep his factory
turning over for the next few weeks, hoping things will improve.
Perhaps he's nursing some plot, like to get all the Rawlinson's business
for himself and then, next time they re-order, increase the prices without having to bother about competition from us." He gave a dry bark
of a laugh. "Or perhaps he knows he's for the high jump and couldn't
care less what his figures look like."

"How will you find out?"

Wilcox considered the question for a moment, then reached for a
telephone receiver mounted under the dashboard. "Go and see Ted
Stoker at Rawlinson's," he said, handing her the instrument. "Phone
Shirley for me, will you? It'll save me having to stop."

Robyn, who had never even seen a car phone before, found it rather
fun to use.

"I'm afraid Mr Wilcox is out at the moment," Shirley intoned in a
secretarial sing-song.

"I know," said Robyn, "I'm with him."

"Oh," said Shirley. "Who did you say you were?"

"Robyn Penrose. The shadow." She could not suppress a smile as
she identified herself – it sounded like the name of a comic-book character. Superman. Spiderwoman. The Shadow. She passed on Wilcox's
instruction to arrange a meeting with Ted Stoker, the Managing
Director of Rawlinson's, that afternoon if possible.

"You used me as a pretext to see Norman Cole, didn't you?" Robyn
said, as they cruised along the road, waiting for Shirley to call back.

"You came in useful," he said with a quiet grin. "Don't mind, do you? You owe me after last week."

A few minutes later Shirley rang back to say she had fixed an appointment for three o'clock. "Have a nice trip," she said with, Robyn thought, a slightly bitchy intonation. Wilcox made a U-turn through a gap in the road's central reservation, and began driving briskly in the opposite direction.

"Where are we going?" Robyn asked.

"Leeds."

"What – today? There and back?"

"Why not?

"It seems a long way."

"I like driving," said Wilcox.

Robyn could understand why, given the power and comfort of the big car. The wind of their passage was the loudest noise inside its upholstered shell as they sailed up the motorway in the fast lane. Outside, the frostbound fields and skeletal trees cowered under a steely shield of cloud. There was a kind of pleasure in being warm and mobile in a cold and lifeless landscape. Robyn asked if they could have some music, and Wilcox switched on the radio and invited her to tune it. She found some Mozart on Radio Three, and settled back in her seat.

"Like that sort of music, do you?" he said.

"Yes. Don't you?"

"I don't mind it."

"But you prefer Randy Crawford?" she said slyly, having spotted the empty cassette box in the dashboard recess.

Wilcox looked impressed, evidently supposing that she had identified by ear the snatch of song heard earlier that morning. "She's all right," he said guardedly.

'You don't find her a little bland?"

"Bland?"

"Sentimental, then."

"No," he said.

Somewhere on the outskirts of Manchester he pulled off the motorway and drove to a pub he knew for lunch. It was an undistinguished modern building situated on a roundabout next to a petrol station, but it had a restaurant attached to it done out in mock-Tudor beams and stained imitation oak furniture and enough reproduction antique brassware to stock a gift shop in Stratford-upon-Avon. Each table bore an electric lamp fashioned in the shape of a carriage lantern, with coloured glass panels. The menus were huge laminated cards that garnished every dish with epithets designed to tickle the appetite: "*succulent*", "*sizzling*", "*tender*", "*farm-fresh*", etc. The clientèle were

138

mostly businessmen in three-piece suits laughing boisterously and blowing cigarette smoke in each other's faces, or talking earnestly and confidentially to well-dressed young women who were more probably their secretaries than their wives. In short, it was the kind of establishment that Robyn would normally have avoided like the plague.

"Nice place, this," said Wilcox, looking around him with satisfaction. "What will you have?"

"I think I'll have an omelette," said Robyn.

Wilcox looked disappointed. "Don't stint yourself," he said. "Lunch is on the firm."

"All right," said Robyn. "I'll have a half of luscious avocado pear with tangy French dressing to start, and then I'll have golden-fried ocean-fresh scampi and a crisp farmhouse side salad. Oh, and a home-baked wholemeal roll coated with tasty sesame seeds."

If Wilcox perceived any irony in her pedantic recitation of the menu, he did not betray it. "Some chips as well?" he enquired.

"No thanks."

"Anything to drink?"

"What are you having?"

"I never drink in the middle of the day. But don't let that stop you."

Robyn accepted a glass of white wine. Wilcox ordered a mixture of Perrier water and orange juice to go with his succulent char-grilled rump steak and golden crisp french-fried potatoes. Few of the other diners were so abstemious – bottles of red wine cradled in wickerwork baskets, and bottles of white sticking up like missiles from enormous ice buckets, were much in evidence on or between the tables. Even without alcohol, though, Wilcox became relaxed, almost expansive over the meal.

"If you really want to understand how business works," he said, "you shouldn't be following me around, you should be shadowing somebody who runs his own small company, employing, say, fifty people. That's how firms like Pringle's begin. Somebody gets an idea of how to make something cheaper or better than anybody else, and sets up a factory with a small team of employees. Then if all goes well he takes on more labour and brings his sons into the business to take over when he retires. But either the sons aren't interested, or they think to themselves: why risk all our capital in this business, when we could sell out to a bigger company and invest the money in something safer? So the firm gets sold to a conglomerate like Midland Amalgamated, and some poor sod like me is brought in to run it on a salary."

"Late capitalism," said Robyn, nodding.

"What's late about it?"

"I mean, that's the era we're living in, the era of late capitalism." This was a term much favoured in *New Left Review*; post-modernism was said to be symbiotically related to it. "Big multinational corporations rule the world," she said.

"Don't you believe it," said Wilcox. "There'll always be small companies." He looked round the restaurant. "All the men in here are working for firms like Pringle's, and I bet there's not one of them who wouldn't rather be running his own business. A few of them will do it, and then, after a few years, they'll sell out, and the whole process starts again. It's the cycle of commerce," he said rather grandiloquently. "Like the cycle of the seasons."

"Would you prefer to be running your own business, then?"

"Of course."

When Robyn asked him what kind of business, he glanced around in a slightly conspiratorial fashion, and lowered his voice. "Tom Rigby – you remember, the general manager of the foundry – Tom and I have an idea for a little gadget, a kind of spectrometer, for giving instant readout of the chemical composition of the molten metal, straight onto the shop floor. If it worked, it would save having to take samples to the lab for analysis. Every foundry in the world would have to have one. Nice little business, that could be."

"Why don't you do it, then?"

"I have a mortgage, a wife and three idle children to support. Like most of these poor buggers."

Following Wilcox's sweeping glance at the other diners, Robyn observed how the deportment of the secretaries being entertained by their bosses had mutated under the influence of drink from a demure reserve over the starter to giggling irresponsibility by the time the dessert was served. She was less amused by their waiter's evident assumption that she herself was Wilcox's secretary, being set up for seduction. He referred to her throughout the meal as "the young lady", winked and smirked when Wilcox suggested another glass of wine, and recommended something "sweet and lovely" for dessert.

"I wish you'd drop a hint to that young man that I'm not your dolly-bird," Robyn said at last.

"What?" said Wilcox, so startled by the suggestion that he nearly choked on his portion of home-made orchard-fresh apple pie.

"Haven't you noticed the way he's carrying on?"

"I thought he was just queer. Waiters often are, you know."

"I think he's hoping for a big tip."

"He'll get a big surprise, then," said Wilcox grimly, and nearly bit the unfortunate waiter's head off when he urged them to round off their meal "with a *relaxing* liqueur". "Just coffee, and bring the bill with it," he growled. "I've got an appointment in Leeds at three."

Robyn was rather sorry that she had raised the subject, not so much for the waiter's sake as because Wilcox now relapsed into sulky silence, evidently feeling that he had somehow been compromised or made to look foolish. "Thanks for the meal," she said conciliatorily, though in truth the scampi had tasted of nothing except the oil in which they had been fried, and the cheesecake had glued her tongue to the roof of her mouth.

"Don't thank me," Wilcox said ungraciously. "It's all on expenses."

The drive over the still snow-covered wastes of the Pennines on the rolling M62 was spectacular. "Oh look, that's the way to Haworth!" Robyn exclaimed, reading a roadsign. "The Brontës!"

"What are they?" Wilcox asked.

"Novelists. Charlotte and Emily Brontë. Have you never read *Jane Eyre* and *Wuthering Heights*?"

"I've heard of them," said Wilcox guardedly. "Women's books, aren't they?"

"They're about women," said Robyn. "But they're not women's books in the narrow sense. They're classics – two of the greatest novels of the nineteenth century, actually." There must, she reflected, be millions of literate, intelligent people like Victor Wilcox walking about England who had never read *Jane Eyre* or *Wuthering Heights*, though it was difficult to imagine such a state of cultural deprivation. What difference did it make, never to have shivered with Jane Eyre at Lowick school, or throbbed in the arms of Heathcliff with Cathy? Then it occurred to Robyn that this was a suspiciously humanist train of thought and that the very word *classic* was an instrument of bourgeois hegemony. "Of course," she added, "they're often read simply as wish-fulfilment romances, *Jane Eyre* especially. You have to deconstruct the texts to bring out the political and psychological contradictions inscribed in them."

"Eh?" said Wilcox.

"It's hard to explain if you haven't read them," said Robyn, closing her eyes. The lunch, the wine, and the cushioned warmth of the car had made her drowsy, and disinclined to demonstrate an elementary deconstructive reading of the Brontës. Soon she dropped off to sleep. When she awoke, they were in the car park of Rawlinson and Co.

Another drab reception lobby, another interval spent leafing through trade magazines with titles like *Hydraulic Engineering* and *The Pump*, another walk down lino-tiled corridors behind a high-heeled secretary, another managing director rising from behind his polished executive desk to shake their hands and have Robyn's presence explained to him.

"Dr Penrose understands that everything we say is confidential," Wilcox said.

"If it's all right by you, Vic, it's all right by me," said Ted Stoker with a smile. "I've got nothing to hide." He sat down and plonked two hands the size of hams on the surface of his desk as if to prove the point. He was a tall, heavily-built man with a face composed of pachydermous folds and wrinkles from amongst which two small, pale and rheumy eyes looked out with lugubrious humour. "What can I do for you?"

"You sent us a letter," said Wilcox, taking a paper out of his briefcase.

"Yes, we did."

"I think there was a typing error in it," said Wilcox. "It says you're looking for a reduction of five per cent on our prices for cylinder blocks."

Stoker looked at Robyn and grinned. "He's a caution," he said, jerking his head in Wilcox's direction. "You're a caution, Vic," he repeated, turning back to Wilcox.

"There's no mistake?"

"No mistake."

"Five per cent is ridiculous."

Stoker shrugged his massive shoulders. "If you can't do it, there's others who can."

"What others?"

Stoker turned to Robyn again. "He knows I can't tell him that," he said, grinning with delight. "You know I can't tell you that, Vic."

Robyn acknowledged Stoker's asides with the thinnest of smiles. She didn't relish the role of stooge, but she couldn't quite see how to get out of it. Stoker was in control of this conversational game.

"Is it a foreign firm?" Wilcox said.

Stoker wagged his head slowly from side to side. "I can't tell you that either."

"I could bite the bullet and come down by two per cent on the four-bore," said Wilcox, after a pause.

"You're wasting your time, Vic."

"Two and a half."

Stoker shook his head.

"We've been doing business together for a long time, Ted," said Vic reproachfully.

"It's my duty to accept the lowest bid, you know that." He winked at Robyn. "He knows that."

"The quality won't be as good," said Wilcox.

"The quality is fine."

"You're already sourcing from them, then?" Wilcox asked quickly.

Stoker nodded, then looked as if he wished he hadn't. "The quality is fine," he repeated.

"Whoever it is can't be making any money out of it," said Wilcox.

"That's their problem. I have my own."

"Business not so good, eh?"

Ted Stoker addressed his answer to Robyn. "We sell a lot to the third world," he said. "Irrigation pumps, mostly. The third world is broke. The banks won't lend them any more money. Our Nigerian order book is down fifty per cent on last year."

"That's terrible," said Robyn.

"It is," said Ted Stoker. "We may have to go on to short time."

"I mean for the third world."

"Oh, the third world . . ." Stoker shrugged off the insoluble problems of the third world.

Wilcox was busy with his calculator while this conversation was going on. "Three per cent," he said, looking up. "That's my last offer. I just can't go any lower. Say yes to three per cent and I'll tear your arm off."

"Sorry, Vic," said Ted Stoker. "You're still two per cent adrift of what I'm offered elsewhere."

When they were back in the car, Robyn said, "Why were you doing those calculations if you were already prepared to come down by three per cent?"

"To fool him into thinking he'd pressured me into it, got himself a bargain. Not that it did fool him. He's a shrewd old bugger, is Ted Stoker."

"He didn't tell you who the other company were."

"I didn't expect him to. I just wanted to see his expression when I asked him."

"And what did it tell you?"

"He's not bluffing. There really is somebody offering four or five per cent below our price. More important, they're already supplying Rawlinson's. That means I can find out who they are."

"How?"

"I'll get a couple of our reps to sit in a car outside Rawlinson's and make a note of the name on every wagon that goes into the place. They can sit there all week if necessary. With a bit of luck we'll be able to find out who's delivering cylinder blocks and where from."

"Is it worth going to such lengths?" Robyn asked. "How much is this business actually worth?"

Wilcox thought for a moment. "Not all that much," he admitted. "But it's the principle of the thing. I don't like to be beaten," he said, pressing the accelerator so that the Jaguar surged forward with a squeal of tyres. "If the mystery supplier turns out to be Foundrax, I'll make Norman Cole rue the day."

"How?"

"I'll blast him. I'll attack his other customers."

"You mean assault them?" said Robyn, shocked.

Wilcox guffawed, the first full-blooded laugh she had heard from him. "What d'you think we are – the Mafia?"

Robyn flushed. His melodramatic talk of setting men to spy on Rawlinson's had misled her.

"No, I mean attack 'em with low prices," said Wilcox, "take his business away. Tit for tat, only our tit will be a lot more than his tat. He won't know what hit him."

"I don't see the point of all this jockeying and intriguing and undercutting," said Robyn. "No sooner do you get an advantage in one place than you lose it in another."

"That's business," said Wilcox. "I always say it's like a relay race. First you're ahead, then you drop the baton and someone else takes the lead, then you catch up again. But there's no finishing line. The race never ends."

"So who gains in the end?"

"The consumer gains," said Wilcox piously. "At the end of the day, somebody gets a cheaper pump."

"Why don't you – all of you, you and Norman Cole and Ted Stoker – why don't you put your heads together and *make* a cheaper pump instead of squabbling over a few per cent here or there?"

"What would happen to competition?" said Wilcox. "You've got to have competition."

"Why?"

"You've just got to. How did you get to where you are?"

"What?"

"How did you become a university lecturer? By doing better than other people in exams, right?"

"Actually, I'm opposed to competitive examinations," said Robyn.

"Yes, you would be," said Wilcox. "Having done all right out of them, you can afford to be."

This observation made Robyn angry, but she could not think of a satisfactory reply. "I'll tell you what it reminds me of, your precious competition," she said. "A lot of little dogs squabbling over bones.

Foundrax has stolen the Rawlinson's bone from you, so while they're chewing on that one you're going to steal another bone from them."

"We don't know it's Foundrax, yet," said Wilcox, ignoring the analogy. "Mind if I smoke?"

"I'd rather you didn't," said Robyn. "Could I have Radio Three on?"

"I'd rather you didn't," said Wilcox.

The rest of the journey passed in silence.

On the following Monday morning, Rupert Sutcliffe put his head round Robyn's door in the middle of a tutorial to say she was wanted on the telephone. As part of the economy drive, telephones capable of communicating with the outside world had been removed from the offices of all but the most senior members of the University, and consequently a good deal of expensive academic and secretarial time was wasted running up and down the corridor to and from the phone in the Department Office. Pamela, the Department Secretary, usually avoided interrupting a class, but apparently she wasn't in the office when this call came through, and Sutcliffe, who was, had thought fit to fetch Robyn. "It sounded important," he said to her in the corridor. "Somebody's secretary. I thought it might be your publisher." But it wasn't her publisher's secretary who spoke when she picked up the phone. It was Shirley.

"Mr Wilcox for you," she said. "I'm putting you through."

"It's Foundrax," Wilcox said, without any preliminaries. "I thought you'd like to know. Two of our reps sat in a car outside Rawlinson's for two days and a night, nearly froze to death they said, but they got the name on every wagon that went in. The likeliest was a Midlands firm called GTG. My transport manager used to work for them, luckily, so he gave his old mates a buzz and soon found out what they were delivering to Rawlinson's. Guess what? Four-bore cylinder blocks from Foundrax."

"Have you brought me to the phone just to tell me that?" Robyn enquired icily.

"Don't you have your own phone?"

"No, I don't. Furthermore, I was in the middle of a tutorial."

"Oh, sorry," said Wilcox. "Why didn't your secretary tell Shirley?"

"I don't have a personal secretary," said Robyn. "We have one secretary between fifteen of us, and she isn't in the office at the moment. She's probably in the store-room steaming open letters so we can re-use the envelopes. Is there anything else you'd like to know, or can I go back to my tutorial now?"

"No, that's all," said Wilcox. "I'll see you on Wednesday, then."

"Goodbye," said Robyn, and put the phone down. She turned to find that Philip Swallow had wandered into the office, holding a paper in his hand rather helplessly as if he were looking for Pamela.

"Hallo, Robyn," he said. "How are you?"

"Cross," she said. "That man Wilcox I'm supposed to be shadowing seems to think he owns me."

"Yes, it is depressing weather," Swallow said, nodding. "How's that shadow business going by the way? The VC was asking me only the other day."

"Well, it's going."

"The VC is looking forward to your report. He takes a personal interest in the scheme."

"Perhaps he'll take a personal interest in keeping me on, then," said Robyn. She smiled as she said this, from which Swallow evidently inferred that she had made a joke.

"Ha, ha, very good," he said. "I must remember to tell him that."

"I hope you will," said Robyn. "I must dash now, I'm in the middle of a tutorial."

"Yes, yes, of course," said Swallow. "*Tutorial*" was one of the words he still recognized without too much difficulty, perhaps because it had a lot of vowels in it.

When Robyn Penrose rang off, Vic Wilcox replaced the telephone receiver on its cradle slowly and deliberately, as if trying to convince some invisible observer that that was what he had intended to do. In fact, he prided himself on being a fast gun when it came to using the phone – quick to snatch up the instrument as soon as it rang, and the first to put it down when the conversation had served its purpose. He had a theory that this gave you a psychological advantage over a business adversary. Robyn Penrose wasn't a business adversary, but he didn't like the sensation of having been put in his place by her abrupt termination of his call. Somehow he had miscalculated, supposing that she would be as elated as himself at having solved the mystery of Rawlinson's supplier. He had expected congratulations and had received instead a flea in his ear.

He shook his head, as if he could physically dismiss these irritating thoughts, but they lingered, retarding his progress through the files on his desk. He tried to picture the context in which Robyn Penrose had received his call. Where was the telephone to which she had been called? How far had she walked to come to it? What would she have been doing in the tutorial? He could summon up only the vaguest images to answer these questions. Nevertheless, he began to develop some dim appreciation of why she might not have been overjoyed to receive his news. This did nothing to improve his humour. When Shirley brought him the fruits of that morning's dictation to sign he complained about the layout of one of the letters and told her to do it again.

"I always do quotations that way," she said. "You never complained before."

"Well, I'm complaining now," he said. "Just do it again, will you?"

Shirley went off muttering about some people being impossible to please. Then Brian Everthorpe, who had been off sick the previous Thursday and Friday, came huffing and puffing into Vic's office, having picked up a rumour about the Foundrax–Rawlinson's affair. Vic briefly filled him in.

"Why didn't you tell me you were going to see Ted Stoker?" he said. "I would have come with you."

"There wasn't time. I fixed it up on the spur of the moment, straight after seeing Norman Cole. Did it all through Shirley on the car phone. You weren't available," he lied, though it was a safe lie, since Brian Everthorpe seldom was available when you wanted him.

"Took your shadow with you, though, I hear," said Everthorpe.

"She happened to be with me at the time," said Vic. "It was her day."

"Sounds more like it was yours," said Everthorpe with a leer. "You're a dark horse, Vic."

Vic ignored this remark. "Anyway, as you gathered, we found out that Norman Cole is undercutting us on cylinder blocks at Rawlinson's by five per cent."

"How can he do it at that price?"

"I don't think he can for long."

"What are we going to do – go after him?"

"No," said Vic.

"No?" Everthorpe's bushy eyebrows shot up.

"We'd make ourselves look weak, fighting with Foundrax for the Rawlinson account. Like little dogs squabbling over a bone. Not much meat on the Rawlinson bone, when you work it out. Let Norman Cole have it. Let him choke on it."

"You're going to let him get away with poaching on our business?"

"I'll drop a hint that I know what his game is. That'll worry him. I'll let him twist in the wind a while."

"Looks to me like we're twisting in the wind."

"Then I'll hit him."

"With what?"

"I haven't decided yet."

"That doesn't sound like you, Vic."

"I'll let you know," said Vic coldly. "Feeling better, are you?"

"What?"

"Weren't you off sick last week?"

"Oh, yes! That's right." Brian Everthorpe's illness had evidently not engraved itself on his memory. "Touch of flu."

"I expect you've got a lot of work to catch up on, then." Vic opened a file to signify that the interview was over.

A little later he phoned Stuart Baxter and told him he wanted to let Brian Everthorpe go.

"Why, Vic?"

"He's no good. He's idle. He's stuck in old grooves. He doesn't like me and I don't like him."

"He's been with the company a long time."

"Exactly."

"He won't go without a fight."

"I'll enjoy that."

"He'll want a hefty golden handshake."

"It'll be money well spent."

Stuart Baxter was silent for a moment. Vic heard the rasp and snick of a cigarette lighter at the other end of the line. Then Baxter said, "I think you should give Brian a chance to adjust."

"Adjust to what?"

"To you, Vic, to you. It's not easy for him. I suppose you know he had hopes of your job?"

"I can't think why," said Vic.

Stuart Baxter sighed. Vic imagined plumes of smoke jetting from his nostrils. "I'll think about it," he said at last. "Don't do anything hasty, Vic."

For the second time that day Vic heard the click of a telephone receiver being put down before he was able to replace his own. He frowned at the instrument, wondering why Stuart Baxter was so protective towards Brian Everthorpe. Perhaps they were both Masons. Vic himself wasn't – he had been approached once, but couldn't bring himself to go through all the mumbo-jumbo of initiation.

Shirley came back into the office with the retyped letter. "Is that all right?" she said, with a surprisingly obsequious smile.

"That's fine," he said, scanning the document.

"I believe Brian mentioned to you his idea for a Pringle's calendar," she said, hovering at his shoulder.

"Yes," Vic said, "he did."

"He said you weren't keen."

"That's putting it mildly."

"It would be a great chance for Tracey," said Shirley wistfully.

"A great chance to degrade herself," said Vic, handing her the letter.

"What d'you mean?" said Shirley indignantly.

"You really want pictures of your daughter in the altogether stuck up on walls for anybody to look at?"

"I don't see the harm . . . What about art galleries?"

"Art galleries?"

"They're full of nudes. Old masters."

"That's different."

"I don't see why."

"You don't get blokes going into an art gallery and staring at a picture of Venus or whatever and nudging each other in the ribs saying, '*I wouldn't mind going through her on a Saturday night.*'"

"Ooh!" gasped Shirley, averting her face.

"Or taking the picture home to wank off with," Vic continued remorselessly.

"I'm not listening," Shirley said, retreating rapidly to her office. "I don't know what's got into you."

No more do I, Vic Wilcox thought to himself, feeling slightly ashamed of his outburst, as the door closed behind her. It was in fact several weeks before he realised that he was in love with Robyn Penrose.

2

The winter term at Rummidge was of ten weeks' duration, like the autumn and summer terms, but seemed longer than the other two because of the cheerless season. The mornings were dark, dusk came early, and the sun seldom broke through the cloud cover in the brief interval of daylight. Electric lights burned all day in offices and lecture rooms. Outside, the air was cold and clammy, thick with moisture and pollution. It drained every colour and blurred every outline of the urban landscape. You could hardly see the face of the clock at the top of the University's tower, and the very chimes sounded muffled and despondent. The atmosphere chilled the bones and congested the lungs. Some people attributed the characteristic adenoidal whine of the local dialect to the winter climate, which gave everybody runny noses and blocked sinuses for months on end and obliged them to go about with their mouths open like fish gasping for air. At this time of the year it was certainly hard to understand why human beings had ever settled and multiplied in such a cold, damp, grey place. Only work seemed to provide an answer. No other reason would make anyone come here, or having come, stay. All the more grim, therefore, was the fate of the unemployed of Rummidge and environs, condemned to be idle in a place where there was nothing much to do, except work.

Robyn Penrose was not unemployed – yet. She had plenty of work: her teaching, her research, her administrative duties in the Department. She had survived the previous winter by surrendering herself to work. She drove to and fro between her cosy little house and her warm, well-lit room at the University, ignoring the dismal weather. At home she read, she took notes, she distilled her notes into continuous prose on her word-processor, she marked essays; at the University she lectured, she gave seminars and tutorials, she counselled students, interviewed applicants, drew up reading-lists, attended committee meetings, and marked essays. Twice a week she played squash with Penny Black, a form of recreation unaffected by the climate – or, indeed, any other aspect of the environment: swiping and sweating and panting in the brightly lit cubic court down in the bowels of the Sports Centre one might have been anywhere – in Cambridge, or London, or the South of France. The steady grind of intellectual work, punctuated by brief explosions of indoor physical exercise – that was the rhythm of Robyn's first winter at Rummidge.

But this year the winter term was different. Every Wednesday she left her familiar milieu, and drove across the city (by a quicker and more direct route than she had followed on her first visit) to the factory in West Wallsbury. In a way she resented the obligation. It was a distraction from her work. There were always so many books, so many articles in so many journals, waiting to be read, digested, distilled and synthesised with all the other books and articles she had read, digested, distilled and synthesised. Life was short, criticism long. She had her career to think of. Her only chance of staying in academic life was to build up an irresistibly impressive record of research and publication. The Shadow Scheme contributed nothing to that – on the contrary, it interfered with it, taking up the precious one day a week she had kept free from Departmental duties.

But this irritation was all of the surface. The Shadow Scheme was something to grumble about, to Charles, to Penny Black, something handy to blame for getting behind with other tasks. At some deeper level of feeling and reflection she derived a subtle satisfaction from her association with the factory, and a certain sense of superiority over her friends. Charles and Penny led their lives, as she had done, wholly within the charmed circle of academia. She now had this other life on one day of the week, and almost another identity. The designation "Shadow", which had seemed so absurd initially, began to acquire a suggestive resonance. A shadow was a kind of double, a *Döppelgänger*, but it was herself she duplicated at Pringle's, not Wilcox. It was as if the Robyn Penrose who spent one day a week at the factory was the shadow of the self who on the other six days a week was busy with women's studies and the Victorian novel and post-structuralist literary theory – less substantial, more elusive, but just as real. She led a double life these days, and felt herself to be a more interesting and complex person because of it. West Wallsbury, that wilderness of factories and warehouses and roads and roundabouts, scored with overgrown railway cuttings and obsolete canals like the lines on Mars, itself seemed a shadowland, the dark side of Rummidge, unknown to those who basked in the light of culture and learning at the University. Of course, to the people who worked at Pringle's, the reverse was true: the University and all it stood for was in shadow – alien, inscrutable, vaguely threatening. Flitting backwards and forwards across the frontier between these two zones, whose values, priorities, language and manners were so utterly disparate, Robyn felt like a secret agent; and, as secret agents are apt to do, suffered occasional spasms of doubt about the righteousness of her own side.

"You know," she mused aloud to Charles one day, "there are millions of people out there who haven't the slightest interest in what we do."

"What?" he said, looking up from his book, and marking his place in it with his index finger. They were sitting in Robyn's study–living-room on another Sunday afternoon. Charles's weekend visits had become more frequent of late.

"Of course they don't *know* what we do, but even if one tried to explain it to them they wouldn't understand, and even if they understood what we were doing they wouldn't understand why we were doing it, or why anybody should pay us to do it."

"So much the worse for them," said Charles.

"But doesn't it bother you at all?" Robyn said. "That the things we care so passionately about – for instance, whether Derrida's critique of metaphysics lets idealism in by the back door, or whether Lacan's psychoanalytic theory is phallogocentric, or whether Foucault's theory of the episteme is reconcilable with dialectical materialism – things like that, which we argue about and read about and write about endlessly – doesn't it worry you that ninety-nine point nine per cent of the population couldn't give a monkey's?"

"A what?" said Charles.

"A monkey's. It means you don't care a bit."

"It means you don't give a monkey's fuck."

"Does it?" said Robyn, with a snigger. "I thought it was a monkey's nut. I should have known: 'fuck' is much more poetic in Jakobson's terms – the repetition of the 'k' as well as the first vowel in 'monkey' ... No wonder Vic Wilcox looked startled when I said it the other day."

"Did you pick it up from him?"

"I suppose so. Though he doesn't use that kind of language much, actually. He's a rather puritanical type."

"The protestant ethic."

"Exactly ... Now I've forgotten what I was saying."

"You were saying they don't go in much for poststructuralism at the factory. Hardly surprising, is it?"

"But doesn't it worry you at all? That most people don't give a ... damn about the things that matter most to us?"

"No, why should it?"

"Well, when Wilcox starts getting at me about arts degrees being a waste of money –"

"Does he do that often?"

"Oh yes, we argue all the time ... Anyway, when he does that, I find myself falling back on arguments that I don't really believe any more, like the importance of maintaining cultural tradition, and improving students' communicative skills – arguments that old fogies like Philip Swallow trot out at the drop of a hat. Because if I said we teach students about the perpetual sliding of the signified under the signifier, or the way every text inevitably undermines its own claim to a determinate meaning, he would laugh in my face."

"You can't explain poststructuralism to someone who hasn't even discovered traditional humanism."

"Precisely. But doesn't that make *us* rather marginal?"

There was a silence while Charles pondered this question. "Margins imply a centre," he said at length. "But the idea of a centre is precisely what poststructuralism calls into question. Grant people like Wilcox, or Swallow for that matter, the idea of a centre, and they will lay claim to it, justifying everything they do by reference to it. Show that it's an illusion, a fallacy, and their position collapses. We live in a decentred universe."

"I know," said Robyn. "But who pays?"

"Who pays?" Charles repeated blankly.

"That's always Wilcox's line. '*Who pays?*' '*There's no such thing as a free lunch.*' I expect he'd say there's no such thing as a free seminar on deconstruction. Why should society pay to be told people don't mean what they say or say what they mean?"

"Because it's true."

"I thought there was no such thing as truth, in the absolute sense."

"Not in the absolute sense, no." Charles looked exasperated. "Whose side are you on, Robyn?"

"I'm just being Devil's Advocate."

"They don't pay us all that much, anyway," said Charles, and resumed reading his book.

Robyn caught sight of the title, and pronounced it aloud: "*The Financial Revolution!* What on earth are you reading that for?"

"I told you, I'm going to write an article about what's going on in the City."

"Are you really? I'd no idea you were serious about that. Isn't it terribly boring?"

"No, it's very interesting, actually."

"Are you going to go and watch Basil's Debbie at work?"

"I might." Charles smiled his feline smile. "Why shouldn't I be a shadow too?"

"I didn't think you could ever get interested in business."

"This isn't business," said Charles, tapping his book. "It's not about buying and selling real commodities. It's all on paper, or computer screens. It's abstract. It has its own rather seductive jargon – arbitrageur, deferred futures, floating rate. It's like literary theory."

Pringle's was definitely a business dealing in real commodities and running it was not in the least like doing literary theory, but it did strike Robyn sometimes that Vic Wilcox stood to his subordinates in the relation of teacher to pupils. Though she could seldom grasp the detailed matters of engineering and accounting that he dealt with in his meetings with his staff, though these meetings often bored and wearied her, she could see that he was trying to *teach* the other men, to coax and persuade them to look at the factory's operations in a new way. He would have been surprised to be told it, but he used the Socratic method: he prompted the other directors and the middle managers and even the foremen to identify the problems themselves and to reach by their own reasoning the solutions he had himself already determined upon. It was so deftly done that she had sometimes to temper her admiration by reminding herself that it was all directed by the profit-motive, and that beyond the walls of Vic Wilcox's carpeted office there was a factory full of men and women doing dangerous, demeaning and drearily repetitive tasks who were mere cogs in the machine of his grand strategy. He was an artful tyrant, but still a tyrant. Furthermore, he showed no reciprocal respect for her own professional skills.

A typical instance of this was the furious argument they had about the Silk Cut advertisement. They were returning in his car from visiting a foundry in Derby that had been taken over by asset-strippers who were selling off an automatic core moulder Wilcox was interested in, though it had turned out to be too old-fashioned for his purpose. Every few miles, it seemed, they passed the same huge poster on roadside hoardings, a photographic depiction of a rippling expanse of purple silk in which there was a single slit, as if the material had been slashed with a razor. There were no words on the advertisement, except for the Government Health Warning about smoking. This ubiquitous image, flashing past at regular intervals, both irritated and intrigued Robyn, and she began to do her semiotic stuff on the deep structure hidden beneath its bland surface.

It was in the first instance a kind of riddle. That is to say, in order to decode it, you had to know that there was a brand of cigarettes called Silk Cut. The poster was the iconic representation of a missing name, like a rebus. But the icon was also a metaphor. The shimmering silk, with its voluptuous curves and sensuous texture, obviously symbolised the female body, and the elliptical slit, foregrounded by a lighter colour showing through, was still more obviously a vagina. The advert thus appealed to both sensual and sadistic impulses, the desire to mutilate as well as penetrate the female body.

Vic Wilcox spluttered with outraged derision as she expounded this interpretation. He smoked a different brand, himself, but it was as if he felt his whole philosophy of life was threatened by Robyn's analysis of the advert. "You must have a twisted mind to see all that in a perfectly harmless bit of cloth," he said.

"What's the point of it, then?" Robyn challenged him. "Why use cloth to advertise cigarettes?"

"Well, that's the name of 'em, isn't it? Silk Cut. It's a picture of the name. Nothing more or less."

"Suppose they'd used a picture of a roll of silk cut in half – would that do just as well?"

"I suppose so. Yes, why not?"

"Because it would look like a penis cut in half, that's why."

He forced a laugh to cover his embarrassment. "Why can't you people take things at their face value?"

"What people are you referring to?"

"Highbrows. Intellectuals. You're always trying to find hidden meanings in things. Why? A cigarette is a cigarette. A piece of silk is a piece of silk. Why not leave it at that?"

"When they're represented they acquire additional meanings," said Robyn. "Signs are never innocent. Semiotics teaches us that."

"Semi-what?"

"Semiotics. The study of signs."

"It teaches us to have dirty minds, if you ask me."

"Why d'you think the wretched cigarettes were called Silk Cut in the first place?"

"I dunno. It's just a name, as good as any other."

"'Cut' has something to do with the tobacco, doesn't it? The way the tobacco leaf is cut. Like 'Player's Navy Cut' – my uncle Walter used to smoke them."

"Well, what if it does?" Vic said warily.

"But silk has nothing to do with tobacco. It's a metaphor, a metaphor that means something like, 'smooth as silk'. Somebody in an advertising agency dreamt up the name 'Silk Cut' to suggest a cigarette that wouldn't give you a sore throat or a hacking cough or lung cancer. But after a while the public got used to the name, the word 'Silk' ceased to signify, so they decided to have an advertising campaign to give the brand a high profile again. Some bright spark in the agency came up with the idea of rippling silk with a cut in it. The original metaphor is now represented literally. But new metaphorical connotations accrue – sexual ones. Whether they were consciously intended or not doesn't really matter. It's a good example of the perpetual sliding of the signified under the signifier, actually."

Wilcox chewed on this for a while, then said, "Why do women smoke them, then, eh?" His triumphant expression showed that he thought

155

this was a knock-down argument. "If smoking Silk Cut is a form of aggravated rape, as you try to make out, how come women smoke 'em too?"

"Many women are masochistic by temperament," said Robyn. "They've learned what's expected of them in patriarchal society."

"Ha!" Wilcox exclaimed, tossing back his head. "I might have known you'd have some daft answer."

"I don't know why you're so worked up," said Robyn. "It's not as if you smoke Silk Cut yourself."

"No, I smoke Marlboros. Funnily enough, I smoke them because I like the taste."

"They're the ones that have the lone cowboy ads, aren't they?"

"I suppose that makes me a repressed homosexual, does it?"

"No, it's a very straightforward metonymic message."

"Metowhat?"

"Metonymic. One of the fundamental tools of semiotics is the distinction between metaphor and metonymy. D'you want me to explain it to you?"

"It'll pass the time," he said.

"Metaphor is a figure of speech based on similarity, whereas metonymy is based on contiguity. In metaphor you substitute something *like* the thing you mean for the thing itself, whereas in metonymy you substitute some attribute or cause or effect of the thing for the thing itself."

"I don't understand a word you're saying."

"Well, take one of your moulds. The bottom bit is called the drag because it's dragged across the floor and the top bit is called the cope because it covers the bottom bit."

"*I* told *you* that."

"Yes, I know. What you didn't tell me was that 'drag' is a metonymy and 'cope' is a metaphor."

Vic grunted. "What difference does it make?"

"It's just a question of understanding how language works. I thought you were interested in how things work."

"I don't see what it's got to do with cigarettes."

"In the case of the Silk Cut poster, the picture signifies the female body metaphorically: the slit in the silk is *like* a vagina –"

Vic flinched at the word. "So you say."

"All holes, hollow spaces, fissures and folds represent the female genitals."

"Prove it."

"Freud proved it, by his successful analysis of dreams," said Robyn. "But the Marlboro ads don't use any metaphors. That's probably why you smoke them, actually."

"What d'you mean?" he said suspiciously.

"You don't have any sympathy with the metaphorical way of looking at things. A cigarette is a cigarette as far as you are concerned."

"Right."

"The Marlboro ad doesn't disturb that naive faith in the stability of the signified. It establishes a metonymic connection – completely spurious of course, but realistically plausible – between smoking that particular brand and the healthy, heroic, outdoor life of the cowboy. Buy the cigarette and you buy the life-style, or the fantasy of living it."

"Rubbish!" said Wilcox. "I hate the country and the open air. I'm scared to go into a field with a cow in it."

"Well then, maybe it's the solitariness of the cowboy in the ads that appeals to you. Self-reliant, independent, very macho."

"I've never heard such a lot of balls in all my life," said Vic Wilcox, which was strong language coming from him.

"Balls – now that's an interesting expression . . ." Robyn mused.

"Oh no!" he groaned.

"When you say a man 'has balls', approvingly, it's a metonymy, whereas if you say something is a 'lot of balls', or 'a balls-up', it's a sort of metaphor. The metonymy attributes value to the testicles whereas the metaphor uses them to degrade something else."

"I can't take any more of this," said Vic. "D'you mind if I smoke? Just a plain, ordinary cigarette?"

"If I can have Radio Three on," said Robyn.

It was late by the time they got back to Pringle's. Robyn's Renault stood alone and forlorn in the middle of the deserted car park. Wilcox drew up beside it.

"Thanks," said Robyn. She tried to open the door, but the central locking system prevented her. Wilcox pressed a button and the locks popped open all round the car.

"I hate that gadget," said Robyn. "It's a rapist's dream."

"You've got rape on the brain," said Wilcox. He added, without looking at her: "Come to lunch next Sunday."

The invitation was so unexpected, and issued so off-handedly, that she wondered whether she had heard correctly. But his next words confirmed that she had.

"Nothing special," he said. "Just the family."

"Why?" she wanted to ask, if it wouldn't have sounded horribly rude. She had resigned herself to giving up one day a week to shadowing Wilcox, but she didn't want to sacrifice part of her precious weekends as well. Neither would Charles.

"I'm afraid I have someone staying with me this weekend," she said.

"The Sunday after, then."

"He stays most weekends, actually," said Robyn.

Wilcox looked put out, but after a moment's hesitation he said, "Bring him too, then."

To which there was nothing Robyn could say except, "All right. Thank you very much."

Vic let himself into the administration block. The solid wooden inner door was locked, as well as the glass swing doors. Only a low-wattage security light illuminated the reception lobby, making it look shabbier than ever. The office staff, including Shirley, had all gone home. So, it seemed, had the other directors.

He always liked being alone in the building. It was a good time to work. But this evening he didn't feel like working. He went into his office without switching on any lights, making his way by the dim illumination that filtered through the blinds from the car park. He slung the jacket of his suit over the back of his swivel chair, but instead of sitting down at the desk, he slumped into an armchair.

Of course, she was bound to have a boyfriend, a lover, wasn't she – an attractive, modern young woman like Robyn Penrose? It stood to reason. Why then had he been so surprised, why had he felt so . . . disappointed, when she mentioned the man who stayed with her at weekends? He hadn't supposed she was a virgin, for God's sake, not the way she talked about penises and vaginas without so much as a blush; nor that she was a lezzie, in spite of the cropped hair. But there was something about her that was different from the other women he knew – Marjorie, Sandra, Shirley and her Tracey. Dress, for instance. Whereas they dressed (or, in the case of Tracey, undressed) in a way which said, *Look at me, like me, desire, marry me*, Robyn Penrose turned herself out as if entirely for her own pleasure and comfort. Stylishly, mind – none of your women's lib regulation dungarees – but without a hint of coquetry. She wasn't forever fidgeting with her skirt or patting her hair or stealing glances at herself in every reflecting surface. She looked a man boldly in the eye, and he liked that. She was confident – arrogant at times – but she wasn't vain. She was the most independent woman he had ever met, and this had made him think of her as somehow unattached and – it was a funny word to float into his mind, but, well, *chaste*.

He recalled a painting he had seen once at the Rummidge Art Gallery, on a school outing – it must have been more than thirty years ago, but it had stuck in his memory, and arguing with Shirley the other day about nudes had revived it. A large oil painting of a Greek goddess and a lot of nymphs washing themselves in a pond in the middle of a wood, and some young chap in the foreground peeping at them from behind a bush. The goddess had just noticed the Peeping Tom, and was giving him a really filthy look, a look that seemed to come right out of the picture and subdue even the schoolboys who stared at it, usually all too ready to snigger and nudge each other at the sight of a female nude. For some reason the painting was associated in his mind with the word "chaste", and now with Robyn Penrose. He pictured her to himself in the pose of the goddess – tall, white-limbed, indignant, setting her dogs on the intruder. There was no place in the picture for a lover or husband – the goddess needed no male protector. That was how he had thought of Robyn Penrose, too, and she had said nothing to suggest the contrary until today, which had made it all the more upsetting.

Upsetting? What right or reason had he to feel upset about Robyn Penrose's private life? It's none of your business, he told himself angrily. Business is your business. He thumped his head with his own fists as if to knock some sense into it, or the nonsense out of it. What in God's name was he doing, the managing director of a casting and engineering company with a likely deficit this month of thirty thousand pounds, sitting in the dark, woolgathering about Greek goddesses? He should be at his desk, working on the plan to computerise stock and purchasing.

Nevertheless he remained slumped in his armchair, thinking about Robyn Penrose, and about having her to lunch next Sunday. It had been an unpremeditated act, that had surprised himself almost as much as it had evidently surprised her. Now he regretted it. He should have taken the opportunity, when she mentioned her boyfriend, to let the matter drop. Why had he persisted – why, for God's sake, had he invited the boyfriend too, whom he hadn't the slightest wish to meet? He was sure to be another highbrow, without Robyn Penrose's compensating attractions. The lunch would be a disaster: the certainty of this pierced him like a self-administered dagger-blow. It would be the first worry to rush into his head tomorrow morning, and every morning until Sunday. And his anxiety would communicate itself to Marjorie, who always got into a panic anyway when they were entertaining. She would probably drink too much sherry out of nervousness and burn the dinner or drop the plates. Then imagine her making small talk with Robyn Penrose – no, it was too painful to imagine. What would they discuss? The semiotics of loose covers? Metaphor and metonymy in wallpaper patterns? While his father entertained the boyfriend with the retail price index for 1948, and his children sneered and sulked on the sidelines in their usual fashion? The social nightmare he had conjured up so appalled him that he seriously contemplated phoning Robyn Penrose at once to cancel the invitation. He could easily invent an excuse – a forgotten engagement for next Sunday, say. But that would only be a postponement. Having pressed the invitation upon her, he would have to go through with it, and the sooner it was got over with, the better. Probably Robyn Penrose felt the same way.

Vic literally writhed in his armchair as he projected the likely consequences of his own folly. He loosened his collar and tie, and kicked off his shoes. He felt stifled – the central heating was set far too high considering the building was empty (and even in the throes of his private anxieties he made a mental note to have the thermostat turned down at night – it could save hundreds on the energy bill). He closed his eyes. This seemed to calm him. His mind went back over the argument with Robyn Penrose in the car, about Silk Cut. She was clever, you had to admit, even if her theories were half-baked. A vagina indeed! Admittedly, some people did call it a slit sometimes. And clit of course was like *slit* and *cut* run together . . . *Silk slit clit cut cunt* . . . Silk Cunt . . . That was one she hadn't thought of! Nice name for a packet of fags. Vic smiled faintly to himself as he dropped off.

He woke oppressed with a sense that he had made a terrible mistake about something, and immediately he remembered what it was: inviting Robyn Penrose to lunch next Sunday. At first he thought he must be in bed at five o'clock in the morning, but his clothes and his posture in the armchair soon reminded him where he was. He sat up stiffly and yawned. He glanced at his watch, pressing the button to illuminate the digital display. Nine twenty-three. He must have been asleep for nearly two hours. Marjorie would be wondering where the hell he was. Better phone her.

As he got to his feet and moved towards the desk he was arrested by a strange, muffled sound. It was very faint, but his hearing was sharp, and the building otherwise totally quiet. It seemed to be coming from the direction of Shirley's office. Still in his socks, he moved stealthily across the carpeted floor and through the communicating anteroom into Shirley's office. This was dark, save for the light seeping through the blinds from the car park, and quite empty. The sound, however, was slightly more audible here. There was nothing particularly sinister about a noise at this time of night, but Vic was curious to identify it. Perhaps one of the other directors was working late after all. Or it might be the security man, though usually he only patrolled the outside of the buildings, and in any case why would he be talking or moaning to himself? For that was what the noise sounded like – indistinguishable human speech or someone moaning with pain or –

Suddenly he knew what the sound was, and where it was coming from – from the reception lobby on the other side of the partition wall, with its painted-over windows. His eye flew to the spyhole scratched in the paint, where a spot of light shone faintly like an old penny. Quietly and carefully he placed a chair so that he could climb onto the filing cabinet immediately below the hole. Even as he did so he recalled how he had spied on Robyn Penrose on her first visit, and realised with a guilty pang why he associated her with the picture in the Rummidge Art Gallery: he himself was the Peeping Tom in the foreground. He wondered if perhaps he was dreaming and whether, when he applied his eye to the spyhole, he would see Robyn Penrose, with the robes of a classical goddess slipping from her marbly limbs, glaring indignantly back at him.

What he actually saw, by the dim illumination of the security light, was Brian Everthorpe copulating with Shirley on the reception lobby sofa. He couldn't see Everthorpe's face, and the broad bum going up and down like a piston under his shirt tails between Shirley's splayed legs could have belonged to anyone, but he recognised the sideboards and the bald spot on the top of his head. He could see Shirley's face very clearly. Her eyes were shut and her mouth was open in a dark red O. It was Shirley who was making the noise Vic had heard. He climbed down quietly and carefully from the filing cabinet, went back into his own office and shut the connecting doors. He sat in his armchair and covered his ears.

He hadn't been dreaming, but he went about for the next few days as if he was in a dream. Marjorie remarked on his more than usually abstracted state. So did Shirley, whose eyes he dared not meet when she came into his office the morning after he had watched her and Brian Everthorpe making love. A lot of things had clicked into place when he set eyes on that tableau, a lot of puzzles had been cleared up: why Brian Everthorpe always seemed to know so much, so quickly, about what was going on at Pringle's, and why he had taken such a personal interest in the forwarding of Tracey's career as a model. How long the affair had been going on he had no way of knowing, but there had been something about Shirley's joyful abandonment that suggested it wasn't the first time Brian Everthorpe had had her on the reception lobby sofa. They were taking an extraordinary risk doing it there; though, on reflection, if the building was empty and the inner door of the entrance locked, they were fairly safe from interruption except by the security man, and no doubt Everthorpe had squared him. They must have come into the building by the back door from a restaurant or pub after Vic himself had fallen asleep in his office, or perhaps they had been holed up in Everthorpe's office waiting for everyone else to leave.

Presumably they preferred the reception lobby to Everthorpe's office because of the sofa. Or perhaps the greater danger of discovery there added an extra excitement to their amours.

He had a sense of being on the edge of depths and mysteries of human behaviour he had never plumbed himself, and brooded on them with mixed feelings. He didn't approve of what Everthorpe and Shirley were up to. He'd never had any time for hanky-panky between married folk, especially when it was mixed up with work. By rights he ought to be feeling a virtuous indignation at their adultery and considering how he could use his knowledge to get rid of the pair of them. And yet he felt no such inclination. The fact was that he was ashamed of his own part in the episode. He could tell no one, including the culprits, about what he had witnessed without evoking the ludicrous and ignoble picture of himself standing in the dark in his socks on top of the filing cabinet, squinting through a peephole in the partition wall. And beyond that consideration was another, even more painful to contemplate. In spite of the fact that they were an unglamorous pair of lovers, Brian Everthorpe fat and balding, and Shirley past her prime, with double chin and dyed hair; in spite of the incongruous setting and undignified half-undressed state in which they had coupled, Everthorpe's trousers and underpants and Shirley's skirt, knickers and tights tossed carelessly over the tables and chairs and copies of *Engineering Today*; in spite of all that, it couldn't be denied that they had been transported by genuine passion. It was a passion Vic himself had not experienced for a very long time, and he was doubtful whether Marjorie ever had. Certainly his lovemaking had never drawn from Marjorie the cries of pleasure that had carried to his ears through a partition wall and across the space of two offices. Vic had never imagined that he would envy Brian Everthorpe anything, but he did now. He envied him the full-blooded fucking of a passionate woman, and the woman's full-throated hurrahs. It was a kind of defeat, and with the bitter taste of it in his mouth, he had no spirit to visit retribution on Brian Everthorpe. Vic did not speak to Stuart Baxter again about letting Everthorpe go.

The scene in the lobby replayed itself again and again in his head like a film – not one of the carefully edited and soft-focused bedroom scenes you saw on late-night television, but more like the peep-show he had watched once in a sordid booth in Soho in a moment of furtive curiosity, feeding 50p pieces into the machine to keep the flickering jerking naked figures in motion. Again and again he saw Brian Everthorpe's heaving buttocks, Shirley's splayed white knees, her red lips rounded in that O of pleasure, her long painted nails digging into Everthorpe's shoulders so hard Vic could see the indentations – though

162

it was difficult in retrospect to distinguish what he had witnessed from what his overheated imagination had reconstructed. Sometimes he wondered whether he hadn't been dreaming after all, whether the whole episode wasn't a fantasy that had passed through his head as he dozed in his office armchair. He made a surreptitious examination of the reception lobby sofa, looking for corroborating evidence. He observed a few stains that could have been either semen or milky coffee, and discovered a crinkly black filament that might have been a pubic hair or a fibre from the upholstery, before a curious glance from one of the receptionists moved him on.

The approach of Sunday and its lunch did nothing to calm his state of mind. He badgered Marjorie continually about the menu, requesting a lamb joint rather than beef because it wouldn't suffer so much if she overcooked it, and requiring her to specify exactly what vegetables she proposed to serve. He expressed a preference for apple crumble for dessert rather than the less reliable lemon meringue pie which was Marjorie's other staple pudding. And he insisted on having a starter.

"We never have a starter," said Marjorie.

"There's always a first time."

"What's got into you, Vic? Anybody would think the Queen was coming."

"Don't be stupid, Marjorie. Starters are quite normal."

"In restaurants they may be. Not at home."

"In Robyn Penrose's home," said Vic, "they'd have a starter. I'd take a bet on it."

"If she's as stuck up as that –"

"She's not stuck up at all."

"I thought you didn't like her, anyway. You complained enough."

"That was at the beginning. We got off on the wrong foot."

"So you do like her, then?"

"She's all right. I don't like her or dislike her."

"Why invite her to lunch, then? Why make all this fuss?"

Vic was silent for a moment. "Because she's interesting, that's why," he said at length. "You can have an intelligent conversation with her. I thought it would make a change. I'm sick to death of our Sunday lunches, with the children squabbling and Dad wittering on about the cost of living and –" He cut short an unkind reflection on Marjorie's conversational accomplishments, and concluded limply, "I just thought it would make a change."

Marjorie, who had a cold, blew her nose. "What d'you want, then?"

"Eh?"

"For your precious starter."

"I don't know. I'm not a cook."

"And I'm not a starter cook."

"You don't have to cook starters. They can be raw, can't they? Have melon."

"You can't get melon at this time of year."

"Well, something else then. Smoked salmon."

"Smoked salmon! Do you know what it costs?"

"You don't usually care how much anything costs."

"*You* do, though. And so does your Dad."

Vic contemplated his father's likely comments on the price of smoked salmon, and withdrew the suggestion. "Avocado pear," he said, remembering that Robyn had seemed to enjoy this at the restaurant near Manchester. "You just cut it in half, take out the stone and fill the hole with oil and vinegar."

"Your Dad won't like it," said Marjorie.

"He needn't eat it, then," said Vic impatiently. He began to worry about the wine. It would have to be red to go with the lamb, of course, but should he get some white to go with the avocado and if so how dry should it be? Vic was no wine connoisseur, but he had somehow convinced himself that Robyn's boyfriend was, and would sneer at his choices.

"I could use those glass dishes I got in the Sales for the avocados," Marjorie conceded. This idea seemed to please her, and she accepted the idea of a starter.

"And tell Raymond I don't want him walking in from the pub in the middle of lunch this Sunday," said Vic.

"Why don't you tell him yourself?"

"He listens to you."

"He listens to me because you won't talk to him."

"I'd only lose my temper."

"You should make an effort, Vic. You don't talk to any of us. You're that wrapped up in yourself."

"Don't start on me," he said.

"I've lent him the money, any road."

"What money?"

"For their demo tape. For the band." Marjorie looked defiantly at him. "It's my own money, from my Post Office account."

At another time, in another mood, Vic would have had a blazing row with her. As it was, he merely shrugged and said, "More fool you. Don't forget paper serviettes."

Marjorie looked blank.

"For Sunday."

"Oh! I always have serviettes when we have guests."

"Sometimes we run out," said Vic.

Marjorie stared at him. "I've never known you give a second's thought to serviettes in your life before," she said. In her pale, tranquillised eyes, he saw, like something stirring indistinctly under water, a flicker of fear, a shadow of suspicion; and realised for the first time that she had grounds for these feelings.

3

Half of Vic's apprehension about the Sunday lunch was relieved when Robyn rang on the Saturday morning to say her boyfriend, Charles, had a cold, and wouldn't be coming to Rummidge that weekend after all. She herself arrived rather late, and they sat down at table almost immediately. There were paper serviettes at every place setting and, reposing in blue-tinted glass dishes, halves of avocado pear. These last excited much wonderment and derision from the children.

"What's this?" Gary demanded, sticking a fork into his half, and lifting it into the air.

"It's avocado, stupid," said Sandra.

"It's a starter," said Marjorie.

"We don't usually have a starter," said Raymond.

"Ask your father," said Marjorie.

All looked at Vic, including Robyn Penrose, who smiled, as if she recognised that the avocado was his personal tribute to her sophistication.

"I thought it would make a change," Vic said gruffly. "Don't eat it if you don't want to."

"Is it a fruit or a veg?" said his father, poking doubtfully at his portion.

"More like a vegetable, Dad," said Vic. "You pour oil and vinegar dressing into the hole and eat it with a spoon."

Mr Wilcox scooped out a small spoonful of the yellow flesh and nibbled it experimentally. "Queer sort of taste," he said. "Like candle-grease."

"They cost five pounds each, Grandad," said Raymond.

"What!"

"Take no notice, Dad, he's having you on," said Vic.

"I wouldn't give you five pee for them, to be honest with you," said his father.

"They taste much nicer with the vinaigrette, Mr Wilcox," said Robyn. "Won't you try some?"

"No thanks, love, olive oil doesn't agree with me."

"Gives you the squits, does it, Grandad?" said Gary.

"You're so vile, Gary," said Sandra.

"Aye, it does, lad," said Mr Wilcox. "We used to call 'em the back-door trots when I was a lad. That's because –"

"We know why, Dad, or we can guess," Vic interrupted him with

166

an apologetic glance at Robyn, but she seemed to be amused rather than offended by this exchange. He began cautiously to relax.

Thanks to Robyn, the meal was not the social minefield he had feared. Instead of talking a lot herself and making the family feel ignorant, she drew them out with questions about themselves. Raymond told her about his band and Sandra told her about hairstyling and Gary told her about computer games and his father told her about how he and Vic's mother had married on thirty-five bob a week and hadn't considered themselves poor. Whenever the old man looked like getting onto the subject of "the immigrants", Vic managed to head him off by some provocative remark about the cost of living. Only Marjorie had defeated Robyn's social skills, absorbing all her questions with monosyllabic murmurs or faint, abstracted smiles. But that was Marjorie for you. She always kept herself in the background, or in the kitchen, when they had guests. But she'd served up a cracking good dinner, apart from the avocados, which were underripe and rather hard.

The nearest approach to a snag in the smooth running of the proceedings came when Robyn tried to take a hand in washing-up after the meal, and Marjorie strongly resisted. For a moment there was a polite struggle of wills between the two women, but in the end Vic arranged a compromise by taking charge of the operation himself, conscripting the children to help. He proposed a short walk afterwards before it got dark, but Marjorie excused herself on the grounds that it was too cold, Raymond went off to rehearse with his mates in somebody's garage, Sandra curled up in front of the telly with an emery board to manicure her nails and watch *Eastenders*, and Gary implausibly pleaded a prior commitment to homework. Mr Wilcox agreed to come out, but when Vic returned to the lounge after completing the washing up, he was asleep and snoring faintly in an armchair. Vic didn't wake him, or make any effort to persuade the other members of the family. A walk with Robyn on her own was what he had been secretly hoping for.

"I'd no idea your children were so grown-up," she said, as soon as they were clear of the house.

"We've been married twenty-three years. We started a family straight away. Marjorie was only too glad to give up work."

"What work was that?"

"Typing pool."

"Ah."

"Marje is no intellectual," said Vic, "as you probably noticed. She left school without any O-Levels."

"Does that bother her?"

"No. It bothers me, sometimes."

"Why don't you encourage her to do a course of some kind, then?"

"What – O-Levels? Marjorie? At her time of life?" His laughter rang out in the cold air, harsher than he had intended.

"It doesn't have to be O-Level. There are extra-mural courses she could do, or WEA. And the Open University has courses you can follow without doing the examinations."

"Marjorie wouldn't be up to it," said Vic.

"Only because you've made her think she isn't," said Robyn.

"Rubbish! Marjorie's perfectly content. She has a nice house, with an *en suite* bathroom and four lavatories, and enough money to go shopping whenever she feels like it."

"I think that's an unbelievably patronising thing to say about your own wife," said Robyn Penrose.

They walked on in silence for a while, as Vic considered how to respond to this rebuke. He decided to let it pass.

He led Robyn by an aimless route through the quieter residential streets. It was a cold, misty afternoon, with a low red sun glowing through the branches of the leafless trees. They met few other people: a lone jogger, a couple with a dog, some disconsolate-looking African students waiting at a bus stop. At every intersection, marking the nocturnal passage of marauding vandals, uprooted traffic bollards lay on their sides, with all their wiring exposed.

"It's my kids who should be worrying about getting qualifications," said Vic. "Raymond dropped out of university last year. Failed his first-year exams and the resits."

"What was he doing?"

"Electrical Engineering. He's clever enough, but never did any work. And Sandra says she doesn't want to go to university. Wants to be a hairdresser, or 'hairstylist', as they call it."

"Of course, hair is very important in youth culture today," Robyn mused. "It's a form of self-expression. It's almost a new form of art."

"It's not a serious job, though, is it? *You* wouldn't do it for a living."

"There are lots of things I wouldn't do. I wouldn't work in a factory. I wouldn't work in a bank. I wouldn't be a housewife. When I think of most people's lives, especially women's lives, I don't know how they bear it."

"Someone has to do those jobs," said Vic.

"That's what's so depressing."

"But Sandra could do something better. I wish you'd talk to her, about going to university."

"Why should she take any notice of me?"

"She won't take any notice of *me*, and Marjorie isn't interested. You're nearer her age. She'd respect your advice."

"Does she know I shall probably be out of a job next year?" Robyn asked. "Not much of an advertisement for the academic life, is it? She'd probably make much more money out of hairdressing."

"Money isn't –" Vic pulled himself up.

"Everything?" Robyn completed his sentence, with arched eyebrows. "I never thought to hear you say that."

"I was going to say, money isn't something she understands," he lied. "None of my kids do. They think it comes out of the bank like water out of a tap – or it could if mean old Dad didn't keep his thumb over the spout."

"The trouble is, they've had it too easy. They've never had to work for their living. They take everything for granted."

"Right!" Vic agreed enthusiastically, then saw, too late, by her expression, that she was parodying him. "Well, it's true," he said truculently.

Their stroll had brought them to the landscaped site of the University's halls of residence, and Robyn proposed that they should turn in through the gates and walk round the lake.

"It's private, isn't it?" said Vic.

"Don't worry, I know the password," she said, mocking him again. "No, of course it's not. Anyone can walk around."

In the winter dusk the long buildings, backlit by a red sunset, looked like great liners at anchor, their lighted windows mirrored in the dark surface of the lake. A frisbee flew back and forth like a bat between a group of tracksuited young men, who shouted each other's names as they threw. A couple stood on a curved wooden bridge throwing crusts to a splashing, fluttering throng of ducks and Canadian geese.

"I like this place," said Robyn. "It's one of the University's few architectural successes."

"Very nice," Vic agreed. "Too nice for students, if you ask me. I never did understand why they had to have these massive three-star hotels built especially for them."

"They've got to live somewhere."

"Most of 'em could live at home and go to their local colleges. Like I did."

"But leaving home is part of the experience of going to university."

"And a very expensive part, too," said Vic. "You could build a whole polytechnic for the price of this little lot."

"Oh, but polytechnics are such ghastly places," said Robyn. "I was interviewed for a job at one once. It seemed more like an overgrown comprehensive school than a university."

"Cheap, though."

"Cheap and nasty."

"I'm surprised you defend this élitist set-up, considering your left-wing principles." He gestured at the handsome buldings, the well-groomed grassy slopes, the artificial lake. "Why should my workers pay taxes to keep these middle-class youths in the style to which they're accustomed?"

"The universities are open to everyone," said Robyn.

"In theory. But all those cars in the car park back there – who do they belong to?

"Students," Robyn admitted. "I agree, our intake is far too middle-class. But it needn't be. Tuition is free. There are grants for those who need them. What we need to do is to motivate more working-class children to go to university."

"And kick out the middle-class kids to make room?"

"No, provide more places."

"And more landscaped halls of residence, with artificial lakes and ducks on them?"

"Why not?" said Robyn defiantly. "They enhance the environment. Better these halls than another estate of executive houses with Georgian windows, or is it Jacobean now? Universities are the cathedrals of the modern age. They shouldn't have to justify their existence by utilitarian criteria. The trouble is, ordinary people don't understand what they're about, and the universities don't really bother to explain themselves to the community. We have an Open Day once a year. Every day ought to be an open day. The campus is like a graveyard at weekends, and in the vacations. It ought to be swarming with local people doing part-time courses – using the Library, using the laboratories, going to lectures, going to concerts, using the Sports Centre – everything." She threw out her arms in an expansive gesture, flushed and excited by her own vision. "We ought to get rid of the security men and the barriers at the gates and let the people in!"

"It's a nice idea," said Vic. "But it wouldn't be long before you'd have graffiti sprayed all over the walls, the toilets vandalised and the Bunsen burners nicked."

Robyn let her arms fall back to her sides. "Who's being élitist now?"

"I'm just being realistic. Give the people polytechnics, with no frills. Not imitation Oxford colleges."

"That's an incredibly condescending attitude."

"We live in the age of the yob. Whatever they don't understand, whatever isn't protected, the yobs will smash, and spoil it for everybody else. Did you notice the traffic bollards on the way here?"

"It's unemployment that's responsible," said Robyn. "Thatcher has created an alienated underclass who take out their resentment in crime and vandalism. You can't really blame them."

"You'd blame them if you were mugged going home tonight," said Vic.

"That's a purely emotive argument," said Robyn. "But of course you support Thatcher, don't you?"

"I respect her," said Vic. "I respect anybody with guts."

"Even though she devastated industry round here?"

"She got rid of overmanning, restrictive practices. She overdid it, but it had to be done. Any road, my dad will tell you there was worse unemployment here in the thirties, and much worse poverty, but you didn't get youths beating up old-age pensioners and raping them, like you do now. You didn't get people smashing up roadsigns and telephone booths just for the hell of it. Something's happened to this country. I don't know why, or exactly when it happened, but somewhere along the line a lot of basic decencies disappeared, like respect for other people's property, respect for the old, respect for women —"

"There was a lot of hypocrisy in that old-fashioned code," said Robyn.

"Maybe. But hypocrisy has its uses."

"The homage vice pays to virtue."

"What?"

"Somebody said hypocrisy was the homage vice pays to virtue. Rochefoucauld, I think."

"He had his head screwed on, whoever it was," said Vic.

"You put it down to the decline of religion, then?" said Robyn, with a slightly condescending smile.

"Maybe," said Vic. "Your universities may be the cathedrals of the modern age, but do you teach morality in them?"

Robyn Penrose paused for thought. "Not as such."

As if on cue, a church bell began to toll plangently in the distance.

"Do you go to church, then?" she asked.

"Me? No. Apart from the usual – weddings, funerals, christenings. What about you?"

"Not since I left school. I was rather pious at school. I was confirmed. That was just before I discovered sex. I think religion served the same psychological purpose – something very personal and private and rather intense. Do you believe in God?"

"What? Oh, I don't know. Yes, I suppose so, in a vague sort of way." Vic, distracted by Robyn's casual reference to her discovery of sex, was unable to focus his mind on theological questions. How many lovers had she had, he wondered. "Do you?"

"Not the patriarchal God of the Bible. There are some rather interesting feminist theologians in America who are redefining God as female, but they can't really get rid of all the metaphysical baggage of Christianity. Basically I suppose I think God is the ultimate floating signifier."

"I'll buy that," said Vic, "even though I don't know what it means."

Robyn laughed. "Sorry!"

But Vic didn't resent her high-flown language. That she used it unselfconsciously in conversation with him, whereas she had spoken normal English to the rest of the family, he took as a kind of compliment.

When they returned to the house, Robyn declined to take off her coat and have a cup of tea. "I must be getting back," she said. "I have a lot of work to do."

"On a Sunday, love?" Mr Wilcox protested.

"I'm afraid so. Marking essays, you know. I'm always behind. Thanks for the lovely lunch," she said to Marjorie, who gave a watery smile in acknowledgement. "Sandra – your father wants me to talk to you about the advantages of a university education."

"Oh, does he?" said Sandra, with a grimace.

"Perhaps you'd like to come and see me in the University one day?"

"All right," said Sandra, with a shrug. "I don't mind."

Vic longed to box his daughter's ears or pull her hair or smack her bottom, or better still, to do all three at once. "Say thank you, Sandra," he said.

"Thanks," she said sullenly.

Vic saw Robyn to her car. "Sorry about my daughter's manners," he said. "It's the Yobbish Tendency."

Robyn dismissed the matter with a laugh.

"I'll see you Wednesday, then," said Vic.

"All being well," she said, getting into her car.

Vic went back into the lounge. His father was alone in the room, thirstily sipping hot tea from the saucer. "Nice young wench, that," he observed. "What she call herself Robin for? Boy's name, innit?"

"It can be a girl's. They spell it with a 'y'."

"Oh-ah. Wears her hair like a boy's too. Not one of them . . . you know, is she?"

"I don't think so, Dad. She's got a boyfriend, but he couldn't come today."

"I just wondered, seein' as how she's one o' them university dongs."

"Dons."

"Well, whatever. You get all kinds at them places."

"What do you know about universities, Dad?" Vic said, amused.

"I seen films on the telly. All sorts of queer folk, carrying on with each other something chronic."

"You don't want to believe everything you see on television, Dad."

"Aye, you're right there, son," said Mr Wilcox.

When she got home, Robyn telephoned Charles. "How are you?" she said. He said he was fine. "What about your cold?" she said. It hadn't materialised, he said. "Beast," said Robyn, "I believe you made it up, just to get out of lunch at the Wilcoxes." How had it been, Charles asked, not denying the accusation.

"All right. You would have been bored stiff."

"But you weren't?"

"It was quite interesting to me to see Wilcox in his domestic setting."

"What was the house like?"

"Luxurious. Hideous taste. They actually have that reproduction of the black girl with the green complexion in the lounge. And the fireplace is unbelievable. It's one of those multicoloured rustic stone affairs, stretching all the way up to the ceiling, with all sorts of nooks and crannies for ornaments. Just to look at it makes you want to coil a rope round your waist and start scaling it. Of course they've got one of those *trompe l'oeil* gas fires, logs that burn from everlasting to everlasting, plus, would you believe, a set of antique brass fire-irons. It's like something by Magritte." She felt slightly ashamed, hearing herself going on on this Cambridgey way, but something inhibited her from telling Charles about the rather interesting conversation she had had with Vic Wilcox on their walk. It was easier to entertain him with amusing domestic vignettes of the Rummidge bourgeoisie. "Oh, and they've got four loos," she added.

"Did you have to go that often?" Charles giggled on the other end of the line.

"The old grandfather told me in a stage whisper. He was a bit of a racist, but otherwise rather sweet."

"What about the rest of the family?"

"Well, I couldn't get much out of Mrs. She seemed to be scared stiff of me."

"Well, you are rather scaring, Robyn."

"Nonsense."

"I mean to women who aren't intellectual. Did you talk a lot about literary theory?"

"Of course I didn't, what d'you take me for? I talked to everybody about their interests, but I couldn't discover what her interests were. Perhaps she hasn't got any. She seemed to me the classic downtrodden housewife whose occupation's gone once the children are grown up. The whole scene was like a Freudian sit-com, actually. The eldest son is still working through his Oedipus complex at the age of 22, by the look of it, and Wilcox has repressed incestuous feelings for his daughter which are displaced into constant nagging."

"Did you tell him that?"

"Are you joking?"

"Teasing," said Charles.

"Actually, I did tell him I thought he was oppressing his wife."

"And how did he take that?"

"I thought he was going to lose his temper, but he didn't."

"Ah, Robyn," Charles sighed along the line from Ipswich. "I wish I had your confidence."

"What do you mean?"

"You're a born teacher. You go around the world putting people straight, and instead of resenting it, they're grateful."

"I'm not sure Vic Wilcox was grateful," said Robyn. She sneezed suddenly and violently. "Damn. You may not have a cold, but I think I have."

When Robyn Penrose didn't turn up at the appointed hour on the following Wednesday, Vic was surprised to find how much her absence disturbed him. He was unable to concentrate on chairing a meeting with the sales staff, and was corrected several times by his financial director over figures, much to the delight of Brian Everthorpe. At 10.30, after the meeting had broken up, he phoned Robyn's Department at the University, and was informed that she didn't normally come in on a Wednesday. He phoned her home number. It had rung about fifteen times, and he was just about to put the receiver down, when Robyn's voice croaked, "Hallo?"

She had a cold, probably flu. She sounded extremely cross. She had been asleep, she said.

"Then I'm sorry I disturbed you. But as you didn't send a message . . ."

"I don't have a bedside phone," she said. "I've come all the way downstairs to answer this call. You seem to make a habit of making inconvenient phone calls."

"I'm sorry," said Vic, mortified. "Go back to bed. Take some aspirin. Do you need anything?"

"Nothing except peace and quiet." She rang off.

Later in the day Vic arranged for a basket of fruit to be delivered by Rummidge's major department store, but phoned again almost immediately to cancel the order on reflecting that, to receive it, Robyn would have to get out of bed and go downstairs again.

The following Wednesday she returned, looking a little pale, a mite thinner perhaps, but recovered from the flu. Vic could not repress a grin of pleasure as she came through the door. Somehow, Robyn Penrose had changed, in the space of a few weeks, from being a nuisance and a pain in the neck, to being the person of all his acquaintance he was most glad to see. He counted the days between her visits to Pringle's. His weeks pivoted on Wednesdays rather than weekends. When Robyn was shadowing him he was aware that he performed particularly well. When she was absent he played to her imagined presence and silent applause. She was someone to whom he could confide his plans and hopes for the company, work through his problems and refine the solutions. He couldn't trust any of his staff with such speculative thoughts, and Marjorie wouldn't have had a clue what he was on about. Robyn didn't understand all the fine detail, but her quick wit soon grasped the general principles, and her detachment made her a useful judge. It was Robyn who had made him see the futility of a tit-for-tat policy towards Foundrax. He'd heard on the grapevine that Foundrax was having cash-flow problems – hardly surprising if they were supplying Rawlinson's at a loss. He would just wait for Foundrax to pull out, or fold altogether, then resume negotiations with Ted Stoker for a reasonable price. Brian Everthorpe didn't approve of this waiting game, but then he wouldn't, would he?

Vic tried not to think too much about Brian Everthorpe rogering Shirley on the reception lobby sofa. Having Robyn Penrose around helped with that, too. Her youthful complexion and lissom figure made Shirley look raddled and overblown in comparison. Shirley was jealous of Robyn, that was plain to see, and Brian Everthorpe was piqued by his inability to decide whether Vic was taking advantage of the situation. He was forever throwing out innuendoes about the intimate relationship between a man and his shadow. When Robyn let slip that her temporary post at the University was called "Dean's Relief", he could hardly contain his glee. "What about an MD's Relief, eh Vic?" he said. "No need to slip round to Susan's Sauna, then, for a spot of executive's tonal treatment, eh? Have it laid on." If Robyn had shown any sign of being bothered by this, Vic would have taken Everthorpe aside and told him to leave it out; but she reponded with stony indifference, and Vic wasn't averse to keeping Everthorpe guessing whether he and Robyn Penrose were having an affair, ridiculous as the idea was. Ridiculous, yet there was a kind of pleasure to be got from letting it float idly in the stream of one's thoughts, driving to and from work. He played Jennifer Rush a lot on the car stereo these days: her voice – deep, vibrant, stern, backed by a throbbing, insistent rhythm accompaniment – moved him strangely, enclosing his daydreaming in a protective wall of sound. She sang:

> *There's no need to run away*
> *If you feel that this is for real,*
> *'Cause when it's warm and straight from the heart,*
> *It's time to start.*

She sang:

> *Surrender! It's your only chance, surrender!*
> *Don't wait too long to realise*
> *That her eyes will say, 'Forever'.*

He played the cassette so often that he learned the lyrics by heart. The track he liked best was the last one of side two, "The Power of Love":

> *'Cause I am your lady*
> *And you are my man,*
> *Whenever you reach for me,*
> *I'll do all that I can.*
> *We're heading for something,*
> *Somewhere I've never been,*
> *Sometimes I am frightened,*
> *But I'm ready to learn*
> *About the power of love.*

One day, after sitting through a series of meetings with junior management about rationalising the company's operations, Robyn asked him whether he intended to explain the grand strategy to the workers as well. It hadn't occurred to Vic to do so, but the more he thought about the idea, the more he was taken with it. The men tended to see everything in terms of their own little bit of the factory's operations, and automatically assumed that any change in their work-patterns was an attempt by management to screw more work out of them without giving them more pay. Of course, this was broadly true. Given the bad old work practices the industry had inherited from the nineteen-sixties, it had to be. But if he could explain that the changes related to an overall plan, which would mean greater security and prosperity for everybody in the long term, he would be more likely to get their co-operation.

Vic went to see his Personnel Director about it. George Prendergast was sitting crosslegged on the floor in the middle of his office, with his hands on his knees.

"What are you doing?" Vic demanded.

"Breathing," said Prendergast, getting to his feet. "Yoga breathing exercises for my Irritable Bowel Syndrome."

"You look daft, if you don't mind my saying so."

"It helps, though," said Prendergast. "Your Shadow suggested it."

"Did she teach you herself?" Vic felt, absurdly, something like a stab of jealousy.

"No, I go to evening classes," said Prendergast.

"Yes, well, I should keep it to evening classes, if I was you," said Vic. "Don't want you levitating in the middle of the factory, it might be distracting for the operatives. And speaking of them, I've got a suggestion."

Prendergast was enthusiastic about the idea. "Worker education is very important these days," he said. "Dialogue between management and shop-floor is the name of the game." Prendergast was a graduate in Business Studies, and was fond of this sort of jargon.

"There won't be much dialogue about it," said Vic. "I'll give a speech, and tell 'em what we're going to do."

"Won't there be questions?"

"If there are, you can answer them."

"Perhaps I could arrange small group discussions at work stations afterwards," said Prendergast.

"Don't overdo it, we're not running an evening institute. Just set up a series of lunchtime meetings in the old transport shed, will you? Say three hundred at a time? Starting next Wednesday." He specified Wednesday so that Robyn Penrose would be present at the inaugural meeting.

Brian Everthorpe was sceptical about the idea, naturally, claiming that it would only unsettle the men and make them suspicious. "They won't thank you for taking up half their lunch hour, either."

"Attendance will be voluntary," said Vic, "except for directors."

Everthorpe's face fell. "You mean, we've got to be there at every meeting?"

"It's no use my banging on to the men about all pulling together if they know my directors are down at the Man in the Moon knocking back pints while I'm talking."

The following Wednesday, at one o'clock, Vic sat on a makeshift platform in the old transport shed, a gloomy hangar-like building, obsolete since the company started contracting out its transportation requirements, which was now used for large meetings on the factory site when the canteen was not available. He was flanked by his directors, sitting on moulded plastic chairs. A few rows of chairs and benches had been arranged on the floor, facing the platform, and he was surprised to see Shirley as well as Robyn sitting there. The mass of the audience stood in a great crowd behind these seats, beneath a haze of cigarette smoke and condensing breath. Though Vic had ordered the wall heaters to be turned on that morning, the atmosphere was still damp and chilly. His directors were sitting in their overcoats, but Vic was just in his suit, which he regarded as a kind of uniform that went with his job. He rubbed his hands together.

"I think I'll start," he muttered to Prendergast, who was sitting beside him.

"Do you want me to introduce you?"

"No, they all know who I am. Let's get on with it. It's perishing in here."

He felt an unaccustomed spasm of nervousness as he stood up and stepped forward to the microphone that had been set up, with a couple of portable speakers, at the front of the platform. A hush fell over the assembly. He scanned their faces – expectant, sullen, quizzical – and wished he had prepared some joke to take the tension out of the moment. But he had never been one for jokes – he forgot funny stories five minutes after he'd been told them, perhaps because he seldom found them funny.

"You're supposed to start speeches with a joke," he began. "But I don't have one. I'll be honest with you: running this company is no joke." They laughed a little at that, so it seemed that he had broken the ice after all. "You all know me. I'm the boss. You may think I'm like God in this place, that I can do what I like. I can't. I can't do anything at all on my own."

He grew in confidence as he went on. The men listened to him attentively. There were only a few faces in the audience that looked thoroughly bored and mystified. Then, just as he was hitting his stride, all the faces broke into broad grins. There were cheers, hoots, shrill whistles and much laughter. Vic, who was not conscious of having said anything funny, faltered in his speech and stopped. He looked round and saw a young women advancing towards him, obviously deranged because she was in her underwear. She was shivering from the cold, and her arms and shoulders were covered in goosepimples, but she smiled at him coyly.

"Mr Wilcox?" she said.

"Go away," he said. "This is a meeting."

"I have a message for you," she said, flexing a leg sheathed in a fishnet stocking, and taking a folded paper out of her garter.

The crowd cheered. "Show us yer tits!" someone shouted. Another yelled, "Tek yer knickers off!"

The girl smiled and waved nervously at the audience. Behind her head Brian Everthorpe's grinning face bobbed like a red balloon.

"OFF, OFF, OFF!" roared the crowd.

"Get out of here!" Vic hissed.

"It won't take long," said the girl, unfolding the piece of paper. "Be a sport."

Vic grabbed her by the arm, intending to bustle her off the stage, but such a whoop went up that he let go as if he had been burned. Inclining her head towards the mike, the girl began to sing:

"Pringle bells, Pringle bells, Pringle all the day,
Oh what fun it is to work the Victor Wilcox way!
Oh, Pringle bells —"

"Marion," said Robyn Penrose, who had suddenly appeared just below the front of the platform. "Stop that at once."

The girl looked down at her with blank astonishment. "Doctor Penrose!" she exclaimed. She thrust the message into Vic's hands, turned on her high heels, and fled.

"Hey, let's hear the rest of it!" Brian Everthorpe called after her. The audience hissed and groaned as the girl disappeared through a small door at the back of the shed. Robyn Penrose said to Vic, "Why don't you carry on?" and hastened after the girl before Vic could enquire into the magical power she seemed to have over her.

He tapped on the mike for attention. "As I was saying . . ." The men guffawed good-naturedly, and settled to hear him out.

After the meeting had dispersed, Vic found Robyn sitting in his office, reading a book.

"Thanks for getting rid of the girl," he said. "Know her, do you?"

"She's one of my students," said Robyn. "She has no grant and her parents won't pay for her maintenance, so she has to work."

"You call that work?"

"I disapprove of its sexist aspects, naturally. But it's quite well-paid, and it doesn't take up too much of her time. It's called a kisso-gram, apparently. She didn't get as far as the kiss today, of course."

"Thank Christ for that," said Vic, throwing himself in his swivel chair and taking out his cigarettes. "Or rather, thank *you*."

"It could have been worse. There's also something called a gorilla-gram."

"It was bad enough. Another minute, and the meeting would've collapsed."

"I could see that," said Robyn. "That's why I intervened."

"You saved my bacon," said Vic. "Can I buy you a drink and a sandwich? Haven't got time for a proper lunch, I'm afraid."

"A sandwich will be fine. Thanks. Marion was worried that she wouldn't get paid because she didn't finish the job. I said you'd make it up to her if necessary."

"Oh, you did, did you?"

179

"Yes." Robyn Penrose held him with her cool, grey-green eyes.

"All right," he said. "I'll pay her double if she can find out who set me up."

"I asked her that," said Robyn. "She said the customer's name is confidential. Only the boss of the agency knows. Have you no idea?"

"I have my suspicions," he said.

"Brian Everthorpe?"

"Right. It has his fingerprints all over it."

Vic did not take Robyn to the Man in the Moon or the King's Head, where they would be likely to meet his colleagues. Instead he drove a little further, to the Bag o' Nails, a quaint old pub built on ground riddled with disused mineshafts and subject to chronic subsidence which had twisted every line of the building out of true. Doors and windows had been re-made in the shape of rhomboids to fit the distorted frames, and the floor sloped so steeply you had to hang on to your glass to prevent it from sliding off the table.

"This is fun," said Robyn, looking about her as they sat down near the open fire. "I feel drunk already."

"What will you have?" he asked.

"Beer, I think, in a place like this. Half a pint of best bitter."

"And to eat?"

She glanced at the bar menu. "Ploughman's Lunch with Stilton."

He nodded approval. "They do a nice ploughman's here."

When he came back from the bar with their drinks, he said, "I've never bought draught bitter for a woman before."

"Then you must have had a very limited experience of life," she said, smiling.

"You're dead right," he replied, without returning the smile. "Cheers." He took a long swallow of his pint. "Sometimes when I'm lying awake in the small hours, instead of counting sheep, I count the things I've never done."

"Like what?"

"I've never skied, I've never surfed, I've never learned to play a musical instrument, or speak a foreign language, or sail a boat, or ride a horse. I've never climbed a mountain or pitched a tent or caught a fish. I've never seen Niagara Falls or been up the Eiffel Tower or visited the Pyramids. I've never . . . I could go on and on." He had been about to say, *I've never slept with a woman other than my wife*, but thought better of it.

"There's still time."

"No, it's too late. All I'm fit for is work. It's the only thing I'm any good at."

"Well, that's something. To have a job you like and be good at it."

"Yes, it's something," he agreed, thinking that in the small hours it didn't seem enough; but he didn't say that aloud either.

A silence fell. Robyn seemed to feel the need to break it. "Well," she said, looking round the pub, "Wednesdays won't be the same when term ends."

Alarm bells rang in Vic's head. "When's that then?"

"Next week."

"*What?* But Easter's weeks off!"

"It's a ten-week term," said Robyn. "This is week nine. I must say it's flown by."

"I don't know how you people justify your long holidays," he grumbled, to cover his dismay. Although he had always known the Shadow Scheme had a limited time-span, he had avoided calculating exactly when it would end.

"The vacations are not holidays," she said hotly. "You ought to know that. We do research, and supervise it, as well as teach under-graduates."

The arrival of their food excused him from answering. Robyn tucked into her ploughman's with relish. Vic took out his diary. "You've only got one more week, then?" he said. "It says here that I'm going to Frankfurt next Wednesday. I'd forgotten that."

"Oh well," she said. "In that case *this* is my last week. So let me buy you another drink."

"No it isn't," he said. "You have to come with me to Frankfurt."

"I can't," she said.

"It's only two days. One night."

"No, it's impossible. I have a lot of classes on a Thursday."

"Cancel them. Get somebody else to do them for you."

"That's easier said than done," she said. "I'm not a professor, you know. I'm the most junior member of staff."

"It's the terms of the Shadow Scheme," he said. "You have to follow me around all the time, for one day a week. If I happen to be in Frankfurt that day, then so must you."

"What are you going for?"

"There's a big machine-tool exhibition. I'm seeing some people who make automatic core blowers – I'm going to buy a new one instead of messing about with second-hand. It would be interesting for you. No dirty factories. We'd stay in a posh hotel. Get taken out for meals." It had suddenly become a matter of the greatest urgency and importance that Robyn Penrose should accompany him to Frankfurt. "They have restaurants on river boats," he said enticingly. "On the Rhine."

"The Main, isn't it?"

"The Main, then. I never was much good at geography."

"Who would pay my fare?"

"Don't worry about the fare. If your University won't pay, we will."

"Well, I'll see," said Robyn. "I'll think about it."

"I'll get Shirley to make reservations for you this afternoon."

"No, don't do that. Wait."

"They can always be cancelled," he said.

"I really don't think I can come," said Robyn.

Driving home later that afternoon, Robyn noticed that there was still some light left in the sky. In fact the streetlamps were only just coming on, each slender metal stalk tipped with a rosy blush that briefly preceded the yellow sodium glare. For a few moments these fairy lights bestowed a fragile beauty on the soiled tarmac, concrete and brick of West Wallsbury. Usually it was quite dark when she drove home from Pringle's. But it was the middle of March now. Spring was approaching, even if you couldn't feel it in the air. So, thank God, was the Easter vacation. Only one more week of nonstop preparation, lecturing, tutoring, marking. Interesting as it was, you could only keep up the pace for so long – rushing breathlessly from one literary masterpiece to another, from one group of anxious, eager, needy students to another. Besides, she was itching to get back to *Domestic Angels and Unfortunate Females*, which she'd hardly looked at this term, partly because of the Shadow Scheme. Not that she regretted her involvement in that, especially now that it was drawing to a close. It had been an interesting experience, and she had the satisfaction of knowing that she'd done a good PR job. From being hostile and bullying at the outset, Vic Wilcox had become, in the space of a couple of months, friendly and confiding, positively glad to see her at the factory on Wednesday mornings, and patently dismayed at the imminent termination of the Shadow Scheme. Once again she had proved herself invaluable. If Vic Wilcox was going to write a report too, she ought to come out of it well.

Robyn permitted herself a complacent smile, recalling the way she had despatched Marion Russell earlier that day, Vic's gratitude, and his eager insistence that she should accompany him to Frankfurt. That might be fun, actually, she reflected. Frankfurt was not a name that set the pulses racing, but she had never been there – in fact she hadn't been anywhere outside England for the past two years, so preoccupied had she been first with getting a job, then with trying to hang on to it. She felt a sudden pang of appetite for travel, the bustle of airports, the novelty of foreign tongues and foreign manners, clanging tramcars and pavement cafés. Spring might have already arrived in Frankfurt. But no, it wasn't possible. Thursday was a heavy teaching day for her, including two groups of the Women's Writing seminar, the most important classes of the week as far as she was concerned. She knew from experience that it would be impossible to find alternative hours at which all the students concerned could attend, such were the labyrinthine complexities and infinite permutations of their personal timetables. And no one else in the Department was qualified to take these classes, even if they were willing to do so, which was unlikely. A pity. It would have been a nice break.

Robyn had made up her mind. Mentally she registered her regret, sealed her decision, and filed it away, with a memo to phone Vic Wilcox the next day.

Later that evening she received a surprising phone call from Basil. He said he was phoning from his office after everyone else had gone home. He sounded a little, but only a little, drunk.

"Have you seen Charles recently?" he asked.

"No, not very recently," she said. "Why?"

"Have you two split up, then?"

"No, of course not. He just hasn't been over lately. First he had a cold or thought he did, and then I had flu . . . what are you on about, Basil?"

"Did you know he's been seeing Debbie?"

"Seeing her?"

"Yes, *seeing* her. You know what I mean."

"I knew he was going to watch her at work."

"He's done more than that. He spent the night with her."

"You mean, he stayed in her house?"

"Yes."

"So what? He probably took her out to dinner and missed his last train and she put him up."

"That's what Debbie says."

"Well, then."

"You don't find it suspicious?"

"Of course not." The only thing she found slightly disturbing about the story was that Charles had said nothing about it to her on the telephone, but she did not admit this to Basil.

"Suppose I told you it happened twice."

"Twice?"

"Yes, once last week, and again last night. Missing one train is unfortunate, missing two looks suspicious, wouldn't you say?"

"How do you know all this, Basil? I thought you and Debbie never saw each other in midweek."

"Last Tuesday I phoned her at ten o'clock in the evening and Charles answered the phone. And last night I followed them."

"You *what*?"

"I knew he was up in town again, researching his stupid article or whatever it is. After work I followed them. First they went to a wine bar and then I saw them go into Debbie's house. I waited until the lights went out. The last light to go out was Debbie's bedroom."

"Well, it would be, wouldn't it?"

"Not necessarily. Not if he was sleeping in the guest room."

"Basil, you're being paranoid."

"Even paranoids have unfaithful girlfriends."

"I'm sure there's some perfectly simple explanation. I'll ask Charles – I'm seeing him this weekend."

"Well, that's a relief, anyway."

"Why?"

"Debbie claims she's going to stay with her parents this weekend. I was beginning to wonder. What do you women see in Charles anyway? He seems a cold fish to me."

"I don't want to discuss Charles' attractions with you, Basil," said Robyn, and rang off.

A little later, Charles rang. "Darling," he said, "do you mind terribly if I don't come this weekend after all?"

"Why?" Robyn said. To her surprise and annoyance she found she was trembling slightly.

"I want to write up my article on the City. There's a chap I knew at Cambridge who works for *Marxism Today* and he's really interested."

"You're not going to visit Debbie's mother, then?"

There was a brief, surprised silence. "Why should I want to do that?" Charles said.

"Basil just phoned me," said Robyn. "He says you stayed overnight with Debbie. Twice."

"Three times, actually," said Charles coolly. "Is there any reason why I shouldn't?"

"No, of course not. I just wondered why you hadn't mentioned it."

"It didn't seem important."

"I see."

"To tell you the truth, Robyn, I thought you were a teeny-weeny bit jealous of Debbie, and I didn't see the point of aggravating your hostility."

"Why should I be jealous of her?"

"Because of all the money she makes."

"I don't give a monkey's fuck how much money she makes," said Robyn evenly.

184

"She's been extraordinarily helpful to me over this article. That's why I've been staying with her – to talk at leisure. It's impossible while she's working – it's pandemonium in the dealing room. Unbelievable."

"You didn't sleep with her, then?"

Another pregnant pause. "Not in the technical sense, no."

"What do you mean, in the technical sense?"

"Well, I gave her a massage."

"You gave her a massage?" A vivid and unwelcome image presented itself to Robyn's consciousness, of Debbie's skinny, naked body squirming with pleasure under Charles' oily fingers.

"Yes. She was very tense. It's the nature of her work, of course, continuous stress . . . She suffers from migraines . . ."

While Charles was describing Debbie's symptoms, Robyn rapidly reviewed various questions of a casuistical nature. Did a masssage, their kind of massage, constitute infidelity, if administered to a third party? Could there, in fact, *be* infidelity between herself and Charles?

"I don't really want to know all these details," she said, interrupting him in mid-sentence. "I just wanted to get the basic facts straight. You and I have had an open relationship, with no strings, since I moved to Rummidge."

"That's what I thought," said Charles. "I'm glad to hear you confirm it."

"But Basil doesn't see things the same way."

"Don't worry about Basil. Debbie can handle Basil. I think she was a bit pissed off with him, actually. He tends to be over-possessive. I expect she was using me to make a point."

"You don't mind being used?"

"Well, I'm using her, in a way. For researching my article. And how are things with you?" he said, trying rather obviously to change the subject.

"Fine. I'm going to Frankfurt next week." She uttered this thought without premeditation, as it blossomed irresistibly in her head.

"Really! How's that?"

"The Shadow Scheme. Vic Wilcox is going to a trade fair on Wednesday, so I have to go with him."

"Well, that should be quite fun."

"Yes, that's what I thought."

"How long will you stay?"

"Just one night. In a posh hotel, Vic says."

"Shall I come over the weekend after that?"

"No, I don't think so."

"All right. You're not angry or anything, are you?"

"Of course not." She laughed rather shrilly. "I'll phone you."

"Oh, right." He sounded relieved. "Well, enjoy yourself in Frankfurt."

"Thanks."

"What will you do about your teaching, while you're away?"

"I'll ask Swallow's advice," she said. "After all, this shadow business was his idea."

The next morning, after her ten o'clock lecture, Robyn knocked on Philip Swallow's door and asked if he could spare a few minutes.

"Yes, yes, come in," he said. He held a thick stencilled document in his hand and wore a haggard look. "You don't know what 'virement' means, I suppose?"

"Sorry, no. What's the context?"

"Well, this is a paper on resources for the next meeting of Principals and Deans. '*At present, resources are allocated to each Department for separate heads of expenditure without the possibility of virement.*'"

Robyn shook her head. "I've no idea. I've never come across the word before."

"Neither had I before the cuts. Then it suddenly started appearing on all kinds of documents – committee papers, working party reports, UGC circulars. The VC is particularly fond of it. But I still don't know what it means. It's not in the *Shorter Oxford Dictionary*. It's not in any of my dictionaries."

"How very peculiar," said Robyn. "Why don't you ask somebody who would know? The writer of that paper, for instance."

"The Bursar? I can't ask *him*. I've been sitting on committees with the Bursar for months solemnly discussing virement. I can't admit *now* that I have no idea what it means."

"Perhaps no one knows what it means, but they're afraid to admit it," Robyn suggested. "Perhaps it's a word invented by the Government to terrorise the universities."

"It certainly sounds nasty enough," said Philip Swallow. "*Virement* . . ." He stared unhappily at the stencilled document.

"The reason I wanted to see you . . ." Robyn prompted.

"Oh, yes, sorry," said Philip Swallow, wrenching his attention away from the mystery word.

"It's about the Shadow Scheme," she said. "Mr Wilcox, the man I'm shadowing, is going to Frankfurt on business next Wednesday and he thinks I ought to go with him."

"Yes, I know," said Swallow. "He's been on the phone to me this morning."

"Has he?" Robyn tried to conceal her surprise.

186

"Yes. We've agreed that the University will pay half your expenses and his firm the other half."

"You mean, I can go?"

"He was very insistent that you should. He seems to take the terms of the Shadow Scheme very literally."

"What shall I do about my teaching on Thursday?" Robyn said.

"Oh, it's the usual rather heavy German cuisine," said Philip Swallow. "Pork and dumplings and sauerkraut, you know."

"No, my *teaching* on *Thursday*," Robyn said more loudly. "What shall I do about it? I'd rather not cancel classes in the last week of term."

"Quite," said Swallow, rather sharply, as if she had been responsible for the misunderstanding. "I've been looking at your timetable. You have quite a lot of teaching, don't you?"

"Yes, I do," said Robyn, pleased that he had noticed this.

"The ten o'clock lecture you can swap with one Bob Busby was going to give next term in the same course. And I'm going to ask Rupert Sutcliffe to take the third-year tutorial at three . . ." Robyn nodded, wondering who would be most dismayed by this news, Sutcliffe or the students. "The difficult ones are the two Women's Writing seminars at twelve and two," Swallow said. "There seems to be only one member of staff free at those hours. Me."

"Oh," said Robyn.

"What is the topic, actually?"

"The female body in contemporary women's poetry."

"Ah. I don't know a lot about that, I'm afraid."

"The students will have prepared reports," said Robyn.

"Well, of course, I don't mind just chairing a discussion, if that would . . ."

"That would be fine," said Robyn. "Thank you very much."

Swallow escorted her to the door. "Frankfurt," he said wistfully. "I attended a very lively conference there once."

FIVE

"Some persons hold," he pursued, still hesitating, "that there is a wisdom of the Head, and that there is a wisdom of the Heart. I have not supposed it so; but, as I have said, I mistrust myself now. I have supposed the head to be all-sufficient. It may not be all-sufficient; how can I venture this morning to say it is!"

Charles Dickens: *Hard Times*

1

It was, perhaps, inevitable that Victor Wilcox and Robyn Penrose would end up in bed together in Frankfurt, though neither of them set off from Rummidge with that intention. Vic was conscious only of wanting to have Robyn's company, and to give her a treat. Robyn was conscious only of wanting to be treated, and to be whisked away from her routine existence for an interval, however brief. But subconsciously other motives were in play. Vic's growing interest in Robyn was on the point of ripening into infatuation. Robyn's cool handling of Charles's relationship with Debbie concealed wounded pride, and she was ready to assert her own erotic independence. The trip to a foreign city, safe from the observation of friends and family, provided the perfect alibi, and a luxury hotel the perfect setting, for an *affaire* whose time had come. It hardly needed the extra incitements of the drama of the Altenhofer negotiations, Robyn's susceptibility to champagne, or the hotel disc-jockey's penchant for Jennifer Rush. As Robyn herself might have said, the event was over-determined.

Vic picked up Robyn from her house at 6.30 and drove swiftly through slumbering suburbs to the airport, with her silent and still half-asleep beside him. While he parked the car, she had a cup of coffee and started to come to life. It was her first time in Rummidge Airport. The new-looking terminal impressed her with its stainless-steel and fibreglass surfaces, its vaulted roof, its electronic databoard announcing departures to half the capitals of Europe. Built (so Vic informed her) with the help of a grant from the EEC, it seemed like an interface between the scruffy, depressed English Midlands and a more confident, expansive world. Burly Rummidge businessmen toting overnight bags and burgundy leather briefcases with digital locks checked in nonchalantly for their flights to Zurich, Brussels, Paris, Milan, as if they did so every day of the week.

"Smoking or non-smoking?" the British Airways checker asked Vic, who hesitated and glanced at Robyn.

"I don't mind," she said accommodatingly.

"Non-smoking," he decided. "I can do without fags for an hour and a half."

Only an hour and a half! If one had the money, then, one could rise at six and be in Germany in time for breakfast. Quite a lot of money, though – she sneaked a look at her ticket and was appalled to see that the fare was £280·00. Breakfast was included, however. They were travelling Club Class, and attentive stewardesses served them with a compote of apricots and pears, scrambled eggs and ham, rolls, croissants and coffee, and Dundee marmalade in miniature stoneware jars. Robyn, whose rare flights were undertaken on the cheapest tickets available, and usually spent sitting next to the lavatories in the bucking tail of the plane, trying to eat a trayful of tasteless pap with her knees under her chin, relished the standard of service. "You businessmen do yourselves proud," she said.

"Well, we deserve it," said Vic with a grin. "The country depends on us."

"My brother Basil thinks the country depends on merchant bankers."

"Don't talk to me about the City," said Vic. "They're only interested in short-term profits. They'd rather make a fast buck in foreign markets than invest in British companies. That's why our interest rates are so high. This machine I want will take three years to pay for itself."

"I never did understand stocks and shares," said Robyn. "And after listening to Basil, I'm not sure I want to."

"It's all paper," said Vic. "Moving bits of paper about. Whereas we *make* things, things that weren't there till we made 'em."

Sunlight flooded the cabin as the plane changed course. It was a bright, clear morning. Robyn looked out of the window as England slid slowly by beneath them: cities and towns, their street plans like printed circuits, scattered over a mosaic of tiny fields, connected by the thin wires of railways and motorways. Hard to imagine at this height all the noise and commotion going on down there. Factories, shops, offices, schools, beginning the working day. People crammed into rush-hour buses and trains, or sitting at the wheels of their cars in traffic jams, or washing up breakfast things in the kitchens of pebble-dashed semis. All inhabiting their own little worlds, oblivious of how they fitted into the total picture. The housewife, switching on her electric kettle to make another cup of tea, gave no thought to the immense complex of operations that made that simple action possible: the building and maintenance of the power station that produced the electricity, the mining of coal or pumping of oil to fuel the generators, the laying of miles of cable to carry the current to her house, the digging and smelting and milling of ore or bauxite into sheets of steel or aluminium, the cutting and pressing and welding of the metal into the kettle's shell, spout and handle, the assembling of these parts with scores of other components – coils, screws, nuts, bolts, washers, rivets, wires, springs, rubber insulation, plastic trimmings; then the packaging of the kettle, the advertising of the kettle, the marketing of the kettle to wholesale and retail outlets, the transportation of the kettle to warehouses and shops, the calculation of its price, and the distribution of its added value between all the myriad people and agencies concerned in its production and circulation. The housewife gave no thought to all this as she switched on her kettle. Neither had Robyn until this moment, and it would never have occurred to her to do so before she met Vic Wilcox. What to do with the thought was another question. It was difficult to decide whether the system that produced the kettle was a miracle of human ingenuity and co-operation or a colossal waste of resources, human and natural. Would we all be better off boiling our water in a pot hung over an open fire? Or was it the facility to do such things at the touch of a button that freed men, and more particularly women, from servile labour and made it possible for them to become literary critics? A phrase from *Hard Times* she was apt to quote with a certain derision in her lectures, but of which she had thought more charitably lately, came into her mind: "*'Tis aw a muddle.*" She gave up the conundrum, and accepted another cup of coffee from the stewardess.

Vic, meanwhile, was reflecting that he was sitting next to the best-looking woman on the plane, including the hostesses. Robyn had surprised him by appearing at the door of her little house dressed as he had never seen her dressed before, in a tailored two-piece costume, with matching cape, made out of a soft olive-green cloth that set off her coppery curls and echoed her grey-green eyes. "You look terrific," he said spontaneously. She smiled and stifled a yawn and said, "Thanks. I thought I'd try and dress the part."

But what was the part? The other passengers on the plane had clearly made up their minds. They were businessmen like himself, many of them on their way to the same trade fair, and he had intercepted their knowing, appraising glances at Robyn as she strode into the departure lounge at his side. She was his girlfriend, his mistress, his dolly-bird, his bit of spare, his nookie-cookie, thinly disguised as his secretary or PA, going with him to Frankfurt on the firm's expenses, nice work if you could fiddle it, lucky bastard. And the Germans would presumably think the same.

"How shall I explain you to the Germans?" he said. "I can't go through all that rigmarole about the Shadow Scheme every time I introduce you. I don't suppose they'd understand what I was on about anyway."

"I'll explain," she said. "I speak German."

"Go on! You don't!"

"*Ja, bestimmt. Ich habe seit vier jahren in der Schule die Deutsche Sprache studiert.*"

"What's that mean?"

"Yes, I do. I studied German for four years at school."

Vic stared in wonderment. "I wish I could do that," he said. "*Guten Tag* and *Auf Wiedersehen* are about the limits of my German."

"I'll be your interpreter, then."

"Oh, they all speak English . . . As a matter of fact," he said, struck by a thought, "it might be useful if you don't let on that you understand German when we meet the Altenhofer people."

"Why?"

"I've done business with Krauts before. Sometimes they talk German to each other in the middle of a meeting. I'd like to know what they're saying."

"All right," said Robyn. "But how will you explain what I'm doing there?"

"I'll say you're my Personal Assistant," said Vic.

Altenhofer's had sent a car to meet them at the airport. The driver was standing at the exit from Customs holding a cardboard sign with MR WILCOX on it. "Hmm, giving us the treatment," said Vic, when he saw this.

"How much would this sale be worth to them?" Robyn asked.

"I'm hoping to get the machine for £150,000. *Guten Tag*," he said to the chauffeur. "*Ich bin Herr Wilcox.*"

"This way, please sir," said the man, taking their bags.

"You see what I mean?" Vic murmured. "Even the bloody chauffeurs speak better English than I do."

The driver nodded approvingly when Vic gave the name of their hotel. It was on the outskirts of the city because it hadn't been possible to get an additional room for Robyn in the downtown hotel where he'd originally been booked. "But this one should be comfortable," said Vic. "It's pricey enough."

It was in fact the most luxurious hotel Robyn had ever entered as a guest, though the ambience was more like that of an exclusive country club, with a great deal of natural wood and exposed brick in the decor, and all kinds of facilities for recreation and body-maintenance: a beauty salon, a gymnasium, a sauna, a games room, and a swimming pool. "*Schwimmbad!*" Robyn exclaimed, seeing the direction sign. "If I'd known I'd have brought my costume."

"Buy one," said Vic. "There's a shop over there."

"What, just for one swim?"

"Why not? You'll use it again, won't you?"

While Vic was registering, she strolled over to the sports boutique on the other side of the lobby and flicked through a rack of bikinis and swimsuits. The more exiguous they were, the dearer they seemed to be. "Much too expensive," she said, coming back to the reception desk.

"Let me treat you," he said.

"No thanks. I want to see my room. I bet it's enormous."

It was. It had a monolithic bed, an immense leather-topped desk, a glass-topped coffee table, a TV, a minibar and a vast wardrobe system in which the few items of her modest luggage looked lost. She plucked a grape from the complimentary bowl of fruit on the coffee table. She switched on the radio at the bedside console and the strains of Schubert filled the room. She pressed another button and the net curtains, electrically operated, whirred apart to reveal, like a cinemascope establishing shot, landscaped grounds and an artificial lake. The bathroom, gleaming with sophisticated plumbing, had two washbasins carved out of what looked convincingly like marble, and was provided with more towels of diverse sizes than she could think of uses for. Behind the door were two towelling bathrobes sealed in polythene covers. Schubert filtered into the bathroom from an extension speaker. It was the only sound in the suite: double glazing, deep-pile carpets, and the heavy wooden door, absorbed all sound of the outside world. Two weeks here, she thought, and I could finish off *Domestic Angels and Unfortunate Females*.

The chauffeur had waited to take them into the centre of the city. Sitting in the back seat of the swift, silent Mercedes, Robyn was struck by the contrast between the streets of Frankfurt and their equivalents in poor old Rummidge. Everywhere here looked clean, neat, freshly painted and highly polished. There were no discarded chip cones, squashed fried-chicken cartons, dented lager cans, polystyrene hamburger containers or crumpled paper cups in the gutters. The pavements had a freshly rinsed look, and so had the pedestrians. The commercial architecture was sleek and stylish.

"Well, they had to rebuild from scratch after the war, didn't they," said Vic when she commented on this. "We pretty well flattened Frankfurt."

"The centre of Rummidge has been pretty well flattened too," said Robyn.

"Not by bombing."

"No, by the developers. But they haven't rebuilt it like this, have they?"

"Couldn't afford to. We won the war and lost the peace, as they say."

"Why did we?"

Vic pondered a moment. "We were too greedy and too lazy," he said. "In the fifties and sixties, when you could sell anything, we went on using obsolete machines and paid the unions whatever they asked for, while the Krauts were investing in new technology and hammering out sensible labour agreements. When times got harder, it paid off. They think they've got a recession here, but it's nothing like what we've got."

This was an unusually critical assessment of British industry, coming from Vic. "I thought you said our problem was we bought too many imports?" she said.

"That too. Where was that outfit of yours made, as a matter of interest?"

"I've no idea." She looked at the label inside the cape and laughed: "West Germany!"

"There you are."

"But it's nice, you said so yourself. Anyway, you can't talk. This cost me all of eighty-five pounds. You're just about to spend a hundred and fifty thousand on a German machine tool."

"That's different."

"No, it isn't. Why don't you buy a British machine?"

"Because we don't make one that will do the job," Vic said. "And that's another reason why we lost the peace."

The exhibition centre housing the trade fair was rather like an airport without aeroplanes: a vast multi-levelled complex of large halls, connected by long walkways and moving staircases, with bars and cafeterias dotted about the landings. They registered inside the entrance hall. Robyn put down on the form, "J. Pringle & Sons" under *Company* and "Personal Assistant to Managing Director" under *Position*, and received an identity card recording these false particulars.

Vic frowned at a plan of the exhibition. "We have to go through CADCAM," he said, adding for her benefit: "Computer-aided design and computer-aided manufacture." Robyn stored away the information for future reference: she intended to compose her URFAIYS report as far as possible in acronyms.

They threaded their way though a hot and crowded space where computers hummed and printers chattered and screeched on stands packed as close together as fairground booths, and passed into a larger, airier hall where the big machine tools were displayed, some in simulated operation. Wheels turned, crankshafts cranked, oiled pistons slid up and down, in and out, conveyor belts rattled round, but nothing was actually produced. The machines were odourless, brightly painted and highly polished. It was all very different from the stench and dirt and heat and noise of a real factory. More like a moving toyshop for grown men; and men in large numbers were swarming round the massive machines, squatting and bending and craning to get a better view of their intricacies. Robyn saw very few women about, except for professional models handing out leaflets and brochures. They wore skintight Lycra jump-suits, heavy make-up and fixed smiles and looked as if they had been extruded from the Altenhofer automatic core-moulding machine.

The sales director of Altenhofer's, Herr Winkler, and his technical assistant, Dr Patsch, welcomed Vic and Robyn warmly at the company's stand, and ushered them into a carpeted inner sanctum for refreshment. Champagne was offered, as well as coffee and orange juice.

"Coffee for me," said Vic. "I'll leave the bubbly till later."

Herr Winkler, a portly, smiling man, with small, perfectly shod feet and a springy step like a ballroom dancer, chuckled. "You wish to keep a clear head, of course. But your charming assistant . . .?"

"Oh, she can drink as much as she likes," said Vic offhandedly, presumably to encourage the supposition that her presence on this occasion was purely decorative. He had already stripped her of her doctorate, introducing her to the Germans as "Miss Penrose". With her false identity card on her lapel, Robyn felt she had no option but to go along with the role assigned to her, and enjoy the fun of it. "I'm rather susceptible to champagne," she simpered. "I think I'd better mix it with orange juice."

"Ah, yes, the Buck Fizz, isn't it?" said Herr Winkler.

"Buck's Fizz, actually," she said, ever the teacher, even in disguise. "As distinct from Buck House, where the Queen lives."

"Buck's Fizz, Buck House – I must remember," said Herr Winkler, waltzing over to the drinks table. "Heinrich! a glass of Buck's Fizz for the lady! And coffee for Mr Wilcox, who wishes to buy one of our beautiful machines."

"If the price is right," said Vic.

"Ha ha! Of course," Winkler chuckled. Dr Patsch, tall, saturnine and dark-bearded, measured orange juice and sparkling wine into a champagne flute, holding it level with his eyes like a test-tube. Winkler snatched the drink from him and sashayed back to Robyn. He presented the glass to her with a slight bow and a perceptible click of his heels. "I am informed that your boss is a hard bargainer, Miss Penrose."

"Who told you that?" Vic said.

"My spies," said Dr Winkler, beaming merrily. "We have all spies in business these days, do we not? Will you take cream in your coffee, Mr Wilcox?"

"Black with sugar, please. Then I'd like to take a closer look at the machine you've got out there."

"Of course, of course. Dr Patsch will explain everything to you. Then you and I will talk money, which is so much more complicated."

The next hour was rather tedious for Robyn and she had no difficulty in simulating bored incomprehension. They went out into the exhibition hall and examined the huge moulding machine at its phantom task. Dr Patsch gave a detailed commentary on its operation in excellent English, and Vic seemed impressed. When they went back inside the stand to discuss terms, however, there appeared to be a wide gap between the asking price and Vic's limit. Winkler suggested that they adjourn for lunch, and pranced them out of the exhibition centre and across the road to a high-rise hotel of ostentatious luxury where a table had been reserved. It was the kind of restaurant where the first thing the waiters did was to take away the perfectly serviceable place settings already on the table and substitute more elaborate ones. Robyn submitted to being guided through the German menu by Dr Winkler, and compensated herself by choosing the most expensive items on it, smoked salmon and venison. The wine was excellent. There was light conversation about differences between England and Germany in which Robyn avoided giving any impression of suspicious intelligence by attributing her every opinion to something she had read in a newspaper. But as the meal drew to its conclusion the talk turned back to the matter of business. "It's a beautiful machine," said Vic, puffing a cigar over the coffee and cognac. "It's exactly what I need. The trouble is, you want a hundred and seventy thousand pounds for it, and I'm only authorised to pay a hundred and fifty."

Dr Winkler smiled, a shade desperately. "We might be able to arrange a small discount."

"How small?"

"Two per cent."

Vic shook his head. "Not worth talking about." He glanced at his watch. "I have another appointment this afternoon . . ."

"Yes, of course," said Winkler despondently. He motioned to a waiter for his bill. Vic excused himself and went off to the men's cloakroom. Winkler and Patsch exchanged some remarks in German to which Robyn listened attentively, while accepting a second cup of coffee from the waiter and indulging herself in a chocolate truffle. After a little while she stood up and, with a little charade of embarrassment, asked the way to the Ladies. She loitered outside the door until Vic emerged from the adjacent *Herren*.

"They're going to accept your price," she said.

His face brightened. "Are they? That's terrific!"

"But there's a catch in it, I think. Patsch said, '*We can't do it with a* something *system*,' – it sounded like '*semen*', And Winkler said, '*Well, he hasn't specified semen.*'"

Vic frowned and pushed his fingers through his forelock. "The cunning bastards. They're going to try and fob me off with an electro-mechanical control system."

"What?"

"The machine we saw this morning has a Siemens solid-state control system with diagnostic panels for identifying faults. The older type is electromechanical – all switches and relays, and no diagnostic facility. Nowhere near as reliable. The Siemens system would add nearly twenty thousand to the total cost – exactly the margin we're haggling about. Nice work, Robyn." While he was talking Vic was moving back towards the restaurant.

"Wait for me," said Robyn. "I don't want to miss anything, but I must go to the loo."

When they returned to the restaurant, Robyn wondered whether Winkler and Patsch would have seen anything suspicious in their long absence, but Vic had had a story ready about phoning his divisional boss in England. "No dice, I'm afraid. My ceiling is still a hundred and fifty thousand."

"We have been discussing the problem," said Winkler with a genial smile. "After all, we think we can meet your requirements for that figure."

"Now you're talking," said Vic.

"Excellent!" Winkler beamed. "Let us have another cognac." He waved to the wine waiter.

"I'll send you a letter as soon as I get back," said Vic. "Let's just get the deal straight." He took a notebook from his inside pocket and leafed through it with a wetted finger till he reached a certain page. "It's your 22EX machine, right?"

"Correct."

"With Siemens solid-state systems."

Herr Winkler's smile faded. "I do not think we specified that."

"But the demonstration model in the exhibition has Siemens solid-state."

"Very likely," said Winkler with a shrug. "Our machines are available with a variety of control systems."

"The 22EX is also supplied with Klugermann electromechanical controls," said Dr Patsch. "That is what we had in mind for the price."

"Then it's no deal," said Vic, closing his notebook and stowing it away. "I'm only interested in solid-state."

The wine waiter came up to the table. Winkler swatted him away irritably. Vic stood up and put his hand on the back of Robyn's chair. "Perhaps we shouldn't waste any more of your time, Mr Winkler."

"Thanks for the lovely lunch," said Robyn, getting to her feet and giving a vacant smile of which she was rather proud.

"One moment, Mr Wilcox. Sit down, please," said Winkler. "If you will excuse us, I should like to discuss further with my colleague."

Winkler and Patsch went off in the direction of the cloakrooms, deep in conversation. The former's step seemed to have lost some of its spring, and he collided clumsily with one of the waiters as he threaded his way through the tables.

"Well?" said Robyn.

"I think they might just bite the bullet," said Vic. "Winkler thought he had the deal sewn up. He can't bear the thought of it slipping out of his grasp at the last moment."

After five minutes, the Germans came back. Patsch was looking glum, but Winkler smiled gamely. "One hundred and fifty-five thousand," he said, "with Siemens solid-state. That is absolutely our final offer."

Vic took out his notebook again. "Let's not make any more mistakes," he said. "This is the 22EX with Siemens solid-state, for one hundred and fifty-five thousand, to be paid in sterling in stages as per your outline quotation: 25% with order, 50% on delivery, 15% on being commissioned by your engineers, and 10% after two months satisfactory operation, right?"

"Correct."

"Can you write out the new quotation and let me have it today?"

"It will be delivered to your hotel this afternoon."

"It's a deal, Mr Winkler," said Vic. "I can find the odd five thousand from somewhere." He shook Winkler's hand.

"I was not misinformed about you, Mr Wilcox," said Winkler, with a slightly weary smile.

They all shook hands again when they parted in the foyer of the hotel. "Goodbye, Miss Penrose," said Winkler. "Enjoy yourself in Frankfurt."

"*Auf Wiedersehen, Herr Winkler,*" she replied. "*Ich wurde mich freuen wenn der Rest meines Besuches so erfreulich wird wie dieses köstliche Mittagessen.*"

He gaped at her. "I did not know you speak German."

"You didn't ask me," she said, smiling sweetly.

"Goodbye, then," said Vic, taking Robyn's arm. "You'll be getting a letter next week. Then my technical people will be in touch." He hurried her away towards the revolving doors. "What did you say?" he muttered.

"I said I would be happy if the rest of my stay was as enjoyable as the delicious lunch."

"That was cheeky," he said, keeping his grinning face hidden from the Germans. As the door spun them into the open, he punched the air triumphantly, like a footballer who has scored a goal. "Turned the tables on the buggers!" he cried. "At a hundred and fifty-five, it's a snip!"

"Ssh! They'll hear you."

"They can't back out now. What do you want to do?"

"Haven't you got another appointment?"

"No, I invented that to concentrate their minds, I've got no more meetings till tomorrow. We could go and have a look at the Old Town if you like – it's all fake, mind. Or go on the river. Whatever you fancy. It's your treat. You deserve it."

"It's raining," Robyn observed.

He held out a hand and looked up at the sky. "So it is."

"Not much fun sightseeing in the rain. I think what I'd like to do is buy a swimming-costume and go back to that nice hotel and have a swim."

"Good idea. There's a taxi!"

So they went back to the hotel by taxi and Robyn chose a blue and green one-piece swimming costume in the sports boutique and allowed Vic to pay for it. He bought a pair of trunks for himself at the same time. He was not a great enthusiast for this form of exercise, but he had no intention of letting Robyn out of his sight any longer than was necessary to change into a pair of trunks.

It was years since he had bought such a garment, and in the meantime either he had got bigger or swimming costumes had got smaller. Robyn's appearance when she emerged from the changing-room suggested that the latter was the case. Her pointed nipples were sharply embossed on the tight-fitting satiny cloth, and the bottom part of her costume was cut away so steeply that tendrils of red-gold hair crept out from under the fabric at the vee. He would have enjoyed all this more if he hadn't been so conscious of his genitals bulging like a bunch of grapes at the crotch of his own costume.

They had the pool to themselves, apart from a couple of kids splashing about at the shallow end. Robyn dived gracefully into the water, and began a tidy crawl up and down the length of the pool. He might have guessed she would be a good swimmer. He jumped in, holding his nose, and tailed her with his slower breaststroke. When she offered to race him, he stipulated the breaststroke, but she still beat him easily. She climbed out of the pool, water streaming from her long white flanks, and tried vainly to lever the cheeks of her buttocks under the skimpy costume with her thumbs. She stood at the end of the diving board, bounced once, twice, and somersaulted into the water with a great splash. She surfaced, laughing and spluttering, *"Made a hash of that!"* and hauled herself out to try again. Vic trod water and watched her, entranced.

There was a jacuzzi at one end of the pool, a foaming whirlpool of hot water that gently pummelled your muscles into a state of blissful relaxation. They sat in it up to their necks, facing each other like cartoon characters in a cannibal's pot. "I've never been in one of these before," said Vic. "It's magic."

"An item to tick off your list," said Robyn.

"What list?"

"The miss list. The list of things you've never done."

"Oh, yes," said Vic. He thought of another item, that she did not know about. Jennifer Rush burst into song inside his head:

> *There's no need to run away,*
> *If you feel that this is for real,*
> *'Cause when it's warm and straight from the heart,*
> *It's time to start.*

"We shouldn't stay in here too long," said Robyn. She clambered out and took a running dive into the pool. He clumsily followed suit, gasping with the shock of the cool water after the hot jacuzzi. Into the jacuzzi they went once more, and once more into the pool. Then they separated to shower and dry themselves. The locker-room was supplied with an abundance of towels, robes, track suits, soaps, shampoos, body lotions and talcum powders. They emerged pink, gleaming, and odoriferous from these ablutions, and ordered tea in the games room. They played table-tennis and Vic won the best of five games. Then he taught her how to play snooker, a heady experience. Apart from the occasional handshake, or a guiding hand placed on her arm, he had never touched her before. Now he encircled her with his arms, almost embraced her from behind, as he corrected her posture and adjusted her handling of the cue. Jennifer Rush murmured:

> *I hold on to your body,*
> *And feel each move you make,*
> *Your voice is warm and tender*
> *A love that I could not forsake.*

They explored the gymnasium and played with the exercise bicycle and the rowing-machine and a kind of inverted treadmill that looked as if it had been invented by the Spanish Inquisition, until they worked up such a sweat that it was necessary to go and shower again. They agreed to rest for an hour or so in their rooms.

Vic lay on his bed, feeling tired but relaxed after all the exercise, his eyes shut, his head a mere amplifier now for Jennifer Rush. The lobes of his brain were two spools on which her tape played and replayed in an endless loop.

> *But it makes you feel all right,*
> *Just to think of doin' her right,*
> *The road to choose is straight ahead in the end.*
> *Surrender! It's your only chance, surrender!*
> *Don't wait too long to realise*
> *That her eyes will say 'Forever'.*

He rose after an hour and shaved for the second time that day. In the mirror his hair looked as light and fluffy as a baby's from all the washing and drying. He parted it carefully, and combed it back, but the limp forelock fell forward inevitably across his forehead. Other men's hair didn't do that, he reflected irritably. Perhaps all his life he had been combing it the wrong way. He tried parting it on the other side, but it looked queer. Then he combed it forward without a parting at all, but it looked ridiculous. He rubbed some Vaseline into it, parted and combed it in the usual style. As soon as he moved, the forelock fell forward.

He put on a clean shirt and anxiously inspected his tie, which had got splashed with a bit of gravy at lunch. He dabbed at it with a wet face-flannel without much effect, except for creating a damp halo around the original spot. It was the only tie he had, though, and he could hardly wear an open-necked shirt with his striped suit. For the first time in his life, Vic wished he had brought more clothes with him on a business trip. Robyn, he felt sure, would have brought a change for the evening. *"I thought I'd dress the part."*

He was not disappointed. When he knocked on the door of her room at the appointed time, she appeared at the threshold wearing a dress he had never seen before, something silky and filmy and swirling, in a muted pattern of brown, blue and green, with different shoes and different earrings, even a different handbag, from the ones she'd worn earlier that day.

"You look wonderful," he said. His voice sounded strange to his own ears: it had assimilated some of the passionate timbre of Jennifer

Rush. Robyn seemed to notice, for she blushed slightly, and rattled away in reply:

"Thanks – shall I come straight away? I'm ready, and hungry, believe it or not. Must be all that exercise."

"Do you want to go out somewhere to dinner? Or shall we eat here?"

"I don't mind," she said. "Do you know somewhere special?"

"No," he said. "Wherever we go will be crowded with people from the trade fair."

"Then let's eat here."

"Good," he said.

Vic insisted on ordering champagne at dinner. "A celebration," he said. "We deserve it." He raised his glass. "Here's to the Altenhofer 22EX automatic core blower with Siemens solid-state diagnostic controls at the bargain price of a hundred and fifty-five thousand pounds."

"Here's to it," said Robyn, feeling the bubbles explode pleasantly in her nostrils as she drank. "Mmm, delicious!"

Robyn hadn't been joking when she told Herr Winkler that she was peculiarly susceptible to champagne. It had no perceptible effect on her at first, apart from tasting nice, so that she tended to drink more of it, more quickly, than she would another wine. Then, suddenly – woomph! She would be high as a kite. This evening she ordered herself to drink slowly, but somehow the bottle had emptied itself before they had finished their main course of trout *meunière*, and she weakly acquiesced in the ordering of a second. After all, why shouldn't she get a little high? She was in a holiday mood: carefree, hedonistic, glowing with physical wellbeing. Rummidge and its attendant worries seemed infinitely remote. The curved crystal-lit dining room, filled with the civilised sounds of tinkling glassware, the soft clash of cutlery on china plate, subdued laughter and conversation, might have been the cabin of a spaceship, with portholes behind the thick velvet curtains from which the Earth would look no bigger or more substantial than a milky-coloured balloon. There was no gravity here, and one breathed champagne bubbles. The sensation was exhilarating.

Across the table, Vic talked ramblingly about the difference the new machine would make to Pringle's competitive edge. She responded with phatic murmurs, not really attending. He hardly seemed to be attending himself. His dark eyes gazed intently at her from under the falling forelock. He was, after all, she thought, a not unattractive man, in spite of his short stature. If only he had clothes that fitted him properly, he could look quite handsome. He certainly looked better without any. She recalled his white, broad-shouldered torso in the pool that afternoon, the flat belly and sinewy arms, the masculine bulge under his briefs. Under the table she slipped off her shoe and briefly rubbed her foot against his calf, keeping a straight face with difficulty as she watched a startled question fill his eyes, like the face of a prisoner who comes to the door of his cell and grips the bars, only to discover that it is unlocked, and does not know whether the prospect of release is genuine or not. Robyn herself had not decided, she was suspended in time and space, but she teased him mischievously.

"I suppose if I hadn't been here, Herr Winkler would have fixed you up with a call-girl tonight. Isn't that what goes on at these trade fairs?"

"So they tell me," he said, gripping the bars more tightly. "I wouldn't know."

The waiter presented the bill, and Vic signed it. "What d'you want to do now?" he said. "A drink in the bar?"

"No more drink," she said. "I'd like to dance." She laughed at the look of dismay on his face. "There's a discothèque in the hotel – it said so in the lift."

"I can't do that sort of dancing."

"Anyone can do it after that much champagne," she said, getting a little unsteadily to her feet.

There turned out to be two discothèques in the hotel; one a booming, strobe-lit cell in the basement designed for young people, occupied at this hour only by the disc-jockey and the two children who had been in the swimming-pool: and another, situated in an annexe to the bar, that was more like a nightclub, offering music of a less frenzied tempo to a more mature clientèle. Vic looked round with relief. "This is all right," he said. "There are even people dancing together."

"Together?"

"Holding on to each other, I mean. The way I learned to dance."

"Come on, then," she said. She took him by the hand and led him onto the floor. A song of sublime silliness and repetitive melody was in progress, sung by a female vocalist with a high-pitched girlish voice.

> *I'm in the mood for wooing, and doing*
> *The things we do so well together . . .*

Vic led off with a kind of modified quickstep, holding her at arm's length. Then Robyn executed a few jive twists and turns and broke away so that he was forced to jig up and down on his own, facing her across two yards of floor.

205

"Come back," he said, with comical pathos, shuffling his feet awkwardly, his torso rigid, his arms held stiffly at his side. "I can't do this."

"You're doing fine," she said. "Just let yourself go."

"I never let myself go," he said. "It's against my nature."

"Poor Vic!" She shimmied up to him and, as he reached for her like a drowning swimmer, backed away.

At last, after several records, she took pity on him. They sat down and ordered soft drinks. "Thanks, Vic, that was lovely," she said. "I haven't danced for ages."

"Don't you have balls at the University?" he said. "May balls." He dredged up the phrase as if it belonged to a foreign language.

"May balls are Cambridge. I believe they have dances at the Rummidge Staff Club, but I don't know anybody who goes to them."

The lights dimmed. Music of a slower tempo commenced. The couples on the dance floor drew together. A strange expression came over Vic's face that she could only describe as awe.

"This tune," he said hoarsely.

"You know it?"

"It's Jennifer Rush."

"You like her?"

He stood up. "Let's dance."

"All right."

It was a slow, smoochy ballad with an absurd, sentimental refrain about *I am your lady and you are my man* and *the power of love*, but it did amazing things for Vic's dancing. His limbs lost their stiffness, his movements were perfectly on the beat, he held her close, firmly but lightly, nudging her round the floor with his hips and thighs. He said nothing, and with her chin resting on his shoulder she couldn't see his face, but he seemed to be humming faintly to himself. She closed her eyes and yielded to the languorous rhythms of the silly, sexy tune. When the record finished she gave him a quick kiss on the lips.

"What was that for?" he said, startled out of his trance.

"Let's go to bed," said Robyn.

2

They do not speak to each other again until they are inside Robyn's room. Robyn has nothing to say, and Vic is speechless. As, hand in hand, they tread the carpeted corridors of the hotel, as they wait for the lift, and rise to the second floor, their states of mind are very different.

Robyn's mood is blithe. She feels mildly wanton, but not wicked. She sees herself not as seducing Vic but as putting him out of his misery. There is of course always a special excitement about the first time with a new partner. One never knows quite what to expect. Her heart beats faster than if she were going to bed with Charles. But she is not anxious. She is in control. Perhaps she feels a certain sense of triumph at her conquest: the captain of industry at the feet of the feminist literary critic – a pleasing tableau.

For Vic the event is infinitely more momentous, his mood infinitely more perturbed. The prospect of going to bed with Robyn Penrose is the secret dream of weeks come true, yet there is something hallucinatory about the ease with which his wish has been granted. He regards himself with wonderment led by the hand by this handsome young woman towards her bedroom, as if his soul is stumbling along out of step behind his body. In the mirrored wall of the lift he sees himself standing shoulder to shoulder beside Robyn, who is three inches taller. She catches his eye and smiles, lifts his hand and rubs it against her cheek. It is like a watching a puppet being manipulated. He smiles tensely back into the mirror.

Robyn opens the door of her room, hangs the *Do Not Disturb* sign on the outside, and locks it from the inside. She kicks off her shoes, bringing her height down nearer to Vic's. He pushes her against the door and begins to kiss her violently, his hands clutching and groping all over her. Only passion, he feels, will carry him across the threshold of adultery, and this is what he supposes passion is like.

Robyn is surprised, and a little alarmed, by this behaviour. "Take it easy, Vic," she says breathlessly. "You don't have to tear the clothes off me."

"Sorry," he says, desisting at once. His arms drop to his sides. He looks at her humbly. "I haven't done this before."

"Oh, Vic," she says, "don't keep on saying that, it's too sad." She goes to the minibar and peers inside. "Good," she says, "there's a half bottle of champagne. You don't have to do anything if you don't want to."

"Oh, I want to," he says. "I love you."

"Don't be silly," she says, handing him the bottle. "That song has gone to your head. The one about the power of love."

"It's my favourite song," he says. "From now on it will be our song."

Robyn can hardly believe her ears.

Robyn holds out two glasses. Vic fills only one. "Not for me," he says.

Robyn looks at him over the rim of her glass. "You're not worried about being impotent, are you?"

"No," he says hoarsely. He is, of course.

"If it happens, it doesn't matter, OK?"

"I don't think it will be a problem," he says.

"You could just give me a massage, if you like."

"I want to make love," he says.

"Massage is a way of making love. It's gentle, tender, non-phallic."

"I'm a phallic sort of bloke," he says apologetically.

"Well, it's also a nice kind of foreplay," says Robyn.

The word "foreplay" gives him a tremendous hard-on.

Robyn puts her hands behind her back, undoes a catch on her dress, and pulls it over her shoulders. As she hangs it up in the wardrobe, she inspects the label. "'*Made in Italy.*' Failed the patriotic test again." She pulls her slip over her head. "'*Fabriqué en France.*' Dear, dear." This is her way of keeping the tone light. She glances at Vic, who is staring at her, still holding the champagne bottle. "Aren't you going to get undressed?" she says. "I feel a little shy standing here like this." She is wearing vest, pants, tights.

"Sorry," he says, struggling out of his jacket, wrenching at his tie, tearing off his shirt.

She picks the shirt up from the floor and searches for its label. "Ha! '*Made in Hong Kong.*'"

"Marjorie buys my shirts."

"No excuses . . . The suit seems to be British though." She hangs his jacket on a wooden valet. "All too British, if I may say so, Vic."

The only British-made garment Robyn is wearing is the last to come off. "I always buy my knickers at Marks and Spencer's," she says with a grin.

She stands before him, a naked goddess. Small, round breasts with pink, pointed nipples. A slender waist, broad hips, and gently curving belly. A tongue of fire at her crotch. He worships.

"You're beautiful," he says.

"Shall I make a terrible confession? I wish I had bigger breasts. Why? I ask myself. There's absolutely no reason except the grossest sexual stereotyping."

"Your breasts are beautiful," he says, kissing them gently.

"That's nice, Vic," she says. "You're getting the idea. Gently does it."

She turns back the sheets on the bed, places a bottle of oil to hand on the night table, switches off all the lights except one lamp. She lies down on the bed, and stretches out her hand. "Aren't you going to take your shorts off?" she says.

"Can we have that light out?"

"Certainly not."

He turns away from her to slip off his boxer shorts, then comes to the bed, shielding his erection with his hands.

"My, what a knobstick," she says.

"Why do you call it that?"

"Private joke." As quick as a lizard she darts out her tongue and licks his cock from root to tip.

"God Almighty," he says. "Can we skip the massage?"

"If you like," she says, beginning herself to be excited by the urgency of his desire. "Have you got a condom?"

Vic looks at her with blank dismay. "Aren't you on the pill or something?"

"No. Came off the pill for health reasons. And the coil."

"What shall we do? I haven't got anything."

"Fortunately I have. Pass that sponge-bag, will you?"

He passes her the sponge-bag. "Here we are," she says. "Shall I put it on for you?"

"Good God, no!" he exclaims.

"Why not?"

He laughs wildly. "All right."

Deftly she rolls the condom onto his penis. When she releases the teat it falls sideways like a limp forelock.

"I don't believe this," he says.

Ever the teacher, Robyn is, of course, trying to make a point, to demystify "love".

"I love you," he says, kissing her throat, stroking her breasts, tracing the curve of her hip.

"No, you don't, Vic."

"I've been in love with you for weeks."

"There's no such thing," she says. "It's a rhetorical device. It's a bourgeois fallacy."

"Haven't you ever been in love, then?"

"When I was younger," she says, "I allowed myself to be constructed by the discourse of romantic love for a while, yes."

"What the hell does that mean?"

"We aren't essences, Vic. We aren't unique individual essences existing prior to language. There is only language."

"What about this?" he says, sliding his hand between her legs.

"Language and biology," she says, opening her legs wider. "Of course we have bodies, physical needs and appetites. My muscles contract when you touch me there – feel?"

"I feel," he says.

"And that's nice. But the discourse of romantic love pretends that your finger and my clitoris are extensions of two unique individual selves who need each other and only each other and cannot be happy without each other for ever and ever."

"That's right," says Vic. "I love your silk cunt with my whole self, for ever and ever."

"Silly," she says, but smiles, not unmoved by this declaration. "Why do you call it that?"

"Private joke," he says, covering her body with his. "Do you think we could possibly stop talking now?"

"All right," she says. "But I prefer to be on top."

3

"Imagine," Robyn whispered. "He had never done it that way before."

"Really?" Penny Black whispered back. "How long did you say he had been married?"

"Twenty-two years."

"Twenty-two years in the missionary position? That's kind of perverted."

Robyn sniggered, a mite guiltily. She didn't like to expose Vic to Penny Black's ridicule, but she felt she had to confide in somebody. It was ten days since the expedition to Frankfurt, and she and Penny were having a sauna after their Monday evening game of squash, on the highest, hottest bench, and they were whispering because Philip Swallow's wife, wrapped modestly in a towel, was sitting on the lowest.

"Well, I don't think there's been a lot of sex in the marriage in recent years," said Robyn.

"I'm not surprised," said Penny.

Mrs Swallow rose to her feet and went out of the sauna, nodding curtly to the two young women as she closed the door.

"Oh dear," said Robyn, "d'you think she thought we were talking about her and Swallow?"

"Never mind the Swallows," said Penny, "tell me about your fling with Wilcox. What possessed you?"

"I fancied him," said Robyn, cupping her chin in her hands, and supporting her elbows on her knees. "At that particular conjuncture, I fancied him."

"I thought you couldn't stand him? I thought he was a bully, a philistine and a male chauvinist."

"Well, he did seem a bit like that at first. In fact he's really quite decent, when you get to know him. And by no means stupid."

"That doesn't sound like enough reason to go to bed with him."

"I told you, Penny, that night I fancied him. You know how it is: you're in a strange place, you have a few drinks, a smooch on the dance floor . . ."

"Yeah, yeah, I know, I've taught Open University Summer School. But Robyn, for heaven's sake – a middle-aged factory owner!"

"Managing Director."

"Well, whatever . . . it's like rough trade."

"He wasn't a bit rough. On the contrary."

"I don't mean physically, I mean psychologically. I think the idea of this man's power and money is a turn-on for you. He's the antithesis of everything you stand for." Penny Black shook her head reproachfully. "I'm afraid it's the old female rape-fantasy rearing its ugly head again, Robyn. When Wilcox screwed you, it was like the factory ravished the university."

"Don't be absurd, Penny," said Robyn. "If anyone did any ravishing, it was me. The trouble is, he wants to make a great romance out of it. He insists that he's in love with me. I tell him I don't believe in the concept, but it doesn't make any difference. He keeps ringing me up and asking to meet. I don't know what to do."

"Tell him you're committed to Charles."

"The trouble is, I'm not. We're not seeing each other at the moment."

"Tell him you're a lesbian," said Penny, with a sly, sideways glance. "That should put him off."

Robyn laughed, a little self-consciously, and pressed her knees more closely together. She had a suspicion that Penny Black herself had tendencies of this kind. "He knows I'm not a lesbian," she said, "all too well."

"What does he have in mind?" said Penny. "Does he want to set you up as his mistress or something?" She chuckled. "Maybe you should consider it seriously, it might be useful when your job runs out."

"He claims he wants to marry me," said Robyn. "He's prepared to get a divorce and marry me."

"Wow! That's heavy!"

"It's quite ridiculous, of course."

"All because of a single fuck?"

"Well, three actually," said Robyn.

The first time he came almost as soon as she straddled him and bore down on him – came with a great groan, like a tree being torn out of the ground by the roots. A little later he was sufficiently hard again to allow her to reach an orgasm, but couldn't come himself until she helped him with the aid of a little massage oil. He wept at that, whether from mortification or gratitude or a mixture of both, she couldn't be sure. And in the early hours of the morning, with the grey dawn light just beginning to seep through the curtains, she woke to find his hand between her legs, and she rolled over onto her back and, still half asleep, let him have her in his own direct way, under the bedclothes, without a word exchanged – only inarticulate cries and moans to which she contributed her quota. When she woke again, in broad daylight, he had gone back to his own room, much to her relief. She gave him credit for unsuspected tact. They could carry on as if the events of the night were bracketed off from their normal relationship. Sober and wide awake, she had no wish to be reminded of them.

But at breakfast in the restaurant he looked at her from under his forelock with worried, doggy devotion, hardly responding to her small talk, eating little but drinking cup after cup of coffee and chainsmoking his Marlboros. When they went back upstairs to pack he followed her into her room and asked what they were going to do. Robyn said she thought she might look at the Old Town while he did his business at the trade fair, and he said, I don't mean that, I mean what are we going to do about last night? And she said, we don't have to do anything about it, do we? We both got a bit carried away, but it was nice. Nice, he said, nice, is that all you can say about it? It was wonderful. All right, she said, to humour him, it was wonderful. I slept beautifully, did you? I hardly slept at all, he said, and he looked it. But it was wonderful, he said, especially the last time, we came together the last time, didn't we? Did we, she said, I don't really remember, I was half-asleep. Don't mock me, he said. I'm not mocking you, she said. It means nothing to you, I suppose, he said, it was just a, what do they call it, a one-night stand, I expect you do it all the time, but I don't. Neither do I, she said hotly, I haven't slept with anyone except Charles for years, and I'm not seeing Charles at the moment. Not that it's any of your business, she added. But a look of relief had come over his face. Well then, he said, so it was love. No it wasn't, she said, I keep telling you there's no such thing. Love, that sort of love, is a literary con-trick. And an advertising con-trick and a media con-trick. I don't believe that, he said. We must talk more. I'll meet you for lunch at the Plaza, where we ate yesterday.

"So I ran away," said Robyn to Penny Black, after giving her a précis of this scene. "I phoned up the airport and found I could get back to Rummidge that morning via Heathrow on my ticket, and I took off."

"Without telling Wilcox?"

"I left a message for him at the Plaza. I couldn't face a sentimental inquest over lunch about the night before. And, you know, I was feeling frightfully guilty about missing my classes in the Department. I got back to Rummidge surprisingly early, because of the time difference. I took a taxi to the University and arrived just in time to take my second Women's Writing seminar. Swallow was very relieved to see me. The first group had given him a hard time over menstruation, I think – he was looking distinctly queasy. And I was able to take my third-year tutorial group back off Rupert Sutcliffe, to their great relief. So I went home that evening by bus quite pleased with myself. But of course, when I turned the corner of the street, there he was, waiting for me."

"Were you frightened?" Penny Black said. "Did you feel he might attack you?"

"Of course not," Robyn said. "Anyway, you can't feel really frightened of someone three inches shorter than you are."

As she approached her house, Vic got out of his car, his face white and tense. Why did you run off like that, he said. I had things to do in Rummidge, she said, rooting in her handbag for her keys. If I'd known how easy it was I'd have flown back yesterday evening, instead of staying overnight, it would have been better all round. Can I come in, he said. I suppose so, she said, if you must, but won't they be expecting you at home? Not yet, he said. I must talk to you. Alright, she said, as long as it's not about love and not about last night. You know that's what I want to talk about, he said. That's the condition, she said. Alright, he said, I suppose I have no choice.

She led him into the living-room and lit the gas fire. He looked round the room. You ought to get a woman in to clean for you, he said. I would never employ a woman to do my dirty work, she said, it's against my principles. Well a man then, he said, I believe they have male cleaners these days. I can't afford it, she said. I'll pay for it, he said, and she gave him a warning look. I like my house like it is, she said. It may look like chaos to you, but to me it's a filing system. I know exactly where everything is on the floor. A cleaning woman would tidy everything up, and then I'd be lost.

She offered to make a pot of tea, and he followed her out into the kitchen. He stared appalled at the heap of soiled dishes in the sink. Why don't you get a dishwasher, he said. Because I can't afford it, and no, you can't buy me one, she said. Anyway, I quite like washing up, it's therapeutic. You don't seem to need therapy very often, he said.

"Cheeky," Penny Black commented.

"I didn't mind," said Robyn. "I took it as a good sign, actually – that he was getting over his maudlin mood." She clambered down over the benches to splash water from a plastic bucket on the stove. Steam hissed angrily and the temperature rose a few degrees higher. She climbed back to her perch. "I tried to keep his mind off the love stuff by talking about the business side of the Frankfurt trip. But then I got a very unpleasant shock."

*

So when will you get this new toy of yours, then, she said, when they carried their tea back into the living-room. Oh, I should think six to nine months, he said. Could be twelve. That long, she said. It depends, he said, whether they've got something already built that's suitable or whether they have to start from scratch. I hope it won't be more than nine, he said, I have a hunch the recession has bottomed out. Business is going to pick up next year and with the new core blower coupled to the KW we'll be all set to exploit a rising market. I suppose you've got to produce more if the machine is to pay for itself, she said. Yes, he said, but there are savings on costs too. There'll be fewer breakdowns, less overtime to make up for breakdowns, and of course I'll be able to lose several men. What do you mean, lose, she said. Well, the new machine will replace half a dozen old ones, he said, so most of the operators will be redundant. But that's terrible, she said, if I'd known that, I'd never have helped you buy the wretched thing. But it stands to reason, he said, that's why you buy a CNC machine, to cut your labour costs. If I'd known it was going to cause redundancies, I'd never have had anything to do with it, she said. That's silly, he said, if you want to stay in business at all, you can't afford to be sentimental about a few men being laid off. Sentimental, she cried, look who's talking! The man whose knees go weak at the sound of Jennifer Rush, the man who believes in love at first fuck. That's different, he said, flinching at the word fuck, I'm talking about business, you don't understand. I understand that some men who have jobs today aren't going to have them this time next year, she said, thanks to you and me and Herr Winkler. Those old machines had to be renewed sooner or later, he said, they're always breaking down, and they're very tricky to operate, we're always having trouble with them, well, you know yourself . . . He faltered and stopped, seeing the expression in her face. Robyn stared at him. You don't mean to say that Danny Ram, operates one of those machines, she said. I thought you knew, he said.

"Well, you can imagine what a fool I felt," Robyn said. "After all the trouble I took back in January keeping Danny Ram's job for him, now I discovered I'd helped to lose it for him again."

"Sickening," Penny Black agreed. "How is it you didn't know?"

"I never knew exactly what job it was he had," said Robyn. "I mean, I don't know the names of all these machines, or what they do. I'm no engineer."

"Well I wouldn't brood on it," said Penny Black. "I bet Wilcox would have got rid of him anyway, as soon as your back was turned. He sounds like a real hard-nosed bastard."

"Hard-nosed and soft-centred. When he saw how upset I was he started to backtrack and pretend that it might not be necessary to lay men off after all, if things went very well, he said, they might be able to have a night shift – imagine working at night in that place, it's bad enough in the daytime . . . but that's by the by. And then he said he would guarantee to find Danny Ram another job somewhere in the factory."

"Just to please you? At the expense of some other poor sod, presumably."

"Exactly. That's what I told him."

You're playing with people's lives as if they're things to be bought and sold and given away, she said. You're offering me Danny Ram's job as a sop, as a bribe, as a present, like other men give their mistresses strings of pearls. I don't want you to be my mistress, he said, I want you to be my wife. She gaped at him for a moment, then threw back her head and laughed. You're out of your mind, she said, have you forgotten that you're married already? I'll get a divorce, he said. I refuse to listen to any more of this, she said, I think you'd better go home, I have a lot of essays to mark. Term ends tomorrow. Listen to me, he said, my marriage has been dead for years, we have nothing in common any more, Marjorie and me. And what do you think *we* have in common, she demanded. Not a single idea, not a single value, not a single interest. Last night, he said. Oh, shut up about last night, she said. That was just a fuck, nothing more or less. I wish you wouldn't keep saying that, he said. Anybody would think it had never happened before, she said, the way you go on about it. It never did happen to me before, he said, not like that. Oh, shut up, she said, go away, go home, for God's sake. She sat up very straight in her armchair, closed her eyes, and did some yoga breathing exercises. She heard a floorboard creak as he got to his feet, and felt his presence like a shadow falling over her. When will I see you again, he said. I've no idea, she said, without opening her eyes. I don't see any reason why we should ever meet again except by accident. That ridiculous scheme is finished. I don't have to go to your ghastly factory ever again, thank God. I'll be in touch, he said, and taking advantage of her closed eyes, kissed her quickly on the lips. She was on her feet instantly, glaring at him from her full height, hissing: *Leave me alone!* All right, he said, I'm going. At the door, he turned and looked back at her. When you're angry, he said, you look like a goddess.

"A *goddess*?" Penny Black repeated wonderingly.

"That's what he said. Heaven knows what he was on about."

Penny Black shifted her weight from one massive haunch to the other, making her pendulous breasts tremble. Runnels of sweat ran down between them and vanished into the damp undergrowth at her crotch. "I must say, Robyn, putting ideology aside for a moment . . . I mean, it's not every day of the week a women gets to be called a goddess."

"It's just a nuisance, as far as I'm concerned, a nuisance and an embarrassment. He keeps phoning me up, and he writes every day."

"What does he say?"

"I don't know. I put the phone down immediately and I throw the letters away without reading them."

"Poor Vic!"

"Don't waste your pity on him – what about poor me? I can't get on with my research."

"Poor lovesick Vic. Next thing you know, he'll be outside your house serenading you."

"Playing his Jennifer Rush and Randy Crawford cassettes under my window." They giggled together. "No, but it isn't funny really," said Robyn.

"Does his wife know?"

"I think not," said Robyn, "But she must suspect something. And I had a visit from his daughter today."

"His *daughter*?"

Sandra Wilcox had turned up in the Department without an appointment, but Robyn happened to be in her room checking the proofs of a Finals paper at the time. The girl was fashionably dressed all in black, with a mask of white make-up, and her hair was expensively contrived to look as if she had just been electrocuted. Oh, hallo Sandra, said Robyn, come in, aren't you at school today? I had to go to the dentist's this afternoon, Sandra said. It wasn't worth going back to school so I thought I'd drop in. Fine, said Robyn, what can I do for you? It's not for me, it's my Dad, said Sandra. Why, what's the matter with him, said Robyn anxiously. I mean it's my Dad who made me come, said Sandra. Oh I see, said Robyn, with a light laugh, but she had given something away to the girl, and it was a subtext of their conversation about the pros and cons of going to university. Why not apply for admission in 1988, said Robyn, and take a year off after leaving school to make up your mind? I could, I suppose, said Sandra, I could get a job at Tweezers – I already work there Saturdays. Tweezers, Robyn said, what's that? Unisex hairdressers, said Sandra. She looked round the room. Have you read all these books, she said. Not all of them, Robyn said, but some I've read several times. What for, said Sandra. You're not thinking of applying for English, are you, Sandra, said

Robyn. No, said Sandra. Good, said Robyn, because there's a lot of re-reading in English. I thought I'd do psychology, if I did anything, said Sandra. I'm interested in the way people's minds work. I'm not sure psychology will help you there, said Robyn, it's mostly about rats as far as I can make out. You'd probably learn more about how people's minds work by reading novels. Like my parents, said Sandra. I'd love to know what makes them tick. My Dad is acting most peculiar, lately. Is he, said Robyn, in what way? He doesn't listen to a word anyone says to him, said Sandra, he goes about in a dream. He banged into another car the other day. Oh dear, I hope he wasn't hurt, said Robyn. No, it was just a bump, but it's the first accident he's ever had in twenty-five years' driving. Mum's worried about him, I can tell, her Valium consumption's gone up. Does your mother take Valium regularly? said Robyn. Does she, said Sandra, pick her up and shake her and she rattles. And now he's reading books, novels, he never did that in his life before. What kind of novels? said Robyn. My school copy of *Jane Eyre* for one, said Sandra, we're doing it for A-Level. I was looking for it everywhere the other day, it made me late for school. Eventually I found it under a cushion on his armchair in the lounge. What's he want with *Jane Eyre* at his age?

"He's obviously trying to study your interests," said Penny Black. "It's rather touching, in a way."

"Touched, you mean," said Robyn. "What shall I do? Next thing you know, I'll have Mrs Wilcox in my office, stoned on Valium, begging me not to entice her husband away from her. I feel as if I'm getting dragged into a classic realist text, full of causality and morality. How can I get out of it?"

"I've had enough," said Penny Black, getting to her feet.

"I'm sorry, Penny," said Robyn, contritely.

"I mean, I've had enough of this heat. I'm going to shower."

"I'll come too." said Robyn. "But what shall I do?"

"You'd better run away again," said Penny Black.

4

So Robyn piled her books and her notes and her BBC micro in the back of the Renault, and locked up her little house and went to spend the remainder of the Easter vacation with her parents in their house with a view of the sea on the South Coast. She instructed Pamela, the Department Secretary, not to divulge her whereabouts to anybody except in the direst emergency, explaining that she wanted to get on with her research free from any distraction. She gave the same reason to her somewhat puzzled parents for descending upon them so abruptly and for so extended a visit. Her old bedroom was much as she had left it on going up to the university; the photos of David Bowie and The Who and Pink Floyd had been taken off the walls, and the wallpaper renewed, but the woodwork was still painted the rather violent pink she had chosen in late adolescence. She set up her word-processor on the scratched and stained desk where she had swotted for her A-Levels, under the window from which, when you looked up from your work, you could see the horizon of the English Channel ruled like a faint blue line between the roofs of two neighbouring houses.

She spent most of her time in this room, but when she went out into the town to shop, or just to stretch her legs, she couldn't help reflecting that although she was only a hundred and fifty miles from Rummidge, she might as well have been in another country. There was no visible industry here, and no visible working class. Black and brown faces were rare, mostly belonging to students from the University, or to tourists who came in motor coaches to stare at the fine old cathedral set serenely among green lawns and venerable trees. The shops were small, special-ised, and served by suavely deferential staff. The customers seemed all to be wearing brand-new clothes from Jaeger and to be driving brand-new Volvos. The streets and gardens were well-groomed, the air soft and clean, smelling faintly of the sea. Robyn thought of Rummidge sprawled darkly and densely in the heart of England, with all its noise and fumes and ugliness, its blind-walled metal-bashing factories and its long, worm-like streets of tiny terraced houses crawling over the hills, its congested motorways and black canals, its hideous concrete core, awash with litter and defaced with graffiti, and she wondered whether it was by luck or cunning that the English bourgeoisie had kept the industrial revolution out of their favourite territory.

"You don't know what the real world is like down here," she told her parents at supper one day.

"Oh, but we do," said her father. "That's why we chose to stay. I could have had the Chair at Liverpool years ago. I went up there and walked about the streets for a morning, and I told the Vice-Chancellor, thanks very much, but I'd rather be a Reader all my life than move up here."

"I don't suppose you'll be sorry to leave Rummidge, will you dear?" said her mother.

"I shall be extremely sorry," said Robyn. "Especially if I can't get another job."

"If only something would turn up here," her mother sighed. "Your father could use his influence."

"On the contrary," said Professor Penrose, "I should have to declare my interest and have nothing to do with the appointment." Professor Penrose always spoke in a formal and deliberate manner, in an effort, Robyn sometimes thought, to disguise his Australian origins. "But the problem will not arise, I'm afraid. We're suffering the same cuts as everywhere else. There are no prospects of any new posts in the Arts Faculty, unless our UGC letter is very much better than expected."

"What letter is that?" Robyn asked.

"The UGC is going to announce, probably some time in May, the distribution of the available funds to each university, based on an assessment of their research record and the viability of their departments. There are rumours that one or two universities will be closed down completely."

"They wouldn't dare!" Robyn exclaimed.

"This Government is capable of anything," said Professor Penrose, who was a member of the SDP. "They are systematically destroying the finest university system in the world. Whatever happened to the spirit of the Robbins Report? Higher education for everyone who could benefit. Did I ever tell you," he said, smiling reminiscently at his daughter, "that someone once asked me if we called you Robyn after the Robbins report?"

"Many times, Daddy," said Robyn. "Needless to say I deplore the cuts, but don't you think, in retrospect, that the way Robbins was implemented was a mistake?"

Professor Penrose laid down his knife and fork and looked at Robyn over his spectacles. "What do you mean?"

"Well, was it a good idea to build so many new universities in parks on the outskirts of cathedral cities and county towns?"

"But why shouldn't universities be in nice places rather than nasty ones?" said Mrs Penrose plaintively.

"Because it perpetuates the Oxbridge idea of higher education as a version of pastoral, a privileged idyll cut off from ordinary living."

"Nonsense," said Professor Penrose. "The new universities were carefully sited in places that, for one reason or another, had been left out of the development of higher education."

"That would make sense if they served their own communities, but they don't. Every autumn there's this absurd migration of well-heeled youth going from Norwich to Brighton or from Brighton to York. And having to be accommodated in expensive halls of residence when they get there."

"You seem to have acquired a very utilitarian view of universities, from your sojourn in Rummidge," said Professor Penrose, who was one of the very few people Robyn knew who used the word sojourn in casual conversation. Robyn made no answer. She was well aware that she had adopted some of the arguments of Vic Wilcox, but she had no intention of mentioning him to her parents.

When they were washing up, Mrs Penrose asked Robyn if she would like to invite Charles down for the weekend.

"We're not seeing each other at the moment," she said.

"Oh dear, is it off again?"

"Is what off?"

"You know what I mean, dear."

"There was never anything 'on', Mummy, if you mean, as I presume, getting married."

"I don't understand you young people," Mrs Penrose sighed unhappily. "Charles is such a nice young man, and you have such a lot in common."

"Perhaps too much," said Robyn.

"What do you mean?"

"I don't know," said Robyn, who had spoken without premeditation. "It's just a bit boring when you agree about everything."

"Basil brought a most unsuitable girl down here," said Mrs Penrose. "I do hope he doesn't intend to marry her."

"Debbie? When was that?"

"Oh, some time in February. You've met her, then?"

"Yes. I believe it's all off, as you would say."

"Oh, good, she was a frightfully common little thing, I thought."

Robyn smiled secretly.

Basil himself confirmed Robyn's speculation when he came home for the Easter weekend. He was loudly pleased with himself, having just moved to a new job with a Japanese bank in the City at a greatly increased salary. "No, I'm not seeing Debbie any more," he said, "socially or professionally. Is Charles?"

"I don't know," said Robyn. "I'm incommunicado at the moment, trying to finish my book."

"What book is that?"

"It's on the image of women in nineteenth-century fiction."

"Does the world really need another book on nineteenth-century fiction?" said Basil.

"I don't know, but it's going to get one," said Robyn. "It's my chief hope of getting a permanent job somewhere."

When Basil went back to London on Easter Monday evening, peace and quiet returned to the house, and Robyn resumed work on her book. She made excellent progress. It was a house that respected scholarship. No radios played. The telephone bell was muted. The cleaning lady's vacuuming was strictly controlled. Professor Penrose worked in his study and Robyn worked in her bedroom, and Mrs Penrose padded quietly to and fro between the two of them, bringing coffee and tea at appropriate intervals, silently setting the fresh cups down on their desks, and removing the soiled ones. To minimise distraction, Robyn denied herself her daily fix of the *Guardian*, and only the occasional late news on television brought her tidings of events in the great world: the American raid on Libya, riots in British prisons, violent confrontations between striking printers and police at Wapping. These public outrages and conflicts, which would normally have stirred her to indignation and perhaps action (signing a petition, joining a demonstration), hardly penetrated her absorbed concentration on the book. By the end of the vacation, it was three-quarters written in draft.

She drove back to Rummidge in buoyant mood. She felt pleased with what she had written, though she hankered for confirmation from some other person, some kindred spirit, some knowledgeable but sympathetic reader, someone like Charles. They had always relied on each other for such help. It was a pity, in the circumstances, that they were not seeing each other any more. Of course, nothing decisive or final had been said. There was no reason why she shouldn't ring him up when she got home, and ask if he would read her draft, no reason at all. It would not even be necessary to meet, though obviously it would be more convenient if he could come over for a weekend and read the manuscript there and then. Robyn decided she would phone Charles that evening.

When she got back to her house in Rummidge, there was a letter from Charles on the doormat, along with nine from Vic Wilcox which she threw straight into the waste-bin. She opened Charles's letter, which was quite bulky, at once, and read it standing in the kitchen with her outdoor coat still on. Then she took off her coat and made a cup of tea and sat down and read it again.

★

My dear Robyn,

I've tried to phone you several times without success, and the Secretary of your Department refuses for some reason to admit that she knows where you are, so I am writing to you – which is probably the best thing to do, anyway, in the circumstances. The telephone is an unsatisfactory medium for communicating anything important, allowing neither the genuine absence of writing nor the true presence of face-to-face conversation, but only a feeble compromise. A thesis topic there, perhaps? "Telephonic communication and affective alienation in modern fiction, with special reference to Evelyn Waugh, Ford Madox Ford, Henry Green . . ."

But I've finished with thesis topics. What I have to tell you is that I have determined upon a change of career. I'm going to become a merchant banker.

"Have you done laughing?" as Alton Locke says to his readers. I am of course rather old to be making such a change, but I feel quite confident that I can make a success of it and I'm very excited by the challenge. I think it's the first *risky* thing I've ever done in my life, and I feel a new man in consequence. I've got to undergo a period of training, of course, but even so I shall start at a higher salary than my present one, and after that, well, the sky's the limit. It's not just the money, though, that has led me to this decision, though I *am* rather fed up with the constant struggle to make ends meet, but a feeling that, as a university teacher, especially at a place like Suffolk, I've been left behind by the tide of history, stranded on the mudflats of an obsolete ideology.

You and I, Robyn, grew up in a period when the state was smart: state schools, state universities, state-subsidised arts, state welfare, state medicine – these were things progressive, energetic people believed in. It isn't like that any more. The Left pays lip-service to those things, but without convincing anybody, including themselves. The people who work in state institutions are depressed, demoralised, fatalistic. Witness the extraordinary meekness with which the academic establishment has accepted the cuts (has there been a single high-level resignation, as distinct from early retirements?). It's no use blaming Thatcher, as if she was some kind of witch who has enchanted the nation. She is riding the *Zeitgeist*. When trade unions offer their members discount subscriptions to BUPA, the writing is on the wall for old-style socialism. What the new style will be, I don't know, but I believe there is more chance of identifying it from the vantage-point of the City than from the University of Suffolk. The first thing that struck me about the City when I started observing Debbie at work was the sheer *energy* of the place, and the second was its democracy. A working-class girl like Debbie pulling down thirty-thousand-odd a year is by no means an anomalous figure. Contrary to the stereotype of the ex-public-school stockbroker, it doesn't matter what your social background is in the City these days, as long as you're good at your job. Money is a great leveller, upwards.

As to our universities, I've come to the conclusion that they are élitist where they should be egalitarian and egalitarian where they should be élitist. We admit only a tiny proportion of the age group as students and give them a very labour-intensive education (élitist), but we pretend that all universities and all university teachers are equal and must therefore have the same funding and a common payscale, with automatic tenure (egalitarian). This worked all right as long as the country was prepared to go on pumping more and more money into the system, but as soon as the money supply was reduced, universities could only balance their books by persuading people to retire early, often the very people they can least afford to lose. For those who remain the prospects are bleak: bigger classes, heavier work-loads, scant chances of promotion or of moving to a new job. You know as well as I do that, apart from the occasional chair, new appointments are always made, if they're made at all, at the bottom of the scale. I reckon I would be stuck in Suffolk for another fifteen years, possibly for ever, if I stayed in academic life. I don't think I could face that.

The opportunity to change direction came, curiously enough, from my developing these thoughts, or something like them, in the company of a big wheel in Debbie's bank, at a party she took me to. I began rather fancifully to propose the idea of privatising the universities, as a solution to their financial crisis, and as a way of promoting healthy competition. Staff could buy shares in their own universities and have a financial stake in their success. I was only half serious, in fact I was half pissed, but the big wheel was rather impressed. We need men with bold ideas like that, he said, to spot new investment opportunities. That's what started me thinking about a change of career. When I went to see the big wheel a few days later, he was very encouraging. He wants to set up a kind of strategic planning team within the bank, and the idea is that I will join it when I've acquired some basic experience in securities etc. I have to admit, in spite of the stuff about democracy above, that it helped that I was at Westminster, because his son is there. Also that I had Maths to A-Level.

But, you will ask, what about the ideas to which we have dedicated our lives for the last ten years, what about critical theory and all that?

Well, I see no fundamental inconsistency. I regard myself as simply exchanging one semiotic system for another, the literary for the numerical, a game with high philosophical stakes for a game with high monetary stakes – but a *game* in each case, in which satisfaction comes ultimately from playing rather than winning, since there are no absolute winners, for the game never ends. Anyway, I have no intention of giving up reading. I don't see why deconstruction shouldn't be my hobby as other men have model railways or tropical fish as hobbies, and it will be easier to pursue without the anxiety of integrating it into one's work.

To be honest, I have had my doubts for some time about the pedagogic application of poststructuralist theory, doubts that I've suppressed, as a priest, I imagine, suppresses his theological doubts, hiding them away one by one until one day there is no space left in which to hide them and he finally admits to himself and to the world that he has lost his faith. There was a moment when we were talking in your house a couple of months ago, and you were putting the case against teaching poststructuralism as a kind of Devil's Advocate – do you remember? You wanted reassurance – your factory manager friend had got you rattled – so I told you what you wanted to hear, but it was a close thing. You were articulating so many of my own doubts that I nearly "came out" there and then.

Poststructuralist theory is a very intriguing philosophical game for very clever players. But the irony of teaching it to young people who have read almost nothing except their GCE set texts and *Adrian Mole*, who know almost nothing about the Bible or classical mythology, who cannot recognise an ill-formed sentence, or recite poetry with any sense of rhythm – the irony of teaching them about the arbitrariness of the signifier in week three of their first year becomes in the end too painful to bear . . .

So, I've resigned from Suffolk – taken severance, actually, they're desperate to lose staff, so I have a nice lump sum of £30,000 which I confidently expect to enhance by at least 25 per cent in the equity market by the end of the year. I'm moving in with Debbie, so living expenses will be modest. I hope you and I can still be friends. I shall always think of you with the greatest admiration and affection. Good luck in the future – if anyone deserves a tenured university job, it's you, Robyn.

Love, Charles

"You shit," Robyn said aloud, when she had finished reading the letter. "You utter shit." But the "utter" was a hyperbole. There were things in this letter which struck a nerve of reluctant assent, mixed up with things she found false and obnoxious. 'Twas all a muddle.

Meanwhile, Vic Wilcox was having a hard time, nursing his unrequited love. The weekdays were not so bad, when he could distract himself with work. He pushed on faster than ever with the rationalisation programme at Pringle's, harried his managers mercilessly, chaired endless meetings, doubled the frequency of his surprise swoops on the shop floor. You could almost hear the effect of all this pressure when you pushed through the door into the machine shop: more decibels clashing to a brisker rhythm. In the foundry, they started clearing a space for the new core blower, and Vic made this the occasion for a full-scale good housekeeping campaign. Under his personal supervision, the debris of years was swept away.

But there was a limit to the number of hours even Vic could work. There were still too many left over – driving to and from work, at home in the evenings and at weekends, and, above all, lying awake in the early morning in the darkened bedroom – when he couldn't keep his thoughts from Robyn Penrose and their night of love (for so he persisted in regarding it). There is no need to record these thoughts in detail. They were for the most part repetitive and predictable: a mixture of erotic fantasy and erotic reminiscence, wish-fulfilment and self-pity, accompanied by snatches of Jennifer Rush. But they made him more than usually silent and abstracted around the house. He was subject to fits of absent-mindedness. In the kitchen he washed up cups that had just been cleaned and dried. He would go to the garage for a tool and, when he got there, would have forgotten what he wanted it for. One morning he drove halfway to West Wallsbury, dimly registering that the traffic was unusually light, before he remembered that it was a Sunday morning and he was supposed to be picking up his father. One evening he went upstairs to change his trousers and proceeded mechanically to take off all his clothes and put on his pyjamas. It was only when he was about to get into bed that he snapped out of his reverie. Marjorie came into the room at this moment and stared at him. "What are you doing?" she said.

"I'm having an early night," he improvised, turning back the bedclothes.

"But it's only half-past eight!"

"I'm tired."

"You must be ill. Shall I call the doctor?"

"No, I'm just tired." He got into bed and closed his eyes to shut out Marjorie's worried frown.

"Vic, is there anything wrong?" she said. "Any trouble at work?"

"No," he said. "Work is fine. The factory is on song. We'll make a profit this month."

"Well, what's the matter then? You're not yourself. You've not been yourself since you went to Germany. D'you think you caught a bug or something?"

"No," said Vic. "I haven't got a bug." He had not told Marjorie that Robyn had accompanied him to Frankfurt.

"I'll get you an aspirin."

Vic heard her moving about the room, drawing the curtains, and telling Raymond to turn down his hi-fi because his father wasn't feeling well. To save a lot of argument, he swallowed the aspirin and, shortly afterwards, fell asleep. At three in the morning he was wide awake. With hours to go before the alarm, he played blue movies in his head featuring himself and Robyn Penrose, and crept guiltily to the *en suite* bathroom to seek a schoolboy's relief.

"Marjorie's worried about you," his father said the following Sunday evening, when Vic was driving him home after tea.

Vic feigned surprise. "Why?"

"She says you're not yourself. Nor more you are."

"I'm fine," said Vic. "When was this?"

"This afternoon, when you was out. What d'you want to go off on your own like that for?"

"You were asleep, Dad," he said. "And Marjorie doesn't like walking."

"You could've asked her."

Vic drove in silence.

"It isn't a wench, is it?" said his father.

"What?" Vic forced an incredulous laugh.

"You're not carryin' on with some young wench, are you? I seen it happen enough times," he went on rapidly, as if he feared having his question answered. "Bosses and their secretaries. It always gets round at work."

"My secretary is a pain in the arse," said Vic. "Anyway, she's made other arrangements."

"I'm glad to hear it. The game's not worth the candle, son, take my word for it. I seen it happen many a time, blokes that left their wives for a young wench. They ended up penniless, paying for two families out of one pay packet. Lost their homes, lost their furniture. Wives took it all. Think of that, Vic, next time some flighty piece makes eyes at you."

This time Vic did not have to force his guffaw.

227

"You can laugh," said Mr Wilcox huffily, "but you wouldn't be the first one what's made a fool of himself for a pretty face or a trim figure. It don't last though. It don't last."

"Not like furniture?"

"Definitely."

This conversation, absurd as it was, had the effect of putting Vic on his guard. He wrote his letters to Robyn at work, in the lunch break when Shirley was out of the office, and posted them himself. He telephoned her from call-boxes on the way to and from work. Not that these efforts to communicate succeeded, but they relieved his pent-up feelings somewhat, and his secret remained safe.

Marjorie, though, was plainly disturbed. Her shopping developed a manic intensity. She brought home a new dress or pair of shoes every day, and as often as not exchanged them the next. She had her hair done in a new style and wept for hours at the result. She started a diet that consisted entirely of grapefruit and abandoned it after three days. She bought an exercise bicycle and could be heard puffing and wheezing behind the door of the guest bedroom where it had been erected. She rented a sunbed from the Riviera Sunbed company, who delivered and collected at home, and lay under it in a two-piece swimsuit and dark glasses, anxiously gripping a kitchen timer in case the built-in time switch failed, in mortal terror of overcooking herself. Vic realised that she was doing all this to make herself attractive to him, probably following the advice of some trashy woman's magazine. He was touched, but in a distant, detached way. Marjorie looked at him from the far side of his obsession, with dumb affection and concern, like a dog on the hearth. He felt as if he had only to stretch out his hand and she would jump all over him, licking his face. But he could not do it. Awake in the early hours of the morning, he no longer sought the animal comfort of her body's warmth. He lay on the edge of the mattress, as far as possible from the humped, Valium-drugged shape that groaned and whimpered in its sleep, wondering how to get back in touch with Robyn Penrose.

SIX

The story is told. I think I now see the judicious reader putting on his spectacles to look for the moral. It would be an insult to his sagacity to offer directions. I only say, God speed him in the quest!

Charlotte Brontë: *Shirley*

1

The new term began with a spell of fine weather. Students disported themselves on the lawns of the campus, the young girls in their bright summer dresses sprouting like crocuses in the warm sunshine. There were laughter and music in the air, and dalliance under the trees. Some tutors elected to hold their classes outdoors, and sat cross-legged on the grass, discoursing on philosophy or physics to little groups of reclining ephebes, as they did in the Golden Age. But this idyllic appearance was deceptive. The students were apprehensive about their forthcoming examinations, and the world of uncertain employment that lay beyond that threshold. The staff were apprehensive about the forthcoming UGC letter, and its implications for their future. For Robyn, though, the letter was her last hope of a reprieve. If Rummidge, and more particularly its English Department, received strong support from the University Grants Committee, there was just a chance, Philip Swallow told her, a sliver of a chance, that when Rupert Sutcliffe retired the following year (not an early retirement – on the contrary, Swallow tartly observed, it was if anything overdue), they would be allowed to fill the vacancy.

Because she had worked on her book up till the last moment of the vacation, Robyn was less well prepared than usual for her teaching, and the first week was hectic. She was obliged to sit up late each night, urgently refreshing her memory of *Vanity Fair* and *The Picture of Dorian Gray* and *The Rainbow* and "The Waste Land" and *1984*, texts on which she had rashly committed herself to giving tutorials all in the same week, not to mention revising a lecture on Virginia Woolf and reading Dorothy Richardson's *Pointed Roofs* for the first time in her life for her Women's Writing seminars. This gruelling work-load made it easier, however, to forget Charles and his apostasy. As to Vic Wilcox, her abrupt flight from Rummidge a month before seemed to have had the desired effect, for he no longer pestered her by letter or telephone. Robyn suddenly found herself liberated from the attentions of the two men who had laid claim to her affective life in the recent and long-term past. She was her own woman once more. If this consciousness did not kindle the glow of satisfaction that might have been expected – if, perversely, she felt a little lonely and neglected by the end of the week – this was no doubt because she had been overworking.

Saturday offered a welcome social diversion. A friend of Philip Swallow's, Professor Morris Zapp, had touched down briefly in

Rummidge on his way from the West Coast of the United States to somewhere else, and the Swallows were giving a party for him to which Robyn was invited. She was familiar with his publications: originally a Jane Austen specialist in the Neo-Critical close-reading tradition, he had converted himself (rather opportunistically, Robyn thought) into a kind of deconstructionist in the nineteen-seventies, and enjoyed an international reputation in both guises. He was also something of a local legend at Rummidge, having steered the Department safely through the student revolution of '69, when he had exchanged posts with Philip Swallow. The two men had swapped more than their jobs, according to Rupert Sutcliffe, who whispered to Robyn that there had been an affair between Zapp and Hilary Swallow at the same time that Swallow was carrying on with Zapp's then wife Désirée, subsequently famous as the author of *Difficult Days* and *Men*, big best-selling books written in a mode Robyn sometimes called "vulgar feminism". She was curious to meet Professor Zapp.

Robyn arrived a little late at the Swallows' modernised Victorian villa, and their living-room was already crowded, but she had no difficulty in identifying the guest of honour as she glanced through the window on her way up the garden path to the front porch. He was wearing a seersucker jacket in canary yellow with a bold blue check, and was smoking a cigar the size of a small zeppelin. He was bulky rather than big, with grizzled, receding hair, a wrinkled, sun-tanned face, and a grey moustache that drooped downwards at each end rather lugubriously, perhaps because at that moment he was having his ear bent by Bob Busby.

Philip Swallow opened the door to Robyn and ushered her into the living-room. "Let me introduce you to Morris," he said. "He needs rescuing."

Robyn obediently followed Swallow as he pushed his way through the throng and nudged Bob Busby away from Morris Zapp with a light shoulder-charge. "Morris," he said, "this is Robyn Penrose, the girl I was telling you about."

"Girl, Philip? Girl? Men have been castrated for less at Euphoric State. You mean woman. Or lady. Which do you prefer?" he said to Robyn, as he shook her hand.

"Person would be fine," said Robyn.

"Person, right. Are you going to get this person a drink, Philip?"

"Yes, of course," said Swallow, looking flustered. "Red or white?"

"Why don't you get her a proper drink?" said Zapp, who appeared to have a tumbler of neat scotch in his fist.

"Well, er, of course, if . . ." Swallow looked even more flustered.

"White will be fine," said Robyn.

"I always know when I'm in England," said Morris Zapp, as Philip Swallow went off, "because when you go to a party, the first thing anyone says to you is, '*Red or white?*' I used to think it was some kind of password, like the Wars of the Roses were still going on or something."

"Are you here for long?" Robyn asked.

"I'm going to Dubrovnik tomorrow. Ever been there?"

"No," said Robyn.

"Neither have I. I'm breaking a rule: never attend a conference in a Communist country."

"Isn't that a rather bigoted rule?" Robyn said.

"There's nothing political about it, it's just that I've heard such terrible things about East European hotels. But they tell me Yugoslavia is half-Westernised, so I thought, what the hell, I'll risk it."

"It seems a long way to travel for a conference."

"There's more than one. After Dubrovnik I go to Vienna, Geneva, Nice and Milan. Milan is a private visit," he said, brushing the ends of his moustache upwards with the back of his hand. "Looking up an old friend. But the rest are conferences. You been to any good ones lately?"

"No, I'm afraid I missed the UTE conference this year."

"If that's the one I attended here in '79, then you did well to avoid it," said Morris Zapp. "I mean real conferences, international conferences."

"I couldn't afford to go to one of those," said Robyn. "Our overseas conference fund has been cut to the bone."

"Cuts, cuts, cuts," said Morris Zapp, "that's all anyone will talk about here. First Philip, then Busby, now you."

"That's what life is like in British universities these days, Morris," said Philip Swallow, presenting Robyn with a glass of rather warm Soave. "I spend all my time on committees arguing about how to respond to the cuts. I haven't read a book in months, let alone tried to write one."

"Well, I have," said Robyn.

"Read one or written one?" said Morris Zapp.

"Written one," said Robyn. "Well, three-quarters of it, anyway."

"Ah, Robyn," said Philip Swallow, "you put us all to shame. What shall we do without you?" He shuffled off, shaking his head.

"You leaving Rummidge, Robyn?" said Morris Zapp.

She explained her position. "So you see," she concluded, "this book is very important to me. If by any chance there should be a job advertised in the next twelve months, I ought to stand a fair chance of getting it, with two books to my credit."

233

"You're right," said Morris Zapp. "There are full professors at large in this country who have published less." His eye strayed in the direction of Philip Swallow. "What's your book about?"

Robyn told him. Morris Zapp vivaed her briskly about its contents and methodology. The names of prominent feminist critics and theorists crackled between them like machinegun fire: Elaine Showalter, Sandra Gilbert, Susan Gubar, Shoshana Felman, Luce Irigaray, Catherine Clément, Susan Suleiman, Mieke Bal – Morris Zapp had read them all. He recommended an article in the latest issue of *Poetics Today* which she hadn't seen. Finally he asked her if she had made arrangements to publish her book in America.

"No, my British publishers distributed my first book in the States themselves – the one on the industrial novel. I suppose the same will happen with this one."

"Who are they?"

"Lecky, Windrush and Bernstein."

Morris Zapp pulled a face. "They're terrible. Didn't Philip tell you what they did to him? Lost all his review copies. Sent them out a year late."

"Oh, dear," said Robyn.

"How many did you sell in America?"

"I don't know. Not many."

"I'm a reader for Euphoric State University Press," said Morris Zapp. "Send me your manuscript and I'll have a look at it."

"That's extremely kind of you," said Robyn, "but I already have a contract with Lecky, Windrush and Bernstein."

"If Euphoric State make an offer for the American rights, it would be in their interest to go along with it," said Morris Zapp. "They could sell them the camera-ready copy. Of course, I may not like it. But you look like a smart girl to me."

"Person."

"Person, sorry."

"How shall I get the manuscript to you?"

"Could you drop it here tomorrow morning before eight-thirty?" said Morris Zapp. "I'm catching the 9.45 shuttle to Heathrow."

Robyn left the party early. Philip Swallow intercepted her as she wormed her way through the crowded hall on her way to the front door. "Oh, leaving so soon?" he said.

"Professor Zapp has kindly offered to look at my work-in-progress. It's still on floppy discs, so I'm going home to print it out."

"What a pity, you should have brought him," said Philip Swallow.

"Who?"

"That young man of yours from Suffolk."

"Oh, Charles! I'm not seeing Charles any more. He's become a merchant banker."

"*Has* he? How very interesting." Philip Swallow swayed slightly on his feet, whether from inebriation or fatigue she couldn't tell, and supported himself against the wall with a locked arm, which had the effect of barring her progress. Over his shoulder Robyn saw Mrs Swallow regarding them suspiciously. "Isn't it extraordinary how interesting money has become lately? Do you know, I've suddenly started reading the business pages in the *Guardian* after thirty years of skipping straight from the arts pages to the sports reports."

"I can't say it interests me much," said Robyn, ducking under Swallow's arm. "I must go, I'm afraid."

"I suppose it started when I bought some British Telecom shares," said Swallow, swivelling on his heel and following her to the front door. "Do you know, they're worth twice what I paid for them now?"

"Congratulations," said Robyn. "How much profit have you made?"

"Two hundred pounds," said Swallow. "I wish I'd bought more, now. I'm wondering whether to apply for British Gas. D'you think your young man would advise me?"

"He's not my young man," said Robyn. "Why don't you write and ask him?"

Robyn sat up all night printing out her book. She considered the effort would be worthwhile if she could secure the endorsement of a prestigious imprint like Euphoric State University Press. Besides, there was something about Morris Zapp that inspired hope. He had blown into the jaded, demoralised atmosphere of Rummidge University like an invigorating breeze, intimating that there were still places in the world where scholars and critics pursued their professional goals with zestful confidence, where conferences multiplied and grants were to be had to attend them, where conversation at academic parties was more likely to be about the latest controversial book or article than about the latest scaling-down of departmental maintenance grants. She felt renewed faith in her book, and her vocation, as she crouched, yawning and red-eyed, over her computer.

Even at draft speed, it took a long time to spew out her sixty thousand words, and it was nearly eight-fifteen in the morning when she finished the task. She drove quickly through the deserted Sunday streets to deliver her manuscript. It was a bright sunny morning, with a strong wind that was stripping the cherry-blossom from the trees. A taxi trembled at the kerb outside the Swallows' house. In the front porch Hilary Swallow, in a dressing-gown, was saying goodbye to

235

Morris Zapp, while Philip, carrying Morris Zapp's suitcase, hovered anxiously halfway down the garden path, like a complaisant cuckold seeing off the lover of the night before. But whatever passion there might have been between Zapp and Mrs Swallow had cooled long ago, Robyn inferred, from the merely amicable way they brushed each other's cheeks. Indeed, it was difficult to imagine these three almost elderly figures being involved in a sexual intrigue at all.

"Come on, Morris!" Swallow called out. "Your taxi's waiting." Then he swung round and caught sight of Robyn. "Good Lord – Robyn! What are you doing here at this hour of the morning?"

As she was explaining all over again, Morris Zapp came waddling down the garden path, an open Burberry flapping round his knees. "Hiya Robyn, howya doin'?" He drew a cigar like a long-barrelled weapon from an inside pocket and clamped it between his teeth.

"Here's the manuscript."

"Great, I'll read it as soon as I can." He lit his cigar, shielding the flame against the wind.

"It's unfinished, as I told you. And unrevised."

"Sure, sure," said Morris Zapp. "I'll let you know what I think. If I like it, I'll call you, if I don't I'll mail it back. Is your phone number on the manuscript?"

"No," said Robyn, "I'll give it to you."

"Do that. Haven't you noticed that in the modern world good news comes by telephone and bad news by mail?"

"Now that you mention it," said Robyn, scribbling her phone number on the outside of the package.

"Morris, the taxi," said Philip Swallow.

"Relax, Philip, he's not going to run away – are you, driver?"

"No sir," said the taxi-driver, from behind his wheel, "it's all the same to me."

"There you are," said Morris Zapp, stuffing Robyn's manuscript into a briefcase bulging with books and periodicals.

"I mean, the meter is ticking over."

"So what?"

"I'm afraid I've become a bit obsessive about waste since becoming Dean," Philip Swallow sighed. "I can't help it."

"Well, hang in there, Philip," said Morris Zapp. "Or as you Brits say, keep your pecker up." He wheezed with laughter and coughed cigar smoke. "You should come back to Euphoric State for a visit some time. It would do you good to watch us spending money."

"Are you going to stay there till you retire?" said Philip Swallow.

"Retire? I hate the sound of that word," said Morris Zapp. "Anyway they've just discovered that compulsory retirement is unconstitutional, it's a form of ageism. And why should I move? I have a contract with Euphoric State that says nobody in the humanities is to be paid more than me. If they want to hire some hotshot from one of the Ivy League schools at an inflated salary, they have to pay me at least one thousand dollars more than he's getting."

"Why restrict it to the humanities, Morris?" said Swallow.

"You have to be realistic," said Zapp. "Guys that can cure cancer, or blow up the world, deserve a little more than us literary critics."

"I've never heard such modesty from your lips before," said Swallow.

"Ah well, we all mellow as we get older," said Morris Zapp, clambering into the cab. "*Ciao*, folks."

Blossom swirled in the road like confetti as the taxi drew away. They stood on the edge of the pavement and waved until the car turned the corner.

"He's fun, isn't he?" said Robyn.

"He's a rogue," said Philip Swallow. "An amiable rogue. I'm surprised that he wanted to see your book."

"Why?"

"He can't stand feminists, usually. They've given him such a rough time in the past, at conferences and in reviews."

"He seemed well up in the literature."

"Oh, Morris is always well up, you have to grant him that. I wonder what his game is, though . . ."

"You don't think he would plagiarise my book, do you?" said Robyn, who had heard of such things happening.

"I shouldn't think so," said Philip Swallow. "He'd find it rather difficult to pass off a piece of feminist criticism as his own work. Will you come in for a cup of coffee?"

"Thanks, but I've been up all night, printing off my book. All I want to do at this moment is fall into bed."

"As you wish," said Philip Swallow, walking her to her car. "How are you getting on with your report, by the way?"

"Report?"

"On the Shadow Scheme."

"Oh, that. I'm a bit behind with that, actually," said Robyn. "I've been working flat out on my book, you see."

"Yes," said Philip Swallow, "I suppose you might as well leave it until after the next stage, now."

Robyn didn't understand this remark of Philip Swallow's, but she attributed the obscurity of its reference to his deafness, and was too tired at the time to try and sort it out. She went home and slept until late afternoon, and when she woke she had forgotten all about the matter. It wasn't until she arrived at the University the following morning, and saw Vic Wilcox talking to Philip Swallow on the crowded landing outside the English Department office, that she remembered it again, with instant misgivings. Vic, standing with his hands clasped behind his back in his dark business suit and polished black leather shoes, with the students in their bright loose clothes swirling and fluttering round him, looked like a crow that had strayed into an aviary for exotic birds. Even Philip Swallow, dressed in a crumpled beige linen jacket and scuffed Hush Puppies, looked dashingly casual in comparison. Swallow, spotting Robyn, beckoned.

"Ah, there you are," he said. "I discovered your shadow outside your door, 'alone and palely loitering'. Apparently he's been here since nine o'clock."

"Hallo, Robyn," said Vic.

Robyn ignored him. "What do you mean, *my* shadow?" she said to Swallow.

"Ah, that explains it," he said, nodding.

"*What do you mean, my shadow?*" Robyn repeated, raising her voice against the surrounding babble.

"Yes, the second stage of the Shadow Scheme. We talked about it yesterday."

"I didn't know what you were referring to," said Robyn. "And I still don't," she added, though she could now have made a good guess.

Philip Swallow looked helplessly from one to the other. "But I thought Mr Wilcox . . ."

"I wrote to you about it," Vic said to Robyn, with a hint of smugness.

"The letter must have gone astray," said Robyn. Across the landing, beside the Third Year noticeboard, she saw Marion Russell staring at them, as if she was trying to place Vic Wilcox.

"Oh dear," said Swallow. "So you weren't expecting Mr Wilcox this morning?"

"No," said Robyn, "I wasn't expecting him any morning."

"Well," said Swallow, "in the vacation – I think you were away at the time – Mr Wilcox wrote to the VC suggesting a follow-up to the Shadow Scheme. It seems that he was so impressed by the experiment" – Swallow exposed his tombstone teeth to Vic in a complacent smile – "that he thought it should be continued, in reverse so to speak."

"Yes, me shadowing you, for a change," said Vic. "After all, if the idea is to improve relations between industry and the University, it should be a two-way process. We in industry," he said piously, "have a lot to learn too."

"No way," said Robyn.

"Jolly good," said Swallow, rubbing his hands.

"I said I WON'T DO IT," Robyn shouted.

"Why not?" Philip Swallow looked worried.

"Mr Wilcox knows," said Robyn.

"No I don't," said Vic.

"It's not fair on the students, with the examinations coming up. He'd have to sit in on my classes."

"I'd just be a fly on the wall," said Vic, "I wouldn't interfere."

"I really don't think the students would object, Robyn," said Philip Swallow. "And it's only one day a week."

"One day a week?" said Robyn. "I'm surprised Mr Wilcox can spare a whole day away from his factory. I thought he was indispensable."

"Things are running smoothly at the moment," said Vic. "And I have a lot of holidays owing to me."

"If Mr Wilcox is giving up his holidays to this project, I really think that . . ." Swallow turned his slightly bloodshot eyes appealingly in Robyn's direction. "The VC is *most* enthusiastic."

Robyn thought of the impending UGC letter and the chance, slender as it was, that it might open the way to a permanent job for her at Rummidge. "I don't seem to have much choice, do I?" she said.

"Good!" said Philip Swallow, beaming with relief. "I'll leave you in Robyn's capable hands, then, Mr Wilcox. Metaphorically speaking, of course. Ha, ha!" He shook hands with Vic and disappeared into the Departmental office. Robyn led Vic Wilcox along the corridor to her room.

"I consider this an underhand trick," she said, when they were alone.

"What d'you mean?"

"You're not trying to pretend, are you, that you're genuinely interested in finding out how University Departments of English operate?"

"Yes I am, I'm very interested." He looked round the room. "Have you read all these books?"

"When I first came to Pringle's, you expressed utter contempt for the kind of work I do."

"I was prejudiced," he said. "That's what this shadow scheme is all about, overcoming prejudice."

"I think you fixed this up as an excuse to see me," said Robyn. She hoiked her Gladstone bag onto the desk and began to unpack books, folders, essays.

"I want to see what you do," said Vic. "I'm willing to learn. I've been reading those books you mentioned, *Jane Eyre* and *Wuthering Heights*."

Robyn could not resist the bait. "And what did you think of them?"

"*Jane Eyre* was all right. A bit long-winded. With *Wuthering Heights* I kept getting in a muddle about who was who."

"That's deliberate, of course," said Robyn.

"Is it?"

"The same names keep cropping up in different permutations and different generations. Cathy the older is born Catherine Earnshaw and becomes Catherine Linton by marriage. Cathy the younger is born Catherine Linton, becomes Catherine Heathcliff by her first marriage to Linton Heathcliff, the son of Isabella Linton and Heathcliff, and later becomes Catherine Earnshaw by her second marriage to Hareton Earnshaw, so she ends up with the same name as her mother, Catherine Earnshaw."

"You should go on 'Mastermind'," said Vic.

"It's incredibly confusing, especially with all the time-shifts as well," said Robyn. "It's what makes *Wuthering Heights* such a remarkable novel for its period."

"I don't see the point. More people would enjoy it if it was more straightforward."

"Difficulty generates meaning. It makes the reader work harder."

"But reading is the opposite of work," said Vic. "It's what you do when you come home from work, to relax."

"In this place," said Robyn, "reading is work. Reading is production. And what we produce is meaning."

There was a knock on the door, which slowly opened to the extent of about eighteen inches. The head of Marion Russell appeared around the edge of the door like a glove puppet, goggled at Robyn and Vic, and withdrew. The door closed again, and whispering and scuffling on the other side of it were faintly audible, like the sounds of mice.

"That's my ten o'clock tutorial," said Robyn.

"Is ten o'clock when you usually start work?"

"I never stop working," said Robyn. "If I'm not working here, I'm working at home. This isn't a factory, you know. We don't clock in and out. Sit in that corner and make yourself as inconspicuous as possible."

"What's this tutorial about, then?"

"Tennyson. Here, take this." She gave him a copy of Tennyson's *Poems*, a cheap Victorian edition with sentimental illustrations that she had bought from a second-hand bookshop as a student and used for years, until Ricks' Longman's Annotated edition was published. She went to the door and opened it. "Right, come in," she said, smiling encouragingly.

*

It was Marion Russell's turn to start off the tutorial discussion, by reading a short paper on a topic she had chosen herself from an old exam paper; but when the students filed into the room and seated themselves round the table, she was missing.

"Where's Marion?" Robyn asked.

"She's gone to the cloakroom," said Laura Jones, a big girl in a navy-blue track suit, who was doing Joint Honours in English and Physical Education, and was a champion shot putter.

"She said she didn't feel well," said Helen Lorimer, whose nails were painted with green nail-varnish to match her hair, and who wore plastic earrings depicting a smiling face on one ear and a frowning face on the other.

"She gave me her essay to read out," said Simon Bradford, a thin, eager young man, with thick-lensed spectacles and wispy beard.

"Wait a minute," said Robyn, "I'll go and see what's the matter with her. Oh, by the way – this is Mr Wilcox, he's observing this class as part of an Industry Year project. I suppose you all know this is Industry Year, don't you?" They looked blankly at her. "Ask Mr Wilcox to explain it to you," she said, as she left the room.

She found Marion Russell hiding in the staff women's lavatory. "What's the matter, Marion?" she said briskly. "Pre-menstrual tension?"

"That man," said Marion Russell. "He was the one at the factory, wasn't he?"

"Yes."

"What's he doing here? Has he come to complain?"

"No, of course not. He's here to observe the tutorial."

"What for?"

"It's too complicated to explain now. Come along, we're all waiting for you."

"I can't."

"Why not?"

"It's too embarrassing. He's seen me in my knickers and stuff."

"He won't recognise you."

"Course he will."

"No he won't. You look entirely different." Marion Russell was wearing harem pants and an outsize teeshirt with Bob Geldof's face imprinted on it like the face of Christ on Veronica's napkin.

"What did you do your paper on?"

"The struggle between optimism and pessimism in Tennyson's verse," said Marion Russell.

"Come on, then, let's hear it."

If Vic had been explaining Industry Year to the other three students, he had been very brief, for the room was silent when Robyn returned with Marion Russell. Vic was frowning at his copy of Tennyson, and the students were watching him as rabbits watch a stoat. He looked up as Marion came in, but, as Robyn had predicted, his eyes signalled no flicker of recognition.

Marion began reading her paper in a low monotone. All went well until she observed that the line from "Locksley Hall", *"Let the great world spin for ever, down the ringing grooves of change,"* reflected the confidence of the Victorian Railway Age. Vic raised his hand.

"Yes, Mr Wilcox?" Robyn's tone and regard were as discouraging as she could make them.

"He must have been thinking of trams, not trains," said Vic. "Train wheels don't run in grooves."

Simon Bradford gave an abrupt, high-pitched laugh; then, on meeting Robyn's eye, looked as if he wished he hadn't.

"D'you find that suggestion amusing, Simon?" she said.

"Well," he said, "trams. They're not very poetic, are they?"

"It said the Railway Age in this book I read," said Marion.

"What book, Marion?" said Robyn.

"Some critical book. I can't remember which one, now," said Marion, riffling randomly through a sheaf of notes.

"Always acknowledge secondary sources," said Robyn. "Actually, it's quite an interesting, if trivial, point. When he wrote the poem, Tennyson was under the impression that railway trains ran in grooves." She read out the footnote from her Longman's Annotated edition: *"'When I went by the first train from Liverpool to Manchester in 1830 I thought that the wheels ran in a groove. It was a black night, and there was such a vast crowd round the train at the station that we could not see the wheels. Then I made this line.'"*

It was Vic's turn to laugh. "Well, he didn't make it very well, did he?"

"So, what's the answer?" said Laura, a rather literal-minded girl who wrote down everything Robyn said in tutorials. "Is it a train or a tram?"

"Both or either," said Robyn. "It doesn't really matter. Go on, Marion."

"Hang about," said Vic. "You can't have it both ways. 'Grooves' is a whadyoucallit, metonymy, right?"

The students were visibly impressed as he brought out this technical term. Robyn herself was rather touched that he had remembered it, and it was almost with regret that she corrected him.

"No," said Robyn. "It's a metaphor. *'The grooves of change'* is a metaphor. The world moving through time is compared to something moving along a metal track."

"But the grooves tell you what kind of track."

"True," Robyn conceded. "It's metonymy inside a metaphor. Or to be precise, a synecdoche: part for whole."

"But if I have a picture of grooves in my head, I can't think of a train. It has to be a tram."

"What do the rest of you think?" said Robyn. "Helen?"

Helen Lorimer reluctantly raised her eyes to meet Robyn's. "Well, if Tennyson thought he was describing a train, then it's a train I s'pose," she said.

"Not necessarily," said Simon Bradford. "That's the Intentional Fallacy." He glanced at Robyn for approval. Simon Bradford had attended one of her seminars in Critical Theory the previous year. Helen Lorimer, who hadn't, and who had plainly never heard of the Intentional Fallacy, looked despondent, like the earring on her left ear.

There was a brief silence, during which all looked expectantly at Robyn.

"It's an aporia," said Robyn. "A kind of accidental aporia, a figure of undecidable ambiguity, irresolvable contradiction. We know Tennyson intended an allusion to railways, and, as Helen said, we can't erase that knowledge." (At this flattering paraphrase of her argument, Helen Lorimer's expression brightened, resembling her right earring.) "But we also know that railway trains don't run in grooves, and nothing that *does* run in grooves seems metaphorically adequate to the theme. As Simon said, trams aren't very poetic. So the reader's mind is continually baffled in its efforts to make sense of the line."

"You mean, it's a duff line?" said Vic.

"On the contrary," said Robyn, "I think it's one of the few good ones in the poem."

"If there's a question about the Railway Age in Finals," said Laura Jones, "can we quote it?"

"Yes, Laura," said Robyn patiently. "As long as you show you're aware of the aporia."

"How d'you spell that?"

Robyn wrote the word with a coloured felt-tip on the whiteboard screwed to the wall of her office. "*Aporia*. In classical rhetoric it means real or pretended uncertainty about the subject under discussion. Deconstructionalists today use it to refer to more radical kinds of contradiction or subversion of logic or defeat of the reader's expectation in a text. You could say that it's deconstruction's favourite trope. Hillis Miller compares it to following a mountain path and then finding that it gives out, leaving you stranded on a ledge, unable to go back or forwards. It actually derives from a Greek word meaning 'a pathless path'. Go on, Marion."

A few minutes later, Vic, evidently encouraged by the success of his intervention over *'grooves'*, put up his hand again. Marion had been arguing, reasonably enough, that Tennyson was stronger on emotions than on ideas, and had quoted in support the lyrical outburst of the lover in *Maud*, "*Come into the garden, Maud,/For the black bat night has flown.*"

"Yes, Mr Wilcox?" said Robyn, frowning.

"That's a song," said Vic. "'Come into the garden Maud'. My grandad used to sing it."

"Yes?"

"Well, the bloke in the poem is singing a song to his girl, a well-known song. It makes a difference, doesn't it?"

"Tennyson wrote 'Come into the garden, Maud', as a poem," said Robyn. "Somebody else set it to music later."

"Oh," said Vic. "My mistake. Or is it an aporia?"

"No, it's a mistake," said Robyn. "I must ask you not to interrupt any more, please, or Marion will never finish her paper."

Vic lapsed into a hurt silence. He stirred restlessly in his seat, he sighed impatiently to himself from time to time in a way that made the students stall nervously in the middle of what they were saying, he licked his fingers to turn the pages of his book, and flexed it so violently in his hands that the spine cracked noisily, but he didn't actually interrupt again. After a while he seemed to lose interest in the discussion and to be browsing in the Tennyson on his own account. When the tutorial was over and the students had left, he asked Robyn if he could borrow it.

"Of course. Why, though?"

"Well, I thought if I have a read of it, I might have a better idea of what's going on next week."

"Oh, but we're not doing Tennyson next week. It's *Daniel Deronda*, I think."

"You mean, you've finished with Tennyson? That's it?"

"As far as this group is concerned, yes."

"But you never told them whether he was optimistic or pessimistic."

"I don't tell them what to think," said Robyn.

"Then how are they supposed to learn the right answers?"

"There are no right answers to questions like that. There are only interpretations."

"What's the point of it, then?" he said. "What's the point of sitting around discussing books all day, if you're no wiser at the end of it?"

"Oh, you're *wiser*," said Robyn. "What you learn is that language is an infinitely more devious and slippery medium than you had supposed."

"That's good for you?"

"Very good for you," she said, tidying the books and papers on her desk. "Do you want to borrow *Daniel Deronda* for next week?"

"What did he write?"

"He's not a he, he's a book. By George Eliot."

"Good writer, is he, this Eliot bloke?"

"He was a she, actually. You see how slippery language is. But, yes, very good. D'you want to swap *Daniel Deronda* for the Tennyson?"

"I'll take them both," he said. "There's some good stuff in here." He opened the Tennyson, and read aloud, tracing the lines with his blunt forefinger:

"Woman is the lesser man, and all thy passions, matched with mine,
Are as moonlight unto sunlight, and as water unto wine."

"I might have guessed you would lap up 'Locksley Hall'," said Robyn.

"It strikes a chord," he said, turning the pages. "Why didn't you answer my letters?"

"Because I didn't read them," she said. "I didn't even open them."

"That wasn't very nice."

"I knew all too well what would be in them," she said. "And if you're going to get stupid and sentimental, and sick Tennyson all over me, I'm going to call off The Shadow Scheme Part Two right away."

"I can't help it. I keep thinking about Frankfurt."

"Forget it. Pretend it never happened. Would you like some coffee?"

"It must have meant something to you."

"It was an aporia," she said. "A pathless path. It led nowhere."

"Yes," he said bitterly. "It left me stuck on a ledge. I can't go forward, I can't go back."

Robyn sighed. "I'm sorry, Vic. Surely you can see that we're too different? Not to mention the fact that you have other ties."

"Never mind them," he said. "I can take care of them."

"We're from two different worlds."

"I could change. I already have changed. I've read *Jane Eyre* and *Wuthering Heights*. I've got rid of pin-ups at the factory, I've –"

"You've what?"

"We've been cleaning up the place – I took the opportunity to have the pin-ups taken off the walls.'

"Won't they just put up new ones?"

"I got the unions to put it to a vote. The shop stewards weren't keen, but the Asian membership was overwhelmingly in favour. They're a bit prudish, you know."

"Well! I'm impressed," said Robyn. She smiled a benediction on him. This proved to be a mistake. To her dismay he seized her hand, and dropped to his knees beside her chair, in a posture reminiscent of one of the engravings in her old Tennyson *Poems*.

"Robyn, give me a chance!"

She snatched her hand away. "Get up, you fool!" she said.

At that moment there was a knock on the door and Marion Russell blundered breathlessly into the room. She stopped on the threshold and stared at Vic on his knees. Robyn slid off her chair and on to the floor. "Mr Wilcox has dropped his pen, Marion," she said. "You can help us look for it."

"Oh," said Marion. "I'm afraid I can't, I've got a lecture. I came back for my bag." She pointed to a plastic shopping-bag full of books under the chair where she had been sitting.

"All right," said Robyn, "take it."

"Sorry." Marion Russell retrieved her bag, backed towards the door and, and with a last stare, left the room.

"Right, that's it," said Robyn, as she got to her feet.

"I'm sorry, I got carried away," said Vic, dusting his knees.

"Please leave now," said Robyn. "I'll tell Swallow that I've changed my mind."

"Let me stay. It won't happen again." He looked embarrassed and helpless. She was reminded of when they had gone back to her room at the Frankfurt hotel and how he had sprung on her behind the door, and just as abruptly desisted.

"I don't trust you. I think you're a bit mad."

"I promise."

Robyn waited till he looked her in the eye before she spoke again. "No more references to Frankfurt?"

"No."

"No more love-stuff?"

He swallowed, and nodded glumly. "All right."

Robyn thought of the tableau they must have presented to Marion Russell, and giggled. "Come on, let's get some coffee," she said.

As usual at this hour of the morning, the Senior Common Room was crowded, and they had to join a short queue for coffee. Vic looked about him in a puzzled way.

"What's going on here?" he said. "Are these people having an early lunch?"

"No, just morning coffee."

"How long are they allowed?"

"Allowed?"

246

"You mean they can doss around here as long as they like?"

Robyn looked at her colleagues lounging in easy chairs, smiling and chatting to each other, or browsing through the newspapers and weekly reviews, as they drank their coffee and nibbled their biscuits. She suddenly saw this familiar spectacle through an outsider's eyes, and almost blushed. "We all have our own work to do," she said. "It's up to us how we do it."

"If you don't start till ten and you knock off for a coffee-break at eleven," said Vic, "I don't see where you find the time." He seemed to recognise no intermediate point in manners between self-abasement and truculence. The first having failed, he switched straight into the second.

Robyn paid for two cups of coffee and led Vic to a couple of vacant chairs beside one of the full-length windows that overlooked the central square of the campus. "Surprising as it may seem to you," she said, "a lot of the people in this room are working at this moment."

"You could've fooled me. What kind of work?"

"Discussing university business, settling committee agendas. Exchanging ideas about their research, or consulting about particular students. Things like that."

It was unfortunate that at this moment the Professor of Egyptology, who was sitting nearby, said very audibly to his neighbour, "How are your tulips this year, Dobson?"

"If I was in charge," said Vic, "I'd shut this place down and have that woman behind the counter going up and down the corridors with a trolley."

The Professor of Egyptology turned in his seat to stare at Vic.

"Scruffy lot, aren't they, the men in here? No ties, most of 'em. And look at that bloke over there, he's got his shirt hanging out."

"He's a very distinguished theologian," said Robyn.

"That's no excuse for looking as if he'd slept in his clothes," said Vic.

Philip Swallow approached them with a coffee cup in one hand and a thick sheaf of committee papers in the other. "May I join you?" he said. "How are you getting on, Mr Wilcox?"

"Mr Wilcox is scandalised by our lax habits," said Robyn. "Open-necked shirts and open-ended coffee-breaks."

"It wouldn't do in industry," said Vic. "People would take advantage."

"I'm not sure that some of our colleagues don't take advantage," said Swallow, looking round the room. "You do tend to see the same faces in here, taking their time over coffee."

"Well, you're the boss, aren't you?" said Vic. "Why don't you give them a warning?"

247

Philip Swallow gave a hollow laugh. "I'm nobody's boss. I'm afraid you're making the same mistake as the Government."

"What's that?"

"Why, supposing that universities are organised like businesses, with a clear division between management and labour, whereas in fact they're collegiate institutions. That's why the whole business of the cuts has been such a balls-up. Excuse my French, Robyn."

Robyn waved the apology aside.

"You see," said Philip Swallow, "when the Government cut our funding they obviously hoped to improve efficiency, get rid of overmanning, and so on, like they did in industry. Well, let's admit that there was room for some of that – it would be a miracle if there hadn't been. But in industry, management decides who shall be made redundant in the labour force, senior management decides who shall go from junior management, and so on. Universities don't have that pyramid structure. Everybody is equal in a sense, once they pass probation. Nobody can be made redundant against their will. Nobody will vote to make their peers redundant."

"I should think not," said Robyn.

"That's all very well, Robyn, but nobody will even vote for a change of syllabus that threatens to make anyone redundant. I wouldn't like to count the hours I've spent on committees discussing the cuts," said Philip Swallow wearily, "and in all that time I can't remember a single instance in which anybody admitted that there was any aspect of our existing arrangements that was dispensable. Everybody recognises that there have to be cuts, because the Government controls the purse-strings, but nobody will actually make them."

"Then you'll soon be bankrupt," said Vic.

"We would be already, if it wasn't for early retirements," said Swallow. "But of course the people who have volunteered to take early retirement are not always the people we can most afford to lose. And then the Government had to give us a lot of money to make the terms attractive. So we ended up paying people to go away and work in America or for themselves or not at all, instead of spending the money on bright young people like Robyn here."

"It sounds like a shambles," said Vic. "Surely the answer is to change the system. Give management more muscle."

"No!" said Robyn hotly. "That's not the answer. If you try to make universities like commercial institutions, you destroy everything that makes them valuable. Better the other way round. Model industry on universities. Make factories collegiate institutions."

"Ha! We wouldn't last five minutes in the marketplace," said Vic.

"So much the worse for the marketplace," said Robyn. "Maybe the universities are inefficient, in some ways. Maybe we do waste a lot of time arguing on committees because nobody has absolute power. But that's preferable to a system where everybody is afraid of the person on the next rung of the ladder above them, where everybody is out for themselves, and fiddling their expenses or vandalising the lavatories, because they know that if it suited the company they could be made redundant tomorrow and nobody would give a damn. Give me the University, with all its faults, any day."

"Well," said Vic, "it's nice work if you can get it." He turned his head and looked out of the full-length window, which was open to the warm day, at the central square of the campus.

Robyn followed the direction of his gaze with her own eyes. The students in their summer finery were scattered like petals over the green lawns, reading, talking, necking, or listening to their discoursing teachers. The sun shone upon the façade of the Library, whose glazed revolving doors flashed intermittently like the beams of a lighthouse as it fanned readers in and out, and shone upon the buildings of diverse shapes and sizes dedicated to Biological Sciences, Chemistry, Physics, Engineering, Education and Law. It shone on the botanical gardens, and on the sports centre and the playing fields and the running track where people would be training and jogging and exercising. It shone on the Great Hall where the University orchestra and choir were due to perform "The Dream of Gerontius" later in the term, and on the Student Union with its Council Chamber and committee rooms and newspaper offices, and on the privately endowed art gallery with its small but exquisite collecton of masterpieces. It seemed to Robyn more than ever that the university was the ideal type of a human community, where work and play, culture and nature, were in perfect harmony, where there was space, and light, and fine buildings set in pleasant grounds, and people were free to pursue excellence and self-fulfilment, each according to her own rhythm and inclination.

And then she thought, with a sympathetic inward shudder, of how the same sun must be shining upon the corrugated roofs of the factory buildings in West Wallsbury, how the temperature must be rising rapidly inside the foundry; and she imagined the workers stumbling out into the sunshine at midday, sweatstained and blinking in the bright light, and eating their snap, squatting on oil-stained tarmac in the shade of a brick wall, and then, at the sound of a hooter, going back in again to the heat and noise and stench for another four hours' toil.

But no! Instead of letting them go back into that hell-hole, she transported them, in her imagination, to the campus: the entire workforce – labourers, craftsmen, supervisors, managers, directors, secretaries and cleaners and cooks, in their grease-stiff dungarees and soiled overalls and chain-store frocks and striped suits – brought them in buses across the city, and unloaded them at the gates of the campus, and let them wander through it in a long procession, like a lost army, headed by Danny Ram and the two Sikhs from the cupola and the giant black from the knockout, their eyes rolling white in their swarthy, soot-blackened faces, as they stared about them with bewildered curiosity at the fine buildings and the trees and flowerbeds and lawns, and at the beautiful young people at work or play all around them. And the beautiful young people and their teachers stopped dallying and disputing and got to their feet and came forward to greet the people from the factory, shook their hands and made them welcome, and a hundred small seminar groups formed on the grass, composed half of students and lecturers and half of workers and managers, to exchange ideas on how the values of the university and the imperatives of commerce might be reconciled and more equitably managed to the benefit of the whole of society.

Robyn became aware that Philip Swallow was talking to her. "I beg your pardon," she said, "I was daydreaming."

"The privilege of youth," he said, smiling. "I thought for a moment you might be getting a little hard of hearing, Robyn."

2

"The next question," said Philip Swallow, "is what we do about the Syllabus Review Committee's report."

"Throw it in the wastepaper basket," Rupert Sutcliffe suggested.

"It's easy for Rupert to sneer," said Bob Busby, who was Chairman of the Syllabus Review Committee, "but it's no easy matter, revising the syllabus. Everybody in the Department wants to protect their own special interests. Like all syllabuses, ours is a compromise."

"A thoroughly unworkable compromise, if I may say so," said Rupert Sutcliffe. "I calculate that it would entail setting a hundred and seventy-three different Finals papers every year."

"We haven't gone into the question of assessment yet," said Bob Busby. "We wanted to get the basic structure of courses agreed first."

"But assessment is vital," said Robyn. "It determines the students' whole approach to their studies. Isn't this an opportunity to get rid of final examinations altogether, and go over to some form of continuous assessment?"

"Faculty Board would never accept that," said Bob Busby.

"Quite right too," said Rupert Sutcliffe. "Continuous assessment should be confined to infant schools."

"I must remind you," said Philip Swallow wearily, "as I shall have to remind the full Department Committee in due course, that the object of this exercise is to economise on resources in the face of the cuts. Three colleagues will be leaving, for various reasons, at the end of this year. It's more than likely that there will be further losses next year. If we go on offering the present syllabus with fewer and fewer staff, individual teaching loads will rise to intolerable levels. The Syllabus Review Committee was set up to confront this problem, not to devise a new syllabus that all of us, in ideal circumstances, would like to teach."

"Rationalisation," said Vic from the far end of the table.

The others gathered in Philip Swallow's room, including Robyn, turned their heads and looked at Vic in surprise. He did not normally speak at the committee meetings to which he followed her – nor, since his first day, had he intervened in tutorials. On his weekly visits to the University he sat in the corner of her room, or at the back of the lecture theatre, quietly attentive, and followed her about the corridors and staircases of the Arts Faculty like a faithful dog. Sometimes she wondered what he was making of it all, but most of the time she simply forgot he was there, as she had done this morning. It was the fourth week of term, and they were attending a meeting of the Department Agenda Committee.

Like everything else in the Department, the Agenda Committee had a history, and a folklore, which Robyn had gradually pieced together from various sources. For decades the Head of Department had been a notorious eccentric called Gordon Masters, who spent every available moment pursuing field sports and had never been known to convene a Department Committee except for the annual Examiners' Meeting. As a result of the student demonstrations of 1969 (which had contributed to Masters' abrupt retirement in a disturbed mental condition) his successor, Dalton, was obliged by a new University statute to hold regular Department Committee meetings, but had cunningly defeated the democratic intention behind this rule by keeping the agenda of such meetings a secret unto himself. His colleagues were therefore able to raise important matters only under Any Other Business, and Dalton invariably contrived to spin out the discussion of his own agenda of yawn-inducing trivia for so long that by the time the meeting reached AOB it was no longer quorate. To counter this strategy, Philip Swallow, then a Senior Lecturer freshly energised by his exchange visit to America, had managed to secure the establishment of a new subcommittee called the Agenda Committee whose function was to prepare business for discussion by the full Department Committee. Swallow had inherited this apparatus when he himself became Head of Department following the sudden death of Dalton in a car accident, and he used the Agenda Committee as a kind of kitchen cabinet, to consider the Department's policy on any given issue, and how it might be presented to the full Department Committee with the minimum risk of contentious debate. The Agenda Committee consisted of himself as *de facto* chairman, Rupert Sutcliffe, Bob Busby, Robyn, and a student representative who seldom attended, and was absent on this occasion.

"Rationalisation is what you're talking about," said Vic. "Cutting costs, improving efficiency. Maintaining throughput with a smaller workforce. It's the same in industry."

"Well, that's an interesting thought," said Philip Swallow politely.

"Perhaps Mr Wilcox would like to design a new syllabus for us," said Rupert Sutcliffe with a smirk.

"No, I couldn't do that, but I can give you some advice," said Vic. "There's only one surefire way to succeed in business: make something people want, make it well, and make it in one size."

"Henry Ford's formula, I believe," said Bob Busby. He wagged his beard from side to side, preening himself on this *aperçu*.

"Wasn't he the one who said 'History is bunk'?" said Rupert Sutcliffe. "It doesn't sound like a very promising model for an English Department."

"It's absurd," said Robyn. "If we followed it we would have just one standard course for all our students, with no options."

"Oh, well, there's a lot to be said for that, actually," said Rupert Sutcliffe. "That was the sort of syllabus we had under Masters. We seemed to have more time to think in those days, and time to talk to each other. The students knew where they were."

"It's no use hankering after the good old days, which were actually the boring old days," said Bob Busby impatiently. "The subject has expanded vastly since you started in it, Rupert. Now we have linguistics, media studies, American Literature, Commonwealth Literature, literary theory, women's studies, not to mention about a hundred new British writers worth taking seriously. We can't cover all of it in three years. We have to have a system of options."

"And you end up with a hundred and seventy-three separate Finals papers, and endless timetable clashes," said Rupert Sutcliffe.

"Better that than a syllabus which gives the students no choice," said Robyn. "Anyway, Mr Wilcox is being disingenuous. He makes more than one thing at his factory. He makes lots of different things."

"True," said Vic. "But not as many as we made when I took over. The point is, a repeatable operation is always cheaper and more reliable than one which has to be set up differently each time."

"But repetition is death!" Robyn cried. "Difference is life. Difference is the condition of meaning. Language is a system of differences, as Saussure said."

"But a *system*," said Rupert Sutcliffe. "The question is whether we have a system any more, or just a muddle. A muddle this document" – he slapped the report of the Syllabus Review Committee with the palm of his hand – "will only exacerbate."

Philip Swallow, who had been listening to this debate with his head bowed and cradled in his hands, straightened up and spoke: "I think that, as usual, the truth lies between the two extremes. Of course I take Robyn's point that if we all taught the same thing over and over again we should all go mad or die of boredom, and so would our students. On the other hand, I think it's fair to say that we are trying to do too many things at the same time and not doing any of them particularly well."

Philip Swallow seemed to be in rather good form today, Robyn thought to herself. A small transparent plastic worm curling out of his right ear, and disappearing under a silver grey wing of hair, suggested that this might have something to do with his having adopted a hearing aid.

"It's partly a matter of history," he went on. "Once upon a time, as Rupert remembers, there was a single syllabus, essentially a survey course on Eng. Lit. from Beowulf to Virginia Woolf, which all the students followed in common, through lectures and a weekly tutorial, and life was very simple and comfortable, if a little dull. And then in the sixties and seventies we began to add all kinds of exciting new ingredients, like the ones Bob mentioned – but without subtracting anything from the original syllabus. So we ended up with an elaborate system of seminar options piled on top of a core curriculum of lectures and tutorials. Well, that was just about workable, if a little frantic, as long as there was plenty of cash to recruit more teachers, but now that the money is running out I think we have to face the fact that the present syllabus is top-heavy. It's like a three-masted ship with too many sails aloft and a diminishing crew. We're exhausting ourselves scrambling up and down the rigging, just trying to keep the damn thing from capsizing, never mind getting anywhere, or enjoying the voyage. With respect, Bob, I don't think your committee has addressed itself to the fundamental problem. Could I possibly ask you to have another look at it before we bring the matter before the Department Committee?":

"All right," Bob Busby sighed.

"Good," said Philip Swallow. "That should make room for another item on the agenda: DEVs."

"What in God's name are they?" said Rupert Sutcliffe.

"Department Enterprise Ventures. A new idea of the VC's."

"Not another!" Bob Busby groaned.

"He wants every Department to put forward projects for raising money from the private sector to support its activities. Any suggestions?"

"Do you mean something like a jumble sale?" said Rupert Sutcliffe. "Or a flag day?"

"No, no, Rupert! Consultancies, research services, that sort of thing," said Swallow. "Of course, it's much easier for the sciences to come up with ideas. But I understand Egyptology is planning to offer guided package tours down the Nile. What we need to ask ourselves is, what do we have as a Department that's marketable in the outside world?"

"We have a lot of pretty girls," said Bob Busby, with a hearty laugh that faded as he caught Robyn's eye.

"I don't understand," said Robyn. "We're already overstretched teaching our own students and doing our own research. Where are we supposed to find the time and energy to make money on the side as well?"

"The theory is that with the additional income we shall be able to hire more staff. The University will take its twenty per cent cut and the rest we can spend as we like."

"And supposing we make a loss," said Robyn. "What will happen then?"

Philip Swallow shrugged. "The University will underwrite any approved scheme. Of course, in that case, we shouldn't get any new staff."

"And we should have wasted a lot of valuable time."

"There is that risk," said Philip Swallow. "But it's the spirit of the times. Self-help. Venture capitalism. Isn't that right, Mr Wilcox?"

"I agree with Robyn," said Vic, to her surprise. "It's not that I don't believe in the market, I do. But you people don't belong in it. You'd be playing at capitalism. Stick to what you're good at."

"How do you mean, playing at capitalism?" said Philip Swallow.

"You can't really lose because the University would underwrite any failures. You can't really win because, as I understand it, there are no individual incentives for success. Suppose, for the sake of argument, Robyn here was to come up with a commerical project for the English Department – say, a consultancy on the wording of safety notices in industrial plant."

"That's not a bad idea, actually," said Philip Swallow, making a note.

"And supposing it proved to be a terrific money-spinner. Would she get a bonus? Would she get a salary raise? Would she advance faster than Mr Sutcliffe, who is clearly not going to have anything to do with it?"

"Well, no," said Philip Swallow. "But," he added, triumphantly, "in that case we should be able to keep her on here!"

"Terrific," said Vic. "She knocks herself out to earn the money to pay for her own lousy salary while the University takes all the profit and redistributes it to drones like Sutcliffe."

"I say, I resent that," said Rupert Sutcliffe.

"It would make more sense for her to set up as a consultant on her own," said Vic.

"But I don't want to be a consultant," said Robyn. "I just want to be a university teacher."

The telephone on Swallow's desk rang, and he tilted his chair backwards from the head of the table to reach the receiver. "I did say no phone calls, Pam," he said irritably; then his expression changed to one of expectant gravity. "Oh. All right. Put him through." He listened for what seemed a very long time, though it was probably only a couple of minutes, saying nothing except, "Oh," "I see," and "Oh, dear." As this one-sided conversation proceeded, he tilted his chair further and further back, as if he was being drawn away from the table by the magnetic force of his interlocutor. Robyn and the others watched helplessly as the chair approached an angle of no return. Sure enough, as Philip Swallow twisted to replace the receiver he crashed to the ground, and banged his head on the wastepaper bin. They hurried to assist him to his feet. "It's all right, it's all right," he said, rubbing his forehead. "The UGC letter has arrived. It's bad news, I'm afraid. Our grant is going to be cut by ten per cent in real terms. The VC thinks we shall have to lose another hundred academic posts." Philip Swallow did not meet Robyn's eye as he made his announcement.

"Well, that's that," said Robyn, when they were back in her room. "There goes my last chance of keeping my job."

"I'm sorry," said Vic. "You're really good at it."

Robyn smiled wanly. "Thank you, Vic. Can I use you as a referee?"

Raindrops trickled down the pane, distorting her vision like tears. The fine weather at the beginning of term had not lasted. There were no golden lads and girls disporting themselves on the sodden lawns today, only a few people hurrying along the footpaths under umbrellas.

"I mean it," he said. "You're a natural teacher. That stuff about metaphor and metonymy, for instance. I see them all over the shop now. TV commercials, colour supplements, the way people talk."

Robyn turned and beamed at him. "I'm very glad to hear you say that. If *you* understand it, anybody can."

"Thanks very much," he said.

"Sorry, I didn't mean to be rude. The point is, it means Charles was wrong to say that we shouldn't teach theory to students who haven't read anything. It's a false opposition. Nobody's read less than you, I imagine."

"I've read more in the last few weeks than in all the years since I left school," he said. "*Jane Eyre* and *Wuthering Heights* and *Daniel Deronda*. Well, half of *Daniel Deronda*. This bloke" – he took a paperback edition of Matthew Arnold's *Culture and Anarchy*, assigned for a tutorial that afternoon, from his pocket, and waved it in the air – "and Tennyson. Funnily enough, I like Tennyson best. I never thought I'd like reading poetry, but I do. I like to learn bits off by heart and recite them to myself in the car."

"Instead of Jennifer Rush?" she said, mischievously.

"I've got a bit tired of Jennifer Rush."

"Good!"

"Her words don't rhyme properly. Tennyson's a good rhymer."

"He is. What bits have you memorised, then?"

Looking into her eyes, he recited:

"In my life there was a picture, she that clasped my neck had flown.
I was left within the shadow, sitting on the wreck alone."

"That's rather beautiful," said Robyn, after a pause.

"I thought it was rather appropriate."

"Never mind that," said Robyn briskly. "Where's it from?"

"Don't you know? A poem called 'Locksley Hall Sixty Years After'."

"I don't think I've ever read that one."

"You mean, I've read something you haven't read? Amazing." He looked childishly pleased with himself.

"Well," she said, "if you've acquired a taste for poetry, the Shadow Scheme hasn't been in vain."

"What about you?"

"I've learned to thank my lucky stars I don't have to work in a factory," she said. "The sooner they introduce those lightless factories of yours, the better. Nobody should have to earn their living by doing the same thing over and over again."

"How will they earn it, then?"

"They won't have to. They can be students instead. Robots will do all the work and produce all the wealth."

"Oh, so you admit somebody has to do that?"

"I recognise that universities don't grow on trees, if that's what you mean."

"Well, that's something, I suppose."

There was a knock on the door and Pamela, the Department Secretary, put her head round it. "Outside call for you, Robyn."

"Hi," said the voice of Morris Zapp when she picked up the phone in the Department Office. "How are you?"

"I'm all right," she said. "How are you? *Where* are you?"

"I'm fine and I'm at home in Euphoria. It's a warm starry night and I'm sitting out on my deck with a cordless phone enjoying the view of the Bay while I make some calls. Listen, I read your book. I think it's terrific."

Robyn felt her spirits lift like an untethered balloon. "Really?" she said. "Are you going to recommend it to your university press?"

"I already have. You'll be getting a letter from them. Ask for double the advance they're offering."

"Oh, I don't think I'd have the nerve to do that," said Robyn. "How much is it, anyway?"

"I've no idea, but whatever it is, insist they double it."

"They might say no, and back out."

"They won't," said Morris Zapp. "It will only make them more eager to sign you up. But I'm not calling you about the Press. I'm calling you about a job."

"A job?" Robyn covered her unengaged ear to shut out the noise of Pamela's typewriter.

"Yeah, we're making a tenure-track appointment in Women's Studies here, starting in the fall. You interested?"

"Well, yes," said Robyn.

"Great. Now what I need is your CV, fast as possible. Could you fax it to me?"

"Facts?"

"F-a-x, fax. Fax? OK, forget it. Send it airmail, special delivery. You'd have to come over here for a few days, meet the faculty, give a paper, the usual sort of thing – that all right? We'd pay your airfare, naturally."

"Fine," said Robyn. "When?"

"Next week?"

"Next *week*!"

"The week after then. The point is – I'll level with you, Robyn – there's another candidate some of my dumber colleagues are backing. I want to get you into the ball-game as fast as I can. I know they'll all be knocked out by your accent. We don't have another Brit in the Department at the moment. That's a plus for you, we have a lot of Anglophiles here, it must be because we're so far from England."

"Who's the other candidate?"

"Don't worry about her. She's not a serious scholar. Just a writer. Leave it to me. Do what I tell you, and the job's yours."

"Well . . . how can I thank you?" said Robyn.

"We'll work on it together," said Morris Zapp, but the innuendo seemed harmless, it was so obviously a conditioned reflex. "Don't you want to know what the salary is?"

"All right," said Robyn. "What is it?"

"I can't tell you exactly. You're young, of course. But I'd say, not less than forty thousand dollars."

Robyn was silent while she did some rapid mental arithmetic.

"I know that's not a lot –" said Morris Zapp.

"It seems very reasonable to me," said Robyn, who had worked out that it was exactly twice as much as she was earning at Rummidge.

"And it should go up very quickly. People like you are very hot right now."

"What do you mean, people like me?"

"Feminists who can do literary theory. Theory is all the rage here.

Your life would be one long round of conferences and visiting lectures. And Euphoric State has just put in a bid to be the home of a new Institute of Advanced Research on the West Coast. If that works out, we'll have all the fat cats from Yale and Johns Hopkins and Duke lining up to spend semesters with us."

"Sounds exciting," said Robyn.

"Yeah, you'll love it," said Morris Zapp. "Don't forget the CV, and tell your referees to write immediately to our chairman, Morton Ziegfield. Speak to you soon. *Ciao!*"

Robyn put down the telephone receiver and laughed aloud.

Pamela looked up from her typing. "Your mother's all right, then?"

"My mother?"

"She was trying to get you earlier, when you were in the Agenda meeting."

"No, it wasn't my mother," said Robyn. "I wonder what's the matter with her."

"She said not to worry, she would phone you this evening."

"Why did you think it was her then?" Robyn said, irritated by the secretary's interest in her private life. Pamela looked hurt, and Robyn was immediately stricken with guilt. To make amends she shared her good news. "At last someone's offered me a job. In America!"

"Ooh, fancy that!"

"But keep it to yourself, Pamela. Is Professor Swallow free?"

"Désirée Zapp!" said Philip Swallow, when she told him her story. "The other candidate must be Désirée."

"You think so?" said Robyn.

"I'd take a bet on it. She wrote on the back of her Christmas card that she was looking for an academic post, preferably on the West Coast. Imagine Désirée in Morris's Department!" He guffawed at the scenario thus summoned up. "Morris would do anything to stop her."

"Even hiring me?"

"You should feel flattered," said Philip Swallow. "He wouldn't run you as a candidate if he didn't think you could win. He must have been really impressed by your book. Of course, that was why he wanted to read it in the first place. He must have been over in Europe scouting for talent. I expect Fulvia Morgana turned him down . . ." Philip Swallow stared abstractedly out of the window, as if trying to think himself through the labyrinthine ways of Morris Zapp's mind, and tenderly fingered a bump on his forehead caused by the wastepaper bin.

"How can I compete with Désirée Zapp? She's world-famous."

"But, as Morris said, she's not a serious scholar," said Philip

259

Swallow. "I imagine that will be his pitch. Scholarly standards. Theoretical rigour."

"But there must be scores of good academic women candidates in America."

"They may not feel inclined to compete with Désirée. She's something of a hero to feminists over there. Or they may just be scared of her. She can fight dirty. You'd better know what you're letting yourself in for, Robyn. American academic life is red in tooth and claw. Suppose you get the job – the struggle only begins. You've got to keep publishing to justify your appointment. When the time comes for your tenure review, half your colleagues will be trying to stab you in the back, and not speaking to the other half. Do you really fancy that?"

"I have no choice," said Robyn. "There's no future for me in this country."

"Not at the moment, it seems," Swallow sighed. "And the devil of it is, once you go, you won't come back."

"How do you know?"

"People don't. Even if they can face returning to the English salary scale, we can't afford to fly them over here for interview. But I don't blame you for seizing the opportunity."

"You'll write me a reference, then?"

"I'll write you a glowing reference," said Philip Swallow. "Which is no more than you deserve."

Robyn went back to her room with a spring in her step and a confused swirl of thoughts, mostly agreeable, in her head. Philip Swallow had taken some of the shine off Morris Zapp's proposition, but it was a pleasant change to be courted by a potential employer under any conditions. She had forgotten all about Vic, and was, for an instant, surprised to find him hunched in a chair by the window, reading *Culture and Anarchy* by the grey rainy light. When she told him her news, he looked less than delighted.

"When did you say this job starts?" he said.

"The fall. I suppose that means September."

"I haven't got much time, then."

"Time for what?"

"Time to, you know, get you to change your mind . . ."

"Oh Vic," she said. "I thought you'd given up that foolishness."

"I can't give up loving you."

"Don't go soppy on me," she said. "This is my lucky day. Don't spoil it."

"Sorry," he said, looking at his shoes. He flicked a speck of dried mud from a toecap.

"Vic," she said, shaking her head sadly, "how many times do I have to tell you: I don't believe in that individualistic sort of love."

"So you say," he said.

She bridled a little at that. "Are you suggesting that I don't mean it?"

"I thought it was impossible to mean what we say or say what we mean," he said. "I thought there was always a slippage between the I that speaks and the I that is spoken of."

"Oh, ho!" said Robyn, planting her hands on her hips. "We *are* learning fast, aren't we?"

"The point is," he said. "If you don't believe in love, why do you take such care over your students? Why do you care about Danny Ram?"

Robyn blushed. "That's quite different."

"No, it's not. You care about them because they're individuals."

"I care about them because I care about knowledge and freedom."

"Words. Knowledge and freedom are just words."

"That's all there is in the last analysis. *Il n'y a pas de hors-texte.*"

"What?"

"'There is nothing outside the text.'"

"I don't accept that," he said, lifting his chin and locking his gaze on hers. "It would mean we have no free will."

"Not necessarily," said Robyn. "Once you realise there is nothing outside the text, you can begin to write it yourself."

There was a knock on the door and Pamela's head appeared round it again.

"My mother?" said Robyn.

"No, it's for Mr Wilcox," said Pamela.

"Sit down, Vic. Thanks for coming in so quickly," said Stuart Baxter, from behind the sparsely covered expanse of his desk, which was elegantly veneered, like his wall units, in black ash, the latest executive fashion. The higher up the ladder people went in the conglomerate, Vic had observed, the bigger their desks became and the less paper and other impedimenta they had on them. The curved rosewood desk of the Chairman of the Board, Sir Richard Littlego, had been, on the one occasion when Vic met him in his penthouse suite, completely bare except for a leather-bound blotter and a silver-mounted quill pen. Stuart Baxter hadn't achieved that conspicuous simplicity yet, but his In-tray was virtuously empty and only a single sheet of paper reposed in his Out-tray. Baxter's office was on the eighteenth floor of Midland Amalgamated's twenty-storey tower block in the centre of Rummidge. The plateglass window behind his head faced south-east and overlooked a drab and treeless segment of the city. The grey, rain-wet roofs of factories, warehouses and terraces stretched to the horizon like the waves and troughs of a sullen, oily sea.

"I wasn't far away," said Vic. He sat down in an easy chair which was more of an uneasy chair, since it was low-slung and forced the occupant to look up at Stuart Baxter. Looking at Baxter was not something Vic particularly enjoyed doing from any angle. He was a handsome man, complacently aware of the fact. His shave was perfect, his haircut immaculate, his teeth white and even. He affected boldly coloured shirts with white collars, above which his plump, smooth face glowed healthily pink.

"The University, wasn't it?" he said. "I gather you've been spending a lot of time there lately."

"I'm following up that shadow scheme," said Vic. "In reverse. I sent you a memo about it."

"Yes, I passed it to the Chairman. Haven't had a reply yet. I thought it was just a suggestion."

"I mentioned it to Littlego myself, at the CRUM dinner dance. He seemed to think it was a good idea, so I went ahead."

"I wish you'd told me, Vic. I like to know what my MDs are up to."

"It's in my own time."

Baxter smiled. "I gather she's quite a dish, this shadow of yours."

"I'm the shadow now," said Vic.

"You seem to be inseparable. I hear you took her with you to Frankfurt."

Vic stood up. "If you've brought me in here to discuss office gossip – "

"No, I've brought you in for a much more important reason. Sit down, Vic. Coffee?"

"No thanks," said Vic, sitting down on the edge of the seat. "What is it?" He felt a cold qualm of fear in his guts.

"We're selling Pringle's."

"You can't," Vic said.

"The deed is done, Vic. The announcement will be made tomorrow. It's confidential till then, of course."

"But we made a profit last month!"

"A small profit. A very small profit, given the turnover."

"But it will improve! The foundry is coming on a treat. What about the new core blower?"

"Foundrax regard it as a good investment. You got a good price on it."

"Foundrax?" Vic said, hardly able to draw the breath into his lungs to speak.

"Yes, we're selling to the EFE Group, they own Foundrax, as you know."

"You mean, they're going to merge the two companies?"

"I gather that's the idea. There'll be some rationalisation, of course. Let's face it, Vic, there are too many companies in your field, all chasing the same business."

"Pringle's is rationalised already," said Vic. "*I* rationalised it. I was hired to turn the company round. I said it might take eighteen months. I've done it in under a year. Now you tell me you've sold out to a competitor that was on its fucking knees."

"We all think you've done a fantastic job, Vic," said Baxter. "But the Board just didn't see Pringle's fitting into our long-term strategy."

"What you mean," said Vic bitterly, "is that by selling off Pringle's now, you can show a profit on this year's accounts at the next AGM."

Stuart Baxter examined his nails, and said nothing.

"I won't work under Norman Cole," said Vic.

"Nobody is asking you to, Vic," said Baxter.

"So it's goodbye and thankyou and here's a year's salary and don't spend it all at once."

"We'll let you keep the car," said Baxter.

"Oh, that's all right then."

"I'm sorry, Vic, I really am. I said to the EFE people, if you had any sense you'd keep Vic Wilcox on to run the new company. But I understand it will be Cole."

"I wish them joy of the double-dealing bastard."

"To be honest with you, Vic, I think they were put off by some of the stories that have been flying around about you."

"What stories?"

"Like having all the pin-ups taken down at the factory."

"The unions backed it."

"I know they did, but it seems a bit . . . eccentric. And then spending one day a week at the University."

"In my own time."

"That's eccentric too. Somebody asked me the other day if you were a born-again Christian. You're not, are you?"

"No, not a Christian," Vic said, getting up to leave.

Baxter stood up too. "You might find it convenient to move your stuff out this afternoon. I don't suppose you want to be around when Cole takes over tomorrow." He extended his hand across the desk. Vic left it there, turned on his heel, and walked out.

Vic drove slowly back to Pringle's – or rather the car took him there, like a horse under slack reins, following the route it knew best. His mind was too choked with anger and anxiety to concentrate on driving. He didn't know what was worst – the thought of all that hard slog over the past year being wasted, or the irony that Norman Cole would profit by it, or the prospect of having to break the news to Marjorie. He settled for that one. A yellow Bedford van he was following along the inside lane of the motorway, with "RIVIERA SUNBEDS" blazoned on it in orange lettering, evoked a poignant image of his wife vainly beautifying herself at home, unaware of the thunderbolt that had already struck her life. They would have to cancel the summer holiday in Tenerife for starters. If he didn't get another job within the year, they might have to sell the house and move to something more modest, without an *en suite* bathroom.

Vic followed the yellow van off the motorway at the West Wallsbury intersection and tailed it through the drab deserted streets that only filled when the shifts changed over, past silent factories with forlorn For Lease notices on their gates, past blind-walled workshops like oversized lock-up garages on the new industrial estate, past Susan's Sauna and down Coney Lane. The van seemed to be following a route that would take it past Pringle's, but to his surprise it turned into the firm's car park and stopped just outside the administration block. Brian Everthorpe climbed down from the passenger seat and waved a thankyou to the driver as the van moved away. He did a double-take on seeing Vic getting out of his car, and came over.

"Hallo, Vic. I thought this was one of your adult-education days."

"Something cropped up. What happened to your car, then?"

"Broke down on the other side of the city. Alternator, I think. I left it with a garage and hitched a lift over here. Serious, is it?"

"What?"

"The something that cropped up."

"You could say so."

"You look a bit shook up, Vic, if you don't mind my saying so. Like somebody that's just had a shunt."

Vic hesitated, tempted to confide in Brian Everthorpe – not because of any charitable impulse to forewarn him about the takeover, but simply to relieve his own feelings, to pass on his own sense of shock to another, and observe its impact. And if Everthorpe should leak the information to others – so what? Why should he worry about the possible embarrassment to Stuart Baxter and Midland Amalgamated? "Come into my office for a minute," he said recklessly.

The reception lobby was full of furniture and cardboard packing-cases. In the middle of the confusion, Shirley, Doreen and Lesley were tearing sheets of protective plastic off a long beige sofa, squealing with excitement. On catching sight of Vic, the two receptionists scuttled back to their posts. Shirley, who was on her knees, struggled to her feet and tugged down her skirt.

"Oh, hallo Vic. I didn't think you were coming in today."

"I changed my mind," he said, looking round. "The new furniture arrived, then?"

"We thought we'd unpack it. We wanted to give you a surprise sort of thing."

"It's ever so nice, Mr Wilcox," said Doreen.

"Lovely material," said Lesley.

"Not bad," he said, prodding the upholstery, thinking: another little bonus for Norman Cole. "Get rid of the old stuff, will you, Shirley?" As he led the way to his office he wondered whether the three women would survive the merger. Probably they would – there always seemed to be a need for secretaries and telephonists. Brian Everthorpe, however, almost certainly wouldn't.

Vic closed the door of his office, swore Brian Everthorpe to secrecy, and told him the news.

Brian Everthorpe said, "Hmm," and stroked his sideboards.

"You don't seem very surprised."

"I saw this coming."

"I'm buggered if I did," said Vic. Already he regretted telling Everthorpe. "I shan't be staying on. I don't know about you, of course."

"Oh, they won't keep me on, I know that."

"You seem remarkably cheerful about it."

"I've been here a long time. I qualify for redundancy."

"Even so."

"And I've made contingency plans."

"What contingency plans?"

"Some time ago, I put some money in a little business," said Brian Everthorpe. "It's not so little any more." He took a card from his wallet and presented it.

Vic looked at the card. "Riviera Sunbeds? That was the van that dropped you just now."

"Yes, I was over there when the motor packed up."

"Doing all right, is it?"

"Marvellous. Especially at this time of year. There are all these women, see, all over Rummidge, getting ready for their annual fortnights on Majorca or Corfu. They don't want to go down to the beach on their first day looking white as lard, so they rent one of our sunbeds, to give themselves a pre-holiday tan at home. Then when they come back, they rent again to keep the tan. We're expanding all the time. Bought another fifty beds last week. Made in Taiwan, amazing value."

"You're involved in the day-to-day running, then?"

"I keep an eye on things. Give them the benefit of my experience, you know," said Brian Everthorpe, preening his whiskers. "And I use my contacts to drum up trade. A card here, a card there."

Vic struggled to control his anger, so as to coax a full confession out of Everthorpe. "What you mean is, you've been looking after the interests of Riviera Sunbeds when you should be giving all your attention to Pringle's. Is that ethical?"

"Ethical?" Brian Everthorpe guffawed. "Do me a favour, Vic. Is it ethical, what Midland Amalgamated are doing to us?"

"It's cynical, it's shortsighted, in my opinion. But I don't see anything unethical about it. Whereas you've been working for yourself on the company's time. Jesus, no wonder we could never find you when we wanted you!" he burst out. "I suppose you were delivering sunbeds."

"Well, I have dropped off the odd bed at peak times – anything to make a sale, you know. It's different when it's your own money, Vic. But no, my role is a bit higher-level than that. In fact I wouldn't be surprised if I don't end up running the business. I'll be able to buy a bigger share with my golden handshake."

"You don't deserve a golden handshake," said Vic. "You deserve a golden kick up the arse. I've a good mind to report you to Stuart Baxter."

"I shouldn't bother," said Brian Everthorpe. "He's one of the chief shareholders in Riviera Sunbeds."

Vic found he had very few personal belongings to move from his office. A desk diary, a framed photograph of Marjorie and the kids taken ten years ago on the beach at Torquay, a table lighter given to him when he left Rumcol, a couple of reference books, an old sweater and a broken-winged folding umbrella in a cupboard – that was about it. It all fitted into a plastic supermarket bag. Nevertheless, Shirley stared curiously when he passed through her office on his way out. Perhaps Brian Everthorpe had already told her he was leaving.

"Going out again?" she said.

"I'm going home."

"I phoned an auctioneers, they're coming to collect the old furniture tomorrow."

"I hope the new stuff is just as strong," said Vic, looking her in the eye. "That sofa gets a lot of wear and tear."

Shirley went white, and then very red.

Vic felt slightly ashamed of himself. "'Bye Shirley, thanks for seeing to it," he said, and hurried out of the office.

★

He drove home fast, straight down the outside lane of the motorway, overtaking everything, wanting to get it over with. Marjorie sensed something was wrong as soon as she saw him in the kitchen doorway. She was standing at the sink, wearing an apron, scraping new potatoes. "You're early," she said, letting a potato fall into the water with a splash. "What's the matter?"

"Make us a cup of tea, and I'll tell you."

She stared at him, knitting her wet, podgy fingers together to stop herself from trembling. "Tell me now, Vic."

"All right. Pringle's has been sold to the EFE Group, and merged with Foundrax. I've got the push. As from tomorrow."

Marjorie came over and put her arms round him. "Oh Vic," she said, "I'm so sorry for you. All that work."

He had steeled himself for tears, perhaps hysterics. But Marjorie was strangely calm, and he himself felt strangely moved by the unselfishness of her response. He looked over her shoulder at the smooth surfaces of the fitted kitchen and all the shining gadgetry arrayed upon them. "I'll get another job," he said. "But it may take time."

"Of course you will, love." Marjorie sounded almost cheerful. "You knew, didn't you? You've known for some time this was going to happen. That's why you've been so strange."

Vic hesitated. He had been deceived so comprehensively himself, he was so sick with the sense of betrayal, that he was tempted to tell her the truth. But the least her loyalty deserved, he decided, was a merciful lie. "Yes," he said, "I knew it was on the cards."

"You should have told me," she said, drawing back her head and shaking him gently. "I've been that worried. I thought I'd lost you."

"Lost me?"

"I thought there might be another woman."

He laughed, and slapped her lightly on the bottom. "Make us that cup of tea," he said. He realised, with a slight shock, that till now he hadn't thought of Robyn Penrose once since Stuart Baxter had given him the news.

"I'll bring it into the lounge. Your Dad's in there."

"Dad? What's he doing here?"

"He just dropped in. He does occasionally, to keep me company. He knows my nerves've been bad."

"Don't tell him," said Vic.

"All right," said Marjorie. "But it'll be in the evening paper tomorrow, won't it?"

"You're right," said Vic.

So they woke up the old man, who was dozing in an armchair, and revived him with a cup of strong tea, and broke the news to him. He took it surprisingly well. He seemed to think that the year's salary Vic would get was a small fortune on which he could live indefinitely, and Vic did not disillusion him – not immediately. As the three children came in one by one, and were told, the gathering turned into a sort of family council, and Vic spelled out the implications. "I've got no assets except this house, and there's a big mortgage on that," he said. "We're going to have to tighten belts until I get a new job. I'm afraid we'll have to cancel the holiday."

"Oh, *no!*" Sandra whined.

"Don't be so selfish, Sandra," Marjorie snapped. "What's a holiday?"

"I'll go away on my own, then, with Cliff," said Sandra. "I'll work at Tweezers all summer and save up."

"Fine," said Vic, "as long as you contribute something to the housekeeping."

Sandra sniffed. "What about university? I suppose you don't want me to apply now."

"Of course I want you to apply. I thought you weren't interested."

"I changed my mind. But if you're going to make a fuss about money all the time –"

"We'll find the money for that, don't worry. It would help if you applied locally, mind . . ." He turned to his eldest son. "Raymond, I think it's time you gave your mother some of your dole money, too."

"I'm moving out," said Raymond. "I've been offered a job."

When the mild uproar that followed this announcement had died down, Raymond explained that the studio where his band had recorded their demonstration tape had offered him a job as assistant producer. "They hated our music, but I impressed the hell out of them with my electronic knowhow," he said. "I went for a drink with Sidney, the owner, afterwards, and he offered me a job. It's just a small outfit, Sidney's only just started it up, but it has possibilities. There are dozens of bands round here looking for somewhere to record without being ripped off in London."

"Hey, Dad, why don't *you* start up your own business?" said Gary.

"Yeah, what about that idea you had for a spectrometer?" said Raymond.

Vic looked at his sons suspiciously, but they weren't teasing him. "It's a thought," he said. "If Tom Rigby gets made redundant, he might invest his lump sum in a partnership. We'd still need a whacking great bank loan, but it's definitely a thought."

"Sidney got a loan," said Raymond.

"Trouble is, I've got no equity to speak of. The house is mortgaged up to the hilt. It would look risky to a bank. There's a lot of research to be done before we could even make a prototype."

"Ay, it's risky, going it alone," said Mr Wilcox. "You'd do better to look for another job like the one you had. Rumcol'd probably be glad to have you back, or Vanguard."

"They've already got managing directors, Dad."

"Doesn't have to be a managing director's job, son. You needn't be proud."

"You mean like a storesman's job, Grandad?" said Gary.

"Don't be cheeky, Gary," said Vic. "Any road, I'm not sure I want to work for a company again. I'm fed up with flogging my guts out for companies and conglomerates that have about as much human feeling as a wagon-load of pig-iron."

"If you started up on your own, Vic," said Marjorie, "I could be your secretary. That would be a saving."

"And I'll do the accounts on my Atari," said Gary. "We'll make it a family business, like a Paki corner shop."

"You could do worse," said Mr Wilcox. "They work 'ard, them buggers."

"I wouldn't mind having a job again," said Marjorie. "I'm bored at home here all day, now you lot are grown up. And if it was our own business . . ."

Vic looked at her in astonishment. Her eyes were bright. She was smiling. And there were dimples in her cheeks.

When Robyn let herself into her house that evening, the telephone was ringing as if it had been ringing for hours. It was her mother.

"Is anything wrong?" said Robyn.

"No, something rather nice, I hope. A registered letter came for you from a law firm in Melbourne. I signed for it and posted it on to you this afternoon."

"What on earth could it be about?"

"Your uncle Walter died recently," said Mrs Penrose. "We heard just after you went back to Rummidge. I meant to tell you, but I forgot. We hadn't been in touch for years, of course. I don't think anybody in the family had. He became a bit of a recluse after he sold his sheep farm to that mining –"

"Mummy, what has all this to do with me?" Robyn interpolated.

"Well, I think he might have left you something in his will."

"Why? He wasn't a real uncle, was he?"

"A sort of uncle-in-law. He married your father's sister, Ethel, she died very young, of a bee-sting. She was allergic and didn't know it. They never had any children of their own, and he always had a soft spot for you, ever since you made him put all his money in the crippled children's box when you were three."

269

"Is that story really true?" Robyn remembered the painted plaster figure of the little boy, with short trousers and a peaked cap and one leg in irons, holding out a box with a slot in it for coins – it had been unique in Melbourne, brought there by an English immigrant shopkeeper – but she had never been quite sure about the incident with her uncle Walter.

"Of course it's true." Her mother sounded hurt, like a believer defending scripture. "Wouldn't it be nice if Walter had remembered you in his will?"

"It would certainly come in useful," said Robyn. "I've just received my rates bill. By the way, Mummy, I'm probably going to America." Robyn told her mother about Morris Zapp's proposition.

"Well, dear," said Mrs Penrose, "I don't like to think of you being so far away, but I suppose it would only be for a year or two."

"That's the snag, actually," said Robyn. "If I go, it will be difficult to get back. But who knows if there'll be any more jobs to get back to in England?"

"Well, dear, you must do what you think best," said her mother. "Have you heard from Charles lately?" she added wistfully.

"No," said Robyn and brought the conversation to an end.

The next morning, when she came downstairs, there were two envelopes on her doormat. One was from her mother, enclosing the letter from Melbourne and the other was addressed in Charles' hand. To extend the rather pleasurable suspense about the putative will, she opened the letter from Charles first. It said that he was getting on well at the bank though the hours were long and he felt exhausted at the end of the day. But things hadn't worked out between him and Debbie, and he had moved out of her house.

She was such a novel sort of person to me that I was rather taken in at first. I mistook quickwittedness for intelligence. Frankly, my dear, she's rather stupid. Most foreign exchange dealers are, in my experience – they have to be to play that electronic roulette all day. And they think of nothing else. When you come home from a hard day's work at the bank, you need some civilised conversation, not more talk about positions and percentages. After a while I took to watching television just to have an excuse not to listen. Then I decided I would have to get my own place. So I've bought a nice little maisonette in a new development on the Isle of Dogs – mortgaged to the hilt, of course, but the average London property is going up by £50 a *day* at the moment, so you can't really lose. I was wondering if you would like to come down and spend a weekend. We could do a show and some galleries.

I know what you will be thinking – "Oh, no, not all *that* again," and I agree, it is rather absurd the way we keep splitting up and coming back together, because it seems that nobody else will do, in the end. I wonder whether it isn't time we bowed to the inevitable, and got married. I don't mean to live together, necessarily – obviously as long as I'm working in London, and you're in Rummidge, that's impossible anyway – but just to put a sort of seal on things. And if you can't find another job when your contract at Rummidge runs out, you might find it pleasanter to be unemployed in London than in Rummidge. I'm fairly confident that I shall be earning enough by then to support you in the style to which you have become accustomed, if not rather better. There's no reason why you shouldn't go on doing research and publishing as a lady of leisure. Think about it. And do come down for a weekend, soon.

Love, Charles

"Humph!" said Robyn, and tucked the letter back into its envelope. She opened the second letter. It informed her in longwinded legal language that she was sole beneficiary of her uncle Walter's will, and that he had left an estate estimated at A\$300,000 after tax. Robyn whooped and ran to consult the rates of exchange in the *Guardian*. Then she telephoned her mother. "You were right, Mummy, Uncle Walter has left me something in his will."

"How much, dear?"

'Well," said Robyn, "when I've paid the rates, I reckon I should have about one hundred and sixty-five thousand, eight hundred and fifty pounds left, give or take a few."

Mrs Penrose screamed, and seemed to drop the phone. Robyn could hear her shouting the news to her father, who was apparently in the bathroom. Then she came back on the line. "Daddy says congratulations! I'm so pleased for you, dear. What a sum!"

"I'll share it with you, of course."

"Nonsense, Robyn, it's your money. Uncle Walter left it to you."

"But it's so eccentric. He hardly knew me. It should have gone to Daddy if he's next of kin. Or equally to me and Basil."

"Basil has more money than is good for him already. And your father and I are quite comfortable, though it's very generous of you to offer, dear. Now you won't have to go to America."

"Why not?" said Robyn, her elation subsiding a little.

"Well, you won't need to. You could live off the interest on a hundred and sixty-five thousand."

"Yes, I suppose you're right," said Robyn. "But I don't really want to give up work."

The rain cleared in the night. It is a calm, sunny morning, without a cloud in the sky – one of those rare days when the atmosphere of Rummidge seems to have been rinsed clean of all its pollution, and the objects of vision stand out with pristine clarity. Robyn, wearing a cotton button-through dress and sandals, steps out of her house into the warm, limpid air and pauses a moment, looking up and down the street, filling her lungs as joyfully as if it were a beach.

Her dusty, dented Renault creaks on its springs as she throws her Gladstone bag onto the passenger seat and gets behind the wheel. The engine wheezes asthmatically for several seconds before it coughs into life. It crosses her mind, with a little acquisitive thrill, that very soon she will be able to swap the Renault for a brand-new car, something swish and powerful. She could put Basil's nose out of joint by buying a Porsche. No, not a Porsche, she thinks, remembering Vic's homily about foreign cars. A Lotus, perhaps, except that you can hardly get into them in a skirt. Then she thinks, how absurd, the Renault is perfectly adequate for my purposes, all it needs is a new battery.

Robyn drives slowly and carefully to the University. She is so conscious of carrying a precious freight of good fortune that she has an almost superstitious fear that some maniac driver will come tearing out of a side turning and smash it all to smithereens. But she reaches the campus without incident. Passing the Wilcoxes' house in Avondale Road, glimpsing a hand, perhaps Marjorie's, shaking a duster from an upstairs window, she wonders idly why Vic was called away so suddenly from the University the day before, and why he did not return. She parks her car under a lime tree – the space is vacant because other drivers avoid the sticky gum that drops from its branches, but Robyn rather likes the patina it imparts to the Renault's faded paint-work – and carries her Gladstone bag to the Arts Faculty building. The sun shines warmly on the red brick and glints on the shiny new ivy leaves. A faint breath of steam rises from the drying lawns. Robyn walks with a blithe, springy gait, swinging her Gladstone bag (lighter than it was in January, for the examinations are about to begin, and her teaching load is tailing off) smiling and greeting the colleagues and students that she recognises in the lobby, on the stairs, on the landing of the English Department.

Bob Busby, pinning a notice to the AUT board, beckons to her. "There's an extraordinary General Meeting next Monday to discuss the implications of the UGC's letter," he says. "It doesn't look good."

He lowers his voice to a confidential murmur: "I hear you may be leaving us sooner than expected. I can't say I blame you."

"Who told you that?" says Robyn.

"It's just a rumour."

"Well, I'd be glad if you wouldn't spread it any further," says Robyn. She walks on, down the corridor, momentarily annoyed by Bob Busby's inquisitiveness and Pamela's indiscretion – for the secretary must have been the source of the rumour. Robyn makes a mental note, heavily underlined, not to tell anyone in the Department about her legacy.

As usual, there is somebody waiting to see her, standing by her door. When she gets closer she sees that it is Vic Wilcox: she didn't recognise him immediately because he is not wearing his usual dark business suit, but a short-sleeved knitted shirt and neatly pressed light-weight trousers. He is carrying two books in his hand.

"I wasn't expecting you," she says, unlocking the door of her office. "Are you making up for what you missed yesterday?"

"No," he says, following her into the room, and closing the door. "I've come to tell you that I won't be coming any more."

"Oh," she says. "Well, it doesn't matter. Teaching is nearly over now. You wouldn't find it much fun watching me mark exam scripts. Is there some crisis at Pringle's, then?"

"I'm finished with Pringle's," he says. "Pringle's has been sold to the group that owns Foundrax. That's what the phone call was about yesterday. I'm unemployed, as from today." He raises his hands and gestures at his casual clothes as if they are a sign of his fallen state.

When he has related all the details to her, she says, "But can they do that to you? Chuck you out, just like that, without notice?"

"Afraid so."

"But it's monstrous!"

"Once they've made up their minds, they don't mess around. They know I could screw up the entire company if I stayed another week, in revenge. Not that I would be bothered."

"I'm very sorry, Vic. You must feel devastated."

He shrugs. "Win some, lose some. In a funny sort of way it's had a good side. Misfortune draws a family together."

"Marjorie's not too upset?"

"Marjorie's been terrific," says Vic. "As a matter of fact" – he rakes back his forelock and looks nervously away from her – "we've had a sort of reconciliation. I thought I ought to tell you."

"I'm glad," says Robyn gently. "I'm really glad to hear that."

"I just wanted to get things straight," he says, glancing at her apprehensively. "I'm afraid I've been a bit foolish."

"Don't worry about it."

"I've been living in a dream. This business has woken me up. I must have been out of my mind, imagining you would see anything in a middle-aged dwarf engineer."

Robyn laughs.

"You're a very special person, Robyn," he says solemnly. "One day you'll meet a man who deserves to marry you."

"I don't need a man to complete me," she says, smiling.

"That's because you haven't met him yet."

"As a matter of fact, I had an offer this very morning," she says lightly.

His eyes widen. "Who from?"

"Charles."

"Are you going to accept?"

"No," she says. "And what are you going to do now? Look for another job, I suppose."

"No, I've had enough of the rat-race."

"You mean you're going to retire?"

"I can't afford to retire. Anyway, I'd be lost without work."

"You could do an English degree as a mature student." She smiles, not entirely serious, not entirely joking.

"I'm thinking of setting up on my own. You remember that idea I mentioned to you for a spectrometer? I talked to Tom Rigby last night, and he's game."

"That's a marvellous idea! It's just the right opportunity.'

"It's a question of raising the necessary capital."

"I've got a lot of capital," says Robyn. "I'll invest it in your spectrometer. I'll be a – what do they call it? A sleeping partner."

He laughs. "I'm talking six figures here."

"So am I," says Robyn, and tells him about her legacy. "Take it," she says. "Use it. I don't want it. I don't want to retire, either. I'd rather go and work in America."

"I can't take all of it," he says. "It wouldn't be right."

"Take a hundred thousand," she says. "Is that enough?"

"It's more than enough."

"That's settled, then."

"You might lose it all, you know."

"I trust you, Vic. I've seen you in action. I've shadowed you." She smiles.

"On the other hand, you might end up a millionaire. How will you feel about that?"

"I'll risk it," she says.

He looks at her, holding his breath, then exhales. "What can I say?"

"'Thank you' will be fine."

274

"Thank you, then. I'll talk to Tom Rigby, and have my lawyer draw up a document."

"Right," says Robyn. "Aren't we supposed to shake hands at this point?"

"You should sleep on it," he says.

"I don't want to sleep on it," she says, seizing his hand and shaking it. There is a knock on the door and Marion Russell appears at the threshold, wearing an oversized tee-shirt with ONLY CONNECT printed on it in big letters. "Oh, sorry," she says, "I'll come back later."

"It's all right, I'm going," says Vic. He thrusts the books abruptly at Robyn. "I brought these back. Thanks for the loan."

"Oh, right, are you sure you've finished with them?"

"I haven't finished *Daniel Deronda*, but I don't think I ever will," he says. "I wouldn't mind keeping the Tennyson, if it's a spare copy. As a souvenir."

"Of course," says Robyn. She sits at her desk, writes in the flyleaf in her bold, flowing hand, "*To Vic, with love, from your shadow*", and gives it back to him.

He glances at the inscription. "'With love'," he says. "*Now* you tell me." He smiles wryly, shuts the book, nods goodbye, and goes out of the room, past the hovering Marion.

Marion pulls a chair up close to Robyn's desk, and sits on the edge of it, leaning forwards and peering anxiously at her. "It's not true, is it, that you're going to America?" she says.

Robyn throws down her pen. "Good God! Is there no privacy in this place? Where did you hear that?"

Marion is apologetic, but determined. "In the corridor. Some students were coming out of a tutorial with Mr Sutcliffe . . . I heard them talking. Only I wanted to do your Women's Writing course next year."

"I can't discuss my plans with you, Marion. It's a private matter. I don't know myself what I'll be doing next year. You'll just have to wait and see."

"Sorry, it was a bit rude, I suppose, only . . . I hope you don't go, Robyn. You're the best teacher in the Department, everybody says so. And there'll be nobody left to teach Women's Studies."

"Is there anything else, Marion?"

The girl sighs and shakes her head. She prepares to leave.

"By the way," says Robyn. "Does your Kissogram firm deliver to London."

"No, not usually. But they have the same sort of thing there."

"I want to send a Gorillagram to somebody in London," says Robyn.

"I could get you the name of an agency," says Marion.

"Could you? Thanks very much. I want the message delivered to a bank in the City, in the middle of the morning. How would a man in a gorilla suit get past the reception desk?"

"Oh, we always change in the loos," says Marion.

"Good," says Robyn. "As soon as you can, then, Marion."

When Marion has gone, Robyn gets out a pad of A4 and begins composing a little poem, smiling to herself as she does so. Soon there is another knock on her door, and Philip Swallow sidles into the room.

"Ah, good morning, Robyn. Can you spare a moment?" He sits down on the chair vacated by Marion Russell. "I've sent off that reference to America."

"That was quick! Thank you very much."

"It implies no eagerness to get rid of you, I assure you, Robyn. In fact, I don't know how we shall manage without you next year. A lot of students have signed up for your courses."

"You did say, back in January," says Robyn, "that if a job came up, I should apply for it."

"Yes, yes, you're quite right."

"I don't particularly want to emigrate. But I do want a job."

"Ah, well, that's what I wanted to talk to you about. You see, I've found out what 'virement' means."

"Virement?"

"Yes, you remember . . . I found it in the revised Collins. Apparently it means the freedom to use funds that have been designated for a particular purpose, in a budget, for something else. We haven't had virement in the Faculty before, but we're going to get it next year."

"What does that mean?"

"Well, it means that if we decide to curtail certain operations in the Faculty, we could redirect the resources. Since the English Department is bulging with students, and some of the smaller Departments in the Faculty are on the brink of disappearing altogether, there's a chance that we may be able to replace Rupert after all, in spite of the new round of cuts."

"I see," says Robyn.

"It's only a chance, mind you," says Philip Swallow. "I can't guarantee anything. But I was wondering whether, in the circumstances, you would consider staying on next year, and see what happens."

Robyn thinks. Philip Swallow watches her thinking. To avoid his anxious scrutiny, Robyn turns in her chair and looks out of the window, at the green quadrangle in the middle of the campus. Students, drawn out of doors by the sunshine, are already beginning to congregate in pairs and small groups, spreading their coats and plastic bags so that they can sit or lie on the damp grass. On one of the lawns a gardener, a young black in olive dungarees, is pushing a motor mower up and down, steering carefully around the margins of the flower beds, and between the reclining students. When they see that they will be in his way, the students get up and move themselves and their belongings, settling like a flock of birds on another patch of grass. The gardener is of about the same age as the students, but no communication takes place between them – no nods, or smiles, or spoken words, not even a glance. There is no overt arrogance on the students' part, or evident resentment on the young gardener's, just a kind of mutual, instinctive avoidance of contact. Physically contiguous, they inhabit separate worlds. It seems a very British way of handling differences of class and race. Remembering her Utopian vision of the campus invaded by the Pringle's workforce, Robyn smiles ruefully to herself. There is a long way to go.

"All right," she says, turning back to Philip Swallow. "I'll stay on."